Xavier Wallace

SHAW INTERVENTION

Xavier Wallace

Xavier Wallace was born and raised in regional New South Wales, Australia. He attended public primary and high schools, before studying business at the University of Newcastle. He worked in Canberra for the Australian Government in both the public service and politics for over a decade. He has a Master of Politics and Public Policy from Deakin University. Xavier's interests include politics, government, national security, media and communications, philosophy, ancient history and mythology. He is an advocate for equality and human rights, including LGBTI+ rights. Live music, thriller novels and action movies occupy his time outside writing and work. He loves spending time with his family and friends, and his groodle, Atlas.

Xavier Wallace is the author of the Max Shaw spy thriller series.

Dedication

For the Canberra Crew.

Acknowledgements

This book is dedicated to my amazing friends in Canberra.

We have had some wild adventures and amazing experiences together. From the frequent long weekend coast trips to the wild nights at the karaoke bars, I could not have asked for a better bunch of people to spend time with and have as part of my life.

It's crazy to think we have known each other for well over a decade now – how time flies – but our friendship keeps getting stronger and I'm so grateful for it!

I feel so privileged to be a small part of your lives and to be given the opportunity to share your most incredible moments, including your beautiful weddings, but also to share the joy of meeting and watching your kids grow up. It's truly wonderful.

Thank you from the bottom of my heart for all your love, support and friendship!

I love you all!

The Max Shaw Spy Thriller Series

Shaw Vengeance

Shaw Initiation

Shaw Confrontation

Shaw Intervention

Shaw Reclamation

Shaw Salvation

SHAW INTERVENTION

By Xavier Wallace

Fourth Novel of the Max Shaw Spy Thriller Series.

Prelude

He drove his new Chevrolet sedan up to the facility gates and showed his credentials to the heavily armed security guard. The guard checked his photo, then swiped the access card in the slot next to his computer. His profile appeared on the screen and the security guard took a moment to read the details.

Professor Eric Franklin of the University of Southern California was a chemical engineer and physicist. He was cleared for entry as a team member on Project Erebus.

The security guard handed Franklin his credentials and pressed the button opening the gates.

After the heavy steel barriers rolled to the side, Franklin drove onto the compound and found a park.

He gathered his bag and made the short walk from the car up to the large wide concrete stairs leading up to the main entrance. As he climbed the steps, the imposing glass and steel doors came into view across the small landing at the top of the modern building in the middle of the desert.

Franklin made his way to the doors, swiped his access card and entered the building. He passed the security desk and headed for the elevators. He kept his head down and walked with purpose.

He took the lift down deep into the bowels of the building underground. With a ding, the elevator doors opened and he walked out onto the floor which was solely dedicated to Project Erebus. The glass door which led into the laboratory like space was embossed with the proud image of an American eagle and the logo for the United States Department of Defense, Special Projects Division.

Franklin pushed open the glass door and followed the sterile white hallways until he found the office labelled with his name. He entered and closed the door behind him. He made his way over to the computer and inserted a thumb drive into the USB slot. A dialogue box opened on the screen and various white text coding started scrolling rapidly up the black screen. Seconds later, the computer unlocked and a new command window opened with the same sprawling code, followed by a progress bar and the words *Trojan Uploading*.

Franklin sat his bag on the desk and pulled on his white lab coat. He took a small remote sized device from his backpack and a silenced pistol which he placed in his jacket pockets.

Franklin left his bag on his desk and strolled out of the room towards the main laboratory. On his way he passed people busy running between offices with clipboards and tablet computers. He nodded occasionally to anyone who bothered to look at him when they passed in the corridors, but he did not let his gaze linger too long.

At the end of the corridor, he found the room he was looking for. The glass door held a sign indicating it was the main testing laboratory for Project Erebus. Franklin scanned his credentials and pushed open the door.

Inside there were glass rooms with humidifiers and stainless-steel equipment. A number of scientists were standing around a solid looking glass box in one of the side rooms. They watched as one of their peers placed a small disk-like object, no bigger than a nickel into the box with a rat, then closed the lid. There was a burst of mist, with a slight red tinge, which shot out of the nickel. An alarm sounded and a small monitor on the side of the glass humidifier flash a warning. Within seconds, the rat convulsed and died. A short time later, the warning cleared on the side of the box.

The scientists all vigorously shook each other's hands and patted themselves on the back in celebration. Franklin continued through the room to the back where a large steel vault-like door stood securing the main storage chamber of Project Erebus. He approached the door, scanned his credentials and entered a six-digit code into the terminal.

"Franklin!" an old scientist shouted from behind him and marched over. "You missed the final trial, my friend. Where have you been? You should come in and celebrate with us."

"I just have something I need to do first," Franklin said without turning around. "Can you enter your details, so I can get a sample out to try one last test on Erebus, before I sign off on it."

"The trials are done. We have completed the final successful test. You do not need to worry my friend. Come join us."

"No, please. I insist. I have been up all night thinking about it. I think I know how to increase its efficiency. Will you help me out, please?"

"Okay, okay, Eric, if you insist," the scientist said walking over to the vault door and scanning his credentials. "You would think with all the trouble you have to go to, to get in here you would not need a two-person verification, but whatever."

The old man typed in his code and the big vault door groaned as it opened.

"I am not sure why you need to do this test now, Eric, we are done! It is very exciting!" the scientist proclaimed before turning to face Franklin. "Eric? You look different. Are you okay?"

Franklin turned to the old man and his expression changed to one of confusion.

"You are not Eric!" the scientist shouted and turned back towards the room with his peers.

"No, I'm not," Franklin said drawing his pistol and shooting the old man in the back.

The scientists in the side room turned to see their colleague fall, as Franklin opened fire on their room. It was like shooting fish in a barrel. The glass in the first window exploded inwards as the scientists fell one by one with blood staining their white lab coats. The final scientist had made it to the door, but Franklin lined him up and fired three rounds into his back. The bullets burst through his body as the shattered door glass fell. The scientist collapsed into a pile of bloodied glass on the floor and did not move.

Franklin yanked open the vault door and entered the safe. In the centre of the room was a black steel cylinder. It looked like a big beer keg, but it was about the size of an oil drum. It was covered in warning labels and it had a hi-tech computer panel built into its side. He typed a command into the little touch screen and the cylinder unlocked from its base. He loaded a new magazine in his pistol, before placing the cylinder on a nearby trolley and wheeling it from the vault.

He moved quickly through the facility, back to the elevator, and rode with the trolley up to the ground floor wheeling it across the lobby.

"Excuse me, sir," one of the security guards said as he walked passed, "but I will need to see your movement order for that item."

Franklin kept walking, pushing the trolley for the main door.

"Sir, you need to stop!" the guard demanded following his colleague out from behind the desk with their hands on their pistols. "We need to see your movement order."

"Sure, I've got it right here," Franklin said stopping in the middle of the foyer.

People had stopped to watch what was happening as the security guards approached Franklin who had not turned around.

"Your paperwork, sir," the guard said cautiously approaching, "please, hand it over."

"You got it," Franklin said spinning on his heal to face the guards and drawing his pistol.

He fired four shots which hit their marks, the head and chest of each guard. As their bodies fell to the floor, scientists and researchers alike screamed and fled from the scene, worried they would be next.

Franklin turned back to the trolley and pushed it out through the big glass and steel door of the main entrance and found the nearby ramp. He dragged the trolley across the parking lot to his car, crunching the stones under its wheels, and he wrestled the big cylinder into the backseat of his car.

He clicked the door closed and security personnel ran out of the main entrance and opened fire. He shot wildly at the guards taking two down, before climbing into the driver's seat. He continued firing as he kicked over the engine and threw the car into gear. He slammed his foot down on the accelerator, but held the car on the spot, spinning the tyres. The black smoke engulfed his car, blocking the vision of the chasing security men, as the tyres threw the little stones over the yard.

Franklin turned the car slightly then let off the brakes. The powerful sedan lurched forward racing across the parking lot and smashed through the mesh fencing. He dragged three or four panels of sparking and tangled wire fence until it caught and freed itself. He drove through the paddock, weaving the vehicle through the trees and scrub, until he found the road. The dark blue Chevy raced down the country road trailing a cloud of hot orange dust. The road surface was a fine powder which caused the big powerful vehicle to skid and slip on each corner as the driver kept his foot pinned down on the accelerator.

As soon as he was clear, Franklin fumbled in his pocket for the small remote device he had put there earlier. He opened the plastic safety flap and pressed the metallic button. Inside the facility, in the office of Professor Eric Franklin, an explosion rang out from the bag he had left on the desk. The force of the blast gutted the entire floor, turning the glass to powder, splintering the furniture and destroying all the equipment.

After several minutes, the treelined road gave way to an outback highway and Franklin yanked hard on the wheel sliding the car out onto the bitumen and headed west.

Chapter One

Rear Admiral Blake 'Hermes' Smyth was sitting in his well-appointed office in the Australian Intelligence Service Building in Canberra. He was a handsome man with sandy and slightly greying hair, and he was always clean shaven. His military dress uniform was adorned with dozens of medals, likely more than any Navy officer had held at his age. Blake was the youngest person and the fastest to ever reach the rank of Rear Admiral in the Royal Australian Navy's history which had officers, like the other military services, embedded in AIS. Blake had spent years with the organisation and had recently been officially appointed as second-in-command of the agency – a role he had unofficially held for years in support of his boss, General Patrick 'Hulk' Scott.

He took off his reading glasses and tossed them onto the desk, and closed his eyes as he rubbed his temples. He had been reading briefs for hours and he was exhausted. He looked out the large glass windows of his office and saw the night settling in across the grounds of the Royal Military College, Duntroon, where the AIS had hidden their headquarters in plain sight after their original building had been destroyed in a terrorist attack. He decided to call it quits for the night, so he packed up his files in his secure filing cabinet and spun the combination lock. He shut down his computer and headed for the door.

When he got to his car deep in the underground carpark, his phone rang and he juggled his briefcase into the back seat before answering the call.

"Hermes," he answered as he moved to the driver's door, "go ahead."

"Sir, apologies for the hour," an AIS analyst said, "but we have a situation."

"What is it?"

"Well, there was an attack on a facility in the United States. The CIA just called and they have asked for us to send over our files."

"On what?"

"Not what, sir, who."

"Whose files do they want?"

"Well, that's the thing, sir, they want the file on Agent Max Shaw, codename Prince."

Blake stopped in his tracks on hearing that name. It had been many years since Max had officially worked for AIS and there was a current warrant for his arrest. Max had gone rogue, assassinating members of a deadly terrorist organisation, known as The Sixteen, who were responsible for killing thousands of people, including Max's fiancé Lachlan. The series of events following Lachlan's death had tortured Max. He blamed himself, until one day he finally snapped and stopped playing by the rules. He took it upon himself to hunt the group responsible and take them out one-by-one.

On that last faithful day with the AIS, Max killed the British Prime Minister and the Duchess of Cambridge who were the two parties at the top of the terrorist group's hierarchy, calling the shots. Since then, the British had put out an arrest warrant trying to force Max in to give evidence. They were sure AIS had provided the appropriate evidence linking the former Prime Minister and Duchess to the crimes, but they were pissed about due process and that Max had acted without their authority. They were also understandably upset that Max had continued to assassinate members of the same terrorist organisation on United Kingdom soil without authority. As far as they were concerned, he had become no better than the terrorists by taking matters into his own hands and disregarding the law. Given the various treaties and agreements between the countries, including the Five Eyes Intelligence Agreement, Australia, New Zealand, the United States and Canada had issued similar warrants to the UK's for his arrest.

For years, AIS had searched for Max, but to no avail. He was hiding and his training meant that he would not be found, unless he wanted to be found. He had spent year planning for the occasion he would need to disappear, storing money and passports, even weapons around the world.

There was only one person on earth that might be able to find him. Max contacted him occasionally to provide information on his latest target and to hand over all the evidence he had collected on the target. Sometimes before, but most of the time after Max had killed them.

That person was Blake.

Blake had not heard from Max for well over a year. When they last spoke, Max had found fourteen of the sixteen members of the terrorist group's high command. There were only two remaining and from what Blake could work out, they were both in the United States.

"Sir," the analyst interrupted his thoughts, "are you still there?"

"Yes, umm, sorry," Blake replied. "I'm on my way back up."

"Thank you, sir. The director is in her office."

Blake walked back into the AIS building. He made his way through security and through to the North American branch's section of the building. While it was late in the evening, there were still countless teams working their shifts and the building buzzed like it was the middle of the day. He found the United States Division director and walked into her office. She stood when Blake walked into the room, surprised he had come to her. He was two ranks above her in the chain of command and he had recently been promoted to Deputy Head of the Australian Intelligence Service. Protocol would normally dictate she would come to his office to brief.

"Sir," she said standing almost at attention. "I was gathering my files to come to your office."

"That's okay, Sally," Blake dismissed, hating like ever the gravity of his rank. "I was on my way out, so I thought it would be just as easy to come to you."

"Yes, sir. Well, please come in and take a seat. Can I get you anything?"

"No, I'm fine, thank you," Blake said taking a seat.

Sally Morrison was a highly capable analyst with the AIS. She had spent time in North America as the intelligence attaché in Washington and she had developed a network of contacts both on and off the record. AIS promoted her to head up the United States Division when she returned to Canberra and she was responsible for all intelligence sharing with the intel agencies in the United States.

"What can you tell me?" Blake asked.

"Well, sir, forgive me. I know you and Agent Shaw were friends."

"Nothing to forgive, Sally. Max is a wanted man and we have a job to do."

"Yes, sir. A few hours ago, a US Defense base near Carson City, Nevada, was attacked. A lone gunman snuck into the facility. He killed a dozen people and stole a weapon."

"What sort of weapon?"

"The Americans have not been forthcoming with that information, but we do know that the facility is used by one of the science and research divisions of the department. We have always believed that it was one of their weapons research centres."

"I guess we were right. Do we have any files on it?"

"Yes, sir," Sally said sliding the file across the desk to Blake.

"What does this have to do with Max?" Blake asked as he flicked through the file trying to sound impartial.

"They sent me a video," Sally stated in a quiet and nervous tone as she adjusted her jacket.

"Let's see it," Blake said looking towards the television in her office.

Sally typed a command into her computer and the television turned on. She mirrored her computer monitor to the television and hit the play button. Blake watched the CCTV footage of a man walking into the facility. He crossed the foyer with his head down and entered the elevator.

Blake watched him walk, staring intently. The footage cut to another camera and this man walked out of shot into an office. A few minutes later, he came out without his bag, wearing a white lab coat.

Blake studied the rolling images. There was something familiar about the man, but he did not want to believe it.

He watched as the man made his way over to a vault door on the footage coming in from the switching cameras in the lab. He had an exchange with another scientist who eventually stepped up to the same door and unlocked it. There was another short exchange before the violence began. The scientist was shot at point blank range followed by a bloodbath inside the laboratory as the man opened fire on the trapped scientists. Blake had seen a lot, but this was hard to watch. The scientists had no where to go and this man was a talented shot – clearly well trained.

The footage followed the man out and showed his escape with some sort of large cylinder he had taken from the vault, before it cut back to the laboratory floor. Blake was confused as to why this footage was part of the package, until flames and broken glass and furniture blasted across the space. It looked like it originated from the office the man had first entered. He obviously left a bomb inside. The vision went white then snowy when the cameras burned and their signal was cut.

"That's it?" Blake asked turning back to Sally. "What's this got to do with Max?"

"No, sir," Sally said clicking the screen. "There is also this."

Blake turned back to the television to find a second video playing. It showed a new dark blue Chevrolet sedan pulling up to the security gate. There was a snowy cut, before the footage changed to a camera pointed at the driver from the security hut. Blake froze as the driver turned to take back his fake credentials and the footage paused on his face.

It was Max.

A series of facial recognition tools appeared on the screen plotting facial features and with green dots, before a matrix like structure hugged his face. A green wave ran over the screen, before a rectangular box appeared across the image with green writing. *Ninety-Five Percent Match,* the first line said. *Agent Max Shaw, Codename: Prince*, the second line stated. The third line noted he worked for the Australian Intelligence Service, but had been disavowed.

Blake stared at the image of his long-term friend and the man he had loved since the day they had met. He looked a little older and Blake noticed his beard was gone and his hair was short like he used to wear it when they first met all those years ago. His reflective Oakleys hung around his neck.

Blake was in disbelief. It was him. The photo, the car, the glasses all matched.

Maybe after all these years, his friend had finally gone off the rails completely and if that was the case, there was no limit to what he would be capable of.

"I need you to call General Scott and ask him to come in," Blake ordered finally standing and walking for the door. "And, you better get your team to come in too. It is going to be a difficult few days."

Chapter Two

Blake paced around in his office for an hour struggling to comprehend what he had seen. If Max had done this, there would have to be a reason for it. Maybe he found out what the project was and wanted to stop the Americans.

He was not sure. None of it was making sense. Max would not kill unarmed civilians. Yes, he had killed unarmed people before, but they were terrorists. He surely would not just kill a bunch of scientists to stop their research.

There had to be a reason.

Blake had Sally send him the video files and he watched them again, studying every movement, but he could not be sure what he was looking for. The man in the file certainly moved like Max, he had an air of athleticism in every step and a familiar feel. Blake paused the video on the image of Max's face from the security hut. It was grainy and black and white. He could not help but wonder why the department had used such a cheap camera for such an important position on the security hut. The image quality was incredibly low, but it was undeniably Max.

He remembered every moment they had been together. When he first nervously met Max as a young recruit at the Wool Shed – AIS's secret training base in western New South Wales – through to every mission they had planned and been on together. They had become so close over the years. Not only did they spend hours and often days together on missions, but they trained together every morning when they were in the same city at five o'clock every morning, like they had at the Wool Shed, and they had celebrated countless birthdays and other important occasions together, let alone just the quiet dinners and drinks they had had.

Blake had secretly loved Max from the first moment they met, but he had never acted on it or even spoken to anyone about it. The closest he ever got was to speak to Max's best friend and their former colleague, Flash, who was killed on Max's last week with AIS.

Max had gotten engaged to his partner, Lachlan, in the first few years of their friendship and work together. Blake respected that relationship, even though he had to admit he was a little jealous, but he never let his feelings interfere with their friendship or work.

When Lachlan was murdered, Blake and Flash were the two people Max relied on for support. Blake was heartbroken for Max and felt his pain and suffering more than most. Here he was the most highly skilled and tough agent Blake had ever worked with, turned into a shattered and grieving mess. Blake could only image the heartache Max had felt and he felt helpless, he did not know how to help Max other than to be there for him.

In the months following Lachlan's death, Blake could only watch on as Max's resolve and demeaner hardened. He shutdown parts of himself and he became more ruthless and determined. He hunted down leads and did whatever it took to get the job done. He hurt and tortured people for information and he arrested or assassinated anyone linked to terror or foul play. Lachlan's death drove him and motivated him. Blake knew deep down it was because Max did not want anyone else to feel the pain he had felt. He did what he did to stop those who would seek to harm innocent people and he was sure that was still his driving goal.

But, maybe he had gone too far. Maybe he had taken this drive and turned it against even friendly governments who were straying into something he did not like. Blake could not be sure. Although he had to admit 'friendly' probably was not the right term for a government with a warrant out for your arrest, for doing your job. What he did know though, was that his feelings for Max had not changed. Just seeing his photo again made his heart race. He had tried other relationships and dating, he even had a boyfriend for the last two years, but it had ended. His partner had asked him to marry him, but he couldn't say yes. He broke his heart and could not help but wonder if he had doomed himself to life-long loneliness in the process. But, he just couldn't do it, he loved someone else and it was not fair to his partner, so he ended it.

Hulk walked into the room interrupting his thoughts. He was a big man and even though he was getting on in years, he was still tough and fit. His large frame had been conditioned over decades in the Special Air Services Regiment in the Australian Army and he was not going to let time or age undo his hard work. He was using a cane to walk from a recent knee surgery which was taking too long to heal.

Hulk got his codename for being tough and angry, and his army mates said they saw him live through fights which would kill a normal man. He still trained at five every morning and kept his competency training in weapons and explosives up to date annually, although as Head of the AIS, he did not get into the field much, if at all, these days, and the cane was not helping. He spent more time arguing with politicians for funding and about legislation, than hunting down leads.

He had promoted and supported Blake for years, seeing early the leadership, ambition and skills he wanted and needed around him. He had told Blake just recently that he was being promoted officially to be his number two, because he needed to know someone he trusted was getting ready to take over when he retired. He assured Blake, he was not going anywhere, but wanted him to be ready. Blake got his codename, Hermes, for being Hulk's messenger, but one day in the future, he would no longer be the messenger, he would be his replacement.

"What the fuck is going on in the US?" Hulk asked with his trademarked impatience, yet another reason his codename suited him. "Is it him?"

"Take a look for yourself," Blake said pointing to the television. "I've watched it several times. It looks like him."

"Jesus Christ," Hulk said taking a seat and rubbing his hand through his thick grey hair. "What is he doing?"

"He apparently stole a weapon of some sort. It's in some sort of black cylinder, looks like a gas bottle or a big beer keg. Here I'll show you."

Blake watched the footage again twice with Hulk then the two sat in silence reflecting on what they had seen. Hulk had personally recruited Max and trained him. He knew if anyone could do what was done on that tape, it was him, and he knew if anyone had the balls to do it, it was certainly him.

"I wanted a monster," Hulk said softly staring at the little screen. "We needed someone who could get down in the weeds with terrorists and play by their rules. We needed someone who could think like them and get in their heads. We needed someone ruthless and uncompromising, and he delivered."

"Yes, sir," Blake responded taking a seat opposite.

"But, he always knew where the line was," Hulk said turning to Blake. "He always knew how far he could take it and he had a moral compass which made him question everything. I think he had a big heart and a lot of love buried under it all which kept him focused and grounded."

"I agree."

"But, when he shot those two British arseholes and disappeared into the wind, then started assigning himself targets and killing them. Well, fuck, he threw out the rulebook."

"Yes, sir, but I can't explain this," Blake said pointing to the screen. "It doesn't make sense."

"Has he contacted you?" Hulk asked looking at his deputy for a reaction. "About this."

"No, sir, he hasn't."

"But, he has contacted you in the last few years hasn't he?"

"Yes, Hulk, he has," Blake admitted. "He called me before or after he took out The Sixteen's high command and he sent me the evidence he had collected."

"And you put that evidence into the system to prove these seemingly random assassinations were linked to The Sixteen?"

"Yes."

"How can you be sure the information he sent through was correct?"

"I verified it on each occasion before I let any of the teams work on it."

"So, he has been doing our job for us for what six years?"

"Yes."

"Anything else you want to tell me since we are here?"

"After each assassination he also sent me a recording proving each target's link to The Sixteen."

"A recording?"

"Yes, he got a confession out of one of The Sixteen's top guys and recorded it. It details the names and ranks, and roles of each member."

"Why haven't I heard these recordings?"

"We wanted to give you plausible deniably if you were asked about it."

"We?"

"Yes, Max and I agreed to distance you from this in case there was any fallout."

"You shouldn't have done that, Blake," Hulk said looking deep into his deputy's eyes. "But I understand your reasons. Trouble is the fallout could be fast approaching if he's gone rogue, and you could be dragged into it – if anyone finds out about your involvement."

"I don't think he has, Hulk. He wouldn't do this without cause."

"We will find out soon enough," Hulk acknowledged crossing his legs and turning back to the television. "I want to hear the recordings."

"Yes, sir," Blake agreed plugging his mobile into the computer and broadcasting the recordings on his office television.

One by one the files played. The terrorist listed the members of his organisation and their roles, followed by a recording of Max and Blake's conversations over the years. Max provided detailed intelligence reports to Blake and each time Blake tried to convince Max to come in for a debrief. Max had refused each time. 'Not until the job is done,' was his reply.

"You didn't have a problem with this?" Hulk asked turning to Blake.

"No, sir," Blake replied. "They were terrorists with proven links to attacks around the world. It would only be a matter of time before they reformed in some way or another and started their attacks again. Max put a stop to that, while at the same time putting the fear of God into all of these groups."

"I suppose you are right."

"It's what we trained him to do and what you admitted to wanting only a few minutes ago."

"But did we go too far, what is he doing in Nevada?"

"I'm not sure, but if these people were linked to The Sixteen, he would have called me. This feels different, but I just can't put my finger on it."

"Play the footage again," Hulk ordered turning back to face the television.

Chapter Three

The afternoon traffic in downtown Los Angeles had ground to a halt as people rushed about to collect their children from school and take them to afternoon sport. Buses, cars and trucks jostled for position on the long stretches of motorway intersecting the city. Trains were starting to fill up on the metro system and people on the sidewalks danced in and out, hurriedly moving to their next appointments.

Franklin strolled at a leisurely pace stopping occasionally to check if he was being followed. He would pause to look in shop windows, pretending to look at the items on the racks, but in reality he was checking the reflection for anyone who might be looking at him. He was wearing a Lakers cap and reflective Oakley sunglasses, and casual clothes which made him blend in. He was also carrying a small backpack.

When he was satisfied no one was following him, he continued along the footpath. A block away, he found the entrance to the subway and took the stairs down under the street. He paid cash for a ticket and bought a newspaper and cheap cup of coffee in a foam cup, then headed for the platform.

A few minutes later the train arrived, he boarded and found a seat. He read the newspaper, occasionally looking over the top to see if any of his fellow passengers were paying him too close attention. He rode the train through several stops, drinking his coffee and reading the paper, constantly watching as the passengers shuffled on and off.

At one stop, a ticket inspector got on board. He presented his ticket on request and the inspector moved on without another look. On the ride to the following stop, Franklin sat down his paper and retrieved his bag from under the seat. He fumbled around inside for a minute or so, then tossed it on the seat next to him.

When the train arrived at the platform, he stood and walked from the train, bumping into a police officer as he stepped onto the platform. He apologised and quickly marched on. The officer shouted in his direction, but he disappeared into the crowd.

The officer was standing in the train's doorway, holding Franklin's bag as the doors closed. He had shouted for Franklin to come back and get the bag. As the train started to move, the officer opened the small backpack and looked inside. He found a stainless-steel thermos resting at the bottom in the dark and a thin notebook in the bag.

He pulled out the notebook and opened the first page to see if there were any contact details for the owner. The first page said *'I am the darkness, born of Chaos. I reside between the earth and Hades. Like my sister, Nyx, and children, Hypnos and Thanatos, I leave only darkness, night and death in my wake. I am Erebus and I am here to bring about your doom.'*

The black text was written in charcoal and was accompanied by a hand drawn picture in the same charcoal of a shadowy, dark Greek God, that looked like death.

The officer sat the notebook down on a nearby seat as a shiver ran up his spine. He took the thermos out of the bag and studied it closer. It was heavy and it shone brightly as the light hit it. He pulled it up close to his ear as a series of soft mechanical clicks started.

There was a final click then the cannister opened at both ends. Two extreme bursts of liquid and mist exploded from each end of the device, easily reaching both ends of the carriage. The slight red tinge showed the mist surrounding the passengers and sucking up into the air-conditioning system.

The officer immediately fell to his knees shaking and convulsing trying to get air. He scratched at his neck and skin as he choked and rolled onto the floor. The other passengers soon followed suit, falling to the ground in fits.

Within minutes the mist had spread throughout the whole train and was affecting everyone on board. The train shot past the next stop as the driver started to convulse and fell from his chair. Halfway to the next stop the train triggered an emergency brake on the tracks and skidded to a stop with the metal wheels and tracks screeching and screaming.

Inside the train the lights flickered then went out leaving an eerie darkness throughout the carriage. There was no movement from the passengers or crew and the officer laid dead on the floor two metres from the notebook.

Chapter Four

Blake sat at his desk picking at his lunch deep in thought. He had a lot of plates spinning, but he could not take his mind off Max. He had watched the tape over and over of the man at the US Defense base. There was something he was missing, but he could not figure it out. The man moved with such precision and familiarity, but there was something else.

He tapped his fork on the plastic salad bowl and starred at the far wall of his office. There was a knock at the door, but he did not respond, he just kept staring. Eventually, the door opened and Sally walked in.

"Apologies, Admiral," Sally said entering the office, "may I come in?"

"Of course," Blake replied dropping his fork and sitting forward, "I didn't hear you knock, sorry. What can I do for you?"

"I have just been on the phone to my contacts at the CIA. There's been an attack on the subway system in LA."

"What happened?"

"There was a runaway train. It was stopped by the emergency system which is like a little metal switch that the train hits on the tracks and it triggers the train's brakes in the event of system or driver error."

"Okay, so how do they know it was an attack? Sounds like there was an error and the system responded."

"There's more, sir. When the transport system guards arrived and opened the train doors, they were suddenly struck down by some sort of chemical which violently killed them."

"Jesus. What was the chemical?"

"They wouldn't tell me, they only told me the result."

"So, why are they telling us, if they won't share all the information they have, how can we help?"

"Well, that's the thing, sir. They have footage of possible suspects."

"And?"

"They sent me this screenshot," Sally said walking over and handing Blake the photo.

The figure in the picture was wearing a baseball cap, but the reflective Oakleys drew his attention. They were always Max's favourite glasses.

"Did they send an analysis of the photo?" Blake asked sitting the picture down on his desk.

"Yes," Sally replied handing over a second piece of paper, "it's a ninety-two percent match. It's Max Shaw."

"And the CIA thinks he is responsible?"

"Yes. My best guess is he released whatever he stole from the base in Nevada on the train and they are now about to launch a major manhunt across the country for him."

"Max would never hurt civilians. This is not what it seems."

"I'm sorry, sir, but the evidence is building up. I think he has lost it. You may need to prepare yourself for the fact that the friend you knew is gone and in his place is a seriously dangerous terrorist."

Blake let the comment hang for a few moments, while he thought about what to do next.

"Thank you, Sally," Blake finally stated. "I need you to try to find out what the chemical was and I think we should assume it was taken from the Nevada base. But I want to know everything we can. Use whatever channels you can to find out."

"Yes, sir," Sally agreed. "What should we do about Agent Shaw?"

"If the Americans think he is behind all of this he will be hunted. There isn't much more that we can do, other than pray they are wrong."

Sally left the office and Blake stood up and paced back and forth. It was true that he and Max had not spoken for over a year, when Max had taken out his last target, but he had received a text message from an anonymous number only a week ago. He opened his phone and scrolled through the messages until he found it.

It said *'H, you will know when to open this and share it as you see fit. P.'* and it had a link in the message to a privately hosted website.

Blake stared at the message for a few minutes then clicked the link. A browser opened and a video file sat on the screen. Blake took a small breath then hit play.

Chapter Five

Mitchell Simmons. That was the name on the small plastic security tag sitting on the hotel room dining table in front of him. The table was covered in paper and a small suitcase sat open, overflowing with files. A computer and two printers sat on the bench to his right above the minibar.

The hotel room was old, and the first and only impression you got when you walked in was orange and brown. Everything was either orange or brown. From the shaggy tiger print inspired carpet to brown tiles and benches and orange curtains. It certainly had a theme.

It was not the worst place he had ever stayed though. It was clean for its age, rough around the edges for sure, but it had a bed and running water, and an owner who did not mind being paid in cash to forget he was there.

He used a razorblade to gently slice away the tag's label and Mr Simmons' photo, and sat it next to the card. He cleaned the security card with alcohol, then sat it back on the table. He turned to the computer and hit enter. The screen came to life and an image identical to the old security tag label appeared, accept the photo was different. It was a picture of him in a suit and tie.

He checked the details one last time then hit print. The printer on the left slowly and carefully printed a high quality and detailed sticker. When it was done, he moved the sticker into the second printer and with a few clicks of the mouse, it started work. The second printer embossed a high security watermark across the label and the appropriate seal, it then printed the name Mitchell Simmons back on the label with raised text and a security barcode which was also raised from the page.

He checked the new label against the old one, not moving it from the printer to allow it to dry. Satisfied with his work he sliced the old label into tiny pieces then walked to the bathroom. He lifted the lid on the toilet and flushed the old label away.

The bathroom had the same decorator. Brown tiles, orange curtains, brown benchtops, even an orange bathtub and basin. He walked over to the bathtub and drew back the old shower curtain, and turned on the shower.

Laying in the tub, a man with only his underwear on and with his hands and legs tied, and his mouth taped shut, woke with a start as the water hit him. He was about the same age, height and build as the man who had turned on the tap.

It was Mitchell Simmons. He looked frightened and scared for his life.

"If you make a sound, I will kill you, do you understand?" the man asked as he turned off the water.

Simmons' nodded his agreement and understanding, and the man ripped the tape from his lips.

"When does the plane leave?" he asked.

"Wheels up at nineteen hundred hours," Simmons said, his voice trembling. "Who are you? Why are you doing this to me?"

"I'm about to be you," the man said stepping over to the basin and mirror.

"What?"

"I'm about to become Mitchell Simmons. At least for a little while."

"Why? What do you want?"

"I need access and you can give it to me."

"You can't do that."

"I can and I will."

"Is this why you approached me in the bar to lure me into coming back here so you could steal my identity?"

"That's exactly what I did."

"How could I be so stupid?"

"It's a good question. Someone in your position should know better."

"I thought you were into me."

"Don't get me wrong, you're a nice guy, but I'm not the one-night stand kind of guy."

"Did you, do anything to me? I don't remember what happened when we got here."

"No, don't worry. As soon as you walked in, I injected you with a small dose of a high concentrate little serum that put you to sleep. I put you in the tub and you've been there ever since."

He washed his face and tidied up his appearance at the basin, before pulling off his shirt and walking to the cupboard just outside the room to retrieve a new business shirt. He put it on and walked back into the bathroom as he did up the buttons.

"Where do normally sit on the plane?" he asked.

"There's a cabin for staff, it's about halfway along, near the wings," Simmons answered. "Why?"

"I'm taking your place on the flight."

"What? You can't. They will never let you on."

"Is there a place for guests?"

"Yes, just behind the staff area."

"Is it usually full?"

"No, normally only a handful of people who have meetings lined up."

"Good," he said walking back out and changing into his suit pants.

He put on his belt and shoes, before walking back to the printer. The ink had dried, so he carefully cut around the sticker with his razorblade, before pealing it off and sticking it to the security access card on the table. He found the small plastic case and slid in the new card. He put on his suit jacket and clipped the security tag to the pocket, then got a tie and walked to the bathroom.

"I want you to know, I don't intend to hurt anyone who is innocent," he said doing up his tie in the mirror and brushing his hair and teeth. "There is only one person I am after and I'm definitely going to hurt her."

"What are you talking about?" Simmons asked. "You will never get on board, let alone hurt anyone."

"Oh, but you see Mr Simmons," the man said walking over and taping the new access card on his pocket. "I won't be, you will."

Simmons starred helplessly and in shock at his name printed boldly on the new security tag. His face had been replaced with his captor's, but it was his name and card.

"Please don't do this," Simmons' pleaded.

The man ignored him and filled up several glasses of water which he lined along the edge of the bathtub. He ripped off a few inches of duct tape and placed it firmly over Simmon's mouth as he squirmed, but the man just held him in place. He sliced a small hole in the tape and inserted a plastic straw into Simmons mouth before securing it with more tape.

"You could be here a while," the man said standing up. "I have put some water in the glasses on the edge for you to drink using the straw. I have asked the hotel to make up the room, so in a few hours a very shocked maid will find you and let you out."

The man looked panicked and tried to speak.

"Don't worry, you will be fine. I don't hurt innocent people, so count yourself lucky."

He walked out of the bathroom, gathered his phone and wallet, as well as his rings and watch. He put his reflective Oakleys on, clicked his suitcase shut and carried it out of the room. He climbed into a hired V8 Chevrolet sedan and headed for Los Angeles airport, as Mitchell Simmons.

Chapter Six

The man pretending to be Simmons pulled his car into the returns bay at the rental place at LAX. He wheeled his briefcase across the road and into the terminal. He wandered through the terminal doubling back occasionally to see if anyone was following him, but he could not see anyone.

He stopped at a busy café and had a sandwich and coffee. He did not know when he would get the chance again. He had some water and paid his account, before using the bathroom and continuing through the terminal.

A few minutes later, he arrived at the VIP entrance and showed his new security card to the guards at the door. They waved him through and gave him some directions. He found the door they had directed him to, a short walk down the corridor. A young woman was there from one of the major airlines helping out. She checked his security card then unlocked the door for him.

He walked down an external staircase carrying his suitcase until he reached the ground and started wheeling it again. He towed the little suitcase across the tarmac, taking a moment to look up and take in the sight before him.

There were dozens of police officers and security personnel, and a makeshift security checkpoint with a short row of people waiting to move through the metal detector. Behind them stood the gleaming blue and white plane carrying the seal of the President of the United States of America.

It was Air Force One.

The new Simmons joined the queue for the security checkpoint at the rear of the plane. One by one his fellow passengers were scanned and admitted. When they got to him, he acted naturally as if he had done it a thousand times.

"Sir, please step forward," the Secret Service agent said waving him forward. "Please place the suitcase on the conveyor belt and remove all items from your pockets."

"No problem," Simmons said doing as instructed, before striding through the metal detector.

"Please scan your pass on the panel, sir," the agent directed.

He walked over and scanned his pass, and watched the computer go to work. It scrolled through its database looking for the relevant file. Finally, it dinged and brought up the file for Mitchell Simmons.

"Please take off your glasses, sir," the agent at the computer commanded.

"Oh, of course, sorry," he said calmly taking off his glasses and placing them in his jacket pocket.

The agent studied the photo, the card and the man before him. Simmons looked at the screen and was thankful to see his photo, not Simmons' original on the file.

"You are clear to board, Mr Simmons, have a nice flight," the agent said handing him his suitcase.

"Thank you," he said walking off towards the plane.

He waited at the bottom of the rear stairs in queue to board when he heard sirens. He turned to his right to see the President's motorcade racing along the tarmac towards the plane. The three limousines pulled up as well as all the support vehicles and passengers started piling out. Half went towards the front of the plane, while the others joined the queue behind him.

"Have you seen Simmons?" one of the staff behind him asked his colleague as the replacement Simmons started up the stairs. "He was supposed to brief me on Project Erebus and the attack out in Nevada, so I could update the Secretary, but he missed our lunchtime meeting."

"He probably went out partying in LA last night and slept in," the colleague replied as they followed him up the stairs. "You know what these guys are like when they get out here to California. They want to let their hair down and go out with the locals, and hook up. Especially, the gay ones, they love it over here."

"Well, he better not have! This is not a fucking frat house, we work for the Secretary of Defense for fuck sake."

"How is the Secretary this afternoon? He seemed pretty pissed off about something this morning."

"He had an argument with the President. Apparently, she was mad about the attack in Nevada and that she did not know about the group's work on Erebus."

"How did she not know?"

"Maybe she had not gotten to it yet?"

"She has been in office for a year. How is that even possible?"

"Well, maybe the department did not feel the need to tell her about it."

"She's the President."

"I know, fuck. Well, I would know more if fucking Simmons had briefed me. I am fucked when the Secretary calls me in."

"We should have gone on his plane back to Washington instead."

"It's going back empty. He is on here with us."

The man pretending to be Simmons looked down to his left and saw the President and Secretary of Defense climbing the stairs at the front of the plane. They waved to the media and the crowd, as he walked through the doorway into the rear of plane.

Inside the plane, he wandered through the cabin until he found the area for guests which Simmons had referred to, not wanting to sit with the staff because they would not recognise him. He stored Simmons' suitcase in the overhead compartment then took a seat in a large business class chair. Even though the plane was getting old, it was immaculate and well appointed. It had been completely refurbished and smelt like a new plane.

A couple of businessmen were shown to their seats by an attendant who looked at him inquisitively. He held up his pass and said he was just taking a break from his colleagues for a bit. She nodded and smiled showing that she understood and walked to the back of the plane. He acknowledged both of the businessmen, as the pilots asked everyone to take a seat. The President was ready for take-off.

Within minutes the big plane had taxied and climbed into the sky heading east for Washington. The man sat patiently until the seatbelt sign was off, thinking about what the two staffers behind him in the queue had said. Simmons was supposed to brief on Project Erebus and an attack. As soon as he could, he retrieved Simmons' suitcase and clicked it open.

He had tossed some of his own files in on top, which he took out and sat on the desk, then he flicked through Simmons' files. He found a red folder near the top, which was marked Top Secret, and embossed with the logo of the US Defense Department. Inside, he read some vague details about a facility in Nevada. There was a short note inside saying the page on Project Erebus had been removed.

He flicked through a couple of other folders and found nothing on Erebus, other than short mentions of testing and trials. One note suggested Erebus was almost ready and that final trials were underway. He closed the file and tossed it back into the suitcase.

He replaced his files in on top of Simmons' then went to shut the lid, but paused when he saw another file jutting out of a second compartment in the top of the case. He pulled out the file and immediately recognised it as a CIA intelligence alert.

The alert told all agents to be on the lookout for a subject who was armed and extremely dangerous. The suspect was a highly trained spy, a weapons specialist and an expert assassin. He was skilled in intelligence and counter-intelligence procedures, and he had been on the run for several years without detection. He had apparently carried out the attack on a Defense facility in Nevada the previous day.

He starred down at the grainy photo attached to the file and he furrowed his brow.

He was staring intently at his own face.

Former Agent Max 'Prince' Shaw was wanted for murder and an attack on a secret facility, and now he was sitting on Air Force One.

Chapter Seven

Max wandered through to the rear of the plane, like he had done it a thousand times. He smiled a friendly greeting to the flight attendant as she made her way out into the guest cabin with drinks. He ducked into the small space which was reserved for the crew and pressed the call button on the small elevator. He waited patiently before opening the lightweight door and climbing into the elevator, which was normally reserved for food and drink service carts.

When the elevator arrived in the underbelly of the plane, Max stepped out and took in his surroundings. He was standing in a relatively large kitchen with fridges and freezers lining the walls and stainsteel worksurfaces. The kitchen needed to handle meals for a lot of people, potentially for several days, given the plane could be refuelled in mid-air. A couple of cooks were on the far side of the room and did not see him duck out of the lift.

There were rooms either side of the kitchen which housed the communications gear and the plane's operations equipment. In another section, he found the luggage storage space. There were steel cargo containers packed symmetrically against the walls and locked in position on the floor. There was no way of knowing what was in them, so the only way he could find out was to open them one by one.

He checked the first container, opening the roll-up door and dragging out various bags and boxes. It was not there, so he put all the items back and slid the door back down into position and moved to the second container. He checked his surroundings then went to work on the second cargo unit. Towards the bottom of the second row of bags he found a suitcase with a name on it – Felicity Musgrave. He yanked the bag out and tossed the others back in the cargo container and closed the door.

Max knelt on the floor next to the big black suitcase and fumbled around trying to open it. It had a modern travel combination lock built into it. He strode back to the kitchen, careful not to be seen and he found a cutlery draw. Inside the draw the knives were housed in special moulded foam to hold them in place. Max took a large chef's knife and headed back to the cargo hold. He crouched down out of sight as a secret service agent did a quick sweep of the main hallways.

When the agent had left, Max found the suitcase and dragged into the middle of the aisle. He made a large cut across the front of the bag with the chef's knife from up near the left-hand corner to about the centre, then dragged the knife to the right at ninety degrees. He cut away at the stiff fabric trying to make it look like the bag had been caught on a random piece of metal in the baggage area at the airport.

He sat the knife down and started pulling items out of the suitcase. Clothes, suits, a few briefs and books, but nothing that looked what he was searching for. Musgrave must have the item with her.

He tossed all the contents back into the bag and put the bag back into the luggage container.

Max made his way back upstairs to his seat and waited. A few minutes later, one of the President's staff came into the guest area to collect the two businessmen for their meeting. Max got up and followed them down the hallway, as if he was attending the meeting too. Neither party asked questions because they thought he was with the other.

As they walked past the staff quarters, Max heard several of the staffers talking about an attack in LA on a train. One of the staff members who had been lined up behind him to get on the plane was on the phone asking if there was a link to the Nevada attack. He yelled directions down the phone before slamming it down in the cradle.

Max looked around the small room for Musgrave, but she was not there, so he kept following. The group walked on, through the Secret Service area and past a conference room.

Max snuck a peek inside and found Musgrave sitting at the table by herself.

He broke away from the group who were headed for the President's office and entered the conference room, clicking the door shut behind him.

"Hello, Felicity," Max said, "it's been a long time."

"Max!" Musgrave exclaimed getting to her feet, "how the hell did you get on here?"

"I've got a pass" Max said pointing to his Mitchell Simmons fake ID. "What has it been twelve years?"

"Something like that," Musgrave said nervously. "You were working for the Australian Defence Minister, well, at least pretending to. You were actually working for the Australian Intelligence Agency."

"Service."

"What?"

"The Australian Intelligence Service."

"Whatever. And now, well it seems you are a terrorist on the run, not only from this country, but most of the western world."

"Don't believe everything you read, especially in those intelligence briefs."

"Funny you should mention it, I just read a CIA and an FBI alert for your arrest. It seems you blew up a base in Nevada, stole a secret weapon and released it on a train in LA."

Max was about to reply but the door opened. He silently stepped to the side out of sight as the Secretary of Defense walked into the room to meet his senior adviser.

"Felicity," Secretary Christopher Woods said walking into the conference room without looking up from his folder, "I need you to get Langley on the phone. The President wants a full briefing on this Australian agent, Max Shaw."

"Good afternoon, Mr Secretary," Max said shutting and locking the door behind the Secretary. "Won't you join us?"

"My God!" Woods exclaimed. "You're him, the one we are looking for, Max Shaw. What are you doing here?"

Max grabbed Woods by the throat before he could yell for the Secret Service and marched him back towards the conference table. Woods awkwardly half sat on the conference table as Max pushed him, his back was at a low angle above the table-top and his feet were only just touching the floor. One hand was grasping at Max's hand and the other was trying to support his weight.

"Your senior adviser is a terrorist," Max said bluntly. "I am here to ask her a few questions then I'm going to kill her."

"What are you talking about?" Woods struggled to get out as he tried to free himself. "The only terrorist on here is you."

"He is right, Max," Musgrave added with more confidence, standing up. "Why don't you let the Secretary go? This is the most secure plane and one of the most secure places on earth. You cannot do this and even if you did, you would not get away with it."

"You are a terrorist, Felicity. You helped plan the attacks on Australia and in the United Kingdom, and the failed attack on San Francisco. You are part of an organisation which has spread terror around the world and pull the strings for years – overthrowing democracies and bankrolling attacks. You are the second last person on my list."

"Prove it."

Max pulled his phone out, found a file and hit play. The recording was made several years ago in London. One of the ring leaders of the terrorist organisation which had wreaked havoc on the world had confessed to his role and named his co-conspirators.

"Felicity Musgrave is one of our knights in the United States," the recording said. *"She is a senior adviser to the Defense Secretary. She is responsible for intelligence and counter-intelligence for The Sixteen. Her role is perfect for our organisation and she has been leaking information for years. We have helped move her into roles with successive*

governments to keep the information flowing. Nearly all of our operations have used intelligence she has gathered."

"Who is that?" Woods asked confused.

"That was Robert Hardy," Max said. "He was a senior leader in the terrorist organisation known as The Sixteen."

"It proves nothing," Musgrave defied.

"This is just one file, Mr Secretary. When they are pieced together it proves your staff member is a terrorist."

"Mr Shaw, I am having trouble believing anything you say," Woods said shifting uncomfortably. "You have your hand around my throat and I have several briefs on my desk claiming you attacked a Defense base and a commuter train in LA."

"I did not attack the base or the train."

"We have photos of you at the sites."

"Mr Secretary, I can assure you I was not there."

"Then why are you on this plane and how did you even get on here?"

There was a knock at the door and the handle jiggled.

"Mr Secretary are you in there?" the Secret Service agent asked from the other side of the door. "Please open the door, sir."

"Shaw is here!" Musgrave yelled.

Max turned to look at her, but before he could act the agents kicked in the door, guns drawn. He let go of Woods as the agents stormed in.

"Get on the floor!" the agent commanded.

Max put his hands up and knelt to the floor. When he got to his knees, the agents ran forward and threw him onto the carpet and drove their knees into his back.

"Stand clear, Mr Secretary," the agent said dragging Max to his feet.

The agents led Max out of the conference room and down the nearby stairs. They took him to the cargo hold and found a chair which they cuffed him to and left him with one guard to watch him. Neither man said a word and the only noise was the null rumble of the jet engines. A few minutes past before Woods walked in.

"Think very carefully, Mr Shaw," Woods said pacing in front of him. "I need to know why you are on this plane."

"I told you, sir," Max calmly replied, "your adviser, Ms Musgrave, is a terrorist."

"Where did you take the weapon which you stole from Nevada?"

"I didn't take any weapon from Nevada."

"We have footage!" Wood snapped throwing a photo at Max.

Max looked at the image for a few seconds studying it. It was definitely a photo of him, but it was an old photo.

"Mr Secretary, when was this picture supposably taken?"

"Two days ago."

"Sir, how could I grow a full beard in two days?"

Max sat back in his chair. His long brown hair was tied in a bun at the top of his head and his long Spartan-style, brown and grey flecked beard sat nearly on his chin. His skin was dark tanned from years of training outdoors.

"Give it a tug if you want," Max offered tilling his head back to push his beard forward. "It's real."

"How is this possible?" Woods asked.

"Someone planted the photo to set me up."

"But, we have this one too," Woods said producing another picture.

The second photo showed a man who looked like Max, but clean shaven, getting off a train in the subway.

"I'm being setup, Mr Secretary, and I wouldn't be surprised if your adviser is in on it."

Woods walked over and grabbed some of Max's beard and yanked hard. A few hairs came out, as his head was pulled forward.

"Ouch," Max joked. "I told you. You need to call Blake Smyth at AIS, but sir, please do it quickly. I believe you and the President are in danger."

"Why?"

"Call Blake, sir."

Chapter Eight

The live-streamed video filled the conference room televisions. The President of the United States of America, Amanda Torres, and Woods sat watching the screen. An aide finished sorting out the connection and turned on the microphones and speakers, then left the room.

"Madam President, this is Rear Admiral Smyth," Blake said over the high-quality speakers in the President's conference room. "I am here with the Head of the Australian Intelligence Service, General Patrick Scott. We also have the Australian Prime Minister, Bronwyn Ferguson, joining us at any minute. We are parked on the runway at the Canberra Airport in the Prime Minister's plane awaiting take-off."

"Thank you and Hello Admiral, and General Scott it is nice to see you again," Torres said. "When will the Prime Minister be available?"

"She is boarding now, Ma'am."

"Good. What are we about to watch?"

"Ma'am, the Prime Minister has just walked in."

"Hello, Madam President," Ferguson said slightly flustered dumping her bag down and taking her seat. "Sorry for the delay, I was briefed on route."

"Hello, Prime Minister. Admiral Smyth was just walking us through what we are about to see."

"Please proceed, Blake," Ferguson directed taking fastening her seatbelt and giving the thumbs up to the pilot.

"Yes, Ma'am," Blake said. "Ma'am President, Mr Secretary, Prime Minister, thank you for agreeing to meet with me. I received a link to this video from Agent Max Shaw or Prince as we call him at AIS. I would like to play the file for you and then I am happy to take any questions."

"You can play the file, Admiral," the President said as Blake hit play.

The video filled the monitors on Air Force One and the Royal Australian Air Force's Special Purpose Aircraft. The footage was a blank wall with a stool. For a few seconds, nothing happened until a tall, athletic man walked from behind the camera, turned and took a seat on the stool. Max Shaw with a long, but tidy beard and shoulder length hair, sat facing them staring down the camera. He was wearing a Navy suit, white shirt and pink striped tie.

"My name is Maxwell Kenneth Shaw and I am an agent with the Australian Intelligence Service, my codename is Prince," Max stated to the camera, his voice booming over the planes' audio systems. *"Six years ago, a terrorist organisation, known as The Sixteen, unleashed a devastating wave of attacks on the United Kingdom during the Commonwealth Heads of Government Meeting. Several world leaders and civilians were killed, changing the course of our world and throwing into the light the limitations of our democracies and our security agencies to do their jobs and protect our citizens. This same group was responsible for attacks in western countries around the globe. Their mission was to compel the western world over time to take harsh action against framed, innocent nations and religions, while restricting freedoms and democracy to a point where we turned over power to an autocratic leader."*

"This leader was the Duchess of Cambridge, Princess Victoria," Max continued. *"The Sixteen planned everything from the downfall of the previous Royal Family to the nuclear bombs they sent to our nations, including the one which successfully detonated in Perth killing hundreds, and the two AIS helped stop from detonating in London and San Francisco. During the interrogation of one of the senior members of The Sixteen, he gave me the names and details of all of his senior members in the group. I have spent the last six years, hunting down these members and their followers and taking them out."*

"Now, I know you believe in the justice system and the right to trials, but let me tell you, this group operates outside of these structures," Max stated. *"They scheme and manipulate and pull the strings without us even knowing. Their reach is beyond*

anything the world has ever seen and it would be easy for them to escape conviction. Our agencies were hopelessly outgunned and boxed in by the very laws which sort to give us more power, but instead tied our hands. So, I took matters into my own hands. I did so to give you all plausible deniability and to protect you, in case I failed. This needed to be done, so I did it. These terrorists know nothing but destruction, devastation and fear, so I got down in the mud with them and used their own strength against them. I spread fear through their ranks and gave them a reason to spend their lives looking over their shoulders."

"I let you all believe and the terrorists believe, that I was on a personal mission of vengeance for the loss of my fiancé, because I needed these people to believe I was capable of finding them and killing them with brutality and without concern for the rules or my own safety," Max said calmly and matter-of-factly into the camera. *"I needed them to believe this was not about protecting the innocent and doing my job, but that it was personal. I did this to set up a new cover. Given how well-connected this organisation was into all our governments, I needed it to seem real. I could not risk them questioning my real motives. I had been planning on finishing the mission then simply vanishing without a trace, but unfortunately circumstances have changed, and I now come to you seeking your help and support."*

"A few months ago, I was deep undercover with a group of freedom fighters intricately linked to The Sixteen. I traded my services as a spy and assassin to get information on the final members of The Sixteen. The promise was that I would help this group of freedom fighters fill the void left by The Sixteen to supposedly become global peacemakers pulling strings behind closed doors. They would give me the locations and access to the last members of The Sixteen, I would kill them, then they would be free to set up in their place. I had an open invitation to join their crusade which their leaders thought I would be eager to take up given my background and the fact that my own government had abandoned me. They sort to use

my personal tragedy and the fact that the whole western world is searching for me as a motivator. The case was compelling and I have let me them believe I was interested in joining, but I wanted to get my vengeance first."

"They seemed comfortable with that approach and happy in the knowledge that I was considering their offer, no doubt they would love to have someone with my skills and experience in their ranks," Max noted. *"But recently, I came across some information about plans for an upcoming attack. This group had issued invitations to the last two members of The Sixteen to join them. The first member is Ms Felicity Musgrave, senior adviser to the US Secretary of Defense. The second is Mr Greg Henderson, the CEO and Chairman of the Board at Global Works. Together, these two groups and their various remaining supporters are preparing for a series of attacks, including a direct threat to the President of the United States. I could not let them succeed."*

"Before I end this video, Hulk, I wanted to say I'm sorry for keeping you in the dark," Max said to his mentor and friend sincerely, regretfully and almost sadly. *"But it was the only way I could do what needed to be done. During my recovery, following the events in London, Blake and I developed this plan to take out these terrorists and where possible to gain information about any rival groups which sort to replace them. We determined our actions needed to be off the books. I am sorry we didn't include you, but we decided to protect you. I don't need to see your face to know you will be disagreeing with that decision, you stubborn old bastard, but trust me it was necessary – and it's what you want have done. The plan needed to look real and what better way for it to look real than to have my mentor and friend be the one to disavow me. I have kept Blake informed of my progress from day one and we both agree to tender our resignations and hand ourselves in when this is all done – should the Government wish. But, for now, I need you to bring me back in and reinstate me. I need you to remove the warrants and allow me to work with AIS to help track these people down and stop the attacks. You need to get word to the*

President's security team and cancel the Prime Minister's visit to the United States – they are both at risk."

"I have always been and will always be a faithful and loyal servant of the people," Max said. *"When Lachlan died, his final request as he laid dying in my arms was for me to promise I would protect the innocent and stop the terrorists from succeeding. I would never turn my back on my country or our allies, I remain as committed today to achieving our mission as the first day I walked into the Wool Shed. Good luck and Godspeed."*

There was silence in the offices on board both planes as the gathered individuals collected their thoughts. Blake watched as Hulk processed what he had just heard. He had always remained convinced Max was the best agent he had ever recruited and when he supposedly went off the rails it crushed Hulk. He blamed himself for failing to protect Max. And, like Max said, it was Hulk who issued the disavowed notice and instructed AIS to try to bring him in.

Blake had known Hulk for well over a decade and he had never seen his boss break his stoic poker face, other than in times of extreme anger, but he thought he saw heartache and sadness in the old man's face. Maybe he was upset they had not included him. Maybe it was relief he was seeing. Relief that he was right all along, Max was the agent he had recruited. He had been so willing to do his job and what was right, that he had sacrificed everything for it. His fiancé was dead, his friends and colleagues had abandoned him, and he had risked his life more than any other agent. He had given his whole existence to their cause.

Hulk looked to Blake. Blake nodded a sympathetic and remorseful nod. A few seconds passed, until Hulk returned the silent nod. It might not have been forgiveness, but at least it was understanding.

"Admiral Smyth," Ferguson said breaking the silence, "what do you expect us to do?"

"We need to get in touch with Max and find out what exactly the threat is," Blake said.

"And, you expect me to sign off on his reinstatement to AIS?"

"Ma'am, Max would not have contacted us unless it was serious. As he said, he has been providing me with intelligence for years. He didn't go rogue, he has been doing his job."

"We will talk about what you knew later. For now, I want to know if you trust him? He's a fugitive."

"I trust him with my life, Prime Minister. There is no one I trust more."

"Given your history and service to this country, Rear Admiral, it is certainly a ringing endorsement, but how can we know he hasn't been turned by these terrorist groups. Six years is a long time."

"Yes, ma'am, it is. But, I know my friend, better than anyone. He was going to just disappear and after everything he has been through, I would not have blamed him. He lost his fiancé and he lost his best friend, let alone what he went through and the things he had to do for our country. If he walked away, I would have supported that decision. But he couldn't. He was compelled to keep going, to find these people and stop them. He would do anything to win, as he has proven that time and time again."

"General Scott?"

"Blake is right," Hulk said sitting up in his chair. "I personally recruited Max and trained him. Whatever he is doing, he is doing it for us. We need to find him and bring him in."

"Where would we even start? We haven't found him in six years."

"That's because he didn't want us to find him."

"Can I interrupt?" Torres asked. "We might be able to help with that."

A few minutes past before the door of the conference room on Air Force One opened and Max walked in wearing handcuffs. Blake watched on the screen as his friend ambled into the room. He had not seen his face for several years. His beard and hair had grey flecks, and his skin was tanned darker than Blake had ever seen, but under it all he was still as handsome as Blake remembered. His heart skipped a beat as Max looked into the camera. It felt like he was staring right at him. Then he smiled and he knew he was.

"Hi, Blake," Max said, "it's good to see you again."

"Hi, Max," Blake said slightly embarrassed, "good to see you too."

"Hi, Hulk. Sorry about all this."

"You were doing your job, kid," Hulk dismissed. "That's why I hired you. Let's move on."

"You got it, boss."

"I'm sorry to interrupt your reunion," Torres interjected. "But, can we get down to business."

"Yes, ma'am," Max said turning his attention to the leader of the free world.

"Take the cuffs off him," Torres ordered and a Secret Service agent unlocked Max's cuffs. "Take a seat, Mr Shaw."

"Thank you, ma'am."

"Why don't you tell me what I need to know."

"Four days ago, I met with my contact in the United Freedom Front. At one stage of the meeting, he ducked out, but he left his phone on the table. I used my phone to hack into his and downloaded the contents. Has someone got my phone?"

"Yes," Woods said sliding the mobile across the table to Max.

Max clicked away at the phone and Blake's phone dinged. Blake checked the phone, opened the link Max had sent and within seconds the screens on both planes started scrolling through the contents of the UFF leader's phone.

"There's an email, Blake," Max said looking at the screen then to the Secretary of Defense. "From Felicity Musgrave."

"What?" Woods asked looking from Max to the screen.

Blake clicked the email opening it to full screen. An encryption lock flashed on the screen meaning the contents were blocked from access. Blake typed away at some commands before a black screen with white coding started scrolling up the screen like movie credits on fast-forward. A few seconds later, the email decrypted.

It was a reply to the UFF's leader, Dylan Welsh, from Felicity Musgrave. It detailed plans for the remaining elements of The Sixteen to join the UFF. She detailed the remaining numbers of the crews around the world and approximate financial holdings on hand. In Welsh's original email he promised seats on the board of directors for Musgrave and her co-leader of The Sixteen, Greg Henderson, in return for the details and access to their finances and staff.

"It says we have two new assets in the field," Ferguson said. "Do we know who they are?"

"No, Prime Minister," Max said, "but, one of them could be me."

"And, no idea on the other?"

"No, ma'am."

"How do we know this is a real email?" Woods asked. "Felicity could be being set up."

"It's real, sir," Max said, "I verified it. Plus with the details given to me six years ago by Robert Hardy, I know with one hundred percent certainty that Felicity Musgrave is involved."

"Where is she now?" Torres asked Woods.

"There is an agent with her in my office," Woods said.

"Get some extra agents and place her under arrest," Torres ordered the Secret Service agent in the room. "Take her below and start the interrogation."

"Yes, Madam President," the agent said leaving the room.

"Sorry, ma'am," Max interrupted, "but it would be more effective if I did the interrogation. She knows what I have done and if she knows you have allowed me into the room then she will be more afraid of me."

"Mr Shaw, I have not decided what to do with you just yet. You snuck onto Air Force One with a number of live arrest warrants pending. You have been on a one-man crusade across the world for several years without a check on your power and movements. I think for the moment you can just stay right here answering our questions."

"With all due respect, President Torres, we don't have time for the twenty questions bullshit."

"I do not care what you think we have time for Mr Shaw, the only thing I don't have time for is your bullshit. You will sit there until I say you can leave. Am I understood?"

"Do I have a choice?"

"Does it sound like it?"

"No."

"Then shut up and answer my questions."

"Yes, ma'am," Max said trying not to roll his eyes.

"The first thing I want to know is why your face is on footage from two attacks in my country?"

"I can only guess it is because I am being set up."

"Who would want to do that?"

"There are literally hundreds of people who want me dead. It could be any of them and it could take days or even weeks to go through them all."

"With enough access to our networks to put forged photos and videos in our systems?"

"That narrows the field a bit, Blake might be able to help us come up with a list."

"I've already started," Blake interrupted.

"Good. Keep as updated, Admiral."

"Yes, ma'am."

"Can I see the footage?" Max asked.

The two groups sat around their respective conference tables as the file loaded. Max watched the circles fading in and out on the screen, then the footage rolled. Max saw the navy Chevrolet pull up to the gate of the Defense facility. It was the same sort of car as he always drove. The wide angled shot cut away to a camera in the security hut. A still image of a clean shaved Max sat on the screen, then quickly changed to a wide shot of the carpark.

Max watched as the man, supposedly him, walked across the parking lot and through the building. Max watched him closely, his eyes narrowing trying to place him. There was something familiar about him, but the cameras did not catch his face.

Minutes later Max saw the assailant gun down the scientists and leave with the weapon. Max thought he knew the man, but it was impossible. It could not be him. He turned to look at Blake on the monitor. Blake noticed the recognition in his eyes, but before either spoke the plane lurched to the side. The President, Secretary and Max all fell to the side, as the pilot came on the intercom.

"Madam President, we have an emergency, we are heading back to LA," the pilot said. *"I have locked the conference room for your security. The Secret Service is sweeping the plane."*

"For what?" Torres asked steadying herself.

"Sorry, ma'am, it seems Miss Musgrave has escaped. There is a dead agent in the holding room below."

"What how is that possible?"

"We are looking into it. For the moment ma'am, I would ask that you fasten your seatbelt, we are going to push the plane to its full capacity."

"Understood."

Max looked to Blake, then back to the President.

"Madam President, let me help," Max pleaded, "let me prove to you, I'm here for the right reasons."

"Thoughts, Prime Minister?" Torres asked turning to the screen.

"From what I have read about Mr Shaw and the things he has done for our country and our allies," Ferguson said, "I am willing to give him the benefit of the doubt."

"So am I."

"Read him in please General Scott."

"Yes, ma'am," Hulk said, "Max Shaw, as the Commander of the Australian Intelligence Service and commissioned four star General of the Australian Army, through the delegations given to me by the Governor-General of the Commonwealth of Australia as the Crown's representative in our nation, I hereby reinstate you to as a Senior Intelligence Agent of the AIS and from today, Head of Field Operations. Do you swear to uphold the values of the Commonwealth and selflessly serve Australia and our allies in achieving our mission?"

"I do so swear," Max said raising his right hand.

"Welcome back, kid. Get to work."

"Yes, boss."

"Blake, inform our teams that Agent Shaw has been sworn in and is taking over as Head of Field Operations. Our teams are to provide him with their full support."

"Yes, boss," Blake said smiling broadly at Max on the little screen.

"And, tell the Poms, their warrants will not be enforced, that we will not be turning over Agent Shaw and that they should consider removing them altogether."

"Yes, Hulk," Blake said reaching for the phone.

"Admiral Smyth," Torres interrupted, "tell them the United States of America will not be handing him over either. We strongly suggest, given Agent Shaw's history and service, that they withdraw the arrest warrants and move on."

"Yes, ma'am."

"Thank you, Madam President, and thank you, Prime Minister," Max said getting to his feet. "I'm going to need a weapon."

"Captain," Torres said into the intercom, "unlock the door to the conference room. Agent Shaw is being released."

"Are you sure, ma'am?" the pilot asked. *"We have the room locked down for your safety."*

"By my order, Captain, open this door, and please inform the Secret Service that they are to cooperate with Agent Shaw as if he was one of their own and he is to be afforded the privileges of his rank as Head of Field Operations, that of a two star general."

"Yes, ma'am," the pilot said as a small buzz sounded in the cabin.

"Thank you, ma'am," Max said walking for the door. "I won't let you down."

Chapter Nine

As the door clicked shut, one of the Secret Service agents handed him a taser and a pistol. Max holstered the pistol under his jacket in his belt and clicked the taser on.

"Where are the sweepers?" Max asked the agent.

"Sir, they have cleared the rear of the lower deck," the agent said. "A second team is sweeping the upper deck. It should only be a matter of time until we find her."

"What could she be doing? Surely she knew she'd never get away."

"We could ask you the same thing."

"I didn't plan on getting caught."

"No one ever does."

"She knew she was caught and that when she got away, we would be looking for her."

"What's your point?"

"My point is, I don't think she is hiding. Is there any way to get off the plane?"

"There are emergency parachutes, but we are too high at the moment. Within about fifteen minutes we will be low enough though."

"What about an escape pod?"

"How do you know about that?"

"We looked at putting one on the Prime Minister's new plane a few years ago. We got the designs from the CIA."

"The room is Secret Service protected and sealed."

"So is this plane and I got on here and so did she."

"Point taken."

"You need to get me to the pod."

Max followed the agent down a narrow set of stairs not far from the conference room. They wound their way through the underbelly of the plane past the communications room to an unmarked door. The agent swiped his access card and the door rolled to the side. Inside Max saw a gleaming steal escape pod which looked like something NASA would send to the moon.

The door to the pod opened as they walked in, but the room was empty. No sign of Musgrave.

"Stay here," Max ordered, "keep the pod in lockdown."

"Yes, sir. What will you do?" the agent asked.

"I'm going to find her."

Max walked out of the room and started moving towards the back of the plane. He raised the taser and strode quickly letting it lead the way. He quickly stepped through to the luggage and cargo hold, and swept the area. He found Musgrave's bag, the same one he had searched earlier laying open on the floor, but the retractable handle had been pulled completely out and was discarded on the ground. Max checked the handle, there was a small hole cut out of the metal struts which looked almost like the breech of a rifle. It was empty. Musgrave must have taken something.

Max stood back up, raised his taser and made his way to the kitchen. He marched into the now familiar space and checked around, then he heard a commotion beyond the door at the rear. He instinctively spun and started at a quick pace towards the sound.

Four shots rang out and Max heard the Secret Service agents yelling. Another volley of bullets filled the space and then silence, only the sound of the roaring engines filled the air as the pilots brought the plane around aiming for their new landing.

Max rounded the corner and went through the door. There was a short corridor and he could see an agent laying dead about halfway along. He turned sharp right and headed into a small storage room for kitchen items. It was clear, so he turned back for the door.

As he got to the door three bullets slammed into the doorframe. Max instinctively scrambled back into the room, behind cover and kicked the door shut. He crawled along the floor lowering his mass, giving the attacker a smaller target. He found a cupboard and laid flat next to it as bullets traced a line in the wall above him leading all the way back to the door.

Above the roar of the engines, Max could hear someone running in the corridor, no doubt the shooter. They were running for the kitchen. Max waited for a moment, then got to his feet and went back for the door.

He pulled it open and ducked his head out then back in, checking the corridor. He repeated the move, looking in the other direction. He noticed the agent on the floor moving. He was not dead after all. Max stepped out into the corridor and saw the agent was gravely wounded. He was dragging himself with determination towards a room on the left-hand side of the plane, leaving a trail of blood as he went. Max could not tell what he was looking for, but the agent must have known his wounds were too bad to survive, so why was he moving with such determination.

Max thought about chasing the shooter, but there was something about the agent that made him stop. He ran down the short corridor to the agent who had made it halfway into the utilities room.

"What is it, agent?" Max asked.

The agent rolled to his side. He was covered in thick, sticky blood. His shirt was clinging to him and he was sweating from the effort of fighting off death and trying to get to the room. Max saw the relief in his eyes as he pointed to a small box on the wall. It had an assortment of tubes running in and out of it, and an iPad sized screen on the front. Max stepped into the room and pressed the screen, and it came to life. It was the air supply control panel. Max looked back to the agent.

"Right, t," the agent struggled to get out, "t, tube."

Max grabbed the tube on the right. It was a clear hose running back towards the roof. At the point where it connected to the monitoring box, the outflow side, Max saw a bullet shaped object sitting in the tube. He pointed at the bullet.

"This?" Max asked the agent.

"Y, yes," the agent said, "she put it in there."

Max saw a small note swinging from the clamp holding the hose in place. He tore it off and put it in his pocket then looked around the room for something he could use to open the clamp.

"Here," the agent said tossing Max his flick knife.

Max caught the knife. It was soaked in the agent's blood. He pressed the button and the blade shot out into position. The guard collapsed, face down on the floor and laid perfectly still. His job was done and he could let go.

Max turned back to the hose and used the knife to undo the clamp. There was a little light on the bullet which was flashing. With every turn of the knife, the light seemed to be speeding up. He tugged the hose and it came free, the bullet like object dropped into his hand. He quickly checked the casing. Stamped into the metal was the word Erebus.

Max ran back towards the kitchen. He tossed bowls and trays out of the draws looking for an airtight container. Finally, he found a Tupperware draw. He found a container and matching lid, and placed the bullet inside. He checked the rubber seal on the container then clicked it shut. He was not sure if the container would hold, so for extra coverage, he placed the container in a nearby freezer.

As he pushed the glass door freezer closed, he saw the little light flashing rapidly then the bullet smoothly, mechanically, slid open and a burst of red mist filled the Tupperware container. It looked to be holding and Max breathed a sigh of relief.

"Sir, we heard shots," an agent said walking into the room. "What is the situation?"

"We have an agent down in the hallway," Max said. "Musgrave tried to release Erebus into the air supply. I have contained it in this freezer. Do not let anyone open it."

"Yes, sir. Where is Musgrave?"

"She was making her way back towards the front of the plane."

"I'll radio it in."

"Good. I'm going after her. Remember, no one can open that freezer. Tell them Erebus has been released inside."

"Yes, sir."

Max turned for the cargo area and ran.

She was not in the cargo hold, so he continued on down the length of the plane. He found two more dead agents as he made his way through the underbelly of the big jet. Outside the escape pod room, he found the agent who had led him downstairs. He was propped against the wall. Blood was flowing from a chest wound and his mouth. He groggily looked at Max as he made his way down the corridor. His eyes were rolling, but he managed to nod towards the escape pod. Max nodded to acknowledge the agent and moved quickly and silently along the corridor.

Max ducked his head around the door, just as Musgrave was climbing into the pod. He burst through the door and lunged for the escape pod hatch which was starting to close. Musgrave fired two shots which missed Max, but smashed into the wall and the roof as he leapt through the air. She dropped the gun and started pulling the door as his fingers grabbed the edge of the hatch. He quickly put his foot on the escape pod to try to force the door open, but he was too late. His fingers slipped and door slammed shut. He saw a smiling Musgrave pull a lever to lock the pod's hatch into position.

A warning light flashed and an alarm sounded as she strapped herself in, then the floor beneath the pod opened up. In an instant, pressurised air rushed from the room out through the hatch. Max dived for the door, catching the frame with his fingers. He could feel the air rushing past him and pulling him towards the opening. Musgrave laughed as she watched Max struggling to hold on.

There was a small explosive sound and the pod dropped from the plane into the pink and blue evening sky. Max could feel his fingers slipping, it was taking all of his strength to hold on. It took a few seconds for the floor to close again and when it did Max rolled to his side clenched his fists and stretched his fingers. He was not sure how much longer he could have held it.

He looked around the room and saw a row of metal cupboards. He flung one opened and found exactly what he wanted to find, a parachute. He wrestled it on, then hit a button on the room's control panel. The floor opened again and when it was wide enough, he dived through the gap like an Olympic high-diver.

Max's eyes watered and his chest ached as the force of the rushing air pulled at his body. His arms and legs had flung out to the side as soon as he was clear of the plane. It was coming in to land, so was just low enough to make the jump. Any higher and Max would have been severally injured or worse. He saw the escape pod below him and off to the side, and as soon as he could he pulled his arms and legs in by his side to streamline the airflow over his body and pointed himself towards the pod.

Three parachutes burst out of the pod and filled with air slowing its descent, but even still, Max knew he would not catch it. He waited for a few more seconds then pulled his own chute. Max felt the parachute open and he took the handles and started working them to point him towards the pod.

Max watched as the pod hit the ground with a thud. The three parachutes wrapped the pod and Max smiled. Musgrave would not see him land. As soon as his feet hit the ground, he unclipped his parachute and it danced off on the breeze. He pulled out the taser and levelled it at the hatch of the pod.

He saw the door open underneath the billowing green parachutes and watched as Musgrave struggled to haul it open, then he saw her pulling at the chutes. He waited patiently, until the chute lifted and Musgrave stepped out. Her eyes widened and she let out a half-scream in fright on seeing him, but before she could react two barbs lodged in her chest trailing wires back to Max's taser. He pulled the trigger and fifty thousand volts travelled down the electrodes and into Musgrave dropping her in the dirt. She convulsed wildly and saliva dribbled into the dirt. Mud covered her chin as her head involuntarily dragged along the ground. The shock stopped and she groaned, so Max hit her again and she passed out.

Chapter Ten

Max took out the flick knife he had taken from the agent on the plane. He cut two lengths of the parachute cord and tied Musgrave to the side of the escape pod. He tied her wrists tight above her head, her arms outstretched and her back uncomfortably positioned leaving her toes only just touching the ground.

When he was sure she was secured, he slapped her. She started to come to, so he slapped her again. She blinked and grimaced as she started to wake and realise her predicament.

Max pulled the note he had found on the plane out of his pocket and began to read it.

"My sister Gaia represents the earth, brother Tartarus, the underworld, Eros spreads love, and our sister Nyx is the night," Max read. "Born from Chaos we are the originals, balanced to keep the universe in check, but now the darkness is rising. My sons Styx and Charon stand ready to ferry souls to the Kingdom of Hades. My daughter Nemesis has long foretold of the arrogance and hubris you have shown to the world, and now is time for my family to rise up and put an end to you. For I am Erebus, the darkness, and I am coming."

"What is Erebus?" Max asked.

"It will be your reckoning," Musgrave answered. "You may have beaten us before, but we have only gotten stronger and more cunning, and you will not win this time."

"Yeah, yeah, I have heard it all before, Felicity," Max dismissed with the wave of his hand. "Let's just skip the speeches and the ominous warnings and cut to the chase, shall we?"

"Erebus will kill any living creature within the weapon's radius. I am told it is quite a painful death, but for every minute it is exposed to oxygen it loses its potency until it completely disappears. Imagine the power of nuclear weapon to wipe out enemies on a large scale without destroying their resources and infrastructure or placing just enough of the chemical in the vents of Air Force One to take out the President and her team. The plane would fly ferrying the bodies of the most powerful people in the world until it ran out of fuel and crashed back to earth as a symbol of our new power."

"Well, I hate to burst your bubble, but I found the vial and contained it, your chemical didn't release, and the President and Secretary are both safe."

"You could have just stayed in hiding and given up all of this, you know."

"I never gave up and never will, which is why you have spent the last few years looking over your shoulder and wondering when I would come for you. One by one I picked off your terrorist mates and now I have finally caught up with you."

Max pulled out his flick knife and held it an inch from Musgrave's throat.

"You are going to tell me who is involved and where I can find them to stop Erebus," Max said as sirens sounded in the distance.

Musgrave looked towards the sirens weaving their way closer to their position. Police, fire and ambulance, maybe even military would be on their way to locate the Presidential escape pod and secure it.

"You win this time," Musgrave said throwing her head forward and slamming Max's knife into her own throat.

Instantly blood started gushing from the wound and from her mouth. Max frantically tried to get pressure onto it, but the position he had tied her in made it almost impossible, as did the blood pouring through his fingers. He pulled the flick knife out of her neck and cut the ropes tying her wrists and she slumped forward coughing blood and gasping for air as her lungs filled with blood. Max knew it was hopeless, but he laid her on the ground and tried to put pressure on the wound, but she was drowning. She coughed and blood spewed from her mouth, and her eyes went wide in realisation of what was coming. Within seconds, she choked and coughed then went perfectly still.

Max was surrounded by police and military officers who all had their weapons trained on him. Max was covered in Musgrave's blood. His suit and shirt were drenched, and his hands were coated. Even his face had random splatters and drops of blood, which she had coughed on him.

"Put down the knife!" a military officer commanded.

Max turned and looked at the officer, then dropped the knife.

"Interlock your fingers behind your head and lay face down on the ground!" the same officer demanded.

Max complied. He had no other choice. He knew how he looked and what the scene was like. He would have given the same orders.

As Max's face touched the dirt four officers moved in and flexicuffed his arms and legs, before carrying him to one of the green camouflaged painted Air Force Jeeps. They secured him in the rear of the vehicle and two of the officers climbed in either side of him. The other two climbed into the passenger seat and driver's seat, and the car accelerated away.

Several miles later they arrived at an Air Force base outside Los Angeles. The officers had taken Max inside and left him locked in an interrogation room without a word. He sat in silence, waiting for over an hour until the Defence Secretary walked into the room.

"Mr Secretary," Max said without standing. "Is the President safe?"

"Yes," Woods said walking in and taking a seat oppose Max, "but, you have some explaining to do."

"Fire away."

"What happened to Felicity?"

"She planted a vial of some sort in the air-filtration and testing system on the plane, before launching herself out in the escape pod."

"And you?"

"And me, what?"

"How did you get to the ground?"

"Parachute."

"What happened next?"

"When Musgrave was climbing out of the pod, I knocked her out and tied her to the pod."

"Then you slit her throat?"

"No."

"In bloodlust over the loss of your partner?"

"No, sir. I did not."

"Then you better start explaining."

"I threatened her with the knife and she jumped forward and stabbed herself."

"She committed suicide on your knife, you expect me to believe that?"

"Believe what you like Mr Secretary, it is the truth."

"I am finding this awfully hard to believe. First you claim my longest serving and most experienced staffer is a terrorist, then you claim she planted a device to kill the President."

"And you, sir."

"What?"

"The chemical, Erebus. She intended to kill you too."

Woods paused on that comment for a few seconds in thought.

"Even if all of that is true, how can I believe you didn't put your own selfish needs in front of the country's national security? You were so hellbent on killing her you snuck onto Air Force One! The most secure plane and one of the most secure places in the world."

"Your point?"

"If you were willing to risk everything by sneaking on that plane, how can I be sure you did not risk our lives to settle your own scores."

"If I wanted to kill her, I could have done it in the conference room on the plane with my bare hands or in the field where the pod landed. Why would I go to all the trouble of tying her up and then trying to save her?"

"Maybe you heard the sirens and knew you would be in trouble."

"I heard them, but so did she. Musgrave knew she was beaten and she took matters into her own hands. She killed herself, because she knew I would torture her until she broke, then she would either die or die in gaol."

"Is there anything else?"

"Yes, the note in my pocket was found with the vial."

Woods stood and walked over to Max and withdrew the note from his pocket. He read it twice, then sat in silence for over a minute.

"Something you want to tell me, Mr Secretary?" Max asked.

"It's her handwriting," Woods said tossing the note on the table, "and, sadly it is not the first note we had seen like this."

"The subway?"

"Yes, there was a note found with the first device."

"What is Erebus, Mr Secretary?"

Wood sat thinking for a few moments. He looked torn, as if debating his response. Then he conceded.

"Erebus is a Top-Secret Defence project," Wood explained looking Max in the eye for the first time. "It is a powerful chemical weapon which is dispersed in the air and absorbed by the lungs. Seizures and haemorrhaging begin within seconds of exposure and the victim is dead within minutes. It was designed to be able to kill enemies in say a building, quickly and efficiently before completely dissipating into the air as if it was never there making it safe for our teams to enter the building and take control."

"Could it be used on a bigger scale?" Max asked.

"In theory, yes. If you had enough you could wipe out large buildings or even potentially a few city blocks."

"How about a whole city?"

"You would need a vast quantity and probably multiple devices spread across the city."

"But it is possible."

"Yes."

"How much was used on the train?"

"Slightly more than the vial that was on the plane."

"And it wiped out the whole train, every carriage?"

"Yes."

"What would the vial hold, fifty to one hundred millilitres?"

"Yes, about two and a half ounces."

"And, how much was stolen from the Defence facility?"

"Almost sixteen gallons."

"Sixty litres?"

"Yes."

"That's enough for over a thousand trains."

"Yes."

"And you didn't think it was important for your allies to know you possessed this chemical weapon and that it was stolen?"

"I'm telling you now."

"So, I'm your ally now?"

"Yes, I guess so."

"Well, get these fucking handcuffs off me and let me get back to work."

The Secretary had ordered Max's release and he had spent several hours with a team of analysts from the CIA and FBI trawling through databases. On the wall in front of him was a large screen displaying an organisational structure. The names of each terrorist known to be part of The Sixteen were displayed. Max saw the various branches falling below each of their names to other members of the organisation from the pawns to the knights. The vast majority had the word deceased written across them in red like a stamp. Over half a decade of Max's life had been spent wiping these people off the face of the earth. But from the ashes new branches were spreading.

Max found Musgrave on the corporate tree and saw the branches leading up and across to a new organisation. A ragtag bunch of freedom fighters from across the world had started marshalling resources. Max gave the analysts the names of those he knew to be involved and they were slowly being added to the screen. Their faces and names were displayed, followed by various branches in a three hundred and sixty degree web of known associates. Some had only had one or two branches, others had many. The scale of the task was clear. This is why he needed AIS and the global intelligence agencies. If this group got up to strength, he would be back to square one and all those years would have been for nothing.

Max heard a steady tapping sound slowly getting closer to him and he turned towards it. It was a metal cane tapping on the tiles as his mentor, recruiter and long-term friend, Hulk, walked across the open space of the CIA's Los Angeles facility. He looked older, slightly smaller, but no doubt stronger than he appeared. Max stood up and walked across to meet him.

"Hello Hulk," Max said shaking the old man's hand. "It's been a while."

"It sure has," Hulk agreed taking a moment to look over Max's shoulder to the large screen. "It looks like you've been keeping busy."

"I had a job to do, boss."

"You still do, tell me where we are at."

"I guess we are done with the catch up," Max said turning and following Hulk to the row of chairs and computers in front of the screen. "We are trying to piece this all together. It just keeps growing."

"Who is in charge?"

"We are still not sure, but whoever he or she is they are moving quickly."

"What about your contacts?"

"Dylan Welsh is the head of a group called the United Freedom Front. It started out as a small group of former soldiers and spies who had worked together in the Middle East and Africa. When their service ended, they became drinking buddies and started sharing old war stories and soon started holding formal meetings to discuss what was wrong with the world."

"And they came up with a plan to fix it?"

"Yes. They began recruiting people from all walks of life who were disgruntled and angry and wanted change. They started out small, taking out a few local gangs and thugs. Then they moved onto the mafia and other organised crime gangs. Slowly amassing wealth and power as they went. Then they started on the bureaucrats and politicians, and community leaders and businesspeople in several countries, taking them out when they got in the way."

"And our American friends let this all happen under their noses?"

"Well, at first they were fine with it. This group was taking out the bad guys and doing their job for them, but now they have seen the results and realise they may have made some mistakes."

"Understatement."

"The chart is coming together easily enough because they have suspected quite a few of these people have been involved in crime and terror for a while."

"So, what's the plan, kid?"

"We need to put out word that I have killed Musgrave. We need to make it seem like I did it and was then arrested and held for murder. We have to assume they are well connected, so it has to look real. I will then stage a prison break and get free then I'll track Welsh down and agree to join him in establishing his new world order. They want my skills and I will want to seek retribution on the countries who have turned their backs on me for the last time."

"He's not going to just let you just waltz in."

"I know. I need to take him a gift."

Chapter Eleven

Max stood in the change room getting into some civilian clothes to blend in. Blue chinos and a white t-shirt, with a grey hoodie. He put on a pair of Converse All-Stars and a pair of reflective Oakleys hung from his shirt front. He found a blue beanie and tucked his long hair up inside it. Under the hoodie, he had a silenced pistol and hunting knife, roll of duct tape and a pair of handcuffs.

"You don't look like you've aged a day," Blake said walking in behind him. "Unlike some of us."

Max turned to face his closest friend. His only contact with the life he used to know for six years.

"You don't look so bad for a desk jockey," Max joked walking over and hugging Blake, holding him tightly. "I thought all that office work might have made you fat."

"Five o'clock starts every day, until the day I die, Max."

"It's a hard habit to break, but you look great," Max said letting go and stepping back to take him in. "Thank you."

"For what?"

"For being there."

"I'm not sure answering texts and a few phone calls is what I would call being there, Max. I wish I could have done more to help you."

"You did more than you could imagine. It's genuinely great to see you."

"You too, Max. It's great to have you back."

"It's good to be back, but sadly, I have to go already."

"I know, but I wanted to see you before you left. To tell you."

"Tell me what?"

An aide walked into the room and handed Max a small folder.

"Tell me what, Blake?" Max asked looking from the folder to his friend.

"To be careful," Blake said sheepishly.

Max walked over and took Blake's hand.

"I will, Blake, and when this is all over, I'll buy you that drink I promised you all those years ago."

"It's a date," Blake said instantly smiling, remembering Max's words.

"See you on the other side," Max said squeezing Blake's hand before heading out of the room.

Max headed down into the garage and took the car that was waiting for him. A few miles down the road the driver let him out and he scrambled into a nearby parking lot. He knelt next to a row of cars until the vehicle he arrived in was out of sight and he was sure no one was watching. He snuck through the lot checking the makes and models, until he found one he liked. A small sedan, white and boring. Forgettable.

He went to the front of the car and kicked the number plate, really hard. The airbags deployed and the doors all unlocked. He pulled out his hunting knife and cut away the deflated airbag and tossed it on the passenger seat, then hotwired the car and drove out into the street.

Max drove for a few miles, constantly doubling back and checking he was not being followed, before heading downtown. He parked the car and sat reading the folder he had been given by the aide. The file was everything the FBI had on Greg Henderson, the CEO and Chairman of the Board at Global Works and the last person on his list from The Sixteen. Max sat staring up at the huge Global Works building in downtown LA. The sign at the top was illuminated and glowing in the night sky.

Max's phone rang and he pressed the green button to answer the call.

"Prince, it's Hermes," Blake's familiar voice said down the line, just like the old days. *"Can you hear me?"*

"Yes, Hermes," Max replied. "Go ahead."

"We got into Henderson's phone. He's still in the office."

"Good, I'm about to head up."

"Let me know if you need anything."

"Will do," Max said ending the call.

Max got out of his car and made his way to the lobby of the Global Works building. There was only one security guard and Max marched across the expansive charcoal tiled space towards him. Two metres from the large concrete sign-in desk, Max drew his silenced pistol and aimed it at the guard's face.

"Put these on," Max ordered throwing the guard the handcuffs.

The guard complied and Max walked around behind the desk and checked the cuffs.

"Please don't kill me," the guard said. "I've got a family."

"I'm not going to kill you," Max said looking the guard in the eyes. "I just need to get to your boss."

Max punched the guard in the face, knocking him out. He fell at Max's feet and Max duct taped his legs and wrists, and put a piece of tape across the guard's mouth, then dragged him under the concrete desk. He removed the cuffs, happy the tape would hold and put them back in his pocket. He took the guard's security pass and headed for the elevator. He swiped the card on the security panel and hit the button for the top floor.

At the top of the building, the doors opened with a chime and Max strolled into the largest office he had ever seen. It took up the whole top floor of the building and was adorned with expensive furniture and artwork.

There was a sitting area and bookcases with everything from Plato, Homer and Herodotus to Sun Tzu, Machiavelli and Clausewitz. There were even sections for novels, mostly crime thrillers, and biographies. There were large armchairs and an ostentatious lamp which hung over the space.

There was a large conference table and office desk with computers and televisions in the far section. A huge concrete bar with three beer taps ran along one wall with four double door glass fridges sitting behind it full of food and drinks. A large coffee machine and grinder sat on the bench, and there were rows and rows of glassware and coffee mugs. The space was obviously used for VIP parties on occasions.

Henderson had been sitting at the bar having a quiet drink by himself until Max arrived. His glass was still sitting half full on the bar. The condensation was glistening on the side of the pint. The same man was now behind the bar pulling another pint.

"Former Agent Shaw," Henderson said, "pull up a chair."

Max walked over and sat to the right of the half full glass. Henderson walked around the bar and handed Max the beer, before taking his own seat and sipping his beer.

"When I heard Felicity had been killed, tied to the escape pod from Air Force One, I knew you would come for me next," Henderson said taking another sip. "And, I figured if you could get on board that plane, you could easily get in here. I sent my security detail home. Well, except for the man you knocked out in the foyer."

"You seem very calm," Max said sipping the beer.

"I am nothing if not a realist, Mr Shaw. I am the only one left. You won. We failed."

"What do you know about Dylan Welsh?"

"He is the leader of the United Freedom Fighters which is an organisation made up of various people from all walks of life who seek to control the destiny of this country by overthrowing the government."

"You don't seem too impressed by them."

"The Sixteen was a civilised organisation controlled by the world's elite. These people are not that."

"Bit beneath you, are they?"

"Indeed," Henderson said taking another sip of beer.

"Did you know Felicity was making a deal with them to take over what was left of The Sixteen?"

"Yes, I tried to talk her out of it, but you did not leave us much choice."

"I think you will find it is you who left me with little choice."

"Killing Lachlan has proved to be the worst possible decision the organisation could have made, but it is ancient history."

"For you maybe," Max said sitting his beer on the bar and standing up.

"So, bullet to the head and that'll be that I guess."

"No, unfortunately," Max said grabbing the back of Henderson's head and slamming it down on his pint glass.

The glass shattered and sliced into the old man's face. Beer and glass ran to the floor, with a tinge of blood. Henderson fell to the floor and scrambled away from Max.

"Why won't you just kill me?" Henderson asked as blood ran from various wounds on his face.

"Because you're the last one," Max answered, "and you're coming with me."

Max kicked Henderson in the face knocking him out, then handcuffed him. He walked over to the bar, took a long sip of his beer. He jogged around the bar and pulled down several bottles of spirits. He put three bottles in a small bag and sat them on the bench before taking another three and throwing them in the office. He threw one at Henderson's desk and it exploded, showering alcohol and glass all over the big wooden desk. The second he threw at the conference room. It shattered against the wall and threw liquid and glass all over the side cabinets. With the third bottle, he traced a line between the conference room and office desk, then back toward the sitting room.

He took the lid off another bottle and fed the FBI file on Henderson into the opening and sat a lighter next to it. He pulled the bag of spirits over his shoulder then picked Henderson up and fireman carried him to the bench. One handed, he lit the file and headed for the lift. He hit the call button, then threw the makeshift Molotov cocktail at the sitting room's bookshelves. It shattered and exploded into a ball of flames. Within seconds the books started to burn, then the trail he had left caught fire. A line of flame shot through the space, up over the conference table and onto the cabinet then to the ornate wooden office desk, which burst into flames.

The elevator arrived and Max walked in. He turned back as the doors were closing to see Henderson's office completely on fire.

Chapter Twelve

Max pulled into a driveway with a heavy steel security fence blocking access. He wound down the window and pressed the call button on the security panel and waited.

"What?" came the answer from the box in an unfriendly male voice.

"Tell Welsh it's Max Shaw," Max said turning and looking at the camera.

The gate clicked and started rolling to the side. It lumbered slowly on its small wheels given its weight. Max drove in through the gate and up to the front of the big house in the Hollywood Hills. When he turned the car off, he was surrounded by six men in combat fatigues with assault rifles all aimed more or less at his head.

"Throw out your weapons and get out of the car," the same man who had spoken to him through the security box at the gate said from next to his window.

"That was the plan," Max said sarcastically.

He tossed his silenced pistol on the ground next to the guard's feet then speared the knife into the ground even closer to the man's right foot. The man shuffled back with an unimpressed look on his face.

"Get out," he ordered and Max climbed out. "Search him."

One of the other guards came and gave Max a thorough pat down.

"You could get a job with airport security with hands like that," Max joked.

"He's clean, boss," the man said stepping back.

"What do you want?" the original man asked.

"I want to speak to Welsh," Max said scanning the troops. "I've got a proposition for him."

"Maybe he doesn't what to hear it."

"If that's true either you wouldn't have let me in or you would have killed me when I drove up, so why don't you run along son and play with your toys and send daddy out so the adults can talk."

The guard stepped forward and punched Max in the face. It was a solid blow, but not as hard as Max pretended it was.

"Clint, that's enough!" Welsh said walking out onto the deck. "Your reputation for pissing people off is legendary former Agent Shaw. I hope the other rumours are also true."

"They are," Max said spitting some blood onto the concrete driveway. "So, do you want to talk or not?"

"Why should I believe you have left your old ways and turned to the dark side?"

"Because I've got a present for you," Max said nodding towards the car. "It's yours in return for a place on your team and five hundred thousand."

"Five hundred thousand a year? Done."

"A quarter."

"Two million a year? You must be joking."

"I spent years working for the government on shit money. I need to plan for my retirement, plus given my skills and your growing wealth you can afford it."

"Let's see what you brought me first, then we can talk about it."

"Fair enough," Max said walking to the boot of the sedan.

The men surrounding him all tightened their fingers on their triggers as the lid rose. Max dragged Henderson from the boot, his face was covered in blood, so much he was hardly recognisable. Max spat on the old man's face and used Henderson's shirt to wipe away some of the blood. He was conscious, but looked like he could pass out again at any moment.

"Walk!" Max ordered and Henderson started walking towards Welsh.

The guards all followed Henderson, assessing the threat and realising he posed none. Not only was his face badly beaten and cut, he was handcuffed. Not that it mattered, he was also missing three fingers on one hand and the thumb from the other, and he was walking with a heavy limp. As he got closer to Welsh, Henderson looked up and smiled through the pain, showing a mouth full of bloodied teeth and two very obvious gaps in the top row.

Welsh stared at the old man for moment then a loud bang shattered the air from behind Henderson and he was covered from head to toe in Henderson's blood and brain matter as his face exploded. Welsh panicked and started feeling his own body in search of a bullet wound but found none. He cleared the blood from his eyes as best as he could then looked down at his blood-soaked hands.

While he had been searching for a wound, Max had killed five of his guards with the pistol he had taped inside the boot of the vehicle. Five headshots into the distracted guards who had been watching Henderson and froze when they saw him crumple at their boss's feet.

Max currently had his gun pressed against Clint's temple and was using him as a human shield between himself and Welsh.

"What do you think about the rumours now?" Max asked.

"You've made your point," Welsh said still in shock. "Put your gun down."

"And the two million?"

"You killed Henderson, I needed his money and contacts."

"I have them."

"What?"

"Why do you think his fingers and teeth were missing? I tortured him for the money and contacts."

"Why didn't you just take them and disappear, or start your own organisation?"

"Because I don't want that. I want a job and an income."

"Always the faithful solider and follower, you need this work, don't you? You love the hunt and the chase."

"That probably explains some of it and, as you can see, I'm fucking good at it. So, do we have a deal?"

"Yes."

Max shoved Clint forward and threw down his gun. Clint turned and came at Max, levelling his gun at Max's forehead.

"Clint!" Welsh snapped as Clint tightened his finger on the trigger.

"Do it!" Max said unphased. "Pull the trigger you soft cock. You don't have it in you."

"Do not do it, Clint. Put the gun down."

Clint hesitated and Max sprung. He ripped the gun from Clint's hand and turned it back on him in fractions of a second. The barrel was aimed right between his eyes.

"Next time," Max said. "Don't hesitate. It'll get you killed."

Max pulled the trigger and the gun clicked. Clint froze in horror, squeezing his eyes closed. When he opened them, he was staring at the grip of his own pistol. Max had flicked the safety on, on the gun, which is why it had not fired, and he was handing it back.

"We're going to be working together," Max said dropping the gun at Clint's feet. "If you want any more lessons, feel free to ask."

Max shouldered a despondent Clint out of the way and walked up to Welsh.

"What's my first mission, boss?" Max asked shaking his hand.

Welsh patted him on the back and they walked inside.

The house was massive. Polished wooden floorboards with a dark stain and white walls. Open planned and well appointed. The furniture looked expensive too. They walked through the house until they found a set of spiral stairs leading up to the second floor where the bedrooms and bathrooms were.

Welsh jumped in the shower to wash the remnants of Henderson off, while Max stood in the bathroom outlining what Henderson had told him about the remaining assets of The Sixteen. Before he died, he had transferred the authorisations over to Max. A few million dollars spread all over the world and a pretty impressive property collection. Max, of course, had no intention of handing it over to Welsh, but he was happy to use it to gain his trust.

"Are you sure you want to just hand all of that over?" Welsh asked getting out of the shower. "It's a lot of money and assets."

"Consider it an investment in your organisation," Max said. "The government and its allies turned on me. After everything I did and everything I sacrificed for them. Those arseholes. They deserve everything we rain down on them."

"It shows what loyalty means to them. They fuck everyone over eventually. You are doing the right thing, Max. And, I'm sure your fiancé would be proud that you have finally killed the people responsible for his death."

"I agree," Max choked out, genuinely thinking about that comment for the first time.

"Now, you can get some retribution for all your pain and loss on the people who are really responsible. Imagine if they hadn't recruited you. Lachlan would still be here. It is their fault, Max. Let us punish them."

"That's the plan."

"Good lad," Welsh said wrapping the towel around himself. "Follow me."

Welsh dressed then led Max upstairs to the third floor of the mansion. It had been completely converted into an operations centre. Televisions with live news feeds from all over the world ran along the wall and a couple of rows of computers lined the room. There was also a conference table and chairs for about ten people.

"Looks like you guys are ready to run a war," Max said taking in the scene.

"We are in the war already," Welsh said. "For the very soul of our nation and the west. Mass surveillance, Echelon, bureaucracy – it's all just a system built to try to control us and it cannot be allowed to continue."

"What is your reach like into other nations?"

"We have sister organisations across the world in western nations. We are in regular contact, but they run their own show, and so do we. We have a joint management committee and we share intelligence, but we are still individual organisations, for now."

"Who's on the committee?"

"The heads of the organisations in each nation, the US, UK, Australia, New Zealand and Canada."

"The Five Eyes countries?"

"Exactly. That's how Echelon and the treaties work, so that's how we work too. Got to know the system to break the system."

"What are their names?"

"Who?"

"The committee members and organisations."

"One step at a time, Max. You're in, but we still have a way to go before I trust you completely."

"Fair enough."

"So, what's our next move?"

"Our Australian friend is here in the States. He runs an Aussie Patriots group, similar to the UFF. He is running a couple of operations here while your Prime Minister is in town."

"Is the Prime Minister a target?"

"Yes and so is that Mexican bitch, Torres."

"The President?"

"Yes, Max, POTUS herself."

"Great," Max said trying to muster all of his sincerity. "So, when do we strike?"

"We are waiting for the delivery of two devices from the Australian. Once we have them, we will be moving out. I suggest you get some food and water, we have a bit of a drive. We will discuss the details on route."

"Got it," Max said walking out of the operations room and back downstairs to find the kitchen.

Chapter Thirteen

Blake sat at his desk reviewing the footage of the assailant that attacked the train and defence facility. There was a thought niggling in the back of his mind, but he could not believe it to be true. He kept watching it, almost trying to talk himself out of it. It was simply not possible.

"Have you heard from Max?" Hulk asked walking into the office at the Los Angeles Australian Consulate.

"Not yet," Blake said watching his boss walk into the room leaning more than ever on his cane. "But, we know he has Henderson."

"Yeah, I saw he set fire to the building. It's still burning apparently. He's still a fucking lunatic."

"Yeah, but he gets results."

"Can't argue with that."

"I am sorry we kept things from you, Hulk."

"I know I made the right choices in hiring both of you. I trust your judgement. You will be in charge of all this one day, so I'm both impressed and satisfied you are getting strong enough to make your own calls."

"Don't go anywhere, anytime soon, will you."

"I don't plan on going anywhere, but sadly I'm not as fit and healthy as I once was."

"I'm sure you would still kick someone's arse if they needed it."

"Yours included!" Hulk quipped and they both laughed.

"I'm sure you would."

There was a knock at the door and a young aide walked into the room.

"General, Rear Admiral, apologies of the interruption," the aide said walking to the television and turning it on. "But, the Ambassador thinks you need to see this."

The television cut to an image of the Australian Parliament, followed by the Parliaments of New Zealand, the United Kingdom, Canada and Congress in the United States. Each image sat on the screen for a few seconds before the buildings started to age and crumble. The flags fell last each time, filling the screen and swiping down the screen to the next image. An ominous voiceover cut in.

"We have been misled," a male voice said. *"Democracy, the intelligence agencies, corrupt politicians and their business puppet masters, the bureaucracy – the system is not working. It's time for change."*

The images on the screen changed to pictures of the Roman Forum and the Greek Pantheon, and the nose-less sphinx.

"Remember the fall of Greece and Roman, and other ancient civilisations," the voice continued. *"Once proud nations with empires that sort to rule the world and in many ways were better run than our own today. These ancient civilisations ran the world for centuries. But, these ancient nations fell and so too will ours. And, I am going to help it happen."*

The screen cut away to a man in a mask standing in front of the stolen Erebus cylinder.

"By now you are well and truly aware, I stole this," the man said as the camera zoomed in on the cylinder. *"But, what you may not know is what I intend to do with it."*

The camera panned around and showed a room full of different sized dispersal devices all with glass windows in them allowing the camera to see the red liquid inside.

"You'll never see me coming and you'll never stop me," the man declared walking to stand in the shot. *"Tell your analysts not to bother counting, there are eight hundred and fourteen cannisters of various sizes. Just imagine the possibilities."*

The camera zoomed in on the man's mask. It was a white hockey mask with black scratches all over it. There were a series of scratches running from the forehead over one eye, then across, up and over the nose, before it turned sharply mid cheek and ran down on an angle over the mouth, like a lightning bolt.

"I will start releasing Erebus on the general population and some high-profile targets in the coming hours, here in the US and elsewhere," the man stated. *"Unless you bring me the Former Australian Intelligence Service Agent, Max 'Prince' Shaw, and shutdown Echelon. The Five Eyes treaty has failed us and serves only to weaken own citizens privacy while doing nothing to stop terror. We have all lost people we love thanks to your failures and it's time to turn it off. Madam President, Madam Prime Minister and Heads of the Five Eyes nations – you have been warned. The clock is ticking. This link will tell you how to contact me."*

The screen cut to black and a small digital clock started counting down. Eight hours and counting until they needed to deliver Max and turn off Echelon – the US, UK, Australia, Canada and New Zealand's' peak electronic surveillance system. Under the clock was a hyperlink that said 'contact'.

Hulk and Blake exchanged worried looks.

"Who did this message go to?" Hulk asked the aide.

"Sir, it was emailed to the Heads of State and Government in the Five Eyes nations," the aide said. "But, we are assuming it may have gone out wider."

"Good assumption. If they are looking to make us look weak, our enemies might seek to give them a hand to bring on our demise."

"Yes, sir."

"No one is to click the link or under any circumstances let this clip out, am I clear?"

"Yes, sir. I will send out your orders."

"Thank you," Hulk said turning back to Blake as the aide left the room. "Who is this fucking guy? He's starting to piss me off."

"I have an idea," Blake said, the concern evident in his voice.

Chapter Fourteen

The man tossed the white hockey mask on the desk. It was Eric Franklin or the person who had pretended to be him at least.

"Sir, are you happy for us to proceed?" one of his men asked.

"Yes," Franklin said. "Send two of the small cannisters to our American friends and let's see how useful they can be."

"Will they be upset at your video?"

"Probably, but I don't care. This isn't about them. They will still get what they want. I'm just using the United Freedom Fighters. They think they will rise up to take on world powers, but they haven't got the resources or the brains to do it. They are our local muscle and that's all they will ever be. I have plans they could never pull off."

"With Erebus?"

"Yes, I'm going to make them suffer."

"And, Max Shaw?"

"Max Shaw is the one I'm going to make suffer the most. It is his fault. All of this is his fault."

"When are we moving?"

"In a couple of hours. Get the other cannisters ready for transport."

"Yes, sir," the man said jogging from the room.

Franklin picked up the mask and ran his fingers over its scratched surface, tracing its lines from forehead to cheeks and lips. He tossed the mask back onto the table and walked out into the storage hanger.

Chapter Fifteen

Max sat at the bench eating a sandwich and some fruit. He was deep in thought about how he was going to be able to stop an attack without breaking his cover. At some point, he thought, he was going to have to make a choice.

His thoughts were interrupted by the metal gate opening on the driveway. He casually wandered over to the window and gazed down into the yard, leaning on the wall beside the window, not wanting to be seen. A nondescript sedan drove in and shut off the engine.

Two tall white men climbed out of the driver and passenger seats, and started talking to three of the UFF men in the yard. Max was on the second floor, so could only hear a few short bursts of conversation. Mostly they seemed focused on the number of bodies piled up beside the driveway. Then he heard one of the UFF men use his name and the two new arrivals exchanged worried looks.

"We better check in with the boss," Max heard the driver say. "He would want to know about this change in your situation."

"Give us the devices and get going," one of the UFF men demanded forcefully. "That was the deal. You let us worry about our crew."

"Look around you, clearly something is not right. You are dragging dead members of your crew into a pile. You can't think this is right. You can't argue your plans won't have to change. I'm calling the boss."

"Do you have the devices?"

"Of course, but you may not be getting them yet."

The driver turned back to the car and his passenger watched him walk back to get his phone.

Two shots rang out in quick succession and both of the new men crumpled at the knees and fell to the concrete dead. The UFF men searched both the newcomers and removed any useful items from their pockets, then dragged them over into the pile with their fallen comrades from Max's entrance.

One of the UFF men walked over to the car and opened the boot. He pulled out two small steel cannisters and marched them over to the two waiting four-wheel drives. He put one in the rear compartment of each vehicle and shut the doors.

Max watched the man and studied the cannisters as he strode across the yard. There was a small glass window on each of the containers and the red liquid inside was visible even at this distance as the sunlight caught it.

Erebus.

Max had read enough about it at the CIA facility earlier to know what is was.

They were planning an attack on the Prime Minister and President with Erebus, and he was supposed to help them.

Upstairs Welsh too had been observing the arrival of the Australians dropping off the cannisters. It had not gone quite to plan, but he had the devices and that was all that mattered. He knew he would be hearing from the man who was running the Australian operations soon enough. He would have to think of a plan to get himself out of trouble there. Eric Franklin, although he knew that was a bullshit name, was a serious man and he did not want to piss him off. Franklin had seemingly come out of nowhere to rise to the top of their organisation and was starting to pull the strings in every one of their countries. Welsh didn't like that one bit. He wanted control and he was not going to let some fucking Australian takeover everything he had built. But, for now, they needed each other and they had to play nicely. And, until he could find out who he was actually dealing with, it was better to not piss him off too badly.

Clint entered the room and Welsh turned back from the window.

"They shot the two Australians," Welsh stated in a matter of fact way. "He's going to be pissed."

"Franklin?" Clint asked.

"Yes. How are we going on finding out who he really is?"

"We found the real Eric Franklin. He was a chemical engineer and physicist at the University of Southern California. My contact at the FBI says he was working on something Top Secret."

"Erebus?"

"It's likely."

"Where is the real Franklin now?"

"No one knows. He hasn't been seen for days."

"And, the Franklin we know, he somehow assumed his identity in the interim to break into the Defense base and steal Erebus?"

"Yes."

"So, he's well-connected and well trained?"

"Yes, I think that is a safe assumption. We think he is an AIS agent."

"AIS?"

"Yeah, an agent of the Australian Intelligence Service."

"Are you trying to find out for sure?"

"Yes, my contact is on it. He is sending over some possible matches."

"Good, put them on my email when they come in."

"Got it."

"Have they got a photo of him?"

"No, that's the thing. My guy says he planted a virus in the Defense server and altered his image. Basically, he uploaded a photo of someone else in his place. So, they haven't got a picture of him yet."

"So, he's smart too. Do they know who he is framing? Whose picture did he upload?"

"Well, you're not going to like this," Clint said handing over a picture of Max. "It's your new best friend, Max Shaw."

"Why do I feel like you have more to tell me?"

"Apparently, the CIA captured Max yesterday and interrogated him for hours."

"Then how did he get here?"

"He broke out of a federal prison, deep blacklisted by the CIA, completely off the grid."

"He escaped? How?"

"To cut a long story short, he apparently shived a guard, stole his gun and wiped out a bunch of prison officers before stealing a car and escaping."

"Jesus, he's good."

"And, he's on the run. Is that really what we need right now? He is being hunted."

"Yeah, but he has evaded them for years. He can do it again. How many people do you know who have the skills he has? He broke out of a fucking hole in the ground run by the fucking CIA, for Christ's sake. He's a highly trained agent and given all the shit he has been through, I think he wants some revenge on them. The enemy of my enemy is my friend. I think he is going to be a good addition to the team."

"I think he is a liability."

"Let's see how he goes on the SF mission. If you still have concerns after, we can figure it out then."

"Okay, but I'm going to be watching him and if I doubt his motives for one minute, I am going to put a bullet in his head."

"My advice to you is that if you choose to do that, you don't miss."

"I won't."

"Is there anything else?"

"Yes," Clint said moving over to one of the computers. "This video was just sent from Franklin to media all over the western world and to the Heads of Government in all Five Eyes countries."

"What video? I don't know anything about a video."

Clint showed Welsh the video of Franklin in the hockey mask threatening world leaders and asking them to turn off Echelon and asking them to turnover Max Shaw.

"Why weren't we told he was putting this out?" Welsh asked. "Fucking Australian arsehole thinks he can just come in and takeover everything."

"Turning off Echelon is something we all want," Clint said.

"But, they'll never do it," Max said walking in behind them.

"How long have you been out there listening?" Clint asked angrily.

"I only heard the video. I can tell you they will never turn off Echelon."

"Maybe after a few high-profile terror attacks, they'll change their mind?"

"Maybe, but they'll have to be big."

"That's what we want and this why you're here to help us," Welsh said. "But, tell me this, why does he want you?"

"I have no idea."

"Do you know who he is?"

"No, but I presume you do."

"No, we only have a name, but it's a fake, Eric Franklin."

"You got into bed with a complete stranger. That's risky."

"He took over the Australian operation about a year ago. They seem to trust him, so I had no reason not to."

"He just appeared and took over?"

"Almost overnight."

"Can you play the video again?"

Clint played the video and Max watched intently. Franklin's voice had been slightly altered but his Australian accent was still there. Max was aware Clint was watching him, so didn't react as he watched the video. Secretly he was horrified. Eight hundred and fourteen cannisters of Erebus. He'd seen the impact from the train and couldn't help but imagine the devastation eight hundred others could inflict.

Max watched Franklin's body language and his mannerisms, and listened for clues as to who he might be.

"We have all lost people we loved thanks to your failures," Franklin said from the little screen.

Max studied the mask and its black scratches as Franklin continued to speak. A feeling of familiarity ran over him, as it had at the CIA facility when he was watching Franklin on the footage from the train and Defense base. There was something about him. Max couldn't shake the feeling he knew him.

"You know him, don't you?" Clint asked.

"No," Max dismissed.

"Maybe we should just hand you over to him now and be done with you."

"Sure. If you want to agree that he is in charge and become his bitch. Go right ahead."

"Max is right, Clint," Welsh interjected. "We don't work for Franklin or whoever he is, and if he and Max have some sort of bad blood that might work out well for us. Max could take him out and I can finally become the leader of our global network."

"Unless Franklin or the government kill him first."

"They can try," Max said. "They wouldn't be the first."

"I'm worried they will be the last and we'll be the ones left to suffer."

"Enough!" Welsh snapped. "It's my call and I want him here. Both of you go get changed and meet me at the cars. It's time to go."

"You got it," Max said turning obediently and leaving the room.

Chapter Sixteen

Max sat in the rear of the four-wheel drive. It had been five and a half hours since they left Los Angeles and they were not far from San Francisco.

Almost seven years ago, Max and his AIS colleagues had stopped a series of terrorist attacks around the world, including stopping the detonation of a suitcase nuke in San Francisco. Max had gotten the intelligence to the Americans just in time for them to stop the device from wiping out a massive chuck of the city and no doubt thousands of people.

The Australian Prime Minister was in town to commemorate the anniversary of the occasion ahead of several days of official visits and dinners hosted by the American President to celebrate the countries friendship and partnership, especially in defence and intelligence.

The Prime Minister and President were due to open a new joint intelligence facility in San Francisco in the morning. The facility was to become part of the Echelon network and it was the first to be funded jointly by Australia and the United States on US soil. The promise was a new era of global surveillance and counter-terrorism to find and exploit enemy secrets, and protect the Five Eyes countries secrets both at home and abroad. It would employ a large workforce of information technology experts and intelligence agents from all five countries, but primarily Australia and the US.

Max looked through the official itinerary and saw the ribbon cutting event and the tour which would follow. Then he saw the official guest list. It was a who's who of the Five Eyes intelligence and political community, including Hulk. His heart sank with the added risk of his mentor and friend being in the line of fire.

Welsh's plan was simple enough. Gain access to the facility, plant the devices and leave before they went off, while the leaders were touring the site. But, putting the plan into action, that was another thing all together. Max studied the blueprints of the facility. It was without question the most secure building he had seen in years, possibly ever.

"What do you think, Max?" Welsh asked pointing to the blueprints.

"There is one obvious point," Max said turning the plan around and pointing at a small section outside the building. "This is the air intake. We could set one off just near this and it would be sucked inside."

"We'd lose some on the way in though."

"Yeah, but it's not your only problem. There is a filtration system on the airducts and it regularly tests the air. It would detect the chemical in an instant and shut the system down. We need to get into the facility and shut off the filtration system, before we can release the weapon, if we want to use the intake."

"So, what would you do?"

"Well, the security is too tight to get in on a normal day, let alone the one they are about to have."

"So, how do we get it in there? Does someone act as a mule?"

"A mule?"

"Someone to take it in for us."

"The guards will pick it up on the x-ray. They'll be checking all the bags."

"I don't think we take it in. We still use the air intake, but someone goes in and shuts off the ventilation system's sensors."

"How do we get someone inside?"

"We need a distraction at the official ribbon cutting which is going to be held outside on the grounds. They will throw open their doors to get the officials and staff inside. We just need to figure out how to get onto the grounds without being seen. But, I think I have an idea."

"Good, you and Clint will go in, and the rest of the team and I will cause the distraction."

"It would be better if I went in alone."

"Like fuck are you going in alone," Clint interjected angrily. "How many times do I have to tell you, I don't trust you?"

"All I am saying is getting one person in will be difficult. Getting two in increases the risk and lowers the probability."

"I don't care. I'm not letting you go in alone."

"Fine."

Max and the UFF team finalised their plans then made their way to the safehouse. Max had spent the last couple of hours making false invitations for the event from himself and Clint.

He had changed into a new suit, shirt and tie, then rode with Clint to the new facility. Clint parked the car and they walked slowly towards the line at the security check point. Well over half the guests were already in their seats on the lawn outside the massive new glass and concrete intelligence facility. The remaining guests, and Max and Clint, were in a sectioned off line to the left. The guards and Secret Service agents were thoroughly checking everyone, but Max could see they were speeding up trying to get everyone in before the VIPs arrived.

Sirens drew nearer as Max and Clint got closer to the front of the line. They were almost deafening as they reached the front of the queue. Max produced his fake invitation which he had constructed using stolen files from AIS. The security guard was typing away on a tablet computer looking for Max's fake name, as the President's motorcade pulled into position next to the gate.

Max turned to the motorcade and saw President Torres and Prime Minister Ferguson get out of the big black limousine, closely followed by the Director of the CIA and Hulk, the Head of the Australian Intelligence Service. The four VIPs were making their way to the gate and waving to the crowd, as two four-wheel drives screamed up the road and flung open their doors.

"I'm sorry, sir," the security guard said to Max, "but I can't seem to find you on the list. Are you sure you have a right to be here this morning?"

"Look again," Max demanded. "I've come all the way from Australia to be here for this! What's your name? It would be a shame for me to have to call your bosses when this is all done."

"Okay, sir. Please calm down, I will look again now."

As the guard began typing, the two four-wheel drives screeched to a halt. Everyone turned to face them as the doors flung open. Five men dressed in heavy body armour, almost like a modern-day Kelly Gang, jumped from each car and opened fire. The Secret Service began firing back as the crowd screamed and started running for the facility's entrance.

The President, Prime Minister, CIA Director and Hulk were all but carried into the building by a swarm of guards. Once they were inside, the guards began letting the crowd into the bulletproof foyer.

The guard who had been questioning Max, threw open the gate and let Max, Clint and the other guests inside the compound. Max and Clint quickly made their way into the foyer. The security guards inside were all manning the doors with the Secret Service agents to protect the VIPs from the UFF team outside. Max and Clint made their way to the back of the foyer near the guard's sign in desk. When he was sure no one was watching, Max reached over and stole one of the guard's security access cards.

As everyone was watching the commotion outside, Max and Clint slipped into the elevator. When they reached the floor they were after, Max led the way down the corridor to the control room, having memorised the blueprint. There were two men inside the control room monitoring the security cameras and calling in support for the teams outside. They were anxious and their voices were cracking with panic.

Max took the one on the right and Clint the one on the left. Max put his guard into a sleeper hold and lowered him softly to the floor. Clint on the other hand, punched his guard as hard as he could in the back of the head, knocking him out. He fell to the floor, smashing his face on the desk as he collapsed.

"Unnecessary," Max said shaking his head, "and noisy."

"Oh, fuck off, Max," Clint spat. "I knew you hadn't changed. Look at you, upset over one guard."

"There are a bunch of people dying out the front. I couldn't give a shit about them or this guy. He made a noise when he fell. You could be more subtle."

Clint took a gun from the unconscious security guard's belt. He locked eyes with Max and pulled the trigger. The bullet smashed into the guard's face at point blank range and it exploded with blood and brain matter, but neither man blinked. Max had passed Clint's little test.

"Whatever, let's just get this done," Clint said turning away breaking their stare contest. "Do you have the codes?"

"Yes," Max stated, still staring intently at Clint.

"Where did you say you got them from again?"

"I hacked AIS."

"And you're sure they can't trace that?"

"Yes," Max lied.

In fact, not only could they trace it. Max left a coded message in the system telling AIS to move in to stop the attack.

As he started typing on the building system's computer, the door behind him flung open and he heard a familiar voice.

"Stop what you are doing, Max," Kate 'Alpha' Matthews demanded, "and put your fucking hands up."

Max raised his hands without turning around as Clint spun and raised his weapon. It was a mistake. Max heard two rounds slam into Clint and he heard him scream. Max turned to see Kate and Jonnie 'Bravo' Belluci both holding their pistols at Clint's face. Clint was holding his shoulder with one hand and his knee with the other.

"Good to see you, Max," Kate said, "been a long fucking time. You got old."

"Hi Alpha," Max said lowering his hands and smiling broadly. "Good to see you too. Hey, kid."

"Hey Max," Jonnie replied. "How you been?"

"I've been good kid. Thanks for asking."

Max took a moment to study his two former colleagues. Both were a few years older since he had seen them in London. Kate was still as tall and strong as ever, but she had a few more worry lines and a couple of new scars. Jonnie, the rookie Max had been mentoring before he went on the run, had grown into his lanky frame and was fitter and stronger than the last time Max had seen him. He had obviously seen a lot of action since Max had left, but he still had those big eager to please eyes Max remembered.

"I fucking knew it!" Clint spat, "I knew you couldn't be trusted."

"Shut the fuck up," Kate said pistol whipping Clint across the face. "You're lucky I don't just put a bullet in your pathetic skull right here."

"Wait 'til Welsh hears this!"

"How's he going to find out?" Max asked getting down close to Clint's face. "Look around you. You aren't going anywhere."

"Fuck you," Clint managed to get out before his wounds and surroundings seem to overwhelm him into silence.

"Is the President clear?"

"Yes and she took the Prime Minister with her," Kate said. "They are on route to Air Force One, then they'll be heading for Washington."

"And Hulk?"

"He went with the team to secure the devices."

"Is he up to that? I mean, he…"

"Don't let the cane fool you," Jonnie jumped in trying to reassure Max. "He's still a fighter."

"I'm sure he is," Max said noting Kate's non-committal half-shoulder shrug and dip of the head. "Bravo, take this piece of shit to the car. Alpha, come with me to back up Hulk."

"Ack," Kate acknowledged.

"Got it," Jonnie responded.

Kate and Max ran through the building up and out the front door. The gunfire had stopped and it looked like most of the UFF men were dead or had fled the scene. There were a number of dead VIPs, security guards and Secret Service agents, and medical staff were already on scene to start helping the wounded.

Max headed left with Kate close on his heals. They rounded the corner of the building and started to run at a full sprint towards the air intake where Welsh was going to place the Erebus cannister. Max leapt over two dead bodies as he ran to the side of the building and pulled the vent from the wall.

There was no sign of the cannister and no sign of Hulk.

"These are his guards," Kate explained sliding her hand over one of the dead agent's faces to close his eyes.

Max looked around and saw the large cuts in the wire fencing where Welsh and his team had cut through during the commotion. It was Max's plan. He felt the guilt running through his system.

"They took him," Max said turning to face her. "It's my fault, Kate."

"You did what you had to do," Kate said. "And, you stopped the assassination of two world leaders in the process."

"What are we up against here?"

"No fucking idea, kid, but sure as shit we've been up against worse. And, I've got your back, like the good ole days."

"Thanks, Kate. It really is good to see you, even if it's under shit circumstances."

"You too, Prince Charming. Now, how about we cut the sentimental shit and go find our boss?"

"I need to go back."

"I'll drive you."

Chapter Seventeen

Franklin grabbed the table, screamed and violently overturned it. His laptop and phone as well as various files and pieces of stationary scattered on the concrete floor.

"What the fuck are these people doing?" Franklin roared with rage. "One fucking job! Is that too hard, is it too much to ask of them? Fuck!"

"They have the Erebus cannister still," one of his men, Victor Jaeger said.

"Who the fuck cares? I should go over there and pour one down Welsh's throat."

"I think that's a good idea, especially after he killed two of our guys."

"He will get what's coming to him for that, but I cannot fucking believe he missed Torres and Ferguson."

"It was an impossible task, boss, especially given the security."

"Oh, fuck that! The plan was solid."

"He told you the plan?"

"Yes, he said he and his men had worked out how to get the cannister into the air intake using a distraction."

"Sounds too good to be true."

"Clearly! But, when he worked it through with me, I had to admit it is exactly what I would have done."

"So, how did it fail? You did this sort of thing for years. Where was the hole in their plans?"

"I don't know. If I knew that I would have warned them."

"When you spoke to him, did he tell you why he killed our guys?"

"Yes. They were going to refuse to give him the cannisters."

"Why?"

"He said there was a disagreement."

"What sort of disagreement?"

"I don't know. Fuck, what is this? Twenty questions."

"Sorry boss, but it just doesn't make sense. They were two of our best. If they had doubts about giving Welsh the Erebus cannisters, I'm sure it was for a reason."

"Yeah, I agree, but I thought Welsh would be killed at the opening anyway, so that justice would be served. Now, who knows what the fuck is going on."

"In fairness, we only know Torres and Ferguson got away. We have no idea what happened to Welsh and his team."

"They got away," Franklin said tossing his phone to Jaeger who read the latest message.

F, both bitches got off the chain. No go on E release. Going back to the safehouse to regroup and develop a new plan. I know it looks like we fucked up, but I have something for you that I hope will make up for it. W.

"What does he have for you?" Jaeger asked.

"Scroll up," Franklin said. "It's not a what, but a who."

"Who is that?" Jaeger asked studying the picture.

"That's General Patrick Scott, codename Hulk, the Head of the Australian Intelligence Service."

"He is on your list."

"Yes, he is on top of the list. He is Max's mentor and one of very reasons this is all happening. In fact, he is responsible for it all. If it wasn't for him, I wouldn't have to get revenge because I never would have been involved in the first place. She would still be here and I wouldn't be who I am today. I was hoping to break him last, but why wait?"

"So, what's the plan now?"

"This is a gift I can't ignore. I'm going to get Hulk and I'm going to destroy him and everything he has built. It is really the least I can do to return the favour."

Chapter Eighteen

Kate drove Max and dropped him a few blocks from Welsh's safehouse where they had prepared for the mission. She promised to stay put in case he needed back up. Max had taken his flick knife out and cut a gash in his left leg, not deep, but enough to be noticed before he got out of the car.

He hobbled quickly through the streets until he got to Welsh's block. At the neighbour's house, he slipped into the yard and made his way around the back. The blood from his leg had covered his left hand from holding the wound and was running down his leg. He dragged an outdoor table over to the fence and used it to throw himself over into Welsh's yard.

He laid in the garden for a few minutes, playing it up, in case any of the guards had seen him, which it turned out they had. Two guards aimed their weapons at the bushes and native grasses he was laying in.

"Come out with your hands up," one of the men ordered.

"Yeah, yeah," Max replied, "okay, just give me a fucking minute would you. You have no idea the shit I had to do to get out of there."

"I don't care, just come out with your hands up."

"Fine," Max said tossing his pistol at the guard's feet.

Both guards looked down at the weapon as it bounced on the pavers. Max used those precious seconds to spring out of the bushes and disarm both men. One of the men staggered to the left as Max punched him in the neck. The second man staggered to the right as Max threw his elbow back into *his* neck.

Max moved like lightning throwing a series of punches and elbows, one blow for each man in turn, down both their bodies. Neck, neck, rib cage, rib cage, stomach, stomach, kidney, kidney. The two men were clutching at their sides and trying to pull away from Max. He swept his leg around and kicked both men's feet out from under them. The task made easier by the fact they were both off balance falling away from Max. The first guy smacked his head pretty hard on the pavers and moaned as he rolled around holding his ribs and head. The second guy tried to get back up, but Max hit him in the face. He fell to the ground as Max moved to hit him again, but he stopped as someone yelled from the back of the house.

"That's enough!" Welsh bellowed as two more of his men levelled their guns at Max.

"You lads better lower those fucking guns if you want to live," Max stated looking between the two men.

"How did you get out?" Welsh asked as his two flunkies waived slightly.

"It wasn't easy."

"That's not an answer."

"I told you, this isn't my first rodeo, Dylan."

"How did you get out?"

"I got out through the vents and used the confusion to slip out. No thanks to you by the way."

"What does that mean?"

"You were supposed to wait for us. We get in and change the computer settings. We signal you and you place the cannister in the intake, and wait until we arrive to detonate it. Then we leave together. Together! Where the fuck were you?"

"When the reinforcements arrived so quickly and got those two bitches out of there, I guessed you were burnt. No way out."

"Well, you guessed wrong."

"So it would seem. Where is Clint?"

"He didn't make it."

"What?"

"He didn't make it."

"That is unacceptable."

"Well, tough shit, Dylan. You have no fucking idea what I had to do to get out of there. That stupid arsehole didn't listen to me and got his dumb arse shot and got me knifed as I took down his killer. See?"

Max raised his left hand and showed Welsh his bloodied palm which seemed to calm the three men.

"Now, how about we go inside so I can clean and bandage this before I pass out?" Max asked.

"Fine," Welsh said turning to his men, "lower your weapons. Come in the house and let's get you cleaned up."

Max followed Welsh inside and made his way to the bathroom. He took off his pants and sat over the bathtub. He ran the water and rinsed his leg. The cut was a couple of inches long and a bit deeper than he had planned. One of the men who had been pointing a gun at him a few minutes earlier arrived with a first-aid kit and sat it on the steps leading up to the bathtub next to Max then left the room when Max said thanks.

Max stitched the wound and added a couple of staples for extra support. He rewashed the wound and dried it, then tightly wrapped a bandage around his leg and secured it in place. He walked to a nearby room and found a pair of skinny leg jeans which he squeezed into, figuring the pressure might help hold the wound together.

Max headed upstairs, just following the sound of people talking. He didn't go into the room, instead he waited in the hallway listening to the conversation.

"How could you fuck this up, Dylan?" Franklin asked from behind his scratched-up mask on the little computer screen, his voice distorted by the computer software. "I trusted you and you promised me you could handle things."

"We had a setback," Welsh said.

"A setback? It was a fucking catastrophe!"

"You're right, but my team can handle it."

"How? How exactly do you plan to handle it? Torres and Ferguson are halfway to Washington and will be locked in a fortress within hours."

"We'll come up with something."

"We'll, who's 'we'll'?"

"My team and I."

"How many men do you have left after the assault on the facility?"

"Only a few in San Francisco, but more are on their way from LA. And, I've also got an expert to join the team."

"Do you just? And, who would that be?"

"You know him actually."

"Do I detect some smug satisfaction on your face and in your tone? He can't be that impressive given all your fuck ups today."

"It was his plan, that you endorsed by the way."

"You're telling me you have a new member of your team who is experienced enough to develop the assault plan, but you still couldn't execute it?"

"The plan was faultless."

"Clearly not. Well, go ahead then, who is it?"

"Max Shaw."

"Bullshit!"

"I'm not kidding you. Max 'Prince' Shaw, one of the most decorated and skilled agents in the history of the Five Eyes intelligence agencies, is now on my payroll."

"You are a fucking idiot!"

"What? Why?"

"If the person who is claiming to be Max Shaw, is indeed Max, then it is no wonder your plans failed. He is the best for a reason and if it was his plan, he also planned for you to fail."

"He got injured escaping the facility and he escaped CIA custody."

"And?"

"And, he killed a bunch of people on the way out, he is a fugitive. I have been working to recruit him for months. He wanted revenge on The Sixteen for what they did to him. I helped him get it, now he is returning the favour. His skills and experience will be vital for our organisation going forward. I trust him and I need him."

"Don't lecture me about the Prince. I know his history. He has been a fugitive for years and was never found. That is not a coincidence. If he wanted to, he could have disappeared forever. But, he didn't. You yourself said he was in CIA custody and I'm telling you, if he was in custody, it's because that's where he wanted to be."

"But all the people he killed, all the heads of The Sixteen, he did it for personal reasons."

"While I have no doubt he got some closure from killing them, I also have no doubt that he did it out of his sense of patriotic duty. He had dual purposes. This is a man who cannot be turned. Trust me. I know this man, better than you. You have let a wolf into the henhouse."

"I don't believe you."

"Believe what you want to believe, Dylan, but I am telling you it is simply not possible that Max Shaw has turned his back on his nation. If killing his fiancé didn't do it all those years ago, finding and hunting down Lachlan's killers isn't going to do it now. He cannot be turned."

Welsh sat for a moment thinking about what he had just heard.

"If that's true," Welsh said, "what should I do?"

"You should put a bullet in his head, before he puts one in yours," Franklin stated coldly.

A shiver ran down Welsh's spine as the barrel of a pistol was pressed against his temple.

"Hello, Max," Franklin said from the screen. "I wish I could say it is good to see you again, but that would be a lie."

"You wouldn't be the first to think that," Max said starring down the lens of the webcam, "and when we meet again in person, I'm going to show you why."

"Good to see you're still as serious as ever, but I'm holding all the cards and you are not going to win this time."

"Why are you doing this?"

"Because you and Hulk, and the whole intelligence community deserve to be destroyed. You claim to be the good guys and the protectors, but you failed. I'm going to repay you all for failing to keep your promises to me and to the citizens of our nations."

"Broken promises? I don't even know who you are. Why don't you take that mask off and reintroduce yourself to me?"

"Nice try, Max, but that's not how this is going to work. You should feel free to put a bullet in Mr Welsh's head. I don't need him anymore. Oh, Dylan, I'm taking over your organisation. As of today, the UFF's resources are mine and I will be assuming control of our other sister organisations as well. Too many chiefs, Dylan. I need to clean house and take over."

"You can't have them," Welsh snapped.

"I already have, check for yourself if you like."

Welsh moved forward slightly to type on the keyboard. Within seconds the colour drained from his face. The UFF and his own bank accounts had been drained. He logged into another system and saw the deeds to his real estate portfolio had also been taken as well as his whole share portfolio.

"You son of a bitch," Welsh said. "The others won't let you get away with this."

"Oh, I think they will," Franklin countered. "Pull the trigger, Max, and then you probably want to shoot yourself too."

"I think I'll give that a miss," Max replied, "but, I'll keep one for you."

"Suit yourself, but you should know, by my calculations you are out-numbered and out-gunned."

"What are you talking about?"

"I've got a confession. I've been keeping you distracted. My men are in the safehouse. They are on their way up to get you and bring you to me. See you soon."

Franklin stood and threw his mask down onto the chair. His face was out of the camera shot, but the mask stared blankly and ominously at Max.

"Clint was right," Welsh said. "You lied to me."

"I think we have other problems right now," Max said dragging Welsh out of the chair as the door behind him flew open.

Max hauled Welsh to the floor and fired three shots into the two men in the doorway as they fell. Welsh wrestled Max trying to take the gun, but Max slammed his forehead down on Welsh's nose breaking it. Welsh recoiled holding his face, as two more of Franklin's men arrived in the doorway. Max fired two shots, the first hit one of the men in the forehead. The second sliced a chunk out of the second men's neck. He dropped his gun and clutched desperately at the gushing wound. Within seconds he would be dead.

"Get up!" Max demanded, pulling Welsh up onto his feet. "Where is Hulk?"

"You broke my fucking nose!" Welsh spat. "Fuck you!"

Max whipped his pistol into the side of Welsh's head, butt first.

"I don't have time for your bullshit," Max said as he punched Welsh in the nose. "Where is Hulk?"

"Downstairs," Welsh managed to say through the pain.

"Where downstairs?" Max asked raising his fist again.

"Basement. Handcuffed to the radiator."

"Lead the way," Max instructed moving in behind Welsh.

"You could at least give me a gun."

"After the shit you tried to pull in there, no fucking way."

"But I'm exposed."

"You're dead in three seconds unless you start moving and take me to Hulk."

"Fine," Welsh said gingerly leading Max from the room.

When the two men got to the staircase, there were two men starting to climb towards the second floor. Welsh flinched in fear, but Max did not hesitate. He fired the first shot into the leading man. He fell backwards into the second man and the pair stumbled down the bottom few stairs to the floor. The corpse fell on top of the second man pinning him to the floor with dead weight, inches from the gun he had dropped in the fall. Welsh and Max moved down the stairs as the man was trying to reach for his gun. Max kicked the gun away, then pressed his pistol into the trapped man's right eye. He squirmed and groaned in pain as the metal pressed hard against his eye.

"How many are there?" Max asked pushing the gun down harder.

"Twelve," the man said. "There are twelve of us."

"That won't be enough," Max said pulling the trigger.

Blood, brain and skull fragments exploded out of the man's head.

"Jesus Christ!" Welsh said. "You are a fucking psychopath."

"You don't know the half of it, so I suggest you don't fuck with me," Max declared standing and reloading his pistol. "Now, move."

Welsh led Max through the safehouse, towards the kitchen. The pair moved quietly onto the tiled floors of the kitchen, but the silence was interrupted by a volley of bullets from behind them.

Max shoved Welsh forward running him towards the kitchen island. He jumped forward knocking Welsh to the floor, as bullets slammed into the cheap cupboards and benches surrounding them. The bullets ripped holes in the various surfaces and smashed glasses. The kitchen window exploded as a bullet went through, raining glass down over Max and Welsh.

Max knelt behind the bench and blind fired over the top, in the direction he thought the bullets were coming from. When the gun clicked dry, he looked down and saw Welsh was clutching his chest. He had thought the attackers had been bad shots to miss him, but now he realised he was not the target. Max propped Welsh up against a cupboard door and ripped open his shirt. Blood was pumping out of a small hole in his chest with every beat of his fading heart.

"Who is he, Dylan? The man in the mask," Max asked.

Welsh tried to speak, but no words left his mouth. Blood trickled down from the corners of his mouth as tears welled up in his eyes. He again tried to speak, but instead coughed blood onto the floor.

"Please, Dylan, help me stop him," Max pleaded. "He completely fucked you and your men, and your cause, help me return the favour."

"He…" Welsh managed to get out, "…he's one of yours."

"Who is he?"

"AIS Agent…"

"Give me a name."

"I don't…" Welsh said but was interrupted by a flash of bullets rushing overhead.

Max reloaded and fired back over the bench, pushing his attackers back. He looked around the kitchen looking for anything he could use, then he saw the cupboard opposite had a bullet hole in it. Through the hole, he saw the reflective surface of a new steel pot. He opened the cupboard softly and dragged the pot out. He slid it on the floor out into the walkway about a foot from the bench.

He sat against the cupboard, starring at the pot, using its reflective surface to see his attackers. They were starting to inch closer to the bench.

Max let one of the men come within a couple of metres, then he fell to his left, laying on the floor with his arm and head in the gap beside the bench, and fired three shots. The bullets slammed into the approaching attacker and dropped him to the floor. Max scrambled back in behind the bench as bullet hit the floor around him. One hit the pot sending it back a metre or so, it spun and danced on the spot, ringing from the impact until it stopped in its place with a deep, but soft, thud. Max saw the dint the bullet had made. It distorted the reflected images, but he could still see the room.

Max fired over the bench pushing back his attackers again, until his weapon ran dry. He looked down to Welsh, he was dead. Max shook his head. He wasn't sure how he was going to find Franklin now, then he saw Welsh's mobile sitting open in his bloody hand. Max grabbed the phone and looked at the list of emails open on the screen. It was a long list of his former colleagues' files from AIS. The subject of the emails said *Franklin Suspects.* Welsh had wanted revenge on Franklin and with his last moments on earth, he had handed the evidence over to Max knowing he would find Franklin and kill him.

Max quickly forwarded the emails to Blake, then pocketed the phone. His pistol was out of ammo, so the only thing he could do now was draw them in for close combat. He looked around the kitchen again, but didn't find anything useful, until his eyes returned to Welsh.

He moved into position and placed his flick knife between his teeth, then he inched Welsh off the ground. Little by little, until his forehead was over the bench. A bullet smashed into it, spraying blood and brain matter over the bench and cupboards. Max dropped Welsh's lifeless body to the floor, then waited. The two guards inched forward, confident they had killed their target. He waited patiently, watching the room's reflection on the pot.

One of the men got to the kitchen bench and Max sprung up. He pulled the man's gun forward and locked it under his left arm, then he spat the flick knife into his right hand and stabbed it towards the attacker's neck, pressing the blade release as it moved through the air. The blade slid into his neck and Max reefed it forward, tearing it out through the attacker's windpipe. Then he threw the knife end over end at the remaining attacker, using the first guy as a human shield. The knife pierced into the man's eye. He screamed in pain, as the knife lodged firmly in place. He squeezed the trigger of his weapon and bullets flew all over the room, more than one hitting his dead colleague who Max was using as a shield.

His gun clicked dry and he trashed around the room, holding his eye. The knife was still lodged in it and the wound was bleeding badly. The attacker's hand was covered in blood. Max let go of his comrade and the lifeless body fell to the floor. Max leapt the bench and dived over the couch tackling the wounded man. They both wrestled on the floor. The attacker was strong and Max was struggling to get him under control. He got Max into a bear hug and began squeezing hard. Max was finding it hard to breathe. He pulled his head back as far as he could then headbutted the butt of the flick knife. Max's head ached from the impact, but it had done the trick. The knife drove deeper into the guard's head and up into his brain. He instantly went limp and Max rolled to the ground, taking in some deep breaths.

He heard footsteps on the stairs and quickly rolled over the dead attacker and pulled him up as a shield. Bullets slammed into the floor all around him and into the dead attacker. Max used one of the dead men's guns to return fire and took out one of the intruders from the stairs, but not before three men escorting Hulk got through behind the dying attacker.

Max chased the men, dropping, ducking and moving behind cover as the men with Hulk fired in his direction. He didn't fire back, not wanting to hit his boss. They made their way to the front of the safehouse and Max took cover behind the door.

Outside in the yard there were three cars and a number of Franklin's men. A couple of them were arguing about going back in to capture Max. Max decided not to wait, he opened fire. Three men in the grouping on the right, fell as the men from the house bundled Hulk into one of the cars. Bullets impacted the door and Max ducked back behind the frame for cover. He took a knee, peered out and fired again, taking down another one of Franklin's men as the car with Hulk in it reversed up the driveway. Max fired a shot into the front tyre and into the grill hoping to hit the radiator. The wheel exploded, but the shot into the radiator missed. It couldn't get far with a wheel out though, so it stopped on the driveway.

A second car reversed up to the one with Hulk in it, as more bullets hit the doorframe and Max was forced back into cover. While he was sheltering behind the door, Hulk was moved into the second car and a few of the attackers left the scene with the Head of AIS in their trunk.

Clearly the man from the stairs had lied to him, there were more than twelve people onsite. He was glad he had shot him. Five of the intruders were still in the yard, aiming at the door. Max fired at the grouping who were now in cover behind their own car. He took one guy down, but then his gun ran dry. The four men in the yard noticed it too and quickly began to move forward. He took cover as three gunshots rang out from the street. Max ducked his head around to see two of the men dead in the driveway and the other two aiming their weapons back towards the street.

Max ran from the house and across the short distance to the closest man. He punched him in the back of the neck and dropped him to the ground.

Kate came around the corner and shot the remaining man in the face.

"They got Hulk," Max said dragging the unconscious man at his feet up onto his shoulder. "We've got to move."

"Got it," Kate said. "I've got Blake tracking the vehicle."

"Let's move," Max said running up the driveway with the unconscious man over his shoulder and followed Kate to her waiting vehicle.

Chapter Nineteen

"Just like old times, hey Max?" Kate asked as she sped through the city streets trying to catch up to the men who had Hulk. "Did you miss it?"

"Parts of it," Max admitted, "but mostly the team, not the car chases with terrorists."

"Fair enough. Well, we fucking missed you. You left a big hole in the team, mate, that's for damn sure. We could have used your help on more than a few missions too."

"Well, I'm glad you are all in one piece. London was a fucking disaster, but I'm glad you all pulled through. How's the kid going?"

"Bravo?"

"Yeah, Jonnie. How's he going?"

"You should spend some time with him when you can. Christ, Max, he still idolises you. When they said we had to come after you, he was the first one to protest. You should have seen him. He kicked over his chair and slammed his hands down on the table, and started screaming and pointing at Hulk and Blake, accusing them of turning on you. I'll never forget it. We all thought it was bullshit, what they did to you, none of us ever believed you would risk national security for a personal vendetta. Hulk and Blake knew too, but they had a job to do."

"I'm not going to lie, Kate, some of it was personal. They killed Lachlan and Flash. I was struggling. I wanted them all dead. But, you're right, I couldn't risk anyone else getting hurt or ending up in a situation like mine. I couldn't risk the team either. I had to do it on my own. I had to protect you and Jonnie, and Blake and Hulk."

"I get it, Max, but know we would do anything for you, especially to get back at these arseholes for what they did to you and to our team. Flash was a great friend to all of us too and a bloody good agent, we missed him every day too, still do."

"I'm ashamed I missed the funeral."

"It was a very sad day, but we gave him a good send off."

"I checked in on Jane a few times, as much as I could, but I felt she was starting to loath my calls, so I've kept my distance for the last couple of years. How is she, do you know?"

"Oh Christ, Max. You don't know? I'm sorry to be the one to have to tell you, but she died in an accident."

"What? What kind of accident?"

"Her car ran off the road. It was a rainy day and it went through a safety rail and down into a ravine. I'm so sorry, Max. I thought you knew."

"No, that's okay. I didn't know."

They sat in silence for a few minutes as Kate kept pushing the big car to its limits, in and out of traffic to the sound of horns blasting from other motorists.

"Well, at least she's no longer in pain," Max eventually said, "Flash's death hit her so hard. They were so in love. She knew the risks, as we all do, but it was just too much for her to take. She cried with me for hours over the phone. We were all so close, Jane, Flash, Lachlan and I. Those were different times. It feels like a different lifetime now. They were there for me, I'm devastated I couldn't be there for them."

"I'm sure they understood, Max. You can't beat yourself up over it. I was there, you did everything you could to save Flash."

"We all did, but I left him in the street. I'll never forgive myself for that."

"We left him, Max. He was dead and we had a job to do. He, of all people, would understand."

"I've felt guilty about it every day since and now with Jane too," Max trailed off.

"It's a lot to have on your shoulders, Max, but as I said, I was there too and share the burden of decisions we made. You're not alone in this."

"Thanks, Kate. It's been a hard few years without you there to help guide me and I could have used your help on a few missions too."

"That's not what I hear from Blake. He reckons you killed every one of those arseholes with ruthless precision. Well fucking trained I hear."

"Well, you should know, you trained me."

"Fucking oath I did and a bloody good job I did too."

"That's true. Thank you."

"Don't need to thank me, kid. Just get ready to kill some more of these pricks when we find them."

"You got it," Max said managing a smile at his old friend.

"We've got them on satellite, Prince," Blake said over their comms units from the CIA facility. *"You're closing in, about five blocks ahead."*

"Got it, mate," Max noted, "keep tracking them. We need to get him back."

"They're making a turn. Okay, two blocks. One block. Next right, Alpha."

"Ack," Kate said dragging the big four-wheel drive around the corner, screeching the wheels.

"There it is," Max said pointing through the windscreen at the car he had seen not long ago leaving the safehouse with Hulk onboard. "The blue Dodge."

"Yeah, I got the fuckers," Kate said as she weaved the large vehicle in and out of the traffic.

"Get in close," Max ordered lowering his window and clicking the safety off on his MP5.

As Kate moved in behind the fleeing vehicle, Max climbed up onto the doorframe, shouldered his MP5 and opened fire. Bullets slammed into the rear taillights of Dodge SUV and into the bitumen as it weaved hard to avoid oncoming cars and his bullets. One of Franklin's men in the backseat started returning fire blindly out his window at Max and Kate. Kate swerved and a row of bullets slammed into the windshield of the car behind them. The driver of that vehicle stomped on the brakes and caused a chain reaction of rear impacts as other cars slammed into the back of it. The noise was astonishing. Max turned back to see two cars flip after smashing into the tailgate of the stopped vehicle. One landed on its roof and skidded to a stop against the gutter trailing a shower of sparks. The other rolled over twice, before stopping on its side. Its windows shattered and pieces of plastic were flung metres through the air. Behind the crashed vehicles, others rear-ended each other crumpling bonnets and boots.

Max turned back and opened fire, again aiming for the rear wheel. The passenger who had fired at them a moment ago, turned his fire on the vehicles either side of his own. Bullets shot out his window into the windows and doors of cars in Kate and Max's path. The vehicles swerved and braked, while others shot off in other directions pulling away from the incoming fire. Kate was braking and swerving trying to avoid the new obstacles in their path, while Max held onto the doorframe and continued to fire when he got a clear shot.

Finally, his bullet found its mark, the rear right tyre exploded and the car fishtailed as the driver wrestled with the wheel to keep it on the road.

Max climbed back into his seat just as the passenger from the fleeing vehicle unloaded volleys of bullets into each of the cars on either side of it. Both vehicles braked and turned into Kate's path as Hulk's vehicle shot through. Kate ploughed into the two cars. Their airbags went off and Kate and Max were thrown into them. Max had not been wearing his seatbelt and bounced hard into the doorframe as the car came to a stop.

Smoke billowed out from under the hood, as people started getting out of their vehicles to help others.

Max came to in a daze. Kate was at his side. She had pulled open the door and had been checking him for injuries.

"You okay, Max?" Kate asked looking into his eyes.

"Yeah," Max managed to say as he held his aching head.

"How many fingers am I holding up?" Kate asked holding up four fingers.

"I didn't realise this would be a maths quiz," Max joked smiling through the pain.

"How about now?" Kate asked flipping Max the bird.

"I'm getting too old for this shit."

"You'll be right," Kate said pressing the comms unit in her ear. "Hermes, it's Alpha. We had an accident. We're going to need a bunch of paramedics onsite. Any idea where those arseholes have gone with Hulk?"

"Roger that, Alpha," Blake said. *"We've got you on satellite, help is already on its way."*

"Good. What about those other pricks?"

"They turned into a shopping centre carpark two blocks north and one west of your location."

"Right. We're on our way."

"Are you both okay?"

"Yes, I'm fine. Prince Charming hit his head, but he'll be fine. We're moving now."

"Ack. Good to hear."

Kate and Max both went to the rear of the Landcruiser to get more supplies, and found Franklin's man who they had tied up in the back dead. He had been thrown into the backseat violently and his neck was clearly broken.

"Fuck," Kate said pushing him to the side. "There goes that lead."

"Yeah," Max agreed holding onto the tailgate to steady himself. "We need to get to the shopping centre."

"Agreed, let's go, Prince," Kate said tossing him an extra magazine from his MP5.

"After you," Max said still holding his head, but catching the clip with the hand he had been steadying himself with.

The two agents took off in the direction of the shopping centre. When they arrived, they shouldered their MP5s and began scanning the carpark for the Dodge. They moved row by row through the seedy, dark carpark. Lights were flickering above the packed rows of cars, but surprisingly few people were walking about, the few that were screamed and scattered or dropped to the ground when they saw the pair.

They cleared the ground floor and headed up the ramp to the second floor. The upper level was slightly bigger, so they decided to split up to cover more ground. Max made his way down the first row on his side of the carpark. He quickly scanned between the vehicles and moved through to the next row. He looked the line up and down each side, leading with the barrel of his MP5. When he made it to the fifth row, the lights flickered which made him instinctively spin to check behind himself. A group of people were leaving a nearby elevator, laughing and chatting, but they screamed in fear when they saw his weapon aimed right at them. He quickly lowered it and gave a small wave in an attempt to reassure them, but they remained locked in place starring at him.

Max heard the loud revs of an engine coming from behind. He spun on his heal and brought up his gun. It was the Dodge. His vision blurred and felt like he might pass out. He blinked and tried to focus, then fired four shots into the windscreen and through into the driver, before he dived out of the way onto the bonnet of a red Chevrolet which was parked beside him. He yelled to the group from the elevator to move, as he shook his head trying to clear his vision, but they were already running. The out of control Dodge sped past Max and rushed towards the fleeing group. It lined up one of the women running in fear, but at the last second veered into the row of parked cars.

Max leapt off the car and raised his MP5. His world was still turning in his mind, but he knew he had to push on. He noticed the rear passenger using Hulk as a shield pulling him out of the car. Max watched as his mentor was dragged backwards towards the elevator by the passenger. Hulk was limping along, dragging his cane, mouthing the words 'shoot him' to Max, but Max just held his aim. As the elevator arrived, people screamed and ran out, as the passenger dragged Hulk backwards into the lift and pressed a floor.

"That's quite far enough," the passenger said. "You wouldn't want me to blow your precious leader's head off now, would you?"

"Let him go and I promise I'll kill you quickly," Max stated confidently and coldly.

"Good luck," he said as the doors slid shut.

Max watched the elevator's number ticking up. Fourth, fifth, sixth floor, then it stopped on the seventh.

"Seventh floor," Max yelled to Kate who was just arriving at the scene.

"Go!" she yelled as Max spun and ran for the fire escape.

He took the stairs two and three at a time, as fast as he could move. His vision was still blurred and occasionally he stumbled, catching his toe on the step, but he kept moving. When he finally got to the seventh floor, he smashed through the door and ran out into the tiled shopping centre. He scanned around the floor looking for signs of where his boss may have been taken. It was a retail level with fashion boutiques and gourmet food and drink outlets.

Max walked briskly with his MP5 pressed to his shoulder, as Kate joined him mirroring his movements. People had already scattered into the nearby shops for refuge when Franklin's man had dragged Hulk through. Max could see them cowering behind tables and pillars, and running into storerooms and back hallways. He yelled into more than one shop to ask where the men had gone. According to the infrequent points and head nods, he was going in the right direction, but there was no sign of Hulk.

Max and Kate found an open stairway door leading up to the roof. Cautiously they climbed the stairs, taking turns to leapfrog each other, hugging the walls for cover. Max lent against the wall near the door at the top of the stairs. His vision was still blurry and his mind cloudy from the earlier crash.

"You okay, kid?" Kate asked.

"I'll be fine," Max said trying to ignore the pain. "Let's get this son-of-a-bitch."

"On three," Kate said taking the door handle. "Three."

The two agents burst through the door and swung left and right looking for their target. The rooftop was dotted with large commercial air-conditioners and ducts. The ground itself was covered in a thick layer of stones that crunched under foot.

Kate headed left and Max went right, both leading with their MP5s. Max stopped around the first air-conditioner he found and threw up. He held onto the unit trying to steady himself, but was forced down onto one knee. The pain in his head was increasing from the pressure. His vision was worse with every beat of his heart and he felt nauseous, but he forced himself up and kept checking the roof.

There was a sound to his left and he spun trying to place it, even as his ears began ringing. Footsteps on the gravel and someone yelling. It was Franklin's man dragging Hulk towards the elevator doors, closely followed by Kate who was aiming straight at the fleeing pair and yelling for them to stop.

Max could see Hulk and while he could not make out what he was saying, he had no doubt he would be telling Kate to shoot, but she wasn't going to take the risk either.

Franklin's man was about twenty metres away from Max, moving right to left. On a normal day, Max would have made the shot, but he couldn't trust himself. His world was starting to spin out of control.

He kept dragging himself towards his mentor and the terrorist who had him hostage, until he reached their walkway and turned left to follow them, alongside Kate.

Franklin's man had Hulk lined up perfectly between himself and the two agents. Neither Max or Kate had a shot. The elevator arrived and the terrorist staggered in with Hulk.

"Four down, one over!" Hulk yelled out and pointed as the door was closing. "Erebus!"

Kate looked back over her shoulder at the rows of air-conditioning units.

"Fuck!" Kate yelled looking to Max. "We have to find the device."

"Go," Max ordered.

"You look terrible, Max, are you okay?"

"Just go, Kate. Get the device. I'll call Blake."

"Okay," Kate said running for the air-conditioning unit Hulk had mentioned.

"Hermes, it's Prince," Max said into his comms unit. "You there?"

"Yes, Prince, I'm here," Blake replied. *"Have you got Hulk?"*

"No. that arsehole dragged him off, but Hulk got a message to us. They planted an Erebus cannister in the ventilation unit."

"Oh shit. Have you secured it?"

"Alpha's over there now trying to locate it. You need to evacuate the mall."

"If I do that, Hulk and his captor will get away."

"I know. Do what you can to track him."

"I will. Issuing the evacuation warning now."

The building's alarms started ringing and a formal announcement came over the audio-system telling people to evacuate. Like Blake had said, Max knew Franklin's man and Hulk would be able to escape in the crowd. It was no use following them.

Max walked over to Kate, who was standing at one of the large ventilation units. She pulled away from the unit when Max arrived.

"Did you get it?" Max asked steadying himself on the closest row of pipes.

Kate didn't respond.

"What is it, Kate?" Max questioned seeing the look on her face.

"We were too late," Kate said pointing to the empty cannister.

Max dashed forward and grabbed the cannister. It was a small steel tube with a glass window. He peered through the glass trying to focus his vision. Kate was right, it was empty.

His heart started thumbing and his head ached. He stumbled forward, dropping the cannister, but catching himself on the air-conditioner.

"Max, you don't look well," Kate said trying to stand him up. "Max, can you hear me? Are you alright?"

Kate grabbed Max under the arms as his eyes rolled back in his head and he fell towards her unconscious.

"Hermes!" Kate shouted into the comms unit. "Erebus is in the ventilation system, Hulk's gone and Max is down! I need an urgent helo evac on the roof asap!"

"Emergency services are on the way and the building is being evacuated as we speak," Blake responded the concern evident in his voice. *"Is Max okay?"*

"He's been struggling since the accident. I need to get him to a hospital."

Chapter Twenty

Kate and Blake sat in the waiting room. Blake had been on his mobile phone screaming orders at people for over an hour. Kate had ridden in the helicopter Blake had sent with Max to bring him here to the hospital. Every minute or two, Blake's phone would ring again, and he would start yelling and giving commands.

After the first couple of calls, Kate cleared the waiting room, so Blake wasn't overheard. God knows what information he would need to share with people and she did not want the general public to hear it.

He was on another call now, screaming down the line at someone at AIS in Canberra, barking orders at whichever analyst or agent who was in charge of trying to find Hulk. Kate sat there thinking about all the years she had known Blake and she was convinced this was the first time she could remember him shouting and swearing at their colleagues. Hulk and Max were both good at loosening their tempers at people, but not Blake, he was always stoic and respectful.

"Get it done and get back to me!" Blake demanded ending the call and pacing in front of Kate.

"Come and have a seat, Blake," Kate said gesturing to the chair next to her.

"I don't think I can sit still right at this moment, Kate," Blake said tapping his phone anxiously on his hand.

"Look at me, kid," Kate said calmly and reassuringly. "You might be the boss, now, but I still trained your arse and could take you in a fight any day. So, sit your arse down, before I knock you out."

"I don't doubt that," Blake conceded smiling. "Once the Alpha, always the Alpha."

"And, don't you fucking forget it, Mr Acting Big Dick Boss man."

Blake took a seat next to Kate and fidgeted, tapping his phone on his thigh. Kate reached over and put her big hand on the phone and pressed it flat against his leg.

"Just stop, just for a minute and get your breath," Kate said calmly. "You're no fucking good to anyone if you give yourself a heart attack or have a stroke."

"Hulk's still MIA, we've got a lunatic on the run with litres and litres of a deadly chemical weapon, and," Blake's voice trailed off.

"And, Max is in surgery."

"Yeah."

"You love him, don't you?"

"I love all of you," Blake offered shyly.

"Yeah, but you're not *in love* with us. You're in love with him and have been for years."

Blake sat still in his chair for the first time starring at the wall.

"I knew it," Kate said wrapping her big arm around his shoulders. "Fucking Prince Charming. Even after all these years, hey? Bloody hell. I saw it in your eyes all those years ago at the Wool Shed. You fell for him then and have never let it go."

Blake just turned his head slightly towards her, then nodded mostly to himself as he sat forward and starred at the floor.

"It's okay, kid," Kate said squeezing his shoulders. "You're a fucking catch, he would be lucky to have you."

"Thanks, Kate," Blake finally said, "but, after all this time and too many missed opportunities, I don't think we could ever find our moment."

"That's bullshit, Blake. With all the crap thrown at both of you, you both deserve some fucking happiness. I've seen how he looks at you."

"What?"

"You must have seen it too? Even in his cold, hard eyes, when he hears your voice or sees you something stirs within him. A brightness, a softness. I don't know how to explain it, I just know what I see. He becomes less hard edged and lowers his guard a bit. It's more than friendship that's for damn sure."

"I don't know, Kate. I think there is too much water under that bridge. We've known each other for years, surely it would have happened by now if it was going to happen."

"He's been gone, what five, six years? No contact. Not with me or Hulk. He cut himself off from everyone in the world. Except for you."

"He needed to keep me in the loop on his hunt for The Sixteen."

"That's bullshit, Blake, and I think you know that. Max doesn't give a fuck about reporting in and going by the book. He could have just disappeared and never returned once he was done. He could have walked away and never looked back, and God knows none of us would blame him. But, he didn't. He kept a line open to the one person he could trust and the one person he couldn't leave behind."

"He's been through so much. Lachlan, Flash, countless missions and so much death. It surrounds him."

"And who has been there every time to help him through it? To go to your early morning gym sessions together, to wrap arms around him and tell him everything is going to be alright, to pick up the phone and trust him when the whole world was against him? You, Blake."

"What about Lachlan?"

"What about him?"

"Max just assassinated everyone connected to his death. A literal worldwide hunt for the people responsible. Did he not do that for love and vengeance?"

"I have no doubt that it was partly driven by that, but I think it could have also been a way for Max to finally put everything behind him. I think when this is done, you will see that. Will he always have a place in his heart and mind for Lachlan? Yes, of course, he will. But that won't in anyway change how he feels for you. He's not replacing one with the other. If you are both open to it, I think you will both find happiness."

Blake's phone rang interrupting their conversation. He stood up, but before accepting the call, turned back to Kate.

"Thanks, Kate," Blake said smiling. "I knew there was soft romantic under that hard arse Army shell of yours."

"Oh, fuck off!" Kate said nodding towards the door, but smiling to herself.

Blake walked to the far side of the room listening to the agent on the other end of the line as Jonnie marched in with purpose.

"Hey, kid," Kate said, "what are you doing here?"

"I've come to get you," Jonnie replied. "Think we've found Hulk."

"What?" Kate asked standing up. "Where?"

"He's still in a vehicle, some old family sedan. They've been circling the city. We've got them on satellite."

"Well what the fuck are we waiting for? Let's go."

"Following your lead," Jonnie said heading for the door.

Kate turned to face Blake. He pulled the phone away from his ear.

"They are filling me in now," Blake said. "Go get him back."

"You got it, boss," Kate replied.

"Kate," Blake said and she turned back to face him, "thank you."

"Go get yourself a Prince, kiddo," Kate said smiling before leaving the room.

Jonnie drove has little sporty WRX in and out of traffic like a possessed rally driver. He expertly shifted gears, pulled and released the handbrake, and used the clutch to slide the car this way or that. Kate couldn't be sure, but she didn't think he had used the actual brake since they got in the car.

"Don't think I'll ever get used to this," Kate commented shifting in her seat. "Fucking maniac."

"Yeah, sorry about that, boss," Jonnie laughed. "Hope you didn't have a big lunch, not like that time in Adelaide."

"I thought I told you to forget that fucking happened, you jerk."

"Forget you threw up in a McDonald's bag about two minutes after you'd eaten the burger out of it? Not a chance."

"If we don't crash and die in this piece of shit car, you better steer clear of me."

"Oh, come on, Alpha," Jonnie said hauling up the park brake then releasing it, sliding the car round a sharp right. "Bit of a rush, it's fun. Got to have some fun on or we would hate our jobs."

"I hate your fucking driving, that's for damn sure."

"You might, but you can't argue with the fact we are fast approaching Hulk's car," Jonnie said nodding towards the satellite navigation system. "Get your gun ready. You can take out the tyres when we get close."

"As long as I don't have to take my seatbelt off, you've got it," Kate said clipping the safety off on her pistol with her right hand, while refusing to let go of the seatbelt in her left.

"Alpha, Bravo, you there?" Blake asked over their comms units.

"Yes, Hermes, we're here," Kate responded, "although I'm not sure how long I'll be here for with this dickhead at the wheel. I've already been in one accident today, I'd prefer not to be in a second. What can we do for you?"

"You're closing in on the signal from Hulk's phone."

"Yes, we know. What's the car we are looking for?"

"It's a plain family sedan. Looks like am older model white Camry. Licence plate Six-Romeo-Golf-Lima-Two-Five-Zero."

"Got it, thanks Hermes. Are we sure he's in there?"

"We've been pinging his phone. It's definitely in the car."

"Yeah, but is he?"

"I asked them to ping his AIS access key too," Blake said referring to the silver ring each AIS agent wore to store

information, access their vehicles and bases. *"It sends out unique signals via mobile towers to the AIS servers."*

"And, it's in the car too?"

"Yes."

"Hulk's never taken that thing off. He has to be in there."

"I agree. Let me know when you have him back."

"Will do."

Jonnie took another hard corner, drifting the WRX into oncoming traffic before yanking it back into his lane to the aggressive horn blasts of an infuriated driver he nearly clipped.

"Whoops!" Jonnie laughed. "That was close."

Kate just looked over at him and shook her head.

"Dickhead," she said with another shake of the head.

"Look, there he is!" Jonnie said pointing through the windscreen.

"Just keep both those fucking hands on the wheel and get us in close," Kate ordered lowering her window and gripping her pistol.

"Got it," Jonnie said slamming his foot down on the accelerator.

He weaved the small car between two big SUVs, cutting off the second one which blasted its horn. Jonnie saw the male driver giving him the finger and swearing in his rear-view mirror. The old Camry driver must have heard the horn and seen them in his mirrors, because he hit the gas and took a sharp left. Jonnie shot past the turn.

"Fuck!" Jonnie spat pulling hard on the handbrake and skidding the WRX in a wide arc around one hundred and eighty degrees.

He cut off the same guy again, who wore a look of disbelief and frustration in his eyes, just before he slammed into the back of another car. It wasn't a surprise given he was swearing and starring at Jonnie instead of watching the road. He had hit his brakes, so he would be fine, but it still totalled his car.

Jonnie took the right turn and gave chase to the old Camry. It was several blocks ahead of them. Jonnie pushed the accelerator back to the floor, but it was only there for a second as he was forced to jump onto the brake for the first time in their journey. A bus had pulled out right in front of them. Kate clenched her seatbelt and put a hand up on the dashboard. Her body stiffened and she planted both feet down hard, as if pressing her own brake, willing the car to stop. It was Jonnie's turn to jump on the horn as his car came to a stop. The bus driver just gave him the finger out the window and drove on.

The oncoming traffic was too heavy to use that lane and there was a row of parked cars lining the road. Jonnie was boxed in following the bus. He slammed his hand down on the horn, but it had the opposite reaction than the one he was looking for. The bus stopped.

"Hermes, the car got ahead of us, have you still got it?" Kate asked.

"Yes, he's about six blocks ahead of you and pulling away," Blake said through their earpieces. *"You okay?"*

"We will be soon, just keep on him and let us know if he changes course."

"Will do. I've also called in the local police to assist."

"Thanks."

The bus driver climbed out and started aggressively marching back towards them, screaming abuse and telling Jonnie where he can shove his horn in some fairly colourful language. When he got close to the window, he was red with anger, but it quickly turned to fear when Kate pointed her pistol at his face.

The driver ran abandoning his bus in the middle of the road.

Jonnie looked behind him, threw the car into reverse and accelerated. The engine whirled and made a whistling noise as he drove it backwards down the road. He found a gap in the parked cars from a driveway and he reversed between them and up onto the footpath. He scrapped the left side of the car against one of those parked on the road, as Kate pressed the horn as a warning to the pedestrians. They scattered, jumping up onto the other parked cars and in through shop doors.

Jonnie used the brake for only the second time to bring the car to a stop, then slammed the little gear shift into first and sped down the footpath. He took over the sounding of the horn, while dodging pedestrians at high speed on the path ahead. There was a café near the end of the block and pulled the car left smashing through one empty set of tables and chairs, narrowly missing two people at the table next to it. Kate looked at Jonnie and he just grimaced and screwed up his face in a 'that was close' knowing gesture.

He jumped the little rally car off the gutter and back onto the road, screaming through a red light, narrowly missing cars from both his left and right.

"I know, I know," he said before Kate even had a chance.

"Alpha, Bravo, the local police threw down a spike strip and the Camry's come to a halt," Blake explained. *"They are creating a parameter, but I've asked them to wait until you arrive. You are only ninety seconds out."*

"Got it, Hermes," Kate said. "Let's go, kid."

"Don't have to tell me twice," Jonnie said hitting the gas again.

Jonnie pulled the car up next to a row of police cars and the two agents jumped out. They ran to the row of police officers who all had their guns drawn and were using their cars as shields. The police had completely circled the Camry and Kate could see the driver. He still had his hands on the steering wheel.

"Agents Matthews and Belluci, AIS," Kate stated. "Who is in charge?"

"Agent Matthews, I'm Officer Nathan Scott," Scott said. "As you can see, we have the suspect surrounded. He's not going anywhere. We held the parameter as directed."

"Thank you, Officer. Please ask your men to hold their fire. We believe one of our colleagues is in the rear or the trunk of the vehicle."

"Oh ok, yes, ma'am," Scott said before passing on the order to his troops via their two-way radios. "What is the plan, ma'am?"

"Pass me your megaphone."

Scott passed Kate the microphone for the loudhailer on the roof of his vehicle.

"You in the Camry," Kate stated over the loudspeaker. "This is Agent Matthews of the Australian Intelligence Service. As you can see, we have you completely surrounded and you have nowhere to go. Throw any weapons you may have with you out the window and keep your hands where we can see them."

The driver looked at Kate through the window, locked eyes with her and nodded in agreement. He threw a pistol out the window and it bounced on the bitumen, then put his hands into his lap, just under the ledge of the window.

"I told you to keep your hands where I can see them," Kate said, "put them up slowly."

The driver turned back to face her and smiled then a flash of light shot out from his lap, followed by a puff of smoke. He raised his hands and Kate saw he was holding a flare. Before she could react, he threw it over his shoulder and the back seat burst into flames.

Jonnie fired his MP5 and while it wasn't his normal sniper rifle it didn't matter, the bullet nailed Franklin's man right between the eyes.

"Call the fire department and paramedics, now!" Kate shouted at the nearby officers as she ran out from behind the police car towards the smoke and flame filled Camry.

But she only got a couple of metres, before Jonnie grabbed her and tried to drag her back away from the Camry.

"What are you doing?" Kate yelled. "Hulk's in there!"

Jonnie did not get the chance to answer. The windows blew out as the car exploded in a ball of flames. The explosion helped Jonnie change Kate's momentum and direction. The shockwave pushed her back into him and they fell to the ground. Kate watched in horror as the cloud of black smoke stretched several storeys into the air, filled with orange bursts of flame. She tried to crawl towards the Camry, but the searing heat made it impossible. She recoiled, the emotion evident on her face.

Jonnie leant down and put his arms around her, partly in hug and partly to try to protect her from the heat and fire. He eventually felt her resistance fall and he dragged her back to the police cars, and they sat on the bitumen in silence as sirens of the approaching fire brigade began their wail.

Chapter Twenty-One

Max woke.

His head was aching and he had no idea where he was. He tried to open his eyes. The light burned, but he blinked trying to take in the room through the pain. As his other senses came online, he could hear the repeating beeps of the heartrate monitor and could smell the bleach. He was in hospital. He coughed and sat up slightly.

"It's okay, Max," Blake said calmly and reassuringly. "You're in the hospital."

"Hi, Blake," Max said smiling and turning to look at Blake.

Max's heartrate monitor beeped quicker when he saw his long-time friend and felt Blake's hand holding his own.

"How are you feeling?" Blake asked.

"Like I was in a car crash," Max joked.

"You were, do you remember?"

"Yeah, did Kate find Hulk?"

"No, Max, they got away," Blake said slightly choking on his words.

"What is it, Blake?"

"It's nothing, Max. You just focus on getting better."

"Good try, Blake, but you know me better than that and I know you too. It's not nothing. Tell me what I need to know."

"Hulk's dead, Max. I'm sorry. We failed."

Max's heartrate monitor started beeping even quicker.

"What?" Max asked. "How did it happen?"

"We got a lead," Blake explained. "Kate and Jonnie tracked a car carrying Hulk's mobile and ring. With the local cops, they surrounded the car, but the driver set it alight. The backseat had been covered in petrol and jerry cans. He threw a flare into it and it exploded."

"Where was Hulk?"

"The fire department put out the flames and when they opened the boot," Blake said trailing off. "When they opened the boot, they found him."

"How do they know it was him?"

"From what they could tell at the scene, the remains matched his height and weight. Plus the phone and ring were found in with him. I'm sorry, Max."

"No, it can't be him," Max said sitting up and ripping the needle for the drip from his hand, and heart monitoring leads from his chest.

"Max, what are you doing?" Blake asked trying to wrestle him back into the bed.

"I'm getting out of here. Hulk could still be out there."

"Max, we followed the car. He was in it."

"And, there is no chance it was someone else?"

"No," Blake said but Max saw something in his eyes.

"What is it, Blake?"

"It's nothing," Blake dismissed trying to push Max back onto the bed. "You need to get some rest."

"Again, Blake, it's not nothing," Max argued grabbing Blake by the wrist and stopping him from pushing him back onto the bed.

A nurse ran into the room having been alerted by the disconnected cords Max had ripped free.

"Mr Shaw, what are you doing?" she asked. "You need to be in bed."

"No, I need to get out of here," Max said trying to push both Blake and the nurse away. "Please stop. Just stop!"

The pair stopped and let him sit up.

"I'm fine," Max said to the nurse, "please can you just give us a minute?"

"I," the nurse said but was interrupted by Blake.

"It's okay," Blake said. "Just give us a minute."

"Alright, I'll be just outside the door," she said leaving the room.

"What aren't you telling me, Blake?" Max asked.

"The car did stop, just once, but it wasn't for long," Blake said.

"They could have gotten Hulk out, Blake. Where did it stop?"

"We don't believe they got him out, Max. Everything is pointing to him being in that trunk. The phone, the ring, the body."

"Well, until they show me the DNA evidence, I'm not going to stop and either way I presume there's still a fucking terrorist on the run with a tonne of that Erebus shit. We need to find him and keep looking for Hulk."

"Max, there was some pressure on your brain. They drained some of the fluid via your spinal cord. You shouldn't be out of bed, let alone chasing this lunatic."

Max had thrown his legs over the edge of the bed and stood up. He saw the worry and the upset in his friend's eyes and stopped in his tracks.

"I'm sorry, Blake," Max said taking Blake's hands. "I can't just lay here. I have to find these people."

"I know," Blake conceded with a sigh. "But you don't have to. You've done more than enough. Someone else can get this one."

Max felt Blake's hands tighten on his own as if trying to hold him in place and stop him from going. Max locked eyes with Blake and he could see the worry and he could feel his oldest friend's emotions.

"I'll be fine," Max reassured. "I feel fine. The dizziness has gone and I'm back in control. Let me find these people, Blake, and if they did kill Hulk, I'll do what needs to be done."

"Okay, Max," Blake said loosening his grip knowing he could not change Max's mind. "Just promise me this time you will come back. I don't want to do this without you anymore."

"I promise, Blake," Max said putting his hand on the side of Blake's face. "I'm not going anywhere."

Blake lent in and kissed Max, and the pair just held each other closely. Blake rested his head against Max's and kissed his neck. After all these years and without speaking a word, they both knew it was right.

Kate walked into the room and saw Max's arse through the gap in the back of his hospital gown. She also saw Blake's head on his shoulder and one of his hands was inside Max's gown holding him tightly around the waist. She smiled to herself.

"Finally!" Kate yelled bounding into the room and wrapping her arms around them both. "Some fucking good news on this shit day! So, happy for you and I'm really sorry to bust in here right now, but the satellite is back in position."

"It's fine, Kate," Max said smiling and pulling away from Blake, but still keeping hold of his hand. "What satellite?"

"We asked the CIA to move a satellite over the warehouse where the Camry had stopped. The footage shows a number of trucks coming and going, and there's about twenty or so heat signatures present."

"You think it's where they are keeping Erebus?"

"Not sure, but there's a lot of trucks. They'll need a heap of them to move all those cannisters."

"Okay, let's move."

"Are you sure you're alright to join us?"

"I'm fine, Kate," Max said as Blake nodded to Kate.

"Alright, but you need to put some fucking pants on first. As much as I like to see your tight arse, I don't think the gown is very practical. I'll be outside."

"Got it," Max laughed. "I'll be right out."

Max quickly dressed into his tactical gear and holstered his weapons, then walked back over to Blake and hugged him tightly.

"See you soon," Max said before kissing Blake and squeezing his hand.

"Be careful," Blake said, "that's an order."

"Yes, boss," Max smiled before leaving the room and joining Kate. "Let's move."

The nurse was yelling at Max as he ran with Kate down the corridor.

Chapter Twenty-Two

In a dark warehouse, an old family sedan came to a stop and the driver shut off the engine. He climbed out and headed to the rear of the car and opened the boot. General Patrick 'Hulk' Scott of the Australian Intelligence Service looked up through blackened eyes at his captor.

When they had gotten out of the lift in the shopping mall, Franklin's man, Jack Rhodes, had pushed him across the carpark with a gun in his back towards a row of vehicles. People had started to evacuate and were streaming into the carpark. Rhodes picked a young man out of the crowd who had been swinging his keys on his index finger and shot him in the face.

People screamed and ran back into the mall away from Rhodes who made Hulk pick up the keys. The old agent paused for a moment in silent respect for the young man whose life had just been taken, right in his prime. Years ago, Hulk would have done anything to stop it from happening, but even he had to admit he was not what he used to be and could not risk a move.

Hulk walked leaning on his cane pressing the button on the vehicle remote looking for the indicators to flash with Rhodes relentlessly pressing the gun into his back. Finally, the quick double beep and flash of the blinkers let them know the young man's car was unlocked.

Rhodes tied Hulk's hands using a pair of jumper leads from the young man's boot and punched Hulk twice trying to knock him out, but the old agent just took the blows and smiled.

Rhodes dismissed the gesture and told Hulk to climb into the boot. His big frame lumped into the trunk of the car and Rhodes tossed his cane in on top then shut the lid, all while Hulk was still smiling broadly, taunting his abductor.

Hulk was not sure how long they had been driving, but he knew it had been well over an hour. They doubled back and made wide circles around the city. Up and down steep streets, through sharp lefts and rights. There was no way Hulk could know where they were.

When the vehicle finally pulled up, Rhodes dragged Hulk out of the boot and let the old agent use his cane to walk, even though his arms were still tied in front with the jumper cables.

They walked to a small office towards the back of the big old warehouse. Hulk was memorising and cataloguing everything he could see. He was sure it was the same warehouse from the video Franklin sent out earlier, but the floor was mostly clear. The cannisters were few and far between.

The office had been covered from top to bottom in plastic and a metal chair sat perfectly centred. Rhodes tied Hulk to the chair and left the makeshift torture chamber. Just outside the door, he was met by Franklin wearing his scratched mask.

"Boss, the General is in there tied to the chair," Rhodes said almost begging for praise.

"And the cannister?" Franklin asked.

"I used it to get away. I set it off in the shopping mall."

"How many people were in the mall?"

"I'm not sure, hundreds probably."

"Probably?"

"Yes, boss. It was pretty busy. It's a big mall."

"So, we traded a cannister, which was originally set aside to kill Torres and Ferguson at the Five Eyes facility opening, for your life?"

"Well, I, I got the General too."

"That is the only reason you don't have a bullet in your head right now."

"Yes, boss. I'm sorry. I wanted to get him back to you, so we can find out what they know."

"I'm not sure we have the time to break him."

"I thought you said everyone breaks?"

"They do, but some are much more difficult than others. This man has spent decades, not only training people on how to torture and how to delay their breaking points, but perfecting his own techniques and tolerances. It could take days."

"It could take you weeks, you weak little prick!" Hulk yelled through the door. "Better come get started."

"Do you see what I mean?" Franklin asked tilting his head towards Hulk's room. "He's taunting us."

"I am sorry, boss. I thought, given everything, that you would want him."

"He was supposed to die with those two bitches Torres and Ferguson, but now I'll get to do it in person."

"So, it worked out?"

"I guess so. Lucky you."

Franklin pushed past Rhodes and walked into Hulk's room.

"Now fellas," Hulk smiled watching them enter the room. "Any chance I can get my phone call?"

"What?" Rhodes asked. "What are you talking about?"

Franklin turned around and without saying a word punched Rhodes in the face, knocking him out, then turned back to Hulk before Rhodes had even hit the ground.

"Am I supposed to be impressed?" Hulk asked. "Why don't you take off that mask and untie me and we can see if you're as tough as you think you are?"

"Well, Hulk," Franklin said taking off his mask and throwing it onto Hulk's lap, "you should know how tough I am – you trained me."

"You got into bed with the wrong people, son. He's going to kill you."

"Not if I kill him first," Franklin said walking away, but pausing near the door. "And, don't call me son. He has always been your favourite. You both abandoned me and now you will pay."

Chapter Twenty-Three

Hulk sat in the metal chair with blood dripping from his mouth and nose. He had several cuts across his chest from some sort of lashing and his eyes were both black. He had been waterboarded and electrocuted. He had just endured thirty minutes of sight and sound torture which used high pitch sounds and flashes of light putting the victim on edge. It had felt like hours, but it wasn't the first time he had been tortured and he focused his mind to get through it. He had spent most of the time focused on the pain coming from his right hand where only hours before his captor had cut off his ring finger to remove his AIS ring. The wound had been sealed with a soldering iron.

That pain had gotten him through the subsequent torture. With every passing minute he focused his pain into hate and channelled it into thinking about all the ways he could kill everyone who had tortured him, if he could get free.

Franklin walked into the room with two of Hulk's torturers, Rhodes and another guy called Webster, and smiled at the extensive damage.

"The human body is truly amazing," Franklin said. "Capable of so many impressive things. Even now, your body is enduring the pain and starting to work on recovery. Of course, it'll all be for naught, you will be dead soon enough."

Hulk just sat and starred at the man who had assumed the identity of Professor Franklin – his torturer, his captor, his former colleague.

"Why do you persist?" Franklin asked. "You are clearly beaten."

"I'm hoping to be around when they find you, so I can watch you die properly," Hulk said spitting a mouthful of blood onto the floor.

"I've died once already, Hulk," Franklin said pulling his shirt open. "Take a look for yourself."

Franklin's body was covered in scars of various shapes and sizes. Some were purple and lumpy, while overs were white, but many of them still had visible marks from stitches and staples which were obviously not done by a professional.

"Look what they did to me!" Franklin screamed. "And, where were you?"

"The next bullet you get won't miss, you'll get your chance to die again," Hulk said. "And, I'm going to stay around just to see it."

Franklin's face flashed red with anger, but he controlled his temper. Hulk registered the emotion and smiled.

"I can't wait," Hulk said. "I hope I'm the one who gets to pull the trigger and send you off to see your dead wife."

"Fuck you!" Franklin spat backhanding Hulk then grabbing him by the neck. "You don't get to speak about her!"

"She'd die all over again in shame seeing you now," Hulk managed to say.

"I know what you are doing and it won't work. I'm not going to kill you quickly. Especially after that little outburst, I'm going to make you suffer for as long as possible."

An explosion rang out in the distance and Franklin turned to look through the door.

"Ah oh," Hulk said sarcastically, "looks like I will get to see you die after all."

"Get him to the truck and secure him inside, and move out," Franklin ordered moving to the table in the corner.

"What are you going to do?" Rhodes asked.

"I'm going to get the last cannisters and meet you at the plane."

"Got it."

Franklin grabbed his scratched mask and put it back on, before clicking the safety off on his Steyr and leaving the room.

"See you soon," Hulk yelled after him.

Rhodes cut the tape holding Hulk to the metal chair.

"Can you walk?" Rhodes asked.

"Yeah, it's left then right foot, right?" Hulk asked sarcastically. "Or is it right first then left?"

Rhodes punched Hulk in the face.

"Get up," Rhodes ordered.

"I need my cane," Hulk replied.

"Fine, give it to him," Rhodes said pointing to the cane on the table.

Webster grabbed the cane and walked it over to Hulk. He handed it to him then turned back for the door. Hulk used it to get to his feet, then as fast as he could move, slid it through his hand, so he was holding the wrong end, and he whipped it up around Webster's neck. He spun a ring near the bottom of the cane and a small metal blade flicked out of the handle, then he pulled the cane with all his might. The blade pierced Webster's neck and punctured his windpipe, then lodged in his spine. He was dead before he hit the ground.

Hulk thrust the cane forward and dislodged it from Webster's neck then spun around on his heal whipping the cane through the air. He swung it around like a golf stick and slammed the handle into Rhodes' ankle. The blade stabbed through the leather shoe straight into Rhodes' foot, while the crook caught the back of his ankle. Hulk yanked hard on the cane and swept Rhodes off his feet. He fell to the floor, dropping his Steyr and slamming his head on the concrete.

Hulk hustled across the room, picked up the fallen weapon and pressed the barrel against Rhodes forehead. Without blinking or hesitation he pulled the trigger and blood splattered across the concrete under Rhodes' head. Hulk retrieved his cane and retracted the blade before leaving the room to find a place to bunker down.

Chapter Twenty-Four

Max, Jonnie and Kate were joined by a large CIA and FBI assault team only a few blocks from the warehouse. Max was in command, much to the annoyance of the local guys, but they played their part and followed orders. He gave everyone their directions. Four teams, one for each side of the compound. Any vehicles were to be immobilised. Shoot to kill was the order on any hostiles onsite. Anyone thought to be in command or leadership positions were to be taken alive, if possible, but otherwise the shoot to kill order remained in effect.

The groups were divided up and sent to their waiting points, watching their watches. They moved in two minutes.

Max had sent Jonnie up to the roof of a nearby building with his sniper rifle to get a better look at the facility and he was calling in the play.

"Prince, I've got dozens of men moving between the trucks and the warehouse," Jonnie updated the teams over the comms units. *"They are moving cannisters and crates, and a few have large bags. Definitely more than twenty."*

"Roger that, Bravo," Max replied, "Echo team, you need to stop those trucks from leaving the facility as a matter of priority."

"Copy that AIS," the FBI Echo team leader said, *"half my men will work on the trucks. The others will secure the doors."*

"Ack. All teams, thirty seconds."

Max and Kate with the support of six CIA agents were going for the front door. They were planning to sweep the facility's higher offices looking for the man in the mask or any of his senior commanders, while the FBI SWAT teams would clear the ground floors.

"Ten seconds, Bravo," Max said running for the warehouse with his team, "five, four, three, two…"

The air cracked above Max's head as a bullet flew past from Jonnie's sniper rifle. It hit the guard on the door in the face and threw him up off his feet. A second round slammed into the guard beside him, as Max fired his MP5 into the lock on the security gate. He shouldered the gate and the chain and broken lock fell to the concrete as the gate swung open and flung back hard into the fence.

At the same moment, Max could hear shots from the other ends of the facility as the SWAT guys started making their way onto the warehouse grounds. Max had sent more men to the driveway to deal with the biggest known quantity of Franklin's men. They were under heavy fire trying to get onto the compound, as the terrorists started returning fire. Franklin's men were using the warehouse walls and the trucks for cover, while the FBI teams were using their big metal vans.

Kate slapped a chunk of C4 on the lock of the warehouse door and slid a detonator in, while Max and the team fired at any of Franklin's men they could see. Kate moved back to a safe distance then pressed the remote trigger. The door instantly exploded inwards ripping it off its hinges.

Max and his team didn't need to be told, they turned and followed Kate in through the door.

It was a massive warehouse. There were five large roller doors to Max's left for loading cargo on semi-trailers. Two of which were currently in use. There were ten of Franklin's men inside using the steel doorframes and the back of the trucks for cover from Echo team's incoming fire.

A row of offices ran the length of the righthand wall. Foxtrot team had just made entry through the emergency exit door at about the mid-point of the offices and they were only experiencing minimal resistance.

On the far side of the warehouse, Delta team had blown a hole in the steel wall and were streaming in taking down anyone in the open space.

Kate had taken down two of Franklin's men as soon as she came through the door. They had been running to help their comrades at the loading dock, but were caught off guard when Kate burst through. They hadn't even been able to raise their weapons.

Max took down a man on the stairs then bounded up two or three at a time. As he reached the middle of the staircase it turned, and raised his aim, as the stairs doubled back to face the opposite direction.

He held his aim providing cover, as one of the CIA guys ran past him. Max then gave chase, but was forced to drop to a knee as the CIA man was hit in the shoulder and fell. Max reached up to drag him back behind the stairwell wall for cover. He grabbed the agent's arm and pulled him back as a bullet hit the plaster board were the agent's chest had been. Max pulled hard and the CIA man groaned as his wounded shoulder hit the wall as he bounced down a couple of steps to where Max was kneeling.

"You okay?" Max asked.

"I'll be fine," the CIA man said. "Go get that arsehole."

"You got it," Max said moving forward and keying his comms unit. "Bravo, you there?"

"Yes, Prince," Jonnie said after another crack of his big rifle.

"Second floor, just to the right of the entrance door we came through. There's a guy there blocking the stairs. Give him something to think about will you."

"With pleasure, boss," Jonnie said turning his rifle back to the middle of the building and firing at the point Max had asked him to hit.

Max heard the four bullets tear through the metal wall and the guards at the top of the stairs were swearing and firing wildly at the metal wall as if they could hit the sniper across the street.

"That'll do, kid," Max ordered and ran up the next section of stairs as the rifle rounds stopped.

Max found the four terrorists. Amazingly, Jonnie had hit one and he was dead against the hallway wall. Max fired a burst at the two men on his right taking them both down. One of them managed to get a shot off, but it thankfully went wide.

Max spun to fire at the remaining man, but he was running at Max at full speed and launched himself in a dive. He tackled Max causing him to drop his MP5. The two men wrestled on the floor, trading blows and fighting over the lifeless bodies of the fallen guards. The man got his knee between them and kicked Max backward, then scrambled back down the hall. He found a gun grabbed it and stood up, smugly smiling as he brought the gun up to point it as Max.

"Bravo, window!" Max yelled before rolling hard to his right.

The window next to the smug terrorist exploded inwards as his head violently snapped to the side and exploded. The force of the shot took him off his feet and he fell against the wall, dead.

"Thanks, kid," Max said picking up his MP5. "Still the only man I want backing me up with that rifle. Great shot."

"Thanks, Prince," Jonnie said smiling to himself at the complement and still happy after all these years to receive his idol's praise.

Kate and the rest of their team entered the hallway and split in two. Kate and one of the CIA men followed Max and the others went the opposite direction to search the offices.

Max and his team cleared the offices they passed, but their mission was to get to the second staircase at the far end of the big building. Max was one room ahead of Kate and the CIA agent, when a door at the far end of the hallway burst open and several men ran out firing at Max and his team. Max returned fire as he jumped for an open office doorway.

Kate and the CIA agent had both made it into a nearby room, but they found themselves in a showdown with two of Franklin's men. The four of them stood aiming at their two respective targets. A Mexican standoff. Not the place anyone wants to find themselves, because normally everyone dies.

Max had made it into his room and had crawled back to the door. He stuck his phone out on video mode to get a look at the hallway. There were still two men aiming their Steyrs down the hall for cover, as Franklin, the man in the scratched mask, came out of the office and bounded up the stairs. Max grabbed a flashbang from his vest, pulled the pin and threw it around the doorframe. It bounced and skidded its way towards the two guards on the stairs. One had the sense to turn away and start running up the stairs after his boss, while the other ran forward to kick the grenade.

He kicked it and it came back towards Max, but only made it halfway before it exploded. Max had ducked back behind cover and was spared from most of the explosive flash and sound. The guard on the other hand had been so impressed with his kick that he had stayed watching the flashbang.

Max rolled out into the hallway and found the guard blinded holding his eyes and firing wildly. The shots were high and wide, so Max raised a knee and fired two shots. The first pierced through the guard's hand, then his skull. The second hit him in the chest. Max got to his feet and started running for the staircase.

As he got to the door of the room Franklin had left, another man sprung from the shadows and drove a knife down into Max's back, just near his ribs. His vest took most of the blow, deflecting the blade, but it still slashed a big cut into his skin under his arm. Max groaned as the man dashed forward again trying to stab him, but Max caught his wrists and drove his thumbs into pressure points, while twisting his arms. The man was in pain, but was fighting hard still trying to stab at Max. Max kneed his attacker in the balls, then threw his head forward and shattered his nose. Max felt the attacker's strength leave his arms and he twisted the knife welding hand up and stabbed the knife into the man's neck. He coughed blood and his eyes went wide, before starting to fall. As he dropped to his knees, Max saw another man running towards them. He pulled the bloody knife from the guy's neck and threw it end over end at the new attacker. The man tried to duck under the knife, but misjudged the speed of the incoming blade. Instead of hitting his chest or neck, it drove itself into his left eye. He fell to the floor in an instant and remained still.

Max's vest was damaged from the attack. It was flapping as he moved and it was going to get in his way, so he grabbed a spare magazine and put it in his pocket, then tossed the vest on the hallway floor and ran for the stairs.

Kate and the CIA man were still locked in their standoff with the two terrorists, and they held their gaze as a man quietly crept up behind the two terrorists.

Kate had been relieved to see her old boss sneak out of a nearby room, but she did not let it show, she didn't want to two terrorists to know he was there. She watched him move without focusing on him. Hulk's movements were covered by the gunfire downstairs and what he thought could only have been a flashbang grenade exploding in the hallway outside which got the attention of the two terrorists.

As they were distracted, Hulk slid the blade back out of his cane and wrapped it around the neck of one of the terrorists as he had with Webster earlier. In his other hand, he aimed the Steyr at the back of the head of the other terrorist.

"Put your guns down," Hulk ordered.

The two men took a moment to consider their situation, then both dropped their weapons to floor. Kate punch the closest man in the face knocking him out, before flexicuffing him. The CIA man followed suit.

"Fuck, I'm glad to see you boss," Kate said. "I thought you were dead. Are you okay?"

"I've been better," Hulk said showing Kate his injured hand and the space where his ring finger had been removed, "but I've been worse too. Have you got Franklin?"

"Jesus, that must have hurt."

"I'll be fine, Alpha. Do you have him?

"Not yet, any idea where he is?"

"Can't be far from here. Where's Max?"

"He was ahead of us in the hallway."

"Go after him, he's going to need your help. He might not be able to do what needs to be done."

"What?"

"Just trust me. Move!"

"Yes, boss," Kate said running from the room.

Max rounded the mid-section of the stairs, but ducked back behind the wall just in the nick of time as two bullets slammed into the wall behind him. Max noticed they hit high, which meant the shooter was probably further back on the roof.

He got his breath back, then laid flat on his stomach and inched forward. No shots, which meant he was out of the shooter's line of sight. Slowly he brought his knee up, then he sprung up on the far right of the stairs, the last place the shooter was expecting, giving Max precious seconds to act. Max found him several metres back from the door and put two rounds into him, and he dropped from view.

Max ran up the remaining stairs and used the doorframe as cover. He took down two of Franklin's guards, then ducked back behind the doorframe as a barrage of bullets smashed into the walls all around him. He blind fired around the roof spreading his shots. He heard the bullets slamming into the metal roof and various utilities boxes on the rooftop which Franklin's men were hiding behind.

The wall and doorframe were still getting pummelled and Max was not sure how long they would withstand the attack. He kept blind firing until his MP5 ran out of ammo. He quickly changed magazines then waited for a pause in the fire.

As soon as it stopped, he thrust his head out and pulled it back just as quick. The bullets started again, but he had seen everything he needed to see. Most of the crew were scattered at the far end of the roof. There were only two men close to him and luckily enough, they were standing together.

Max dropped to his left knee lowering his profile to make himself a smaller target and to change positions. He found the two men and sprayed a line of bullets at their heads. Both men were hit and taken down.

Max ran as fast as his legs could carry him for the nearest cover. A line of bullets was tearing into the metal at his feet. He dived behind a small wall for a housing unit of some sort, maybe a winch or a generator for the warehouse. Bullets collided with the tin and the sound was deafening, like dozens of open palms slapping the tin as hard as they could muster.

Max made his way around the other side of the metal structure and watched as the man in the scratched mask yelled orders to his troops. Four of the closest men started walking hesitantly towards Max with their weapons pressed against their shoulders. He fired at the man on the left. Three bullets tore into his chest and he dropped. The other three men dived to the right for cover. Franklin did not flinch he just raised his Steyr and sprayed the metal wall next to Max, forcing him back behind cover.

Max moved back behind the metal box and waited for his opportunity. It wasn't long before one of the men surfaced. He watched as his would be attacker dived behind a similar structure almost parallel with his own on the other side of the roof. Max waited but the attacker did not make a move. There was only one thing that could mean – someone was at his flank.

Max spun and ran to the nearest corner of the box. He arrived just in time. The new attacker's gun wielding hand flicked around the corner. Max caught it as his new foe opened fire, spraying bullets all over the roof. He was trying to bring the barrel around towards Max, but was otherwise unaware of his surroundings. Max drove him back then pushed him. Half a metre at first, then another metre opened up between them and the terrorist smiled as he tried to bring his Steyr around to face Max, but Max was too fast. He hurdled forward and jumped into the air and with both feet kicked the attacker off the edge of the roof. The man fell quickly, screaming the whole way down, until Max heard the impact as he hit the ground.

"Bravo, are you still on the roof?" Max asked into his comms unit.

"I'm on the fire escape at the far end," Jonnie replied. *"I moved to get a better line on the end near Echo team."*

"Can you still see the roof?"

"Just. How can I help?"

"I'm pinned down, without support. I'm at the opposite end of the building coming back towards you. Franklin is at your end with a couple of his men. See what you can do, will you?"

"You got it, boss. Moving now."

Max moved back to his original position and waited for the man behind the almost mirrored structure to his own. He saw a mobile poke around the corner and he fired. The bullet smashed the little screen and it flicked out of the voyeur's hand.

Max heard the crack of Jonnie's sniper rifle and used the time to make a run for the far side of the roof knowing Franklin and his men would be distracted. Halfway across the short distance, he saw one of the other men who had been making his way towards Max. He was standing still with his gun at his feet. Both his hands were on his chest and covered in blood. Jonnie had shot him in the back.

Max looked behind the dying man and saw Franklin and the others searching for cover. Jonnie dropped one of the other men as Franklin made it to a small rise in the roof, maybe a ventilation window rising from the iron roof like an old factory. He was laying flat on the surface and trying to lower his profile.

Max made it to the structure on the other side of the building and took two long strides to the far corner. He ducked his head around and the saw his prey kneeling and looking in the direction of Jonnie's rifle fire. Max stepped around the corner and shot him at point blank range. He slumped forward and Max stepped over his lifeless body and made his way to the next structure.

He hid behind a brick smokestack and fired at one of Franklin's men. The pair exchanged fire until Max's gun clicked dry. He tossed it to the ground and drew his pistol moving around the smokestack to look for a new angle and saw Franklin returning fire at Jonnie. His Steyr was no match for the sniper rifle, but he was still landing shots in the right area. Clearly, he was a skilled shooter. Max fired two shots at him, the first only missing by an inch or two. The second shot went wide as Max was forced to move back behind cover by one of

Franklin's men. One of the bullets hit and chipped the bricks right next to his face.

Max heard Franklin yell directions to his men and then the bricks he was hiding behind were battered by bullets. Max held as a still as possible and he did not want to give even a slither of his body as a target. The bullets seemed to be coming from every angle on the far side of the structure. Every now and then a loud crack would ring out over the space as Jonnie shot his rifle. Max was not sure whether he was taking out any of their enemies or just keeping them from moving.

"Prince, you with me still?" Jonnie asked.

"I'm here, kid," Max said blindly firing around the pillar of red bricks. "What have you got?"

"Nothing good, I'm afraid. There's a helicopter on fast approach and I'm almost out of rounds."

"Save the rounds unless you have a shot and you get yourself to cover. Let's not have a repeat of Venice."

"Agree, I'll move to the stairwell."

"Got it. How many more of them are there up here?"

"Only three. Franklin and two of his pals."

"Ack. Thanks, kid. Get to cover."

"Roger that."

Max heard Franklin telling his men to get ready to move. Max ducked his head back out when they stopped firing and saw Franklin throw down his Steyr. Empty. He punched the sloped roof he was leaning on in frustration, then called from one of his men to toss him a weapon. The man stepped out readying to throw the gun, but Max shot him twice and the gun only dropped a metre or so from his feet. Jonnie's rifle fired again and Max looked around the pillar. The last of Franklin's men was staggering across the roof towards his boss holding his neck. Blood was pumping from the wound, but he was still moving.

Max stepped around the smokestack and put two bullets into the man just as he managed to kick the weapon towards Franklin. Franklin dived forward landing hard on his hands and knees, and spider crawled as fast as he could move towards the gun. Max fired two shots into the metal roof in front of him, as he came out from behind the pillar, but he did not stop.

Max was in a full sprint across the roof and tossed his now empty pistol to the ground, as Franklin reached the gun. Max dived forward slapping the gun from Franklin's hand and the two started to wrestle trading successive blows.

Every move Franklin made was blocked and Max found himself equally denied a solid blow. They were evenly matched and neither was getting the better of the other. After a minute of unsuccessful combat, they both rolled away from each other and got to their feet.

As if on cue, they both drew their knives and threw them at each other. Max was shocked, it was like watching himself in the mirror. As the knives left their hands, both men dodged and ducked the incoming blades.

Max ran forward jumped springing himself into the air, drew back his right fist and threw it at Franklin's mask. The mask came off as Max landed and went to throw his left hook into Franklin's sternum, but Franklin caught his hand and twisted it back at an awkward angle, forcing him down to one knee. Max was caught off-guard. Not many people had ever blocked the move. He looked up as Franklin turned to face him now free of his mask.

Max's heart pumped and seconds past like minutes. Grief, shock, despair, disbelief, love and hate all raced through his mind.

"Flash," Max choked out, "how is this possible? I watched you die in my arms?"

"I was dead, but not for long," Flash said. "No thanks to you though."

Flash punched Max in the face and he fell flat on the metal roof.

"You left me in that street to bleed out and to die," Flash said running forward and kicking Max in the ribs. "You and Kate, and our whole team. Whatever happened to not leaving our team behind? What happened to our friendship? After everything I did for you!"

Flash kicked Max again, but Max took some of the incoming blow in his arms, cushioning his chest.

"Everything that happened since has been your fault," Flash said. "You abandoned me and I wasn't there for Jane. She's dead because of you. Because of Hulk and Blake."

Max caught Flash's boot as he came in for another blow and tripped him. Flash fell on his back as Max rolled and scrambled to his feet.

"There's not a day that has gone past where I didn't regret leaving you there, Jacob," Max said holding his ribs. "You were dead and I had a mission to finish. There was nothing I could do."

"That's bullshit, Max! You could have saved me, but you didn't. It took me years to recover from my injuries, but The Sixteen helped me. They showed me how AIS and the Five Eyes agencies were destroying the world. They healed me and promised that Jane would be bought to meet me. But, you went on your one man rampage and started killing them all one by one and Jane slipped further from my reach."

"I checked in on her when I could Flash. I was on the run and working to avenge you."

"You didn't do it for me! Don't lie to me, Max, I know you too well. You did it for yourself. You did it for Lachlan. That burning desire for retribution and vengeance, but you know what, I finally get it. Why you channelled your pain into everything you did and how it gave you purpose and strength. I am going to kill you and Kate, Hulk and, of course, Blake for what you have all done to me."

Max sprinted forward, his pain and anguish turning to anger as he heard Blake's name. Flash dodged the incoming attack and swung a heavy left hook punching Max hard in the side of the face. Max's earlier injuries resurfaced and his world started spinning and his head ached. He felt nauseous again and his vision blurred. He tried to stand, but fell back down.

"So, you have moved on," Flash said smugly. "I merely mention Blake's name and you flash to anger. Well, Max, get ready to lose another one. I'm going to find him and put a bullet in his head, and I'm going to make you watch. You will all pay for what you have done. I will tear this world apart and watch it burn."

"Jacob, please," Max said struggling to get to his feet and reaching out to Flash. "You are my best friend. You don't have to do this. I'm sorry for leaving you to die and I'm sorry about Jane – I only found out today she had died."

"So much for checking in on her you lying son-of-a-bitch! She was my world and you took her away from me! You aren't my friend and I'm going to prove to you I'm no longer yours either."

Flash stepped back and kicked Max in the face. Max's body crumpled, his arms losing the power to support himself as he blacked out and his face hit the metal roof.

"See you soon, brother," Flash said to an unconscious Max as the helicopter arrived and he climbed up the rope ladder which was hanging from the door.

He sighted Jonnie on the nearby roof and gave him a short mocking wave, knowing Jonnie was out of ammo. Flash knew Jonnie loved Max and there was no way he wouldn't have shot him, if he had a spare round.

He smiled and climbed up into the chopper as it banked away.

Chapter Twenty-Five

Max woke.

He was in a white room and again surrounded by various heart monitors and medical equipment. He was hooked up to a drip and felt the Deja vu washing over him. Had it been a dream or more accurately, a terrible nightmare? Was he hallucinating from the drugs and the concussion? No, he couldn't be. The room was different. It was vibrating and a dull roar was rushing his ears in between beeps of the monitors.

He was on a jet.

He looked around the emergency room on the plane and did not recognise it. It was a large space and he could only guess it was a big plane.

"Welcome onboard Australia's version of Air Force One," Blake said from a chair in the corner of the room. "We bought a couple of them about two years ago. Brand new Dreamliners with everything we need to run operations all over the world. AIS bought one which we fitted with an emergency room and armoury, plus the usual meeting rooms, kitchen, bathrooms and storage for quite a bit of cargo we may need from time to time."

"It makes the old Gulfstream look small and obsolete," Max said sitting up and hanging his leg over the side of the bed.

He was still wearing his combat pants, but his torso was bare, except for the multiple wires hanging from his skin. Blake saw the years and years of scars on Max's skin. He had been shot and stabbed, including the recent fight in the warehouse which had been stitched up. Blake strolled over to Max and gently touched the area near the stitches, before moving his hands to softly caress Max's oldest scar, a bullet wound near his shoulder. He studied it, watching his fingers dance over Max's skin. He sighed and looked Max in the eyes.

"How are you feeling?" Blake asked placing his hand lovingly on the back of Max's neck.

"Suddenly, like nothing else in the world matters," Max said pulling Blake closer and kissing him before resting his forehead on Blake's. "I don't want to run anymore, Blake."

"You don't have to, Max. I've got you."

Max cried for the first time in years as Blake wrapped his arms around his shoulders and neck, and provided him the comforted he had denied himself for so long. All those years alone, hunting terrorists while being chased by the governments he had loyally served. In pain and anguish from the losses he had experienced and the isolation. The long relentless hours and days without his friends.

And he cried for his new trauma. Flash. Not only was he alive, Max had to confront the fact that he was now an enemy. He felt like his best friend was dying all over again. He was overwhelmed by guilt and heartache.

After a few minutes holding each other in the relative silence, Blake stepped back a little and looked into Max's eyes.

"It's not your fault," Blake stated as he placed his hands on Max's cheeks. "You did what you had to do."

"No, I abandoned my teammate, my friend," Max replied his face portraying his tormented thoughts. "I could have saved him. I failed, Blake. I left him to die in the street. Alone. There isn't a day that goes by where I haven't regretted what I did, but it's now so much worse."

"You thought he was dead, Max. We all did. You know how much we all loved him as a friend and respected him as an agent. We would never have left him behind if we thought he could be saved. You know that."

"How did he survive? I felt the life drain from him. He died in my arms, Blake. I felt him stop breathing."

"I don't know, Max. The best I can guess is that he was revived by someone connected to The Sixteen and they somehow turned him."

"He wasn't the same person we knew, I mean, it was him, but he was cold and callous. Calculating and somehow insane, but totally in control. He knew what to say and how to say it."

"He knows all of us. He knows our strengths and weaknesses, and he knows our tactics. He is going to be hard to find and stop."

"He knows how I feel about you, Blake," Max said grabbing Blake's hands. "I can't let him get to you."

"He won't, Max. I am constantly surrounded my loyal agents and in high security buildings."

"Promise me you will stay out of the fight and change up your security procedures regularly. I won't lose you, Blake."

"Okay, Max. I will talk to my security team."

"And, add a few more to your team. He is too good. You know how effective he was as an agent. We cannot underestimate him. I need you. I can't do this without you."

"I'm here, Max, and always will be," Blake said leaning forward and kissing Max. "I'm not going anywhere. I'll increase my detail if that will make you feel more comfortable."

"It would."

"Then it's done," Blake said with a reassuring smile. "But, what about you? Maybe you should consider sitting this one out. No one would blame you."

"You said it yourself, he knows us, but I know him too. I can find him."

"And, what will you do when you find him?"

"I will figure it out when it happens."

"I don't think you can save him, Max, if that's what you are thinking."

"I owe it to him to try."

"He's dangerous, Max. I want you to be safe. Just like you asked of me. You may have to make an impossible choice and, when it comes, I want you to be the one that walks away. Promise me, Max. I can't do this without you either. Not now."

Max nodded his head.

"Okay, Blake," Max said taking Blake's hand again. "I promise."

There was a soft knock on the door and they turned to see Jonnie and one of the AIS medical team.

"Sorry to interrupt," Jonnie said seeing his two bosses holding hands for the first time. "Hulk asked me to see if you were free for a briefing."

"Yes, of course," Blake said turning to the doctor. "Check him over, Doc, then send him out, will you?"

"Yes, sir," the doctor said walking over to the machines Max was connected to and inspecting them.

"I'll see you in a minute," Blake said squeezing Max's hand.

"I'll be right out," Max said smiling.

He had always had strong feelings for Blake. There was always a what if thought that had hung over their friendship. In the years following the death of Max's fiancé, Lachlan, he and Blake had grown even closer, and while there were times, he was tempted, he felt like it was a betrayal of his love for Lachlan. He had slept with other people and had some shorter relationships, but he wasn't ready. He had not felt love like this for anyone since Lachlan, but he knew it was right. He knew Lachlan would want him to be happy and to find love again, and he had. He was ready and he would do whatever it took to hold onto that love.

There was just one obstacle and he was not sure how he was going to overcome it, but he knew he had to try.

The doctor removed all of the wires and drip, and gave Max some pills to ease any swelling which he took. She also gave him some painkillers which he just sat on the small table next to the bed.

He pulled on a new black t-shirt which Blake had hung on the chair and checked himself over in the mirror in the small adjoining bathroom and washed his face.

When he was ready, he walked out into the corridor. He was somewhere near the rear of the plane. Blake was right, it was like a new Air Force One, albeit slightly reconfigured for AIS. There was the emergency room at the back of the plane, followed by a small set of offices and a seating area. Max walked past a conference room and a small galley kitchen area with an elevator, no doubt to a bigger kitchen downstairs. There were a couple more bigger offices and then a large conference room, double the size of the previous one, filled with electronics – computers, monitors, televisions, phones. It looked like it was just outside the cockpit.

Inside, Hulk, Kate, Jonnie and Blake were sitting around the table. They stopped talking when he walked into the room. It was the first time they had all been together again, since Max fled London.

"Please, don't stop for me," Max said, "keep it rolling."

"How you doing, kid?" Hulk asked.

"Only slightly better than you by the look of it," Max said gingerly sitting down opposite his old boss and mentor who was still recovering from his earlier torture. "Are you okay?"

"I've been through worse," Hulk said touching his swollen face. "Thanks for getting me out of there."

"I was unconscious, so I think the thanks should go to the others," Max said smiling at each of his colleagues. "Still the only people I ever want to have with me in a tough jam."

"Me too, kid."

Max saw one of the televisions behind Hulk was playing the footage of the attack on the Defense base in Nevada. He watched the man walk across the room. The gait, the rhythm and stride – he knew now why it had felt so familiar when he first saw the footage. It was unmistakeably Flash. Max looked away from the screen.

"I'm sorry about Flash," Hulk said, "we all are. If we had of known, we would have mounted a rescue."

"I know you would have, so would I," Max said looking around the room to each of his colleagues. "He made his choices. We have to acknowledge that our old friend and colleague is dead. This man is a terrorist. The Flash we all knew would put a bullet in this guy's head. He made a choice and we have to make ours too. We have to choose to let him go."

"I got to spend some time up close and personal with him. I can tell you the man we once knew is no longer in there."

Hulk raised his bandaged hand showing Max the gap where his ring finger was missing.

"We have a job to do and it's stopping him," Hulk stated.

The team all nodded in support and Blake nodded a gentle knowing smile to Max. He knew how painful this was going to be for him, but he had made the right choice.

"Where are we going?" Max asked.

"Washington," Blake said. "D.C."

"What's in Washington?"

"The Prime Minister is in D.C. She got a ride with us on this plane over here, but she went with the President on Air Force One when evacuating San Francisco. She ordered us to Washington for a debrief, but we also decided we should be in close proximity to her in case we need to evacuate her back to Australia."

"How far out are we?"

"About two hours."

"And, where are we on finding Flash?"

"We started pulling all of Flash's mission files and known allises," Blake said. "We have shut down all of his foreign accounts and are tracing the money transfers throughout the world, trying to shut them all down."

"That's fast work, how long was I out?"

"A couple of hours."

"We started looking into Flash before the warehouse job," Hulk said bluntly. "Blake saw the footage from the train and Defense base attacks and had a hunch it could have been Flash. Blake used to watch the footage of your missions and review it for ways we could improve our performance. He figured it out, but then you sent through Welsh's emails and Flash's name was among the people they suspected. That sealed the deal."

"Why didn't you tell me?"

"Because I didn't have any proof, Max," Blake said. "I didn't want to bring it up until we were sure."

"Okay. So, what else?"

"We are using financial records to track his movements over the last few years. It looks like he spent most of his time in the United Kingdom. Like you, he was trained to disappear and had set up various safehouses and foreign accounts and safety deposit boxes in known and unknown allises."

"And, he was getting help from The Sixteen."

"Yes, until they started to disappear."

"Welsh mentioned he was leading an Australian freedom fighters type organisation."

"Kate's been looking into it."

"We knew someone had taken over," Kate said, "but they were clearly a crafty fucker. We spent the last couple of years trying to get information on their new leader, but we were blocked every step of the way. He killed two of our guys who we tried to get into the organisation undercover. He found them easily and took them out. We weren't sure how it was possible until now. He knew our fucking moves."

"How many of them are there?"

"We aren't sure, but we think a heap of them are here in the US to help him. It makes sense, you know, bring people who you trust and have vetted to get shit done. Rather than relying on Welsh and his pack of wankers."

"Tell me about Jane."

"What do you want to know?"

"Do we have the investigation files?"

"There wasn't really an investigation," Kate said typing some commands on a keyboard and opening the file on the television screens around the room. "The police ruled it an accident. Wet weather, poor visibility."

Max studied the file on the screen.

"Can you show me the pictures?" Max asked

"Are you sure, mate?" Kate asked. "Couple of them are fucking brutal."

"Show me."

Kate started the cycle of pictures from the police file. He saw the road leading up to the corner, then the damaged guide rail from the impact. There was a series of photos of the hillside, marked with muddy tracks and scared trees with broken limps from where the car had ricocheted between them on its steep descent. Then there was the car. It was a crumbled mess. The boot and most of the bonnet section of the car had torn away. Max had seen the debris in the previous photos. It was resting on its roof in a swallow creek, its windows all shattered. The police had determined it had flipped on impact with the railing and skidded down on its roof.

There was a forensic report on the vehicle which Kate skipped over quickly to a series of photos of Jane. Max saw his friend laying dead on a steel trolley in the morgue. She had been a beautiful woman, not only in appearance, but in personality. Both were tragically ripped from her by the accident. Max was beset by emotion and Kate moved the photos onto the autopsy report. Jane had been severely injured and may well have been dead before the car reached the creek, but there were some signs she may have drowned in the creek, unable to escape the vehicle.

Max sat in thought for a few moments to catch his breath. Kate clicked the keyboard and the first photo of the road sat on the screen.

He starred at it blankly.

"We should move on," Hulk said as Kate clicked the image away.

"Wait," Max said suddenly more alert. "Put that back up."

"It's not going to do us any good going down this path, Max," Hulk said. "It'll only bring you pain."

"Just put it back up," Max said getting to his feet and turning to the screen behind him.

Kate put the photo of the road up.

"Look," Max said dragging his finger along the road. "There are no skid marks."

"Yes, from the rain and poor vision, she probably didn't see the corner, until it was too late," Kate said.

"Even if she didn't see it until she was nearly on top of it, there would still be marks closer to the railing," Max stated pointing to the spot he thought on the picture. "Go to the next photo."

Kate clicked and the photo changed.

"There isn't any sign of hard braking at all," Max said. "There was a forensic report about halfway through Kate, can you go to that please?"

Kate clicked a few times until the screen held the image of the vehicle report.

"What are you looking for, Max?" Kate asked. "The car was totally fucked."

"This," Max said pointing to the screen. "The brake lines were broken."

"That probably happened in the crash."

"Or they were cut. Look here, it says, inconclusive. They couldn't tell how they broke."

"You think someone murdered her?"

"It's a play right out of The Sixteen's playbook. Attack the partner to get to the subject."

"But, why would they want her dead?" Blake asked shifting uncomfortably.

"To give him focus. Remove a distraction and give him a reason to seek retribution. They made us the enemy by telling him he wasn't there to save her and it was our fault. It's the same thing he threatened me with earlier."

"What do you mean?"

"He threatened you to create a distraction and I think, in his mind, to balance the scales."

"He blames you for her death, so wants to kill me to punish you."

"Yes and he told me in advance to distract me. To make me focus on protecting you, rather than looking for him."

"You might be right, Max, but I'm not sure we can overturn a police report on a hunch."

"Maybe if he knew they did this to him. Maybe if he knew they killed her and manipulated him. Well, maybe then he would stop what he is doing."

"There are too many maybes, Max," Hulk said. "And, regardless, he's killed a lot of people and do I have to remind you he still has Erebus?"

"How much of it got out before we arrived?"

"More than half."

"What? How is that possible?"

"We think he may have already moved some before we knew where to look and he used a bunch of trucks and helicopters in a huge shell game to scatter his supplies. It's been nearly impossible to track them."

"He used tunnels and overpasses," Blake added. "The loaded truck would enter the tunnel and an empty one would drive out in its place, giving him enough time to move the cannisters. We stopped a bunch of empty trucks."

"Where is he now?" Max asked.

"We don't know. He fled in the helicopter, then by car, and again he did the same thing. Tunnels to switch cars. Impossible to track."

"Fuck."

"Yeah," Kate said, "he's fucking good."

"Do we have a list of targets?"

"Yes," Blake replied. "They are being locked down as we speak, and we are working with the CIA and FFA to close the airports. You know him better than all of us, Max. What is his next move?"

"I have no idea," Max said deflated.

Chapter Twenty-Six

Max had spent over an hour reading through old mission reports from Flash's career at AIS. There were hundreds of missions which they had completed together and a huge caseload of missions he had completed on his own. Max focused on those individual missions to look for any clues, but he hadn't found anything of interest.

He sat his tablet computer back on the desk and went to stretch his legs. He took the small elevator he had found earlier down to the bottom floor. There was a large kitchen equipped to serve a lot of meals over a long time. Max figured the plane was capable of air-to-air refuelling and could fly for weeks if necessary, and the kitchen was stocked accordingly with rows of fridges, freezers and pantries.

Max wandered aimlessly through the cargo area thinking about Flash and what was to come. He found two SUVs strapped in at the rear and saw the modified back of the plane which could ramp down to the tarmac.

He walked back through the plane towards the front. After the kitchen was a row of private quarters fitted with beds, televisions, computers and small adjoining bathrooms. One of the rooms was fitted with several bunkbeds, no doubt for those missions needing a large team.

In the second room from the front of the plane, he found Blake who was just out of the shower and was pulling on his suit pants. Max took a moment to admire Blake's physique. He was still incredibly fit and his six pack was glistening from the shower. He smiled when he saw Max standing in the doorway and picked up his towel to finish drying his chest. Max walked in and took the towel and softly patted down Blake's chest and abs. He tossed the towel on the bed and the pair embraced for a long and passionate kiss.

They were interrupted before they could go any further by a knock on the door and a beaming Kate.

"Sorry boys," Kate laughed playfully, "no time for that now. We are not far out. Suit up."

"Got it," Max said without turning back to face her.

He kissed Blake and held him close, as Kate walked off chuckling down the hall.

"I guess I better find a suit," Max said.

"I had the crew go and get you some clothes," Blake said walking over and opening another cupboard in his little cabin. "You should find what you need in here."

"Thanks, Blake. Mind if I use your bathroom."

"Go for it."

A few minutes later, Max emerged from the steamed-up bathroom with a towel wrapped around his waist. Blake was dressed in a well-tailored tuxedo and vest. His crisp white shirt had small shiny black balls for buttons running down the centre of his chest and a black bowtie. He was standing next to the bed with a first-aid kit. He watched Max dry off and put on his underpants and black suit pants, then changed Max's bandage which had been covering the row of stitches from the earlier knife attack.

Max pulled on his shirt, socks and shoes, followed by his vest. He hung the bowtie around his neck and Blake tied it for him.

"It fits pretty well," Max said brushing the vest with his hand.

"Luckily you haven't changed much," Blake said. "You look amazing."

"Speak for yourself, Blake. Nothing like a man in a tux."

"I agree," Blake said passing Max his jacket. "We should head upstairs."

"After you."

Max followed Blake towards a small staircase which led up to the hallway outside the big conference room.

"I'm sorry I didn't tell you about Flash," Blake said. "I wanted to be sure."

"It's okay, Blake," Max replied. "I was shocked. I still am. But, I'm not sure any heads-up would have helped. I still can't believe it's him."

Blake stopped on the stairs in front of Max and turned back to face him.

"We will get through this," Blake said grabbing Max's hand. "No matter what happens, I will be here for you."

"Thank you, Blake," Max said squeezing his new partner's hand. "I'm here for you too."

Blake smiled like Max had never seen him smile before, full of such warmth. He could not help but feel the love radiating from him and smiled himself, a real, warm and heartfelt smile which he hadn't done for years. In fact, he was struggling to remember the last time he had smiled and felt genuine happiness.

Max and Blake had joined the team in the conference room as the plane came in to land. It had touched down and quickly taxied to a private hanger before the cargo door was lowered and the teams climbed into the SUVs and sped off for the White House. Kate and Jonnie were in with Hulk, and Max and Blake took their own car.

At the White House, their identification was checked at the gates. Hulk's car was waved through fast and the bollards rose back out of the ground blocking the entrance to Max. He wound down his window as the Secret Service agent approached the window.

"Good afternoon, gentleman," the agent said. "Identification please."

"Good afternoon," Max said handing out their AIS identification to the agent. "Agent Max Shaw and Rear Admiral Blake Smyth of the Australian Intelligence Service we are here to meet with the President and our Prime Minister."

The agent checked his computer and a red warning flashed on the screen over Max's photo. The agent read the message and walked back to the car.

"Agent Shaw," he said handing the passes back through the window. "I have been asked to remind you that this is the White House and your previous indiscretions have flagged you as a risk."

"I've been cleared by the President herself," Max stated coldly. "I am the Head of Field Operations and I have the clearance of a two-star general. I suggest you move aside and let me through."

"I am aware, sir," the agent said, his voice wavering a little. "I apologise, I'm just the messenger."

"Open this gate."

"Yes, sir. I will, sir, but I haven't delivered the message."

"What message and who is it from?"

"The Director of the Secret Service."

"What does it say?"

"It says 'we'll be watching'," the agent said noticeably taking a small step back from Max's window.

"Got it," Max said turning to look back through the front windshield. "Now, open this gate, before I get out and open it myself."

"Yes, sir," the agent said rushing over to the control panel and lowering the barricade. "Please park in the designated space next to your other vehicle to the right."

Max didn't reply, he just raised the window and drove through. He parked next to Hulk's car.

"Fucking dickhead," Max said in frustration looking back towards the gate as Blake joined him to walk up to the entrance.

"What did you expect, Max?" Blake asked. "You dealt the Secret Service and the Director himself an embarrassing blow by sneaking onto Air Force One. He'll be lucky if he even has a job when the fallout settles. Someone will need to take the blame."

"I thought I was supposed to be the political one. You're probably right though. But, he probably should lose his job, there is no way I should have been able to get on that plane."

"The political thinking is probably because I have to spend so much time with them these days. Mostly asking them for more money to run the AIS or briefing countless committees. I would spend at least a day a week at Parliament House."

"Oh God, I feel for you. I spent a lot of years there. Not sure I could do it anymore. I don't have the patience. You on the other hand, have a calming influence and a good poker-face. They would probably love and hate you at the same time."

"Yeah, I don't like to give too much away, but I tell them what they need to hear to get what we need."

"We will make a politician out of you yet."

The pair joined the small cue behind Hulk, Kate and Jonnie at the security checkpoint. The Secret Service agents were taken aback by the sight of Hulk and his swollen face and bandaged hand.

"Do you have a problem?" Hulk asked the closest agent.

"Sorry, sir," the agent said. "Are you okay?"

"I was tortured for several hours. How do you think I am?"

The agent didn't know how to reply or where to look.

"Here is my identification," Hulk said passing over his card. "General Patrick Scott, Australian Intelligence Service."

The agent read Hulk's name and rank as it popped up on the screen and quickly fumbled to give him back his card and wave him through. The metal detectors sounded as Hulk walked through with his cane.

"I have a metal cane and a Glock pistol tucked in a holster under my left arm," Hulk stated matter-of-factly. "You'll see I'm cleared to carry."

"Yes, sir, please go through," the agent said, but Hulk was already gone.

Kate, Jonnie and Blake all got through relatively quickly, but when Max's details were punched into the computer the same warning flashed on the screen. Max starred at the agent with cold, hard eyes.

"I know and I suggest you just let it go," Max said his tone as cold as ice.

The agent just nodded and moved aside.

"Alpha, Bravo," Hulk said as Max joined the team in the foyer. "Go and find the Federal Police guys who have been escorting the PM and see what the plans are."

"Ack," Kate said as the two agents walked off towards the security centre.

"You two, come with me," Hulk said walking left towards the West Wing closely followed by Max and Blake.

The three agents waited as directed in a small foyer for several minutes, before being shown into the Oval Office. Max having been a student of politics was surprised to still feel the impact of the room and the weight of its power and importance. Two men and a woman were sitting on the far sofa and stood when they walked into the room. Hulk led his two most senior agents over to meet the group.

"Hello, Hulk," the FBI Director said. "It's nice to see you. I heard what happened, how are you feeling?"

"Hello, Carl," Hulk said shaking the Director's hand with his good hand. "It will take more than that to kill me."

"I believe it," he said as Hulk walked past to greet the other two Directors.

"Alejandra, Allan, good to see you both," Hulk said shaking their hands. "May I introduce you to Rear Admiral Blake 'Hermes' Smyth, my number two."

Blake moved forward and shook hands with the FBI Director.

"FBI Director Carl Moore," Hulk said as Blake shook hands with the Director.

"Pleased to meet you, Admiral," Moore said. "Hulk has spoken frequently about you and the job you have done in shaping the AIS. I look forward to a long conversation about how our two organisations can continue to work together seamlessly into the future."

"It's an honour, sir," Blake said. "I look forward to the discussion."

"You'll remember Alejandra Hernandez, the Director of Central Intelligence," Hulk said as Blake shook her hand.

"Yes, of course, hello Director Hernandez," Blake said. "It's great to see you again."

"And you, Blake," Hernandez said, "but please call me Alejandra."

"Alejandra, got it. Will do."

"And, this is Allan Lewis, the Director of the Secret Service," Hulk said as Blake shook Lewis' hand.

"Admiral Smyth, we have spoken on the phone many times," Lewis said. "It's good to finally meet you in person."

"Yes, sir," Blake said. "Likewise."

"I would also like to introduce you to my Head of Field Operation, Agent Max 'Prince' Shaw," Hulk said looking over to Max.

"Prince," Moore noted. "I have followed your career for many years through mission reports. Both of our countries owe you a debt of gratitude."

"Thank you, sir," Max said shaking the Director's hand and nodding towards Blake and Hulk. "But, it is a team effort, a lot of which is thanks to these two men."

"After everything that has happened over the last few years, I wasn't sure what to expect. You led some of my teams on some wild goose chases looking for you these last few years."

"Yeah, sorry about that."

"Are you?"

"No," Max admitted with a smile.

"Agent Shaw helped take out some of the worst terrorist groups in our history, Director Moore," Hernandez said shaking Max's hand. "The CIA thought all along we should have been pinning a medal on him, not hunting him. After the links were proven on the first couple of targets, we decided to not look very hard for you, Max."

"Thank you, ma'am," Max said. "A couple of your boys got close in the early days."

"I know," she said with a wry smile. "Regardless, thank you for everything."

"Yes, ma'am. Thank you."

"I, on the other hand, think you were reckless and endangered the lives of millions of people," Lewis said unimpressed by Hernandez's comments. "You are not a law unto yourself, Mr Shaw."

"Oh come on, Carl," Moore interrupted, "you're just pissed off he outwitted your boys."

"I am not the only one who's pissed. The Chief of Staff and Secretary of Air Force are even more annoyed. Mr Shaw better hope he doesn't run into them tonight."

"I think he'll be able to handle himself," Hernandez interjected. "From what I have seen over the years, they should hope they don't run into Max, especially if they are going to give him a lecture. Am I right, Max?"

"I couldn't comment, ma'am," Max said causing Blake to smile at his partner's uncharacteristic poise.

"Well," Lewis said, "Mr Shaw, you should not try to repeat any of your so-called heroics tonight, I won't tolerate it."

"Yes, I got your message," Max said his tone stiffening as Blake's smile faded. "Couple of your boys near shit their pants having to deliver it though."

"What did you say?" Lewis said pushing forward to get in Max's face.

"You heard me. In the future, spare your minions the embarrassment. I'm not impressed and I'm not intimidated. If you have something to say to me, you can say it to my face."

"Who do you think you are speaking to?" Lewis said his face turning red, flush with anger. "I should put you on your ass."

"Who do you think you are speaking to?" Max laughed. "I'd break your arm and have you on the ground unconscious within seconds."

"General Scott," Lewis said looking past Max to Hulk, "are you not going to control your wild dog here?"

"I haven't been able to, to date," Hulk said clearly annoyed the Director had threatened one of his team. "But, if I was you, I would keep the threats to yourself. What you should understand is that Max here has a background in politics and international relations. He no doubt has a great respect for this room and the symbol it represents. I know that because otherwise you would already be on the floor."

"It is indeed a respected symbol, gentleman," Moore said, "and I think we should treat it as such and take a seat to calm down before the President gets here."

"Good idea," Blake added patting Max on the forearm.

The three senior US officials sat on their couch as Max, Blake and Hulk took a seat on the opposite lounge.

No sooner had they sat then one of the doors hidden in the wall opened and Torres marched in closely followed by Ferguson. The group stood.

"Please, keep your seats," Torres said first offering a chair near the fireplace to Ferguson then taking her own next to Ferguson. "Sit, sit. We don't have long. Where are we up to?"

"Madam President, Prime Minister Ferguson," Hernandez said eagerly, "the CIA with the assistance of the FBI and AIS managed to regain a great deal of Project Erebus."

Max looked to Moore who rolled his eyes, unimpressed his colleague was trying to take the credit when he had more men on site and carried a heavier burden on the mission.

"How much was recovered?" Torres asked.

"About six gallons," Hernandez said. "About half."

"Half. I think it is less than half."

"Yes, ma'am," Hernandez said shifting uncomfortably.

"Well, getting some back is something, I guess. Where is it now?"

"The FBI is transporting it to the Vault," Moore said jumping in to reclaim his position. "Kentucky."

"Fort Knox?"

"Yes."

"Why?"

"It is already one of the most secure places on the planet and now it will have an extra layer of protection with four FBI SWAT tanks and two dozen agents."

"Okay, well, your call, Director. What are we doing to find the rest?"

"We are coordinating across agencies, including with the AIS, to try to trace the shipments, but I'm afraid it is proving difficult."

"Why?"

"They are using a number of tactics to throw us off their scent."

"What does that mean?"

"It means he is good, ma'am, but we will find him."

"How good is he, General Scott? He is one of your men I am led to believe."

"He is one of the best, ma'am," Hulk conceded. "He was one of our finest agents with thousands of hours of missions and training under his belt. He operated at the top of our organisation's spy ranks for many years."

"And, do we have any idea why he is doing this?"

"Our working theory is retribution."

"Retribution against whom?"

"All of us. The intelligence community. He feels betrayed and is not going to stop until his scores are settled."

"How is it this Jacob Gordon," Torres asked looking up from her notes like an angry librarian over her glasses, "managed to build such a grudge in the first place?"

Max uncharacteristically squirmed and shifted in his seat.

"During a mission in London," Hulk explained, "Agent Gordon, Flash as we called him, was pinned down defending our then Prime Minister. He ran out of ammunition and sacrificed himself causing a distraction, drawing enemy fire, to give the team enough time to secure the PM."

"If he sacrificed himself, then why am I dealing with him today? He should be dead."

"We thought he was, ma'am," Hulk said as Max's face started to betray his thoughts as it flushed red. "The team was under heavy fire and a large incoming attack force. He presented no signs of life, so they made the difficult choice to leave him behind to secure the Prime Minister."

"Well, that was clearly a mistake," Torres said as Blake felt Max's arm tense up and saw his jaw stiffen. "Any ideas on how he survived?"

"Not at this stage."

"Actually, ma'am," Lewis chimed in looking at his phone, "we believe we may have found a connection."

"Go on," Torres said.

"When Agent Shaw killed Felicity Musgrave," Lewis said as Max's jaw tighten further, "we started a deep dive into her life. We believe she was channelling money into an account for an off the books doctor, of sorts."

"What do you mean?"

"Well, he was a former doctor who lost his medical licence in the UK. MI6 have long suspected the doctor was working for the mob or some other illegal entities. I believe he was providing care to Agent Gordon."

"Well, Max killed her, so she is no use to us now," Torres said as Blake saw Max's expression hard further.

Blake was glad Max was only figuratively bitting his tongue, otherwise he would have bitten it right off

"What else have you got?" Torres asked.

"Nothing ma'am," Lewis said.

"Another proud day for the Secret Service, Director," Torres said before turning to Hulk. "General Scott, what is your assessment of our situation?"

"Unfortunately, Madam President," Hulk said. "We believe we need to increase security and monitoring at all of the airports and ports, and the top possible attack sites."

"That is going to cost a fortune, not only in money, but in political capital. Locking down these sites for this lunatic is a major infringement on people and they won't easily forget it."

"Better than them getting killed," Max said impatiently under his breath as he was elbowed in the ribs by Blake.

"What was that?" Torres snapped.

"Nothing, ma'am," Max said.

"I want this man found, ladies and gentlemen," Torres said standing and forcing the group to their feet. "We need to get Erebus back and put a bullet in former Agent Gordon's head and make sure he is really dead this time, will you?"

The bluntness and quick agreement from Lewis, caused Max to huff out a short laugh.

"Something funny, Agent Shaw?" Torres asked.

"Only your reading of the situation," Max snapped.

"Max," Blake said putting his hand on Max's forearm to try to calm him.

"No, Blake," Max said turning to face Blake, "I'm not going to stand here and put up with this bullshit."

"If you have something to say, Agent Shaw, you better spit it out," Torres said. "We have a dinner to get to."

"Flash was my best friend and a great agent. He was let down by me and deceived by a bunch of terrorists. Your call to just put a bullet in his head is as naive and as it is stupid."

"You should remember your place," Lewis jumped in, but Torres waved him off with her hand.

"What would you suggest, Agent Shaw?" Torres asked.

"We need to rethink everything we know. He knows us. He has been ahead of us at every turn because we are predictable. You won't be able to just find this man and put a bullet in his head."

"So, how do we find him?"

"We don't. He will find us and we need to be ready when he does."

Chapter Twenty-Seven

After their conversation in the Oval Office, the group had all walked together to the East Room for the State Dinner.

The President had already addressed the assembled crowd and extolled the virtues of the US-Australian alliance. She spoke about the strength on the countries' friendship and how together with the other Five Eyes nations they had shared goals – protect our countries and allies, spread democracy and push for lasting world peace.

Ferguson had been speaking for over ten minutes already.

"Yesterday, a group of terrorists tried to take down part of our intelligence infrastructure," Ferguson said. "They tried to destroy our new multibillion-dollar joint intelligence facility in San Francisco, but they failed – thanks to the very intelligence agencies they sort to destroy."

The crowd burst onto their feet in rapturous applause. Ferguson waited, absorbing the accolades like she had defused the situation with her own bare hands.

"San Francisco, as you know, was almost a very different city a few years ago," Ferguson started again as people retook their seats. "A global terrorist organisation took control of a number of nuclear devices. They detonated one in Perth, Western Australia and I remember the feeling of overwhelming pain and sadness that followed the attack. I say this, loud and clear, we will never forget those who lost their lives that day and in the months and years that have followed. We will never forget."

The crowd rose again to applaud as a sign of respect for those killed in the attack.

"As has been reported," Ferguson restarted. "There were almost two other nuclear attacks that day. One in London, which was averted thanks to the Australian Intelligence Service who were on the ground there on that dark day – one of the most horrific days in global history. But a second device was also defused by your very own FBI in San Francisco with the assistance of our AIS."

The crowd jumped to their feet and began clapping and cheering which carried on for over a minute.

"It is examples like this," Ferguson stated, "where our two nations work together to protect our people. That is why the Five Eyes treaty and the joint facility we were to open yesterday are so important. Government's exist to protect the people, it is our first priority. We are here to defend, to shield from harm and where necessary to take the fight to the enemies of freedom, the enemies of democracy and the enemies of life and liberty. And, we won't fail."

"I want to thank President Torres," Ferguson said over the applause raising a glass of wine, "for her hospitality, her friendship and her steadfast and determined leadership in defence of my country, our allies and the United States of America. Our alliance is stronger than ever and may it always remain so. Please raise your glasses, to the President."

"To the President," the crowd said in unison rising to their feet yet again, taking a drink before bursting into thunderous applause.

Max was sitting at a table towards the back of the room. The seats were alternated between officials from each country, supposedly to encourage conversation. Max had a loud, drunk Congressman on his right and his equivalent Head of Field Operations for the CIA on his left. Blake was on the other side of the Congressman and was doing his best to maintain the small talk. Max and his CIA counterpart were mostly sitting in silence, clearly neither was interested in this dinner which seemed like a waste of time for them both. But their respective leaders had ordered their attendance.

Max watched Blake and saw how he adapted in the conversation to play his part, all while smiling and nodding his agreement for the Congressman's gratification. Max could not help but stare at the man he had only hours ago kissed and held close. He had longed for Blake for years, especially those cold and lonely nights where he found himself without a friend on the run from the government. And, he longed to hold him close, to breath him in and let the world pass them by as they enjoyed their time together finally.

He smiled as Blake looked over and found his gaze. Blake beamed with joy, but was quickly interrupted by the Congressman excusing himself to go to the bathroom.

The lights in the East Room flickered, then went out. The crowd gasped and more than one person squealed in fright. The projector screens on either side of the fireplace lowered into position and the audience turned to face the screens.

"Excellent speeches, Madam President and Madam Prime Minister," Flash's voice boomed over the audio system as he appeared on the screens.

Max and Blake looked nervously at each other. Max's heart was pounding in his chest. Any thoughts he was still caught in a nightmare vanished when he saw his old friend's face fill the screen closest to him.

"They were both so full of emotion and patriotism," Flash continued. *"Nothing like some flag waving bullshit to try to pull the wool over everyone's eyes. Wake up you bunch of naive sycophants. You brainwashed morons. You are being lied to. The Five Eyes treaty and the intelligence apparatus which flows from it is nothing but smoke and mirrors. Nothing but an expensive blanket you all use to wrap around yourselves to feel protected. But, let me tell you the truth, you are not safe. Your agencies have failed you and your politicians have done nothing but pedal bullshit to fuel their own causes, while decent men and women are sent to die at the stroke of their pens. You might be asking yourself who I am and how I can make such claims, will let me tell you."*

"My name is Jacob 'Flash' Gordon, formerly of the Australian Intelligence Service," Flash said. *"I was once like you and believed their lies and fought their wars. I killed, I lied, I cheated, I manipulated and I tortured people in the name of protection. I was even shot, thirty times, and laid bleeding to death in a cold London street as part of the team helping to stop the very attack Prime Minister Ferguson mentioned in her*

speech moments ago. It was not until that moment, when I was abandoned by my colleagues and friends. Abandoned by my country and abandoned by our so-called protectors. That is when I realised the error of my ways. I had been helping the governments destroy our world and fuel conflict for their own selfish reasons, be it money, or power, or oil. All in the name of freedom and democracy. It is all a lie. And, I am going to prove they cannot protect you."

The screen cut away to footage from the LA Metro system where Erebus had been released on the train. The people on board started choking and convulsing on the screen.

"This is Project Erebus," Flash explained. *"A charming little concoction dreamed up by the US Defense Department. Does this say defence to you? Does it scream freedom and democracy? Or does it shout terrorism? This is an offensive weapon which would be used to attack the helpless, so your President can get re-elected and the governments can look tough on terror, while using the most hideous weapon created since the atomic bomb to secure your oil supplies and dominance as the world's superpower. The Five Eyes are nothing but a bunch of punks looking to steal everyone's lunch money. They are the big kid in the class, the school bully in the playground, completely incapable of realising their own strength is actually their greatest weakness."*

"You failed to heed my warnings," Flash said. *"Echelon is still running and the Five Eyes continue to operate in the shadows stealing everyone's lunch money. Well, not for much longer. Tonight is the first of many where I will teach you the lessons you need to learn for your arrogance."*

A man took a seat between Max and Flash. At first, Max thought it was the idiot Congressman back from the bathroom. He lent forward and said something to Blake and Blake nodded his head. Through the darkness, in the flickering light from the screens, Max caught a glimpse of the man's face.

It was Flash.

Max reached for his gun, but stopped as Flash lent back and revealed a syringe pressed into Blake's back. The needle was completely through Blake's suit and lodged in his back, and the glass vial was filled with a red liquid which Max could only presume was Erebus.

"Hi, Max," Flash said. "I've come to collect, Blake. I hope you don't mind. I really need him to come with me."

"He's not going anywhere with you," Max said trying not to choke on his words. "Look where you are. There is no way you are going to leave here alive."

"Oh, but I am and you're going to help me."

"How do you figure?"

"Well, all hell is about to break loose in here and while Blake and I run with everyone else for the emergency exit, you are going to secure the President and Prime Minister."

"No, I'm going to kill you."

"Please, Max. We both know what you will do. King, President, country, all that bullshit. You'll protect them and sacrifice your new boyfriend in the process."

Flash lent closer to Blake.

"Congratulations, by the way, Blake," Flash said with a smile. "It only took one dead fiancé and countless years it would seem to get there, but you are persistent, you got there in the end."

Max inched forward, but froze as Flash touched the end of the syringe.

"I wouldn't do that, Max," Flash said with a wave of his finger. "Only a couple of mills of this will kill him. Half the vial will mean that within minutes most of the people in the room will be infected and die as it pours out of his dying body."

"Why are you doing this?" Max asked. "This isn't you, Flash."

"It is now."

"They deceived you, Jacob. Please listen to me. They killed Jane to get to you."

"You don't think that is going to work, do you? How stupid do you think I am?"

"It's true, Jacob," Blake said over his shoulder.

"Shut up!" Flash snapped. "She's dead because of you, both of you, and I am going to make you pay. Okay Blake, it's time for us to leave."

"You're not going anywhere," Max said as the three men got to their feet.

"Oh, I almost forgot, catch," Flash said biting the strap of his watch and dropping it into Max's hand. "Check it out."

Max looked at the small watch screen. It had a timer, four minutes, thirty and counting down.

"You might want to watch this," Flash said pointing to the screen. "Oh and don't try to follow us or I will kill him."

"Do what you have to do, Max," Blake pleaded as Flash spun him around to face Max. "Save the President and Prime Minister."

"I can't lose you," Max said.

"Oh, how sweet," Flash said. "Pity this has been such a short relationship, but I'm sure it was good while it lasted."

"Fuck you," Max said as Flash started to drag Blake back towards the door.

"If you take one more step or try to raise the alarm before we are through that door, I will kill him and everyone in this room," Flash said taking another step back. "Stay, Max. I have nothing to lose now, thanks to you, but you on the other hand could lose the new boyfriend and all of these government arseholes in one foul swoop. You have so much to lose."

"Don't worry about me, Max," Blake said calmly holding out his hand to stop Max. "You know what to do."

"I will find you," Max mouthed as Flash was distracted.

"I know you will," Blake mouthed back.

"Here we go," Flash said pointing to the screen. "Bye, Max."

Flash and Blake walked to the door. Max knew he couldn't go after them. Blake would die and everyone in the building would be at risk, including the President and Prime Minister. He felt sick as Flash's voice boomed over the speakers.

"The light of Helios and Apollo cannot overcome me," Flash said on the screen. *"The Sun God's preoccupation with music, since the beginning, will not be enough to see him able to distract and sooth with his lyre following my visit upon you. He and his son, Asclepius, will try in vein to heal and to mend your wounds, but they have never faced the challenges which I will bring upon the world. It is time for the darkness to rise, for this shining beacon painted in a Holy white trying to embrace and appease the Sun God, to be shrouded in the darkness. I am Erebus and I am here to greet the President and her guests."*

The footage cut to a live feed from a camera in a small dark room. At its centre was a cannister of the red liquid, undoubtedly Erebus, with a menu from tonight's State Dinner and a keyring from the White House gift shop. Then the same countdown timer flashed onto the screen. Max checked the watch Flash had given him. Three minutes, twenty, nineteen, eighteen.

All hell broke loose around him.

People started screaming and running for the exits. He stood for a moment and starred at the door Blake had been dragged through and felt like screaming himself. He knew the only thing he could do was to secure the Prime Minister and President. He had no doubt Flash would kill Blake if he went after them, but he also knew Blake would be horrified and would never forgive Max if he saved him instead of the world leaders. Blake had dedicated his life to the service of the country and would happily accept his fate if he knew they were safe.

Max sighted the Prime Minister with Hulk and Kate. He run through the crowd dodging between frightened guests as he heard machine gun fire outside the room. His thoughts turned to Blake, but he had to push on.

He arrived beside the small group of his colleagues and the President with her Secret Service pretorian guard, including the Director himself.

"We need to secure the room," Lewis ordered the nearest agents.

"No," Max countered. "We need to get the President and Prime Minister to the bunker."

"I don't take orders from you," Lewis spat. "We don't know if that's a real image from in the White House and there is a firefight outside the room."

"It's real."

"How do you know, Max?" Hulk asked.

"Flash was here. He's got Blake."

Max tossed his boss the smart watch Flash had given him.

"Move now!" Hulk ordered.

"But," Lewis went to interject.

"Pegasus," Hulk said cutting him off.

The Secret Service agents didn't need any further instruction. On hearing their protection codeword, they sprung into action and like the mythical winged horse lifted the President and ran towards the far exit. Four Australian Federal Police agents did the same thing with the Prime Minister only metres behind the President. A swarm of other agents grabbed different officials and made their way following the President.

Jonnie had arrived and was all but carrying Hulk with Kate. Hulk was yelling for them to leave him and secure the Prime Minister, but they ignored his order. Max joined the perimeter guards taking out hostiles on their route.

The Secret Service agents had cleared a path and opened all the doors on the route.

"Two minutes," Hulk yelled and the group surged forward even faster.

"Teams one and two," a Secret Service agent ordered, "onto the elevator. Everyone else, down the stairs."

"We'll never make it going down the stairs!" Lewis shouted in panic as his detail and the other officials pealed off down the nearby staircase.

Max was at the back of the pack protecting their flank. He dropped two of Flash's men and saw the guns they were using drop and scatter across the wooden floor. He picked one of them up and put it in his belt. Behind him the massive elevator doors were open and the President and Prime Minister, plus a small group of other officials, and their protective details, as well as Hulk and Jonnie were all jammed in.

Kate and Max were firing on any of Flash's men who dared to come into the hallway.

"Go!" Max ordered the Secret Service agent in the doorway.

The agent didn't need to be told twice. He hit the button and the elevator doors closed, leaving Max and Kate in the hallway.

The elevator plummeted at an astonishing speed, before quickly stopping and opening at the bottom of the shaft. The huge pack of dignitaries was swept through the large vault like door and into the Presidential Emergency Operations Centre, the PEOC or Presidential Bunker as if was often referred to.

The Secret Service agent at the door was pressing buttons to get it to close.

"Wait!" the President ordered. "General, how long?"

"One and a half minutes," Hulk said looking at the watch.

"You close it with fifteen seconds left on that watch and not a second sooner," the President said pointing to the agent.

"Yes, ma'am," he said hovering his finger over the final close button.

Kate and Max had killed another two of Flash's men and had started their decent into the basement of the White House. There was no way of knowing where the device was located, so their best bet was to get to the bunker. They caught up with Lewis' group and a few other important officials from both the US and Australia.

"Move your arses!" Max ordered thinking of his internal clock counting down. "Sixty seconds until the device detonates."

The group panicked and started jumping down the last of the steps and running down the hallway towards the foyer outside the bunker.

Hernandez, the CIA Director, was in the pack and she rolled her ankle trying to run in heels. Max and Kate swept her up and ran supporting her weight between them.

The group burst through the hallway door and ran for the bunker door. The first of them made it through, but it was starting to close.

"Wait!" Torres yelled at the agent controlling the door when she saw Hernandez.

"I'm sorry, Madam President," the agent said. "Once the procedure starts it can't be stopped."

"Run!" Torres screamed down the corridor.

"Go!" Max yelled to Kate as he picked Hernandez up over his shoulder and sprinted closely behind Kate.

Kate ducked into the bunker.

A metre out from the door, Max dived through the narrow opening with the Director on his shoulder. They tumbled to the ground in a mess of limbs as the big door sealed and bolted into place. Hernandez hit the concrete hard, but she was in and safe.

"Are you okay?" Max asked her as he helped her to her feet.

"I've never played football before," Hernandez said slightly winded and holding her hip. "I'm not going to rush out and try it."

"I'm glad you're okay."

"Thank you, Max."

"The Director needs some medical attention," Max said to the nearest agent and they whisked Hernandez off to the medical centre to check her over.

"Madam President," an aide said appearing in the room. "You need to see this."

The group of officials turned away from the door. The space behind them was huge. A large oval conference table ran away from them towards a large projector screen which was framed by four flatscreen televisions on each side. On the main screen, it showed footage from Flash's live camera. The cannister had opened and Erebus was pouring out into the air. Footage on the other screens was variously scrolling through CCTV cameras positioned throughout the White House. Within seconds, several of the screens started to show people coughing then convulsing on the floor as Erebus filled the ventilation system and circulated through the building.

"Status report?" Torres asked.

"Ma'am," Moore, the FBI Director, said. "It looks like quite a few guests made it outside. I have teams coming in to secure the perimeter. They should be fine on the lawns outside away from the building."

"My guys are moving them towards the fence line," Lewis said trying still to catch his breath.

"Show me," Torres said to an aide who typed some commands on the keyboard on the end of the conference table.

The main screen showed footage from the portico's cameras. It zoomed in on the crowd of White House staff and guests being ushered towards the fence line. It then zoomed back out and returned to the doors of the VIP entrance. People were staggering out clutching their necks and starting to convulse in the doorway. Some made it to the steps, but their legs collapsed under them and they violently died on old concrete steps.

"Order your men back from the building," Torres said to Lewis. "They can't get too close. Erebus is still pouring out the doors."

"Yes, ma'am," Lewis said.

"I thought the building's ventilation system was supposed to detect an attack and shutdown?"

"Yes, it does," Moore said. "But, it didn't shutdown fast enough. We are completely safe in here though. We have our own isolated air supply."

"That doesn't help them," Torres said pointing to the screens as more people collapsed throughout the building. "Where is the Vice President?"

"He's on route to Andrew's Air Force Base," Lewis said. "As you know, given our new procedures for continuity of government, he was not at the dinner. He was at the Naval Observatory, as soon as the attack started the order went out to get him in the air. Air Force Two is fuelled and the engines are fired up on the runway. As soon as he gets on board it will take off."

"Good. And the Secretary of Defense?"

"I'm here, ma'am," Woods said walking into the room. "I've been in the Situation Room running our Erebus recovery missions."

"Within the last couple of days, Christopher, I have gone from not knowing a thing about Erebus to it killing dozens of people in my fucking White House! You better have some good news for me or, let me tell you, you will be hung, drawn and fucking quartered as I feed you to the press for all your failings."

"We are getting closer to finding a couple of the deliveries," Wood said sheepishly.

"So no, you don't have any good news," Torres said as Lewis stood a bit taller now there was another scapegoat in the room.

"We have some strong leads and I'm confident we will be able to provide you with more information in the next few minutes."

"Good. Well, everyone should take their seats. We could be in here for a while."

Torres and the other American officials took their traditional seats.

"Madam Prime Minister," Torres said to Ferguson and motioning to the table. "You and your team are welcome to join us. We will need a coordinated effort to get through this."

"Thank you, Amanda," Ferguson said motioning for Hulk and Max to sit at the table, while Kate and Jonnie sat in the seats lining the room behind them. "I am very sorry for your losses. We will do whatever we can to help."

"Thank you. You have likely lost some of your fellow countryman upstairs too, so I'm sorry for your losses too."

"Thank you."

"So, would someone like to tell me what we know? Like how these people got into my White House."

"We are still working on it," Lewis said turning back to his aides on phones behind him who shook their heads to tell him they had no more information yet.

"Under normal circumstances, Allan, you would be looking for a new job. First, someone sneaks onto Air Force One, then a bunch of terrorists set off our own supposedly secret weapon in the White House, all under your nose."

"Well, ma'am, thank you for keeping me in the role. I won't let you down again."

"Don't thank me. I would sack you, but I can't afford the political fallout the chaos of change could create in the service. I need you all focused. Do a good job and I might consider keeping you on."

"Yes, ma'am," Lewis said almost in tears.

"Anyone else more enlightened than Director Lewis?"

"Madam President," Max spoke up. "He was here in the White House."

"Who was here?"

"Flash. Jacob Gordon."

"How do you know he was here?"

"I spoke to him."

"You what?"

"I spoke to him, he sat down right beside me at the table in the East Room."

"And, you let him get away?" Lewis jumped in excitedly.

"Not exactly."

"Why don't you tell us what happened Agent Shaw?" Torres asked looking at Lewis with eyes that told him to shut up.

"He had a vial of Erebus in a syringe, which he had stabbed into the back of Rear Admiral Smyth," Max said choking on Blake's name as aides made their way around the room pouring glasses of water. "He told me if I alerted anyone, he would push the plunger. He took Blake as a hostage."

"So, you saved your colleague and risked the lives of everyone else, including the President?" Lewis said trying to shift the blame.

"Actually," Max said coldly and sternly, "there was enough Erebus in the vial to kill everyone in the room. If he expelled enough into Blake, he would have become infected and spread it to all of us within seconds."

"Is this right?" Torres asked turning to her Defense Secretary. "Can that amount take out a whole room?"

"Yes," Wood said.

"So, why would he risk coming into the building himself and capturing one of your men?"

"Payback," Max said.

"Explain."

"Flash knows that Admiral Smyth and I are more than just friends," Max revealed as calmly as he could, still surprised at how difficult it felt coming out to people even now. "He has him to get back at me. He blames me for everything that happened to him. It was my decision and my order to leave him behind in London. Everything flows back to that moment, including the death of his wife, Jane."

"And he is holding you responsible?"

"Yes ma'am. He apparently made a deal with the terrorist group known as The Sixteen to retrieve Jane, so they could be together when he recovered. But, as you all know, I put an end to them and with every one I took out, the more difficult it was for them to operate and thus Jane couldn't be moved. She died before he recovered enough to reach her himself. I believe she was murdered. Either way, he wants me to suffer, while he lets his other plans run their course.”

“His other plans?”

“While he blames me for Jane’s death and what happened to him, he is also hellbent on bringing down the Five Eyes intelligence system and our nations. He blames all of us for recruiting him and forcing him to do the things we had to do.”

“He chose to join. He could have left anytime he wanted.”

“Ma’am, the Flash I know was a patriot. He would never have quit and would never have done anything like this. He was my best friend. I knew him better than anyone. He had to have been brainwashed.”

“How is this even possible?” Lewis asked pointing his finger at Max. “You said we needed stay ahead of him and be unpredictable. It seems like he has the drop on us at every turn, including here in this building – one of the most secure places on earth. It doesn’t added up.”

“What exactly are you asking, Director Lewis?

“You know what I’m asking.”

“Yeah, I think I do, but for the benefit of the room, why don’t you say it anyway.”

“Something doesn’t smell right in all this. How do we know you aren’t involved in all this? You were a wanted fugitive, what seems like, only hours ago. And, now your best friend is terrorising this nation and your homosexual lover just so happens to be the person taken hostage. Pretty big coincidence.”

“You’re a dickhead,” Max said as his frustration started to get the better of him.

“Just hold on one minute. Does no one around this table think it is awfully convenient that this man, after being missing in action for years, somehow manages to get on board the most secure plane in the world. Then his best friend, who has also been missing for years, turns up and launches a successful attack on the White House?”

Max gritted his teeth. He could feel himself losing it. Flash had Blake and Max was trapped in a room being accused of being a terrorist. He wasn't sure whether he wanted to laugh or cry or jump the table and snap Lewis' neck. He was losing his mind in worry. Was he going to lose Blake too? The thought was killing him. Flash knew exactly what he was doing when he took him.

Psychological torture.

How long was he going to be stuck in here listening to these arseholes? Maybe he should have gone after Blake and let these people die. No, that's not what Blake would have wanted. He knew one thing for sure though, his feelings for Blake were real and he was not going to rest until he found him.

"Madam President, you should arrest this man until we can get to the bottom of all of this," Lewis stated causing Max's temper to flare with each word.

"His partner has been captured, Allan, can't you show even just a trace of empathy?" Torres asked. "It's a big accusation."

"That maybe so, but I won't leave our nation's defence to someone like him," Lewis said his words dripping with scorn.

"Someone like him?" Torres questioned. "What exactly do you mean?"

"You know what I mean, don't pretend like you're some flag waving equality cheerleader now."

"That has nothing to do with this, our national security is more important than any ideological views. You should remember your place. If you want to make accusations, you better be prepared to defend them with fact."

"Well, even if he isn't involved, given its his *boy*-friend," Lewis said with distain, "he's too close to all this. He should not be involved. Maybe he will sacrifice national security to save his fag buddy."

Max had had enough. His anger had been building with every word, but that was the last straw. He bounced out of his chair, knocking it over, and slapped his left hand down on the table, while picking up his glass of water in his right. He stood and threw it like Major League baseball pitcher. The glass flew through the air trailing water over the big conference table and shattered on impact with Lewis' face.

"You fucking narrowminded piece of shit!" Max screamed across the table pointing at Lewis. "First you accuse me of being a terrorist, then you disrespect the man I love. A man who has done more for our countries than you ever will. A man, who for all I know, could be laying dead in a gutter somewhere. You can go fuck yourself!"

A swarm of Secret Service agents surrounded Max as a dazed and bleeding Lewis gave the order to take him into custody. Max drew his pistol and the pistol he had picked up after killing one of Flash's men and aimed them at two of the nearest agents.

"How many of you are willing to try to execute that order?" Max asked looking around at the agents. "He's a piece of shit. Is he worth it? How many do you think I will drop before you can take me down? I suggest you back it up."

"Stand down, everyone," Torres ordered standing up. "I said stand down, that's an order."

The Secret Service agents all backed away from Max, but he still held his weapons in outstretched arms.

"Max," Torres said. "You've made your point, but this isn't going to help us find Blake and Flash."

Max lowered his arms. She was right. He had let his temper get the better of him. He dropped his pistol and tossed the terrorist's gun onto the conference table. It slid over to Torres.

"That's how they got into your White House," Max said. "Ceramic guns. I took this off one of the terrorists I shot upstairs."

"Madam President," Moore injected as Torres examined the ceramic gun and he cradled the desk phone. "My team at the FBI have only in the last twenty minutes confirmed that pictures of Max used at the Defense facility in Nevada were uploaded via Professor Franklin's computer to their servers. It was some sort of virus or trojan horse which Flash must have uploaded when he first got into the office. The same virus allowed him to hack into our networks and doctor footage to make it look like Max was responsible for the train attack in LA. We've shutdown the virus and eliminated it, but for what it's worth, I believe Max's story. If he was involved why would he be the one this organisation was trying to set up?"

"Take them away," Torres ordered and the Secret Service agents moved in to take Max.

"Please Madam President, as soon as you have a location, let me go after them," Max said as he allowed the agents to take him away.

"We'll see. Agents, you can take Director Lewis too. Get him seen to by the doctor, then place him in an office without any external communications until this is all over. Allan, I can't allow your failures, your phobias or your incompetence to jeopardise our nation. You're fired."

"You will regret this you fucking immigrant bitch!" Lewis shouted as he was dragged from the room by his former sub-ordinates.

"I was born in Texas, you jackass," Torres said as he disappeared behind the wall. "Why don't we all take ten minutes to make some calls and get updates from your relevant departments and regroup to see where we are at?"

"Good idea," Ferguson said. "Do you have a room we can use?"

"I'll show you," Moore said leading the Australian delegation out of the room.

Chapter Twenty-Eight

"I can't believe you are alive," Blake said as Flash bundled him into the backseat of the waiting SUV.

One of Flash's men had been waiting in the white SUV just outside the White House. His men had secured one of the driveways allowing them access and exit. Flash had handcuffed Blake and removed the syringe. He had taken Blake's ring and phones, so AIS could not track him. He tossed them out the window into the gutter just outside the presidential fortress which he had just successfully raided and attacked.

"We all grieved the day you died," Blake stated. "Your funeral was painful for all of us."

"Shut up," Flash said turning around to face Blake from the front seat. "You won't get to me, Blake."

"So, what's the plan here? Lure Max into a trap an kill him?"

"I'm not going to tell you my plans, but, more or less, yes. If I know Max, I know right now he is beside himself with anxiety and despair. Lachlan's death nearly killed him, but yours will destroy him. I will watch him suffer then kill him."

"You can kill me, Jacob, and you might just hurt Max in the process, but the one thing I do know is that he will kill you. While there is breath in his body, he will search for you. He will hunt you down and he will kill you."

"When you all left me to die alone in London, I was taken to one of The Sixteen's safehouses. I suffered through months of surgeries and rehab without painkillers and morphine. They limited my access to antibiotics, deliberately allowing me to cycle between healing and sickness, life and near-death. My wounds would be ripped open as they started to heal to torture me, then they would stitch me up and pump me full of drugs to stop me from dying, then they would do it all again a day later. Never being allowed to heal enough to survive without their help, but never allowing me to die. Occasionally, they would try new torture techniques – perfecting their skills and methods on me. All the while asking questions about AIS, and you and Hulk – but mostly they wanted to know about Max. The hero, the selfless, tireless, ruthless agent who had killed their leaders and started to pick them off one by one. With each passing day and every new body he left for them to find, their aggression increased and the torture sessions lasted longer and longer as they got desperate."

"They did this to you, Flash. Max had nothing to do with it."

"The funny thing about long-term torture," Flash said turning back again to look at Blake, "and something we were never taught at the Wool Shed. Your body starts to adapt. Your pain tolerances and its ability to heal, change and that just pisses the torturer off even more. They broke me mentally many times, but my body always found a way to fight on. But, the pain it never stopped, it was just longer and more intricate. But, who cares right? I was dead, so no one was looking for me. None of you cared about me and what was happening to me."

"I care, Jacob, I always have."

"That's bullshit, Blake," Flash spat. "If you cared you wouldn't have let them leave me there. It's just as much your fault. I was tortured for years, Blake. Do you get that?"

"Yes, I do and I am sorry."

"Save it. I don't want to hear it."

"What they did to you is horrific, Flash. If I had of known, you have to know, I would have moved heaven and earth to stop them and get you back."

"But you didn't, did you?" Flash yelled back at him.

"No. I'm sorry we failed you, Jacob."

The car stopped in a tunnel a few kilometres away. Flash pulled Blake out and the pair got into another car, as the original sped off. The new car was a blue sedan and doubled back the way they came.

After a few miles, they drove into a carpark and changed cars again. This time a green van was waiting for them. Flash pushed Blake into the back and he sat up on the metal wheel arch. Flash sat across from him as the van sped out of the carpark.

"I tried to comfort her," Blake said breaking the silence, "at the funeral, she was so strong. Stronger than I could ever be if I was in that situation. She said, 'this was always a possibility in his line of work'. She was right, Flash. We choose this life and all of the ups and downs that come with it. All of the risks and the sacrifices. You could have walked away at any moment and spent the rest of your years with Jane, but you chose to stay on, doing what you believed in."

"Don't you say her name," Flash said launching himself at Blake.

He pinned Blake to the van wall by the neck. Blake felt Flash's grip tighten on his neck. Part of him wished Flash would kill him and that somehow Max would find out and avoid the confrontation, but he knew it was wishful thinking. Max wouldn't stop and his death would only pour fuel on the flames of revenge.

"Jane loved you so much, Flash," Blake choked out. "I'm sorry she was killed."

Flash's grip loosened and he tossed Blake to the floor near the backdoor.

"Don't start that shit with me, Blake," Flash said. "Max tried, but I know you are both full of shit."

"She didn't die in an accident," Blake said sitting up, "and it wasn't suicide. We found evidence the brake lines were cut. Think about it. She had driven that road hundreds of times, in all conditions. She knew that corner was there. She would have braked, but the lines were cut, she didn't stand a chance. I'm sorry, Flash, they manipulated you."

"That's bullshit. I made a deal with them."

"What deal?"

"They agreed the torture would stop and they would deliver Jane. In return, I would help them rebuild The Sixteen and stop Max."

"Okay, but when Max killed them all, you took up their mission."

"No, by the time Max had wiped most of them out, I had a new mission."

"Which was?"

"Takeover."

"Why?"

"Because for years I endured torture protecting Max and the AIS in the hope one day you would find me and rescue me, but you never came. I held out for years without saying a word. Then Jane died. She died alone and no doubt petrified at the bottom of a dark ravine. Hope was lost and only pain remained. I found a way to overcome the pain, I would seek retribution on everyone that had failed me and I would tear down the very structures that had failed her and failed me."

"But without those structures, without the Five Eyes and the intelligence community our nations would crumble as our enemies took advantage of our new weaknesses. Surely, Jane wouldn't want that. She would not want to see innocent people hurt."

"No one is innocent," Flash said his face reddening with anger. "They have let their governments destroy countless lives while living in ignorant bliss. Well, it is time they felt the struggle, time they had to start paying attention and if they don't change, it's time for them to die."

"You're insane."

"I'm sure they will all say that, but this is the only way for the world to change and for all of you to experience my pain."

"You selfish son of a bitch. Think about all the women and children and innocent people you have already killed, let alone those that will come if you succeed. All to settle your own scores. My old friend is definitely dead. He died on that street in London a hero. The man sitting here today is not a shadow of his former self. A terrorist. The very thing he used to hunt and bring to justice."

"You may be right, Blake, but you will die knowing you helped train me. Knowing you helped give me the skills I needed to succeed and knowing that I am going to kill your boyfriend. The man who has been so elusive for so long and just when you finally thought you had him, I going to intervene. You will die longing for a man you will never get to hold."

Blake sprang forward and headbutted Flash, breaking his cheek bone, but Flash was undeterred. He punched Blake in the face knocking him to the floor.

"Years of torture," Flash said smiling, "do have an upside. I no longer feel pain like I used to. Good try though."

Not long later, the pair changed cars again, yet another move in the shell game Flash was playing to throw the intelligence agencies off his scent. This time a black SUV.

After countless wide circuits around the city, occasionally doubling back on itself, the SUV made its way to their final destination or so Blake thought.

Chapter Twenty-Nine

Max had paced for twenty minutes. He felt like a trapped animal. Blake was out there somewhere and he had no idea if he was dead or alive or how to find him.

He was replaying part of the conversation he had been a part of with Lewis. How that man had been appointed with all his bigoted views was hard to fathom. Max had spent years working at Parliament House for politicians as a cover job when he started with AIS. He had studied political science and had always enjoyed politics, but with every passing year and sub-par character he saw take office, he grew more disgruntled about the state of global politics.

It wasn't even just his own country and its allies. In the years he had spent on the run, he travelled extensively throughout the world, trying to stay one step ahead of the agencies and the terrorists who had marked him for death. He lived and breathed his adopted countries to blend in. During his years at AIS with Blake and Hulk's help, he had set up countless deposit boxes and foreign accounts under different allises filled with money recovered from different terrorist organisations, weapons and fake passports. He could literally travel anywhere and be anyone, but regardless of his destination, the newspapers were always the same – the government wasn't delivering and the quality of those in office was constantly called into question. With people like Lewis at the highest rungs of government it was not hard to see why.

Max was flashing between anger and fear to anxiety and sadness. He was not in a good place and the longer he stayed trapped in his office-come-cell, the more helpless he felt. He needed to get out of the office and he needed to find Blake before it was too late. And, he was getting impatient.

The lock clicked and Hulk walked in using his cane.

"How you going, kid?" Hulk asked as one of the agents, turned prison guard, closed the door.

"I'm going fucking crazy, Hulk," Max admitted honestly. "Have they found him yet?"

"No, not yet."

"Fuck!" Max said continuing his pace across the little room.

"We're going to get him back, Max, and we are going to stop Flash."

"I'm not going to do anything locked in this fucking room!" Max said slamming his palm on the door.

"Well, throwing a glass and smashing it on the Secret Service Director's face hasn't helped, nor has drawing your weapons on agents in the presence of the President. Even Ferguson has been arguing to keep you locked in here."

"Well, fuck her too."

"She doesn't know you yet, Max. You've been away for a long time."

"So, what are they doing to find Blake?"

"They aren't looking for Blake, they are looking for Flash and Erebus. You know that."

"Well, what are they doing to find them?"

"We think we have found three of the larger shipments of Erebus."

"Where?"

"That's why I'm here, I convinced them to let you out to observe the missions."

"Good let's go."

"Not just yet," Hulk said putting his hand on Max's chest. "Starting a fight with anyone outside of this room, means you can't go back into the field. I've got Moore and Hernandez on side, even Woods is coming around, but Torres and Ferguson aren't sure. Play nice and when the building is clear and you can get out, you'll take the lead in tracking Flash and getting Blake back."

"Okay, Hulk. I will play nice."

"Blake is relying on you, Max, and so am I."

"So are you?"

"Blake is probably the closest friend I have, Max, and I want him to be home safe. But, I also wanted you to hear it from me first, I'm planning to retire. I have spent years training Blake to take over from me when the day comes. There is no one I trust more to take charge after I'm gone."

"You'll outlive all of us, Hulk, retirement is not an option."

"I'm too old for this shit. It's time, kid. Look what those arseholes were able to do to me. Even I'm not proud enough to try to argue I'm still at my best. Blake is going to take over from me as Head of the AIS and I want you by his side as Head of Operations – my old job, the one I had when I recruited you. You will lead the field operations teams and the recruitment and training branches. Between the two of you, I know I will have put the country in good hands."

"I'm going to get him back, Hulk. Failure is not an option. We can talk about this retirement shit another day."

"I know how you feel about him, kid, and I know how much he cares about you. I'm looking forward to the day I can see that become a reality for you both. God knows, you have both been through enough shit for a thousand lifetimes. You deserve happiness. And, I know you will do what needs to be done to get him back."

"I will."

"Good, let's go," Hulk said banging three times on the door. "Play nice."

Hulk led Max out and back to the conference room. No one turned away from the big screen when they entered, just a couple of the Secret Service agents near the door who eyed him cautiously. He could feel their eyes burning into the back of him as he stood near the back of the room.

The large screen was showing live vision from a dashboard camera in an FBI SUV. Max couldn't be sure, but he thought it looked like Chicago. He had been through there for a few nights when he was on the run.

The car launched down a steep little hill, closely behind a sedan it was chasing. The SUV was tailgating the sedan and every now and then would bump into it, causing it to swerve wildly. Max thought they had him pinned a couple of times, but it would find an impossible gap and get away. The FBI was giving a relentless chase though through small side streets and down major freeways.

"Okay," Moore said into the intercom, "let's try to keep them on the freeway headed out of town. Block the exits."

"Yes, sir," came the reply on the conference room speakers.

"Chicago," Kate said walking over to stand next to Max. "They found this guy on route to the State House, but he didn't get a chance to get close. FBI's been chasing him for fucking ages. They should just pull up next to him and shoot him through the fucking window."

"Guess they can now he's out of town," Max agreed.

"Nah, they are a bit softer, than us and the CIA. They'll try to make an arrest."

"The driver could know where Blake is."

"I doubt it. Flash is too fucking smart to share too much information."

"Probably right. Any news on what's happening upstairs?"

"They cleared the roof of agents and have started the ventilation systems on high, trying to vent the remaining gas into the atmosphere. Apparently, it dissolves fairly quickly, so hopefully we will get the all clear soon."

"I hope so, I want to get out of this fucking building."

"I get it, mate. We'll be on their trail soon enough."

"No, not soon enough."

"You know what I meant. We all want him back, kid. I want to be best man at your big gay wedding."

"Couldn't think of anyone I'd rather have," Max said smiling at Kate.

"Anything on Flash yet?"

"He did the whole shell game bullshit again. We have a bunch of teams trying to trace every car and truck that moved in and out of the tunnel they drove into, then they are tracking every vehicle until they get to shelters, tunnels or carparks. Then tracking each one beyond that. It's a fucking nightmare. Each tunnel or structure creates a dozen or more vehicles to track."

"Fuck," Max said feeling deflated.

"It's okay, kid, we're not giving up. We have AIS and CIA on it. We'll get him."

"Thanks, Kate."

"What about the other two shipments. Hulk mentioned three. One in Chicago, where are the other two?"

"Seattle and San Diego."

"Where are they in taking back the shipments?"

"They have a CIA wet team prepping to board a cargo ship in San Diego. They got some intel on of the shipments could be on board."

"Could be?"

"They tracked one of the trucks from the San Francisco warehouse via multiple yards. Well, more specifically they tracked the shipping container as it was moved from one truck to another."

"Turns out they were moving this shit a lot earlier than we thought, it could be anywhere in the US. Could even be in Canada or Mexico. We think he is trying to get some of it out of the country to release in other countries. Can you fucking believe it?"

"No actually, I can't."

"He's fucking thought of everything, must have been planning this for years."

"Yeah," Max conceded lowering his head.

"I'm sorry, Max."

"It's not your fault, Kate."

"Don't give me that bullshit, I was there that day too. I'm as much to blame as you."

"I appreciate you saying it, Kate, but I was in command. It was my decision."

"If I had to do it a thousand times over, I would have made the same call every time."

"Thanks, Kate."

"White House Situation Room, this is Lieutenant Commander James Ericson of the USS Gerald R. Ford, do you read me?" Ericson asked over the speakers in the conference room.

"Yes, Commander Ericson, it's President Torres," Torres replied. "Situation report?"

"Madam President, the FBI team on the ground in San Diego reported the package made its way onto a private Gulfstream. As ordered, we scrambled a squadron of four F-22 Raptors to intercept. I am leading the mission and we are closing in on the Gulfstream."

"That is good news, Commander. How long until you have a visual?"

"One minute, ma'am. I'm told they can connect your monitors to my helmet camera so you will be able to see what I see."

Torres nodded to a nearby aide the screen cutaway from the FBI chase in Chicago to footage from the Raptor. Max saw all the electronics lit up from the pilot's cockpit and for a brief moment, felt he was living a boyhood dream of being a fighter pilot.

He saw the rolling dark storm clouds through the little windows and saw the plane bouncing around from the turbulence. Lightning flashed out the righthand window and the Commander turned to look at the amazing sight. It forked wildly across the sky, followed by a clap of thunder which was barely audible over the roar of the Raptor's engines.

The Commander turned back to the front and tapped his radar.

"Madam President," Ericson said. *"The plane should be visible in a few seconds. Squadron drop to thirty-five thousand feet."*

"Ack. Dropping to thirty-five thousand," his squadron all called in.

"It's a bit hard to see because of the darker clouds down at this altitude, but the Gulfstream is right ahead of me, Madam President. How would like me to proceed?"

"What is your location, Commander?" Torres asked.

"We are approximately forty miles, bearing West South West over the Pacific Ocean."

"Try to contact the pilot."

"Yes, ma'am. November-Two-Five-Niner-Romeo-Lima, this is the United States Navy, do you copy? Niner-Romeo-Lima, do you copy?"

A full minute past as the Commander tried to hail the pilot of the Gulfstream.

"Madam President," Ericson said. *"Aircraft is unresponsive. Please advise, how you would like me to proceed."*

"Stay on them and keep trying to raise them," Torres ordered muting the call and turning to the conference table. "Thoughts?"

"It's over the ocean," Woods said. "That's better than we thought. We can shoot it down without incident."

"Unless it's a private flight and the substance isn't onboard," Ferguson said. "Then there'll be an incident."

"Good point," Torres acknowledged. "Carl, how confident are we Erebus is onboard?"

"Sixty to seventy percent," Moore said.

"Try to do better."

The room sat in silence for a moment as Moore spoke to his advisers.

"Commander," Torres said unmuting the call. "How are we going?"

"Still no reply, ma'am," Ericson said.

"Maybe someone should try to get a visual into the cockpit," Hulk suggested.

"Good idea, General," Torres said. "Did you hear that, Commander?"

"Yes, ma'am," Ericson said already moving his fighter jet. *"Moving now."*

The footage of the screen showed Ericson pealing his jet off to the right, then levelling off beside the Gulfstream and moving forward. When he came level with the cockpit, he turned his head so the camera could see into the other plane. There was only one pilot sitting in the relative darkness, his face could only be seen by the glow of his electronics. He turned briefly to face the fighter jet on his right wing. Ericson turned on a light in his cockpit and indicated the pilot should speak to him, using the pick up the phone hand signal. The pilot nodded.

"November-Two-Five-Niner-Romeo-Lima, this is the United States Navy, do you copy?" Ericson asked.

"Umm, yes," came the pilot's reply. *"This Niner-Romeo-Lima."*

"Romeo-Lima, please confirm your cargo and numbers."

"Ahh, yes. Ahh, we have around ten passengers onboard, with two crew. Umm, cargo. Yep, cargo is just luggage."

"What is your destination?"

"We, umm, err, we are a private charter heading to Hawaii."

"Why didn't you respond to my earlier calls?"

"I was, umm, distracted momentarily."

"Niner-Romeo-Lima, we believe you or someone on your plane may be in possession of a device belonging to the United States Government. Can you please tell me if anyone was acting strangely when they boarded?"

There was a long silence.

"Niner-Romeo-Lima?" Ericson asked looking back towards the cockpit.

"Where is the co-pilot?" Max asked. "Something is wrong."

Torres looked at Max for a moment thinking about what he had just said.

"Commander, ask him where his co-pilot is," Torres ordered.

"*Niner-Romeo-Lima, where is your co-pilot?*" Ericson asked.

"*He, umm, he went to the bathroom,*" came the reply as Ericson continued to look at the cockpit.

There was a flash of lightening and for a brief second the room could see the pilot's face. It was covered in fear, but Max saw something else. Something in the darkness behind the pilot's seat.

"Keep watching, Commander," Max ordered much to the room's surprise, but no one questioned him.

They waited a painfully long minute before the next flash of lightening across the darkened sky. Max focused in.

"He's under duress," Max stated walking to the front of the room. "There's someone in there with him holding a gun on him."

Another flash of lightening and Max pointed to the gun to the shock of everyone in the room.

"Commander, it's the President," Torres said. "The pilot is a hostage. He has a weapon aimed at him."

"*Yes, I heard, ma'am,*" Ericson said. "*I'm sorry I missed it.*"

"Not at all, we all did. Is there any way you can hail him without anyone else hearing us?"

"*Niner-Romeo-Lima, we are getting some feedback on your line,*" Ericson lied. "*Perhaps you could drop the co-pilot's headset off the line to clear it up.*"

"*Ahh, okay,*" the pilot replied nervously. "*That's done, but I'm sure he'll be back very soon.*"

"*I understand, pilot. I believe your transponder should be at seventy-seven hundred, am I right?*" Ericson asked giving the international air signal code for distress.

"Yes, sir."

"How many of them are there?"

"Four."

"Any other civilians on board?"

"Two others."

"Did they have a cannister with them? Like a steel tube?"

"Yes, two."

"Can you tell me how big they were?"

There was a commotion in the cockpit and Ericson turned back to get a visual. There was a struggle of some kind, followed by a flash of light. Max didn't need to wait, he knew that flash instantly – a gunshot. The plane lurched to the right, towards Ericson's Raptor. He quickly pulled away and for a moment his vision returned to the dark sky and electronics panels inside his cockpit. He started shouting orders for his team to pull back to avoid the erratic plane, while asking where it was. His team let him know the plane was under him making a hard left.

"What happened?" Torres said.

"They shot the pilot," Max said shaking his head. "And now they are trying to get away from four Raptors in the middle of a storm."

"Commander?"

"Yes, ma'am," Ericson said clearly under pressure manoeuvring his plane.

"What is happening?"

"Ma'am, it looks like the pilot has been taken out and the plane is banking in a tight arc."

"What is your heading?"

"He just passed South, South East. I think he is turning around to head back stateside."

"We cannot let him return to the US. Thoughts?"

"You have no choice, Madam President," Woods said. "There is a clear and present danger to the United States. You have to shoot it down."

"There are civilians on that plane," Max reminded them.

"Two civilians compared to how many here on the ground they could kill if they get back here."

"Maybe we can force them down and mount a rescue."

"Even you aren't that good, Agent Shaw. It would be impossible."

"Maybe, but it would be worth trying to save your fellow countrymen."

"We don't even know if they are US citizens."

"Does that matter? They are human beings. Madam President, a life is a life. If there is a chance we can save them, we should try."

"Madam President, the aircraft has adjusted course," Ericson said as the footage from his helmet camera showed he had pulled in behind the Gulfstream at a safe distance as it was regularly changing altitude and moving from side to side. *"It is broadly on course for the West Coast."*

"Back to San Diego?" Torres asked.

"Probably more likely Tijuana if he holds this course, ma'am. He is moving unpredictably and could change heading again."

"How long?"

"About twelve minutes, ma'am."

"We can't risk the country, Amanda," Woods said. "You need to shoot it down."

"Max is right. There are civilians onboard. We should at least consider if it is possible to force them down."

"They have two cannisters of Erebus. We don't know how big they are, but it could be enough to take out half of San Diego if it is dropped in the right place above the city."

"I don't understand, I thought it broke down in the atmosphere?"

"It does, but it spreads and settles first. If they pushed it out the door of the plane and it released, it could settle over several city blocks killing hundreds of thousands, before breaking down – depending on the quantity. I think we should assume it's a lot."

"Max, can you suggest any way we can force the plane to land safely," Torres asked turning to Max.

"Use the Navy boys to send some warning shots, then try to escort it in," Max said.

"And if they don't comply?"

"Try to disable it to get it to land on the water."

"It would tear up on impact," Woods dismissed. "You also need to consider something else, Madam President. What if it isn't coming for us? What if they release a US chemical weapon over Tijuana or another Mexican city? We would be at war with our neighbours within days."

Torres' usual poker face broke. The stress was getting to her. She was genuinely torn.

"Madam President," Ericson said. *"The aircraft has not changed course. It is now my strong feeling that it is heading for Mexican soil. We are only a few minutes out."*

"Shoot it down," Torres ordered. "We cannot let this weapon reach land in either the US or our neighbours."

"Thank you, Madam President," Woods said. "Commander Ericson, the President has given the go order. Fire when ready."

"Yes, sir," Ericson said. *"Order confirmed. Targeting."*

Max watched the screen as Ericson ordered his squadron to fall back. A high pitch sound filled the airwaves as Ericson lined up the plane. It was still flying erratically, but it was nowhere near capable enough to shake the Raptor. A deeper tone rang out as the Raptor's weapons radar locked onto the heat signature of the plane.

"Raptor One, box two," Ericson said as he fired the missile.

The room watched in silent horror as the smoke trail shot into view through the cockpit window. The Gulfstream dived hard, but the trail followed it, constantly gaining until a huge explosion ripped the plane apart. A massive fireball roared into the sky as the av-gas caught fire and exploded. The footage cut away as Ericson pulled up and away from the explosion.

"Confirmed hit, target is down, Madam President," Ericson said. *"Returning to the Ford, ma'am."*

"Thank you, Commander," Torres said trying to sound calm. "Excellent work."

"Thank you, ma'am."

"Someone get me the Mexican President on the line. He's going to want to know what is going on. Secretary Woods dispatch search and rescue."

"Yes, ma'am," Woods said, "but I doubt they will find anything."

"It can't hurt to check."

An aide walked into the room a short time later.

"We have the Mexican President ma'am," an aide said.

"Put him through."

"Madam President," the Mexican President started.

"Ma'am," Moore whispered pointing to the screen.

"Emmanuel," Torres said, "I'm sorry I'm going to have to call you back."

The footage on the screen changed to the grainy green of a night-vision camera as Torres ended the call. The eight screens either side also changed to similar footage. The scene coming in was a collection of live feeds from a CIA wet team. The CIA team were currently in a helicopter travelling across the Seattle night sky.

"My boys are on route to the harbour," Hernandez stated as she limped into the conference room. "One minute out."

"And, we are confident they have the container onboard?" Torres asked.

"Yes."

"Okay, take a seat. How's the ankle?"

"It will heal. Thank you for asking."

"Excuse me, Madam President," a Secret Service agent said.

"Yes?" Torres said.

"The White House ventilation units are only detecting trace amounts of Erebus. A special team is being brought in to flush the system. We should be able to return within the next thirty minutes."

"Thank you for the update," Torres said as Max felt his adrenaline surge knowing he would be out of there soon.

The helicopter had arrived and was hovering above a shipping container. The special ops guys were standing in line waiting for their turn to abseil down. One, two, three men either side began their decent when one of the pilots screamed for everyone to hold on.

"What is going on?" Torres asked as everyone in the room sat up to get a closer view of the footage rolling in.

The main screen was showing vision of the helicopter swinging away from the ship as three men who had made it out of the chopper clung desperately to their ropes. Max noticed two of the other screens were showing the fate of the special ops guys who were wearing the body cameras. One was undoubtedly sinking to the bottom of the harbour, the vision was getting darker and the light further away. He must have fallen in. The other man's camera was facing down a narrow walkway between the containers on the deck. He had fallen through the gap and was not moving. Max realised the first man had fallen from the rope and landed on his back. The camera on his chest was sending through the footage of the helicopter.

A trail of smoke flashed passed the helicopter as it swerved wildly to avoid the incoming rocket. Two men fell out the door as the chopper banked away. Both men fell with their arms and limbs flailing. Max checked the footage on the screens to the right of the projector. One of the men, hit a container and tumbled to the deck. His camera smashing on the metal surface as he hit and blacking out the screen. The second guy had hit the ship's railing and somersaulted end over end down into the black harbour water. He sank without struggle and Max hoped he had died on impact or at least was unconscious to save him the pain of drowning.

Miraculously the men on the ropes all were hanging on, but the miracle did not last.

During the attack the sound had been playing and the room had been filled with the terrified screams of men falling to their deaths and the shouted orders of the pilots.

"Oh fuck!" the pilot shouted. *"Move, move, mo…"*

A trail of smoke snaked across the screen, but this time the chopper couldn't avoid the incoming rocket. It hit and the helicopter burst into flames and exploded. The engines cut and the heaving metal wreckage could no longer fight gravity and it fell from the sky dragging the three men on the ropes with it into the ocean. Their screens and those of the remaining men in the chopper all shone brightly with the red and orange flames, before one by one they lost their signals as the fire took hold.

The conference room sat in silence from the horror they had just witnessed, but it wasn't over. One of Flash's men was walking down the narrow corridor towards the special ops guy who had fallen on his side. Vision from the camera moved over onto the main screen. The terrorist smiled and waved at the camera, then shot the man it was attached to. He picked up the camera and laughed in it, his hand slightly framing the shot, then he spun it around and filmed in front of himself as he walked.

He found the other men who had fallen to the deck and shot them turning the camera around each time to smile. Then he followed a few of his comrades up onto the top of the stacked shipping containers. When he got to the top, he turned the camera to the rest of his crew. The men were assembling something on the container roof.

"Holy shit," Max said seeing the legs getting bolted down.

"What Max?" Torres asked. "Can someone tell me what the fuck I am watching?"

"It's a launcher. Maybe a Javelin?"

"It's a Chu-MAT," Hulk said. "Anti-tank missile."

"What are they going to shot with that?" Torres asked.

"I think we are about to find out."

Another two men arrived on the roof carrying small silver cannisters. One of the cannisters was loaded into a shell, then into the launcher. There was nothing the group could do to stop it. With a hiss the shell sped from the launcher up into the air. The man with the camera did a pretty good job keeping it in the shot. Just as the trail became too hard to follow, a small bright flash shot out of the end of the smoke trail.

The man with the camera walked over to the dead special ops man on the roof and took off his headset.

"Madam President," he said into the microphone. *"I have a message for you. Having escaped Pandora's jar, Morbus, Lues, Pestis, Tabes and Macies spread plague, sickness and death. They join me today to fulfil my destiny. Like the arrows of Apollo and Artemis raining down on the battlefields of Troy to spread illness and disease, today I rain down death on your nation. I am Erebus and I am here for your lives."*

The guy dropped the headset and turned the camera around to watch the next cannister launch into the air above Seattle.

"Madam President," Moore said. "We are getting eyewitness reports of people dying in the streets in Seattle."

"Alejandra," Torres said in shock and disbelief. "Are they up there?"

"Yes, ma'am," Hernandez said.

"How long?"

"We have one in the area, it was watching the mission."

"Take it out."

"Ma'am," Moore cautioned. "It could block the harbour for years."

"What else can I do? We don't know how many more of those cannisters they have. Alejandra, do it."

"Yes, ma'am," Hernandez said picking up the phone. "The President has given the order for Seattle, take the shot."

Max looked questioningly at Kate.

"Reaper," Kate said referring to the MQ-9 unmanned aerial drone which had been circling the city.

"Jesus," Max said watching as the footage changed to a live stream from the drone.

The drone moved fast across the city as a targeting system came up on the screen. A red box appeared and zoomed in. Max had watched drone footage before, but the cameras had clearly been updated in the years he had been away. The images coming in were crystal clear even at the incredibly zoomed in angle and speed. The box filled the screen with the smooth, clear and focused vision of the top of the shipping container. 'Target locked' flashed on the screen then the vision changed to the camera mounted on the missile itself. It looked like the camera was rapidly zooming in, but in fact it was the missile speeding stealthily across the sky. It impacted right on the launcher and pierced through the shipping container into the ship and exploded.

The footage switched back to the drone as a CIA operative unnecessarily confirmed the target had been hit over the conference room speakers. The ship was completely engulfed in flames and the shipping containers had been flung into the shipyard and the harbour. The ship lurched to the side and began to sink as the cranes on the harbour burst into flames. The men who had been raining down Erebus shells were nowhere to be seen, but they had achieved their mission. Several cannisters had been launched at different areas of the Seattle skyline showering the city in the deadly chemical.

Max shook his head and rubbed his face at the complete destruction he had just witnessed. Where Torres might have been hesitant with the jet, she more than made up for it with her decisive call on the ship which was sinking and spilling flaming oil into the harbour.

"Madam President," an aide said interrupting the prolonged silence. "I'm sorry to interrupt."

"Yes," Torres said coming back from her deep thoughts, "what is it?"

"We think we have found the terrorist and the remaining cannisters of Erebus."

Chapter Thirty

Max had had a relatively short argument with Torres and the other officials at the White House as the news came in of a possible location on Flash and Blake. The same old lines were run about being too close to both the hostage and, in this case, the terrorist. In the end, Hulk convinced Ferguson and together they assure the President that Max was the best man for the job.

The White House had been flushed of Erebus and the Secret Service with help from Moore's FBI teams had re-doubled their efforts to secure the building. A CIA helicopter had landed on the front lawn of the White House and quickly collected its cargo before flying off over the city.

Max, Kate and Jonnie were currently on board the little chopper. What it lacked in size, it made up in speed. It was gaining fast on their target.

During the briefing at the White House the various intelligence agencies confirmed their suspicions that Flash had made it to a train and was heading for New York. The train was not far out of town, given how long he had worked to hide his trail in an intricate shell game which was eventually uncovered by hundreds of intelligence agents tracking each vehicle's movement.

Flash and Blake had changed vehicles multiple times which had caused their delay in leaving Washington, but they were currently speeding towards Philadelphia and the agencies could only presume New York on the Amtrak.

"Listen to me, Driver," Max yelled over the noise of the chopper's rotors, "I don't care what you think. I have been authorised by the President of the United States to run this mission. I am also working with the CIA and the FBI."

"It's suicide," the train driver replied.

"That's what they pay me for. Will you be ready?"

"Yes Agent, but what about the people on the train, shouldn't I stop to let them off?"

"No! Under no circumstances can you let passengers know what is happening. My target could detonate the device. Just do what I asked and otherwise drive as normal. Am I understood?"

"Yes, Agent Shaw."

"Good man. Thank you."

Max ended the call and moved into position near the door.

"Bravo, stay on the chopper and give us cover if needed," Max ordered.

"Roger that, boss," Jonnie said.

"Alpha, you're with me."

"Hoo-fucking-rah!" Kate shouted. "I got your back, Prince. Let's do this."

"Agent Shaw," the pilot yelled back, "we are coming up on the train."

"Thank you," Max acknowledged. "You know what to do."

"Yes, sir."

Max and Kate checked their weapons as Bravo took up a position across the doorway from Max with his rifle. The pilot brought the chopper in over the back section of the train and Max kicked a rope out the door. It dangled, flapping in the wind, slapping at the back window of the train.

Max grabbed the rope and wrapped his legs around it, and jumped from the doorway. He pinched the rope between his boots to control his decent, but was down next to the train within seconds. Max bounced off the train with his combat boots and the pilot corrected his course, taking Max two or three metres off to the left away from the speeding Amtrak. He looked up and waved for the chopper to bring him in closer. The pilot did as directed, but this time Max was too far forward and used his legs to bounce off the side windows.

It took another three tries before finally Max was able to swing into the open door of the train.

Inside one of the train conductors had reached out to help pull him in.

"Thank you," Max said to the conductor before switching to his comms unit. "Alpha, I'm in."

"Ack. On my way," Kate said as she jumped out the door of the chopper holding the rope.

Max lent out the door to watch his friend and colleague abseil down to meet him.

"We've got a problem," the pilot said.

"What is it?" Max asked.

"We've got a tunnel only a minute or so out."

Max turned to face the front of the train and saw the fast approaching tunnel entrance.

"Fuck," Max said, "Alpha, you've got one shot."

"You can't do this alone, Prince. I'm coming."

"Well, hurry the fuck up."

Kate slid down and came level with the door. The pilot swung her in towards Max. He tried to grab her, but she had bounced into the doorframe and was moving away. He lost his grip on her vest. Kate flung out from the side of the train, still holding the rope. Max could see her swearing to herself.

"Got to pull up," the pilot said.

"No, get me over there!" Kate yelled.

Max looked back to the front of the train. There was no time.

"Pull out, pilot," Max instructed. "That's an order."

The pilot did not respond he just banked the helicopter away, up and to the left.

"You fucking pussy!" Kate yelled at the pilot still swinging wildly from the rope. *"I could have fucking made it and now he's in there on his own. If anything happens to him, I'm coming for you! Prince, we'll meet you on the other side."*

"No," Max said as the train rushed into the tunnel. "It's too risky and the tunnel is too long. You won't be able to hang on that long."

"Yes, I can!"

"No, you can't. Pilot, land where you can and let Alpha back on board. Once she's back in, chase us down and await instructions."

"Yes, sir," the pilot said.

"Well, that was dramatic," the conductor said behind Max. "Don't see that every day."

"No, I'm sure you don't," Max agreed. "Thank you for opening the door."

"The driver said to expect someone, but I'm still not sure this is what I expected."

"Well, thank you anyway. Did the driver say anything else?"

"Only that there may be some unpleasant people on board."

"He's right, but that's why I'm here," Max said scrolling through his phone. "Have you seen this man?"

The conductor studied the photo of Flash.

"No," she said.

"How about this man?" Max asked passing over a photo of Blake.

"No," she said again after a few seconds of study. "Good looking gentleman though. I wish I had seen him."

"How about these?" Max said showing a photo of the Erebus cannisters. "Have you seen anyone carrying anything that looks like this?"

"I'm sorry, sir, but no I haven't. There are hundreds of people on this train and a lot of them have bags, something that big could be easily stowed in people's luggage."

"Yeah," Max said putting his phone away. "Thanks for your help."

"Hey, listen, is there something I can do to help?"

"No, ma'am. When I leave please lock the door behind me and stay in here in safety."

"Alright."

Max nodded and said thanks again, as the conductor closed and locked the door behind him.

He was standing in a luggage room. It would take hours to go through the bags himself, so he did not bother. He walked through the holding area until he reached the door at the far end. He was about to turn the handle when he was jumped from behind.

One of Flash's men had a luggage strap wrapped around Max's neck and was pulling it tightly, choking Max and cutting off his air supply. Max instinctively drove his thumbs in under the strap to try to take some pressure off his neck, but with his hands busy and oxygen dropping, he was running out of options. He charged back trying to overbalance his attacker, but clearly he was a big guy and moved back controlling Max's weight and drive.

Max tried to kick the guy in the nuts, but he anticipated that attack and wedged Max's leg with a laugh. Max was starting to blackout, he needed to act fast. He dropped his hands from his neck and immediately felt the pressure tighten. He reached behind his head and looped both his arms behind his attacker's head, then pulled forward hard and dropped to one knee. As the pair fell forward, Max used his momentum to bounce on his knee and drive back up, as he dragged the guy's face in over his shoulder and pulled it in hard.

Max's upward movement and the strength he had used to pull the guy's head down, had created an explosive force of energy which released right on his nose. His grip instantly relaxed as he reached for his face. Max fell forward dragging in deep breaths and coughing, but he did not have time to recover, he had to get back to his feet.

The big guy gingerly got to his feet still clutching his nose as Max got to his feet. Max did not wait, he sprung forward into the air, drew back his right fist and slammed it into his attacker's face. As he landed, he dipped down letting the energy build in his legs, before exploding up and across with a savage left hook. The punch landed on the attacker's jaw and Max felt it break, but the big man did not fall. Instead he rushed forward and grabbed Max in a bearhug. The force was incredible. Max felt the air rushing out of his lungs. He kneed

Flash's man in the balls and this time it landed. Max felt the grip weaken and used those fractions of a second to throw a violent headbutt into his already broken nose. The big guy tossed Max like a rag doll into a luggage rack with anger.

Max's vision was blurring again. The headbutt had been a bad choice after everything he had been through, but it was the luggage rack which did the most damage. Max hit the solid metal frame and bounced off it onto the floor. He stayed on all fours trying to steady himself as his attacker wound up for a kick. The rushing boot came at him fast, but Max was ready for it. He dodged left then grabbed the guy's leg with both hands and drove himself up off the floor pulling the leg with him. The big man's momentum made it easier to pull him off his feet and he fell hard to the floor, smashing his head on the luggage rack, but Max was not done. He kept driving the leg through the air and folded it down onto his attacker's torso. There were two obvious cracks as the man's leg went limp. Max could not be sure, but he suspected at least one broken bone and likely a snapped glute. His fallen rival screamed in pure agony.

Max stood up, but kept hold of the man's leg.

"Where is Flash?" Max asked.

"Fuck you!" the guy spat through his tears and pain.

"Wrong answer," Max said as he kicked him in the arse.

The big guy screamed and Max saw tears run down his cheeks. Definitely a busted a glute or hip.

"Where is Flash?" Max asked again.

"He's in first class," his attacker said. "Him and the other guy?"

"The Australian official?"

"Yes."

Max felt both relief and anxiety knowing Blake was onboard the train.

"What about Erebus?" Max asked. "How much is on the train?"

"Lots," came the pained reply from the injured man.

"How much is lots?"

"I have no idea."

"Is it all on here or is there more out there?"

"I have no idea."

"Where is it?"

"With our men."

"Where are they?"

"Everywhere."

"What do you mean?"

"They are spaced out throughout the train."

"How do I find them?"

"You don't. That's the point."

"Are you going to New York?" Max asked but the big guy was starting to fade out from the pain. "Answer me."

Max kicked him again, but this time the pain was too much and the big lad passed out cold.

Max dropped his leg and checked the guy's pockets and found a mobile. There was a message notification on the screen. It was an order to check the rear of the train. Max pulled down on the message and a reply line opened. He quickly typed 'all clear' then tossed the phone on the guy's chest and walked for the door.

He moved between the carriages across a small metal platform with waist height metal railings, out in the open air. The train clicked along in a rhythmic canter as Max opened the door into the next carriage. There were about twenty people in the rail car and Max had a sudden panicked thought. How many men did Flash have onboard?

He walked through the carriage watching people's faces as he made his way past. A few people looked up from their books or phones, but most of them quickly returned to what they were doing. But two women held his gaze then turned and looked at each other and nodded. The two women stood and moved into the aisle behind him.

"You should not have come after him, Agent Shaw," one of the women said as a few people looked up to see what was happening, "but my sister, Taylor, and I will right your wrong."

"Look, I don't know who either of you are and quite frankly I don't care, I'm going to stop him," Max said turning his back on the women and started heading towards the front of the carriage.

The girl named Taylor jumped up onto the seats to her right and used the tops of the rows in front of her like a gymnast on the bars. She was quickly past Max and before he knew it, Taylor spun smoothly on her hands building speed and she swung her leg around and kicked Max hard in the chest.

He stumbled backward, in shock at both the strength of the kick and her speed. As he fell backwards holding his chest, the original sister kicked him in the back of the knees and he dropped to the ground. Taylor then gracefully dismounted the chairs and landed in his path. She stepped forward and kicked him in the face. The blow knocked him back, but he did not have a chance to fall because the other sister kicked him in the spine between the shoulder blades forcing him back forward.

The two sisters then began an assault that had Max bouncing back and forth between vicious blows. Nearby passengers were all cowering in their seats, afraid to make a sound. The sister at his rear came in for another kick, but he caught her leg and dragged her off her feet. She fell as Taylor came in to defend. Taylor launched forward with a side kick, but Max dodged left and she kicked her sister in the face as she was trying to sit up.

"Rina!" Taylor said turning her anger back to Max as she stood. "Look what you've done."

"What I've done?" Max said getting to his feet not knowing which body part to hold from the beating he just received. "You kicked her in the face. Maybe I should thank you."

Taylor angered quickly and jumped up to grab the overhead railings. She swung forward and kicked Max with both feet in the chest. He fell backwards, tripping on Rina and landed in the aisle next to her, as she was coming to. He could not afford to fight both at once again, so he elbowed Rina in the face, knocking her out.

Taylor used the railings to pull herself forward then dropped on top of Max and started punching him relentlessly. He rolled and dodged as many blows as he could, but she was fast and surprisingly strong.

He grabbed her by the arms when the chance came and then used his feet to kick her up over his head. She slammed down on the metal floor on her back and for the first time she was relatively still.

Max got to his feet shaking off the kicking he had received at the hands of the sisters. Taylor quickly rolled forward and did two summersaults to put some distance between the pair. She got to her feet and spun back to face Max, but he did not see her grab the briefcase from the passenger to her right. As she spun, she launched the briefcase at Max and it spun through the air, rotating like a discus. He caught it in front of his face, but the relief that it missed him quickly wore off as the metal case slammed into his face. Taylor had launched herself at him again while the case was raised and kicked it straight into his face.

Max staggered back but held his footing. Taylor was coming for him again. Two rows out, she jumped on the seat and tried her kick again, but Max swatted it away with the briefcase. It did not slow her, instead she used the new momentum to throw her other leg around and kicked him in the sternum. He fell back onto a chair and she took advantage of the situation while his back was turned and dived over two rows. He spun back around, but she was gone. As he looked in the other direction, Taylor's foot connected with the side of his face. He dropped to his knees and used the briefcase to hold himself up.

"You need to come with me," Taylor said pulling a gun on Max. "Flash is going to want to kill you himself."

Max was facing away from Taylor but had seen the gun in the reflection of the door glass.

"Okay," Max said in a defeated tone. "I'll come quietly."

"Good. I knew you would come around with some convincing. I don't know, Max, Flash said you were tough and we should be careful. He said you never give up, but I knew we would kick that out of you."

"Yeah, you've got me," Max said as he saw Taylor inching closer. "I'm sure he will remember what you've done for him."

"I hope so," Taylor said smirking. "I do like him."

Max saw her zone out for just a second to think about the praise she was about to receive from her boss. The second was all he needed. He threw the steel briefcase backwards with astonishing speed and ferocity as he got to his feet. The briefcase tumbled in a backwards spin through the air until it collided with Taylor's face. The force of the impact took her off her feet and she hit the ground with a thud. Max used those precious seconds to scramble in behind a row of seats.

Taylor sat up slightly dazed but completely pissed off. She unloaded six shots into the rows in front of Max as terrified passengers screamed and started moving if they could to the door back to the luggage car. Others were trapped in their seats in pure fear, but they hid down near the floor, curled up in balls.

Max popped up from behind a row of chairs and fired at Taylor, but she was already moving and dived into a nearby row. Max fired two shots into the back of the seats and she blind fired over the top of them back towards Max, hitting two fleeing passengers who screamed and fell in their places, then bellowed in pain and panic.

Max had leapt across the aisle and dropped to the floor, while she was in cover and not watching. He laid on his back and used his feet to inch forward under the rows. Taylor was only three in front of him and still blind firing over the seat at the row she had last seen him in.

Max moved as quickly, but as quietly as possible, until he found himself beneath her chair. He pulled himself into the gap as Taylor got to her knees on the chair facing away from him.

"Put your fucking head up!" Taylor yelled back to where Max had been. "Where are you?"

"I'm right here," Max said sitting up and putting the gun to back of her head.

She flinched, but did not have time to respond. Max shot her in the back of the head spraying blood and brain matter all over the roof of the train.

Max climbed back out into the aisle and told the remaining passengers to move to the luggage carriage. They were terrified, but complied. Max tied Rina to a nearby seat in case she regained consciousness, then headed for the next door.

He crossed to the next carriage and closed the door behind himself. He was in one of the dining cars. There were four men in suits sitting in the car. All four men stood when he walked in. Max did not need to wait long for the men to act. The first on his right dived off the back of his chair to tackle Max. Max managed to fire off three bullets before the tackler's shoulder hit him and took him off his feet. He had seen his bullets rip into one of the men at the far end of the carriage as he fell to the ground.

Max and the tackler wrestled in an open space near the bar. Max could feel his anger building with each blow. He climbed on top of the guy, grabbed his arm and used his own shoulder to tear the tackler's out of joint. He elbowed the tackler in the ribs then threw his head back and shattered his eye socket. As the man squirmed underneath him, he raised his leg then stomped it down on the tackler's right knee breaking the knee cap.

Max got to his feet as the tackler writhed in pain on the floor, but he did not have time to deal with him. The other two men opened fire and Max had no choice but to throw himself over the bar to take cover. Glass, alcohol and other liquids and chips and chocolates exploded over him as the bullets ripped into the display shelves behind the bar.

Max grabbed a bottle of whiskey and stuffed a cleaning rag he found in the neck and lit it on fire with a cigarette lighter from a nearby shelf. He tossed the Molotov cocktail up over the bar in the direction of one of the men. His throw went too high, but it was right in line with one of the men. The bottle shattered on the roof and the whiskey caught fire showering the man with flaming liquid. His clothes quickly took hold in flames and he started patting at them to put them out.

The second man stopped firing, distracted by the sight of his burning comrade. Max took the gift and stood up from behind the bar and fired two shots into the distracted attacker. Head and chest. Textbook.

Max jumped over the bar as the man on fire ran towards him. Max fired one shot which hit the burning man in the forehead. He dropped to the floor and laid there burning. Max did not bother putting him out. Given all the noise, it would be hard to believe Flash did not know he was there, so he had to move.

Max started for the door at the front of the dining car, but stopped in his tracks as it blasted opened, tearing itself to pieces. Max dived behind a dining booth for cover, but snuck a quick look forward. Max could see Flash through the gap where the door had been. He ran out from cover firing wildly at Flash, the bullets slamming into the doorframes and windows as he ran. One bullet hit Flash in the leg as he ducked behind the wall for cover.

Max got to the front wall, but realised the gap between the two carriages was widening. Flash has decoupled the carriages.

"Sorry, Max," Flash yelled from behind his cover, "but, this is your stop."

"Where is Blake?" Max yelled.

"Why don't you see for yourself?" Flash yelled using Blake as a human shield walking backwards into his carriage as the train started to pull away.

"Let him go, Flash."

"It's far too late for that, Max, but don't worry he's going to keep me company for a little while longer yet. Anyway, we've got to go, but I did leave you a parting gift. Good luck."

The distance between the two halves of the train was rapidly increasing and Max could see the terror on Blake's face. Blake managed to point down in a signal to Max. Max was not sure what it meant until he remembered Flash's comment about a parting gift. Max quickly ducked out the front door and looked down. There was a row of C4 planted just under the door. Max looked back up as Flash pulled a remote out.

Max ran for his life back into the dining car. He dived under one of the tables and pressed his back into the booth as the explosion rang out. It ripped the front off the dining car and torn up the tracks. The train shuddered and lurched then jumped the tracks and sped off into the countryside. The tearing metal and screeching wheels tortured anyone in earshot, as the dining car overturned and dragged the other two carriages over the little hill.

The dining car broke free of the other two carriages. Max fell hard and bounced off the table and booth walls, repeatedly, as the dining car tumbled down the hill. Windows shattered and plates and bottles smashed. Alcohol from the bar smashed and caught fire as the fallen attacker fell into the pooling liquids spreading flames wildly with each tumble.

Max hit his head and passed out, turning himself into a ragdoll in the carriage.

As it came to rest in small creek at the bottom of the hill, Max laid perfectly still in the flickering light from the fire.

Chapter Thirty-One

Flash and Blake's train arrived in Philadelphia or what was left of it did anyway. Flash had held a gun to the driver's head the whole way, forcing him to miss stops and power through each station until a few miles from the city's harbour stop where he told him to make the stop.

The doors of the train had opened and Flash shoved a handcuffed Blake through onto the platform. Blake was shocked to see how many men Flash had on the train. They were dressed in a variety of outfits from suits and ties to casual workout wear, no doubt to blend in. They were all carrying briefcases or backpacks. There must have been thirty or more of them. He was sure there were probably a few missing after Max had arrived and he smiled at the thought of Max working his way through the train. His smile quickly faded though as he remembered the train derailing and heading over the hill. His part of the train had made the turn before Blake could see what happened. He was worried about Max, but something told him he was okay.

Maybe it was just hope.

There was a coach waiting and a large black SUV. Both were adorned was the seal of the United States Navy. Flash told Blake to get into the rear of the SUV, then climbed into the passenger seat. His men had all filed into the idling bus behind their vehicle.

"Let's go!" Flash said to his driver.

"Yes, sir," the driver said checking his mirrors to make sure everyone had loaded into the coach.

The SUV moved out into the traffic, closely followed by the bus. When they entered the motorway two SUV's, similar to their own, pulled in front of them taking the lead. Blake didn't know it, but two others had pulled in behind the bus as well taking their convoy to five SUVs and a bus load of men. On the bus, the men were currently changing into Navy camouflage uniforms and readying their weapons.

Flash took off his suit jacket and donned a US Navy black dress uniform jacket, complete with numerous ribbons. His epaulettes indicated he had given himself the rank of Captain. He put on a pair of reflective aviators and his white and black cap, with its gold rope.

"What do you think you are doing?" Blake questioned from the back seat noticing as he sat forward that the driver was also wearing Navy dress uniform of a lower ranked officer.

"Well, *Admiral* Smyth," Flash said turning back to face him, "I thought I would join the Navy. Get my sea legs. You have been in the service a lot of years. Any tips?"

"Yeah, stop now. It's not too late."

"Is that the best you've got?" Flash laughed. "I set off a cannister of Erebus in the White House. Of course, it's too late."

"That's not what I meant. I meant it's not too late to stop your plans, you don't have to do what you are planning. Innocent people are going to be killed."

"The only people I intend to kill in the next little while are people who signed up to be killed. People like you, Blake, who wear the uniform, but who have forgotten what it stands for. You are no longer there to protect the people. You exist to corrupt, to murder, to misinform and to keep the wrong people in power. You are nothing more than puppets these days and I intend to refocus you on what matters."

"You used to believe in this, Flash. Protecting the innocent and stopping terrorists."

"Yes, but in the process I realised the AIS, CIA and all the rest had become the terrorists. We killed the wrong people and failed to live up to our mission and values. We should have existed to protect freedom and save people from death, but instead it followed us wherever we went. So many people died and that blood is on our hands."

"But you have killed more people, the same innocents you claim to be fighting for."

"Yes, but I do it to remind the State of its obligations."

"So, you kill to remind the government to stop people getting killed?"

"You will never understand, Blake. You are part of the system and part of the problem. You need to look beyond what they have told you. Look beyond the brainwashed bullshit they have fed you. The Five Eyes, our governments, politicians, they are all part of a system designed to keep the rich, rich and the poor working in relative slavery on a false promise that one day they can make it too. These people don't care who lives or who dies, as long as they get what they want. Power and wealth. The only way to stop them and right this wrong is to erase the system and start again."

"But millions of innocent people will die as the system crashes. Anarchy will rule and that will be worse for people."

"Worse than spending their lives with no purpose or meaning?"

"People do have purpose and meaning in their lives."

"No, Blake. They don't. They wish and long for it, but the system just keeps them flogging themselves. Always striving, but never making it. A small cog in the powerfuls' wealth creating machine."

"I know you lost someone special to you. What about all those other Janes out there who will die of starvation or war or from Erebus attacks?"

"They are necessary losses to save humanity. This generation will feel the pain and make sacrifices, like I have, to rebuild for future generations. To make this world what it should be for everyone."

"You're talking about millions of lives, probably billions, as the world economy collapses."

"The world can't sustain the population as it stands. I will force those who remain to reconsider the lives they lead and what they want to leave for future generations, while saving the world from itself. Saving the masses from their endless cycle of powering the machine which only serves to work against them and keep them in servitude."

"You are insane."

"Insane is thinking they can continue to operate without restrictions and without restraint. Insane is being the mouse in the wheel on an endless cycle powering nothing, but greed and corruption. Insane is not doing something about it. You have dedicated your life to giving them what they want Blake. You are insane, not me."

"I'm not the one planning to unleash genocide on the world, killing billions. I'm trying to stop people like you from senseless murder. You might be right about the people pulling the strings, The Sixteen and others trying to manipulate the world to their will. But, I'm trying to stop them. You used to believe in that too."

"Oh, I'm going to stop them, but it's in the how where we differ," Flash said turning back to face the front.

Blake was horrified by the conversation. What Flash was planning was not only about vengeance for Jane's death, but about destroying the world as they knew it. Blake could see the radical belief in his eyes. The same belief he had seen in the eyes of religious terrorists. He genuinely thought he could change and save the world by destroying it first.

Blake closed his eyes for a moment. He was not in any way religious, so it was not in prayer, but more in hope. Sending his strength and will to Max, almost calling for him to find them, stop Flash and save humanity.

Blake sighed. Flash was the most organised and prepared adversary they had faced and he knew their plays and all their strengths and weaknesses. He was going to use everything in his arsenal to succeed. He was going to be hard to stop.

Blake opened his eyes and jolted in his seat. He figured out where they were going. The uniforms should have given it away sooner, but before he could speak to Flash again, they arrived.

The two lead SUVs pulled aside and let theirs go through to the gate.

The Naval Inactive Ship Maintenance Facility was one of the United States Navy's shipyards for decommissioned ships. The vessels were striped and processed before being sold or scrapped for parts. Some of them would go on to become diving wrecks or tourist attractions, but not before they were assessed and cleared through a facility like this one in Philadelphia.

Blake knew about the yard because he had visited once before, when he was still working for Navy Headquarters, before joining the AIS. He had been part of a large crew who had been sent to take command of a vessel the US had sold to the Royal Australian Navy. Depending on the ships docked, there could be millions of dollars worth of equipment in the yard and tonnes of weapons. God only knows what Flash could do with them if he got on base.

"Good morning," the driver said to a young Navy guard on the main gate as he wound down his window. "I've got Captain Beaumont and the crew following us. We should be on the list."

"Good morning, sir," the young sailor said. "I'm sorry, but we don't you scheduled for today. We have a boat coming in and only authorised crews and visitors are allowed on site."

"Listen, kid," Flash said looking out the driver's window. "What's your name?"

"Petty Officer, Walter Thomas, sir," the sailor said standing a little bit straighter and with some nerves in his voice seeing Flash's rank.

"Petty Officer, do you think I, a Captain in Navy of these United States, would waste my time and my crew's time coming here if we did not have an invitation."

"Ah, n, no, sir," Thomas said nervously looking back at Blake slightly puzzled by his tuxedo.

"Then open this gate and I will forget this ever happened."

"Y, yes, sir," Thomas said turning back for the guardhouse, but he stopped in his tracks.

He turned back to the car and walked over.

"What is it?" Flash asked. "I'm losing my patience."

"Why is there a man in a tuxedo in your vehicle?" Thomas asked looking at Blake.

"It's a trick, run!" Blake screamed knowing what was coming and trying to warn the young Petty Officer.

Flash raised his pistol and shot Thomas five times in the chest. Alarms sounded and two more guards came out of the guardhouse. Flash shot them both as the driver reversed the car away from the locked gates.

"You didn't have to kill him!" Blake shouted at Flash. "He probably wasn't even twenty yet. You son-of-a-bitch."

"You killed him!" Flash yelled back. "You tried to warn him. His blood is on your hands."

"But the gun is in yours, Jacob. Clearly the man you used to be did die all those years ago in the streets of London. The Flash I know would never kill a young kid like that."

"Shut the fuck up," Flash said spinning around in his seat and pistol-whipping Blake.

Blake fell to the side and as he did, he saw the SUVs which had led them to the base move into position near the gates. The whole roof and top section from just behind the driver's seat to midway down the tailgate zipped off with explosive force and shot into the air before landing behind the SUVs. Two turrets popped up and two men wearing Navy camouflage uniforms stood behind the big weapons.

Blake knew vehicles like this formed part of Presidential and VIP motorcades to protect their officials. Australia had recently added one to each of the Prime Minister and Governor-Generals' motorcades.

The two guns opened up, ripping the imposing metal gates to shreds. Bullets torn into the guardhouses shattering wood and glass and anything inside. Before long, the gates and the guardhouses crumbled, so riddled with holes they could no longer stand. The two SUV's drove over the wreckage, closely followed by Blake's SUV, the coach and the other two turret mounted SUVs in the rear.

The motorcade spread across the base as security and military police vehicles started making their way towards them. One by one the Hummers and civilian sedans were riddled with bullets from the SUVs. One of the attack vehicles from the rear sped past to lead the pack. It flew off and before long was making its way into the little area on base which housed one of the messes and a few shops. It stopped in front of the largest building and Blake watched in horror as its turret turned and opened fire on the building.

Even from the distance, Blake could see the glass shattering out and raining down in the street. Blake had had lunch at the mess in the little town like area of the base. It was the junior officers' mess, so he knew the building opposite which was under attack was the military police barracks.

A military police car raced towards them. The SUV on the left opened fire on the Hummer. Bullets slammed into the bonnet and the road all around it, but it kept coming. A line of bullets hit the Hummer's windscreen, but it kept coming. It was playing chicken with the SUV. The SUV broke right and the Hummer followed mirroring its moves. Blake instinctively flinched as the Hummer deliberately collided headfirst into the SUV and the two vehicles stopped dead on the roadway and burst into flames.

The SUV attacking the MP's building was under assault from all sides as other police vehicles and security arrived on scene. As Blake's SUV took a hard left before getting to the building, he saw the attacking SUV was covered in bullet holes. The turret had stopped, but the security force was making sure everyone inside was dead as the bullets kept flying.

They were two SUVs down by the convoy pushed on, making its way towards the dock.

As they approached, Blake saw there were two old destroyers and a recently retired supply vessel tied in the other bays.

The two attack SUVs had moved to the front and opened fire on a crowd assembled near an empty dock. Blake witnessed what could only be described as a bloody massacre. Naval officials and VIPs as well as family and friends had been gathered in an official seating area with a large stage complete with red, white and blue bunting. The guests young and old were slaughtered in their seats or not far from them if they had managed to move as the bullets flooded the area. The row of VIPs on the stage were violently killed as the turrets unleashed their storm of metal rain.

There was a band to the right of the stage which had been playing, but their instruments were now silent. Cover in blood and damaged beyond repair. The band had fallen in various positions as they tripped on each other to flee their little grandstand.

Within the minute, everyone was dead or dying.

Flash's SUV pulled up only metres from the bloodied seating area and he got out with the driver. Blake watched as the pair gathered their equipment.

The coach pulled up beside them and Blake saw the men had changed into Navy camouflage uniforms. They all had pistols strapped to their thighs and Steyrs over their shoulders, and they were all carrying their bags of various shapes and sizes.

Flash opened the door and pulled Blake from the SUV.

"You can see how well armed we are, Blake," Flash said. "Don't try to be a hero or you will die before I want you to."

"Fuck you!" Blake spat headbutting Flash and causing him to stagger backwards. "Look what you have done."

Flash held up a hand to hold back his men who were ready to take Blake out. He looked at the dead crowd laying on reddening grass. There were old Navy men, battle hardened from various wars and years at sea. There were men in suits and ties stained red with blood. But, the most horrific site was of the women laying dead clutching their children. The women's dresses were ripped and covered in blood from the bullet wounds. Some of the kids had balloons tied around their wrists and they floated in the air as terrifying markers between the rows of smashed plastic seating. Other children had been holding teddy bears or bouquets of flowers, and Blake was overcome by sadness and grief.

"You are a murderer!" Blake yelled again letting the tears turn to hate. "Take a look at your new world! Millions more will die if you keep going. Just look at the horror and think about what you have done. You can't do this. Please, Jacob!"

Flash looked up from the dead bodies and for the briefest of moments Blake thought he saw his old friend, but he vanished.

"Get into position," Flash said to his men before turning back to Blake. "Come with me."

Flash's men ran down to the dock and formed a line between it and the seating area, blocking the massacre site from view. Flash pushed Blake in the back with his pistol, leading him down to the dock. He stepped onto the concrete gangway running between an old destroyer and an empty bay.

"Here they come," Flash said taking a small cannister from one of his men.

Flash's men all started waving small American flags and smiling. One of the men had found the audio controls and plugged in an MP3 player and hit play. The sound of a band playing filled the airwaves, pouring from the loudspeakers.

Blake looked out into the harbour and saw the bridge of the USS Pittsburgh. The submarine's commanding officers were on the bridge waving back to Flash's assembled team. They were completely unaware of what had happened. Blake went to call out, but Flash punched him in the face, knocking him out. One of Flash's men dragged him behind a pillar on the dock.

The big old submarine slowly moved into position at the dock and tossed its ropes up. Flash and one of his men moved a metal walkway into position bridging the gap between the conning tower and the dock. There were four senior officers, including the boat's captain on the bridge at the top of the tower and they smiled warmly as Flash made his way across. He saluted the returning crew who had spent months at sea and were bringing the old submarine in from its final journey. It was to be decommissioned and stripped for parts after almost four decades in service. The crew's families had been gathered to welcome them home.

A series of gunshots rang out from behind Flash's men. More security had turned up and were trying to get to the dock, but the remaining turreted SUVs were blocking their approach. A helicopter also came in over the base, but the turrets opened fire at the big bird and it banked hard and pulled back out of range.

The captain and his crew looked towards the sound of the chopper and gunfire. Flash took his opportunity while they were distracted. He shot the men, starting with the captain, who he shot straight in the temple. They were all dead before the captain hit the ground.

He stepped over the small railing and looked down into the open hatch. Two sailors were looking up excitedly, eager to get out and back on dry land to see their families after months at sea.

Flash stomped down on the lead sailor's face as he got close to the top of the ladder and he fell back down dragging his comrade to the floor with him. Flash dropped the small steal Erebus cannister down onto the sailor's chest and closed the hatch as the sailor looked at the device still in shock from his fall.

Flash checked his watch. Two, one.

The sailor held the cannister and showed it to the other officer, then it detonated spraying them both with the red liquid. Immediately they both started to convulse and seize as the liquid turned to gas and was sucked into the ventilation system. Throughout the boat, sailors started to choke and foam at the mouth as the deadly weapon spread.

An explosion rang out behind Flash and he turned to see what was happening. One of his turreted SUVs was engulfed in flames and the last remaining one was under heavy fire. He checked his watch then signalled his troops.

Half of his men formed a line behind him and the other half moved a second metal bridge into place about halfway down the submarine's length. He held up his gas mask and waited until they had all seen it, then he put it on. He told one of his men to put a mask on Blake and drag him onboard.

Flash opened the hatch and pink mist rose from the opening. He pulled out a small device from his jacket pocket and held it in the mist. It gave a high, but then falling, parts per million count of the Erebus density in the air.

Flash waited for a few seconds then gave his crew the signal to proceed. At the midpoint on the big boat, his crew opened the hatch and started down the ladder. He climbed down his own ladder, through the conning tower to the control centre. He took a seat as his men ran through the boat to their various stations. One of his men dropped an unconscious, but gas masked Blake at his feet.

The last of his men came down the ladder having closed the hatch just before the military police arrived. There were a few gunshots as Flash's men took out any of the sailors who hadn't died yet from the Erebus.

"Pierre," Flash said turning to the Frenchman on his crew, "time to go to work."

"Oui," Pierre responded walking over to the control panel a pressing a number of buttons then he nodded to Flash as a small alarm sounded.

"This is your captain speaking," Flash said his voice booming throughout the sub. "Let's go. Cast off and as soon as we can get us under the water."

Pierre and the crew in the control room started working their stations, while the men in the engine and manoeuvring rooms went to work at their panels.

Flash felt the submarine pulling back from the dock. His crew for this mission had been assembled from all over the world. A good number of them were former submariners who had served in different navies, mostly those not fond of the West, but some just looking for money or other rewards. The majority believed in his cause and were more than happy to help bring down the West.

The air quality device in Flash's hand beeped and he looked at the small screen. The Erebus had broken down in the air and the boat was clear.

"You can remove your masks," Flash told his crew removing his own mask.

Blake stirred at his feet and started to look around.

"What have you done?" Blake asked, the realisation setting in that they weren't just stealing weapons when he saw active the control room.

"Welcome onboard, Admiral," Flash said smiling at his former colleague.

Chapter Thirty-Two

Max woke again in a daze.

He coughed trying to expel some of the smoke which had filled his lungs in the burning carriage. His head was pounding yet again and he could feel the blood pumping through his veins. He could hear and feel his heartbeat in his ears, and could see it in his eyes. He felt the back of his head were a small bandage covered the tiny entry point where the doctors had relieved the pressure on his brain earlier. He felt exhausted and broken, but Blake was relying on him. That was driving him. He knew the governments had put their faith in him to deliver, but he could not help but want to save Blake and hopefully settle into some sort of normal life after so many years on the run.

He had to get up.

Max looked around the destroyed carriage and felt lucky to be alive. He was laying on the table he had been sheltering under. The train was on its roof. He looked over the edge of the table at the smashed bottles and plates on the roof, which was now the floor, of the train. He was laying in a cloud of smoke and needed to get out of it.

He dragged himself forward feeling the pain and stiffness in his muscles and joints. He lowered his legs off the table and lowered himself down.

He ran through his mental checklist to assess the damage as he hunched over coughing the smoke from his lungs. *My head is thumping and my lungs burning,* Max thought to himself. He rolled his shoulders and neck as he stood up, and clenched his fists and arm muscles. *Nothing too major there,* he thought. *My ribs hurt,* Max thought as he held his hand to the tender spot under his left arm where he had also been sliced at the warehouse. *My hips and knees are sore, but nothing I can't handle.*

Max was surprised he had not broken anything. Passing out had probably helped, given he had not been trying to brace himself during the crash.

He limped to the door. China and glass cracked, crunched and crushed under his combat boots. He looked out at the trail of fire and debris leading back towards the railway tracks. The passenger carriage was down in the valley too, but the cargo one was still on the hill having broken free. Both carriages were badly damaged, though his was the worst by far. It had ripped up layers of grass and mud, while leaving behind chunks of metal and glass.

In the distance there was a smouldering hole in the train line from the C4 and some of the heavy metal sleepers and tracks had been blow from the raised line.

He stood for a moment collecting his thoughts, then he remembered the conductor and the passengers in the luggage car. He sprinted up the hill and ran along beside the tracks to where the baggage carriage was on its side. The front end was crumbled and he could not open the door, so he ran around to the far end. There was no door on the rear itself, there was only the door he had swung through on the side. It was now facing the sky.

Max used the undercarriage to climb to the top of the overturned rear of the train. He looked down through the door's window and saw the conductor and several passengers inside. The conductor had a cut above her eye and it was bleeding profusely. She looked up at Max and signalled that the door was jammed. Max tried the handle, but it didn't budge. He quick stepped to the side closest to the door lock and held the handle out, then he started stomping on the door.

After several hard kicks, he felt it start to give. He stomped again and the door flew open. He fell half into the train as his leg followed the door, but he caught himself on the other side of the doorframe.

One of the passengers inside rushed forward to catch him. He grabbed his boot and pushed him back up.

"Thanks, mate," Max said to the passenger. "What's your name?"

"Jim," the passenger said.

"Jim, I'm Max. Nice to meet you."

"You too."

"Jim, I work for the Australian Intelligence Service. There was an explosion on one of the forward carriages and it derailed part of the train. Have we got anyone hurt in there?"

"The guard is bleeding pretty bad and there are a couple of people with some cuts and burses."

"Okay, well, I'm going to need some help to get people out. Do we have a couple of stronger people in there who can help us?"

"Yes, there's a guy here about your height."

"Get him," Max said as Jim looked through the door into the luggage hold and shouted out to one of the other passengers.

"Here he comes."

"Okay, Jim," Max said calmly. "You're going to help our friend here up. What your name buddy?"

"Matt," the new guy said.

"Alright, Matt. Jim's going to help boost you up and I'm going to grab your arm and pull you up, okay?"

"Yeah, that's okay."

"Then I'm going to help lower you off the train and you will need to help everyone down. Is that okay with you?"

"Yes."

"Great. Okay Jim, I need your help mate. You in?"

"Yes, of course," Jim replied.

"You will need to tell people what to expect then help them up."

"Got it."

"Alright Jim, Matt, let's go."

Jim bent his knees and cupped his hands together. On three, Matt stepped into Jim's hands and bounced up. Max had laid down flat on the side of the train, which was now its roof. He had let his right arm and head hang over the edge of the doorframe. He reached down and caught Matt's hand. Jim and Max's combined efforts helped push and pull Matt up to the top.

"Good job, Jim," Max said. "Get the next one ready."

Max helped Matt over the side and down the undercarriage he had used to climb up.

"Stay there and help people down," Max said.

"No problem," Matt replied moving his shoulders and getting ready.

"Okay Jim," Max said laying back down. "How did we go?"

"I think we should get the guard here out first?" Jim said. "She's bleeding pretty bad."

"Alright. Are you ready?"

Both the conductor and Jim said yes, and Jim got back into position. The guard stepped into Jim's hands and Max could see she had not jumped much. Jim was going to have to push hard. Max reached over the doorframe further and just barely caught her outstretched fingers. He spun around and dropped his left arm over too and dragged her up with both. Max checked her head wound when they both stood up.

"You will be okay," Max reassured walking her to the edge of the train. "I'll patch you up when I get down."

"Thank you, Max," the conductor said. "If I knew this was going to happen, I wouldn't have opened the door for you."

"If I knew it was going to happen, I would have found a way to stop it. I am sorry this happened to you."

"You're the good guy, right?"

"I try to be."

"Well, don't blame yourself. Just promise me you will get the bastards responsible."

"I will."

"Good," she said starting to climb down the undercarriage.

Max waited until Matt had hold of her then walked back over to the door.

The three men helped several of the passengers until only Jim was left.

"You did well, Jim," Max said. "I'm going to jump down and boost you up and out."

"What about you?" Jim asked genuinely concerned.

"I'll be fine, I need to find a first-aid kit too."

Max jumped down into the train. Jim had already started opening cupboards in the guard's section of the old train looking for the first-aid kit. He found it in a nearby draw and tossed it to Max. Max opened it and inspected the contents. Satisfied, he zipped it back up.

"Thanks Jim, let's get you out of here," Max said walking over to the space under the door.

"How will you get out?" Jim asked.

"I'll sort it out mate," Max said cupping his hands like Jim had earlier. "I'm going to give this everything I've got. Be ready to catch the edge."

"Got it," Jim said. "Ready?"

"Go."

Jim stepped forward, putting his foot in Max's hands and then bounced as hard as he could off the floor to half-jump into the air to give Max all the help he could. Max used Jim's momentum and a huge squat and push from the floor to boost Jim up fast. Max had Jim's foot at his chest then over his shoulders in seconds. Jim was surprised at the force. His hands went through the door and his elbows got dragged against the doorframe. He scrambled trying to get a grip then he found a lip of metal next to the window. He dragged with all his remaining strength – lifting the others had been quite the workout. Max kept pushing until Jim's feet lifted out of his hands and he could see Jim struggling up. Eventually, Jim managed to get himself out onto the side of the train. He rolled over and looked down to Max through the door.

"Catch," Max said tossing up the first-aid kit.

"Got it," Jim said catching the kit.

"Head down. I'll be out soon."

"Okay, thanks Max."

"No worries, mate."

Max climbed through the sideways door into the luggage room and looked around. Bags had been thrown everywhere. They were pilled one on top of the other on the racks which were making up the new floor. He looked up and saw a window between two of the baggage racks on his new roof.

He stepped to the side and fired three shots into the glass. It cracked, but did not shatter. He threw his pistol as hard as he could into the glass and it shattered, raining small shards down into the carriage and over the bags beside him, but his pistol was nowhere to be seen. It must have shot through and stayed on the roof.

Max got a few of the bags together and climbed up on them. He reached up to the rack which was welded to the roof and pulled himself up to sit on the metal frame. He elbowed out a few remaining shards of glass, then he reached through the window to support himself and used the rack to stand and climb through onto the side of the train.

"Don't move!" Rina snarled standing behind Jim with Max's pistol pointing at his new friend's head.

Max turned to see Rina and a very panicked Jim.

"I'm just going to stand up," Max said calmly, "and we can talk."

"You killed my sister," Rina said, "and you nearly killed me!"

"That's between you and I. Let him go and we can talk."

"Fuck you, I should put a bullet in him right now."

"No, please don't hurt him. You've got me, look I'm raising my hands. Take me instead and let him go."

"I'm getting on my knees," Max pleaded with his hands outstretched and kneeling on one knee. "You can let him go now."

Rina pointed the gun at Max over Jim's shoulder. Jim winked at Max then grabbed Rina's outstretched arm and pistol wielding hand. Shots rang out as Max rolled to the side away from the bullets. Within seconds Jim had forced the pistol from her hands. Rina now without a weapon started pounding Jim in the back and ribs.

Max ran and dived forward tackling her onto the side of the overturned train.

"Get out of here!" Max yelled at Jim, but Jim ran back into the fight.

Rina was strong and she knew what she was doing. She defended herself against the two of them as they each moved in to attack. First, Max's attack went wide and she punched him in the spine as he fell left. He swept with his leg, but she saw it coming and jumped it, and turned to kick him, but Jim ran forward and threw a punch. She caught it and twisted his arm up behind him, kicking him in the back of the knees, then in the back and he fell forward.

Max got to his feet and came in again for another go. The pair traded punches, before Rina out of nowhere did the splits, dropping to the metal train surface like a gymnast and threw a punch at Max's groin. He moved his leg to defend, but the blow still landed and he dropped to his knees and Rina headbutted him. Max fell back as Rina got to her feet.

Jim ran in, coming to Max's defence and tried to land a haymaker. Rina dodged the incoming blow, stepped left, then punched Jim square in the jaw and he fell to the metal surface. While she was distracted Max took his chance. He leapt into the air and drew back his right fist. It collided with the side of her face just as she was turning to attack him. The blow nearly knocked her out. Normally he would follow up with a left hook, but she was done. She laid on her stomach barely conscious as Max helped Jim up.

The two men stood facing each other.

"Thanks," Jim said standing up. "She's a tough bitch."

"She's a terrorist," Max said. "What you did was incredibly brave."

"Thanks, Max. I didn't want to leave you here by yourself, I saw what they did in the carriage earlier."

The pair shook hands and Max saw Jim's eyes shift to look over his shoulder.

"Watch out!" Jim yelled pulling Max to the side.

Rina had found Max's pistol and lined up a shot. The bullet flew through the air, narrowly missing Max, and slammed into Jim's chest. Max hit the metal surface and rolled towards Jim, catching him as he fell to his knees. He laid Jim down and stayed in front of him, taking two slugs in the back from Rina as the pistol clicked empty. Max had been wearing his thin combat vest with Kevlar lining, so he was protected from bullets, but they still hurt like hell.

He rolled to his side and withdrew his knife. As it came free, he threw it like a Frisbee towards Rina. She moved fast, but not fast enough. It pierced through her left arm and she fell to the floor.

Max quickly checked on Jim, he was fading fast.

"You saved my life," Max said sorrowfully and thankfully taking the first-aid kit from Jim. "You are a hero."

"Being a hero sucks," Jim laughed coughing blood as Max tried to pack his wound with gauze making him flinch and moan with pain. "I'm going to die, right?"

"No, you'll be fine," Max lied. "Look at me. You will be fine. Stay with me."

"She's getting up again, Max," Jim said looking past him to Rina who was getting to her feet. "Go kick her arse."

"You got it, kid," Max said getting to his feet. "Keep pressure on the bandage."

Rina ripped the knife out of her arm and came running at Max wielding it wildly above her head ready to stab it down on him. He caught her wrist, but she twisted the blade and it sliced into his forearm. He groaned, but didn't let go. He punched her open wound, then headbutted her, breaking her nose. She staggered back, but didn't let him capitalise. Instead, she moved fast to the side and before he knew it, she had worked her way around behind him and was climbing up his back. Her legs wrapped around his waist and pressed in tight. He immediately felt the pressure on his sore ribs and stitches. His head was aching again from the headbutt he regretted throwing. She pulled the knife in close to his neck, edging the blade closer and closer. Even with one arm badly damaged from the earlier knife wound, she was strong. He grabbed her wrist with both hands stopping the tip of the blade only inches from his neck.

Max clutched her wrist tightly with one hand and grabbed her clenched fingers with the other, then ripped them in opposite directions, shattering her wrist. Max felt her legs loosen their grip around his waist and didn't stop to think as the knife dropped at his feet. Using her broken wrist, he pulled her up over his head and shoulders and slammed her into the train. He kept hold of her arm and drove his knee into her shoulder, tearing it out of joint. The pain was finally too much for her and she passed out.

Max picked up his knife and pistol, loading a fresh magazine as he walked back over to Jim. Max found him laying in a pool of his own blood, clutching his chest, the life gone from his eyes. He could not help but feel an overwhelming sense of guilt. Jim had saved his life and he had failed to protect him. Another innocent death on his conscious, but he was sure this one would remain in his mind for a long time to come.

He turned around and fired a bullet into Rina's head, then holstered his pistol feeling no remorse at the sight of her lifeless body. Max turned back, knelt down and closed Jim's eyes, then after a few moments of silent reflection, he picked Jim up in a fireman carry and headed for the side of the train. He slowly and gently made his way down the undercarriage of the train and laid Jim's body in a small clear patch of grass in the shade, as other passengers from the train came to his side. Some were crying, others were just blank with shock.

Max cleaned and bandaged the conductor's wound, as one of the passengers removed his jacket and covered Jim's face and shoulders. A helicopter could be heard coming in fast as he taped the bandage in place.

"You will be okay," Max reassured the guard.

"Thank you," she said. "Are you okay?"

"I'll be fine. Thank you for asking."

"You killed that lady on the top of the train?"

"Yes, but I'm not sure I would call her a lady."

"I guess you are right there."

"She was a terrorist."

"Yes, she killed that nice young man who helped us out."

"She did," Max said looking over to Jim as the helicopter could be seen in the distance. "I actually need to ask you a favour."

"What is it?"

"His name was Jim. He saved my life. I need you to look after him until the authorities get here, then explain to them what happened. Please ask them to let my office know his details so I can reach out to his family. He died a hero and I would like to tell them myself."

"I will do that for you, but more importantly, I'll do it for him and his family."

"Thank you," Max said as he looked up and saw Jonnie hanging out the door of the helicopter scanning the wreckage until he spotted Max and smiled in relief, but also impatience. "I've got to go now. Do you have a phone?"

"Yes, of course," she said pulling out her old flip phone and passing it to Max.

"This is my number," Max yelled over the sound of the hovering helicopter typing quickly into the phone as a rope ladder dropped and hung beside him. "My name is Max Shaw. My codename is Prince. I'm a Federal Agent and Head of Field Operations with the Australian Intelligence Service. Give these details to the police when they arrive, will you?"

"Of course."

"Thank you."

"Good luck," she said as Max grabbed the ladder and started his climb.

Jonnie grabbed him and helped drag him into the chopper. He nodded his thanks as he grabbed a nearby headset and took a seat as Jonnie dragged in the ladder and the helicopter took off towards Philadelphia.

"How many fucking lives do you have, Prince?" Kate asked turning back to Max.

"I feel like I'm fast running out, that's for sure," Max replied with a smile. "What happened?"

"You were in a major fucking train accident and walked out without a fucking bruise!"

"I know that bit, although I doubt the bruise comment. I meant with the train. Did you follow it?"

"Yeah, we assumed Flash was on that part of the train, so we had to leave you behind and give chase."

"That was the right thing to do. What happened?"

"Well, here's the thing. We lost the train when it got into a few of the tunnels under the city. The locals were completely fucking hopeless in guiding us. Somehow the alerts were turned off and they couldn't track it properly. Anyway, by the time we found the fucking thing they had already gotten away."

"Where are they, Kate?"

"We eventually found them attacking a Naval base."

"What? What were they doing there?"

"Stealing a submarine."

"Sorry?"

"They had a bunch of fucking turrets mounted on SUVs and they destroyed half the base. We came in over the base, but the turrets forced us back. By the time the guns were taken out and we could move, and the MPs on base could move, Flash had gassed out the sub – we presume with Erebus. He and his whole team boarded and sealed it up, before the guys on the ground could get there. Must be a fucking hundred dead on the base and probably the same on the boat. They were coming back from its final mission."

"Jesus."

"That's not all. Flash killed a bunch of men, women and children, Max. They were there to welcome their husbands and wives, fathers and mothers, home."

"Oh God," Max said distraught at the thought of his old friend's barbarism.

"They got the boat out of the dock and disappeared under the water."

"What about Blake?" Max asked after thinking for a few moments.

"He's on the sub."

"But, he's alive?"

"I'm sorry, Max. They carried him on, but we think he was just unconscious. Why take him with them right – if he was dead."

Max looked at Kate, the pain visible in his eyes at the thought.

"Fuck, I'm sorry mate. I'm sure he is fine."

"But, for how long?" Max asked mostly to himself. "Where are they now?"

"We are working with DoD to find them."

"We don't know?"

"Not yet."

Chapter Thirty-Three

Max had spent the better part of the last thirty minutes screaming at various people via videoconference from the Philadelphia Naval Inactive Ship Maintenance Facility, including the Chief of Staff of the Navy and the Chairman of the Joint Chiefs of Staff, the United States' most senior military officer. If he cared about his career, it would have been a career limiting move, but he didn't care, he needed answers.

"Agent Shaw, you need to calm down," one of the Naval officers in the room said. "That was the Chairman you just yelled at. I don't know how you boys do things in Australia, but that's certainly not how we do things here. The Chairman does not answer to you."

"This country and your allies, including my country, are under attack from an evil we have never faced," Max said. "One of our own. He knows more about us than any terrorist or even Russia or China. He is going to take us apart piece by piece and millions are going to die."

"But…"

"But nothing. I don't give a fuck if Torres herself gets on that screen and tells me to be polite. I will tell her and the Chairman, what I am about to tell you right now – fuck your rank and your title! None of it will matter very soon because the world as we know it will end if we don't pull our heads out of our arses! Do you understand?"

"Yes."

"I don't think you do. Flash has a nuclear sub with God knows how much of that Erebus shit which he rained down on Seattle earlier and twelve fucking Tomahawks! He could take out whole cities if he chooses to. So, if you don't like my tone, well that's your fucking problem."

"Alright, I understand."

"Good," Max said. "Now get the Chairman back on the phone and let's get some information flowing."

"Yes, sir."

"Thank you," Max said tensely as the videoconferencing screen displayed the calling symbol and the familiar fading circles rotating in their annoying clockwise motion.

"Agent Shaw," Torres said coming on the screen from the White House bunker. *"The Chairman has just arrived and briefed me. What else should I know?"*

"Madam President," Max started, "right at this point in time, we are nowhere. We have a couple of scenarios, but until the Chairman can find his boat, well, we're fucked."

"Just as blunt as ever, Agent Shaw, but I've got a city with hundreds, potentially thousands, dead. They need my attention and I don't have much patience for your particular brand of bullshit right now."

"Nor I for yours, Ma'am, but unless you want twelve more of those cities, we need to put our personal thoughts to the side to get on with the job."

"You are right, I apologise. I'm under a lot of pressure."

"You are doing fine, ma'am, but I need you to put a rocket up your Chairman's arse before one sails through the roof of the White House."

"Understood," Torres said turning to the Chairman. *"Where are we on finding the submarine?"*

"As I explained to Agent Shaw," the Chairman responded, *"we are hunting for a submarine which is designed to be undetectable."*

"But we have been working on solutions to this particular problem for a number of years. I sat on the Intelligence Committee when I was in the Senate. I got the briefs. We have been developing technology to detect submarines under water."

"Yes, ma'am."

"Well?"

"It's never been used in the field. We have done a lot of tests, but we knew where to look to narrow the search area."

"We know where to look," Max interjected, "but the radius is getting bigger and bigger with every second we waste talking about it!"

"Max is right, General," Torres agreed. *"Why haven't we started the search?"*

"The satellite is still moving into position," the Chairman said.

"And the planes?"

"The Australian's have AP-3C Orions on route and a P-8A Poseidon too. They were on joint exercises nearby. They will be joined by a couple of our P-8A's, plus a couple of Seahawks and Super Seasprites. They will search in a grid pattern, using the satellite to sweep wider areas."

"And when we find it?"

"We aren't sure yet ma'am."

"I have a couple of ideas," Max said, "but you're probably not going to like them."

Chapter Thirty-Four

The mood inside the submarine was jubilant. It was obvious to Blake that not many on Flash's crew had thought their mission to capture the sub was possible. They were full of nervous excitement. It was the same rush Blake had felt on a bunch of missions when things just worked out and went in their favour – sometimes against impossible odds. The team spirit was always high after a success like that, buoyed by triumph. There was also more than a little bit of relief that you and your team had survived, that you had dodged that bullet and held off death for another day.

Flash for his part sat in stoic silence, focused on his mission. Blake had watched for any signs his old friend might be in the battered and broken shell, but his hopes had faded with every passing second. Flash was gone and who ever this man was, full of brainwashed ideals and murderous plots, he was adamant that it was not the man he had once known.

He thought back to the moment he was told Flash had died on that London street and the sadness he had felt. He remembered the sorrow and grief of watching Jane at Flash's funeral saying her goodbyes – full of misery and pain which can only be felt when you lose the love of your life. She was broken and it was heartbreaking. Her funeral was even more profoundly sad, thinking of the horror she must have felt in those final moments.

Blake understood how all of these events could have damaged Flash and caused him immeasurable pain, but nothing that would have turned the man he helped train into a terrorist. The years of torture and indoctrination had played the biggest role, using his pain as a foundation to build the hate.

No, this was not Flash, not the Jacob Gordon he knew. He was dead. This man was a terrorist and Blake knew he could not be saved. He had to die, and soon, because millions would suffer otherwise.

Flash's men had got the sub up and running, then dived below the surface and disappeared from view. They had manned their respective posts and started readying the boat for war. Others on the crew were gathering the dead submariners from the US Navy, who had died during the Erebus attack, and were unceremoniously dumping them in the trash disposal room to be dealt with later. Blake was horrified at the callousness and ruthless efficiency of Flash's crew.

"Sir," Pierre said interrupting Flash's prolonged vacant, almost lifeless, stare at the wall.

"What is it?" Flash asked turning in his chair.

"The weapons room is ready."

"Good," Flash said rising from his seat. "Maintain your course. Blake, get up and come with me."

Blake stood up and followed Flash; there was no point arguing. They walked through the submarine to the forward compartment past the sonar room to an area which was available to access the Tomahawk missiles which were vertically stored in launch tubes just behind the sonar dome at the front of the sub. The Tomahawks could be checked and, if necessary, modified, but the room was mostly for maintenance. They were too big to bring into the space, but sections of the missiles could be detached and brought into this part of the room.

Blake saw a warhead sitting on the large work rack. They had successfully removed the payload section from the missile through a purpose-built hatch in the vertical launch tube which held it. Once on the rack, they had taken out the plutonium in its protective housing unit.

Blake watched as they slid the modified Erebus cannister into the warhead and with the turn of a few screws had it fixed in place. They closed the warhead carefully then used a small crane to move it into position, raising it up to the open hatch. One of the men climbed the nearby ladder and replaced the warhead in the missile, then secured the hatch in the launch tube.

"The first one is in place, boss," the crew member said climbing back down the ladder. "We have eleven more to go."

"Load the cannisters and store the plutonium," Flash ordered. "I want to be ready in the next few hours."

"You got it boss," the man said moving to the second missile tube with the small crane and ladder.

"Why not just use the nukes?" Blake asked as he watched the crew.

"I don't want to destroy the cities," Flash said, "I just want to clear them of some of their people, particularly the politicians and public servants who have wrecked the world."

"So, what exactly is the plan then Jacob? We are in a sub in the middle of the ocean, I'm not going anywhere. I thought you might like to share."

"Now we are onboard I don't see why not. We are going to take out twelve cities with a low altitude detonation of the Tomahawks which, as you have seen, are being fitted with Erebus. The chemical will spread over those cities or parts of those cities, blanketing them with death."

"You will kill thousands."

"I expect several million with these initial strikes, probably somewhere around five or six million."

"Initial strikes?"

"Yes."

"You don't have enough Erebus to launch more than twelve attacks and you only have twelve missiles."

"So, AIS knows a bit more than you let on," Flash smiled smugly. "You are right, onboard we only have enough for these twelve strikes, but you don't think I would put all my eggs in one basket surely?"

"I hate to tell you, but we found your trucks and recovered or destroyed the Erebus they were transporting. And, we shot down the jet on route to Hawaii and sunk the shipping container before it could leave the port in Seattle."

"Oh, Blake," Flash mocked. "You don't give me enough credit. I didn't take all the Erebus to the warehouse you raided.

I sent enough to another one of my teams to start manufacturing it on a much, much bigger scale."

"It's not some basic chemical you can mix in a bucket with goods you pick up at the local hardware store."

"I know that."

"You have someone who can make it for you?"

"Bingo," Flash smiled.

"Franklin," Blake said starring past Flash and thinking of the security pass and identity Flash had used to sneak onto the Defense base and steal the weapon. "You took the Professor hostage?"

"I'm amazed you hadn't asked about him earlier. You might be slipping Blake."

"What have you done with him?" Blake asked quickly embarrassed that not only had he not asked about the Professor, but nor had any of his colleagues – preoccupied with thoughts of Max and getting the cannister back.

"I'm not going to tell you that," Flash laughed, "but, he is safe and working very hard I'm told."

Blake charged forward at Flash leading with his shoulder, because his hands were still cuffed behind his back. Flash stepped aside and punched Blake in the face as he went passed. Blake fell to the metal floor with a thud.

"Maybe you have had too many years behind a desk, old friend," Flash taunted standing over Blake.

"Take the cuffs off me and we will find out," Blake retorted rolling onto his side to face Flash.

"Maybe later."

"Why are you keeping me here? Why not just kill me?"

"I want you to see your failures, but I also want you right by my side in case Max somehow survived that crash. He has nine fucking lives! I want to hurt you and kill you to break him and show him the enormity of his failure."

"He was your best friend."

"No best friend would leave their friend to die, then not support their partner."

"That's not what happened, Flash. It's much more complicated than that."

"Not to me it isn't and certainly not to Jane."

"Max didn't kill Jane, neither did I. You're quick to blame us, but where were you?"

"I was riddled with bullets on the other side of the fucking world!"

"Yeah, but you were alive and you made some pretty powerful friends. Why didn't they help her?"

"They were busy torturing me, all while you and Max did nothing to save me!"

"Max was on the run. He had killed some of your new powerful friends and they were after him, and so were the Five Eyes governments. How was he supposed to get to you?"

"He is a resourceful guy, he survived for six years undetected by all of you. He could have found me if he wanted to."

"He didn't know you were alive, none of us did! You can blame us all you like, but you were the one that failed. You got yourself shot then captured. You are looking for someone to blame for what happened to you and for Jane's death, well look in the mirror and you will see the man responsible!"

Flash stood towering over Blake his face was red with anger and he pulled his gun and rested the barrel against Blake's forehead. At least if he was killed now, it would not happen in front of Max. It would spare him some pain.

Blake closed his eyes and controlled his breathing. He got to his knees, as Flash kept the barrel pressed hard against his head.

With incredible speed, Blake's left hand shot around and took Flash by the wrist, pulling the gun wielding hand off to the side, moving his head in the opposite direction, just as a bullet slammed into the floor behind Blake from Flash's pistol. Blake's right hand clenched into a fist and hammered into

Flash's balls, and he immediately dropped his pistol. Blake caught the weapon as he got to his feet.

He had seen a piece of metal wire laying on the ground when they first walked into the work area and he had set about pissing Flash off so he attack him and Blake would end up on the ground near it. He had used it to pick the lock on his cuffs.

Blake moved in behind Flash, dragged him to his feet and held the gun at his temple, while hanging onto him in choke hold.

"Stop what you're doing!" Blake commanded and the crew all stopped to see what the commotion was. "Get off the ladder and get your arse down here or I will kill this son-of-a-bitch!"

The men all exchanged confused looks.

"Don't you dare!" Flash yelled, causing more confusion.

"I mean it, I will kill him," Blake warned. "Get your arses off the ladder and get on your knees! Hands in the air."

One of the men slowly got down on his knees and others in the room started to comply too. The man on the ladder made a slow climb down and started walking towards Blake with his hands raised.

"You don't want to do this, Mister," the crew member said. "You got nowhere to go. You would be writing your own suicide note in his blood. Just put the gun down."

"Stop right there," Blake said as the man kept approaching. "I will shoot you."

"You won't. Just put the gun down. You have got no other options."

The man kept getting closer. Blake was fast running out of options.

He made his choice. He started to move his pistol wielding hand around to fire at the approaching crewman, when out the corner of his eye he spotted a blur coming in fast. One of the other crew had moved around unseen and was coming for him, while the missile guy had him distracted.

Blake pushed Flash hard in the back towards the approaching crew member and he fell into his arms and the pair tripped over one another and fell to the floor. Blake spun and shot the approaching crewman twice in the face. He fell and skidded to a stop only a foot from Blake.

A bullet crazed his left arm and he swung his right arm back towards Flash and the other crewmen, letting off four shots in their direction as he ran for the door. He fired another couple of shots, as rounds pinged off the metal walls all around him.

He slammed the hatch to the workroom shut and turned the handle to lock the big metal door in place. He quickly looked around, but couldn't find anything useful, so he slid his stolen pistol into the big slide bolt on the door, jamming it in place and for all intents and purposes locking it from the outside.

Blake spun on his heal, clutching his bleeding arm, and he ran.

Chapter Thirty-Five

The wind was rushing past Max at incredible speeds. The sound would have been unbearable without his headset on. He was standing at the rear door of a P-8A Poseidon watching the sonobuoys dropping down into the ocean. The modified Boeing 737 owned by the Royal Australian Air Force was flying low over the rolling and choppy seas. Even in the sunlight the water carried a profound darkness. Obviously, they were flying over deep waters.

The sonobuoys pierced into the sea and deployed their listening devices. They were using both active and passive devices. The active sonobuoys floated on the surface while deploying a series of sensors on wires down into the water. They emitted pings which spread out in sound waves through the water and listened for echoes which were then sent to the plane's signals control centre and interpreted. The passive ones just sat in the water listening for the sound of propellers, engines or even noises as the crew moved about in the submarine. Their data was also being fed back to the plane for analysis.

Max could see the other aircraft moving in their search patterns off in the distance. The US and Royal Australian Air Forces had experience in hunting for submarines, but this was the first time they had done so on this scale. In addition to the Poseidons and Orions, there were also three Triton UAVs and six anti-submarine helicopters from a nearby carrier group, made up of both Australian and United States Navy vessels, which was sailing in to provide support.

"How's it going, would be fly boy?" Kate asked over the Bose headset walking in from the control room. "Spotted them yet?"

"Finding a needle in a haystack is a bullshit, understated cliché," Max said in frustration. "Whoever came up with that never had to find a boat designed to not be found in the middle of the ocean."

"We'll find him, Max."

"I hope so, Kate, because I honestly don't know what will happen if we don't."

"Look out there," Kate said pointing out the door. "Billions of dollars worth of planes and equipment, not even counting the carrier group on its way. We will find Flash and stop him."

"And Blake?"

"I'm sure he is fine, Max. He is as tough as you and twice as smart as both of us put together. I'm sure he is coping and will be fine. You boys will finally get your time together when this is all done."

"I feel sick. I'm the reason he is in this position."

"Oh, fuck that! Flash hates all of us equally. We all fucked him in some way and he's trying to hurt us all. Blake knows the risks of this life, just as much as you and I do. He would be feeling just as guilty for getting you involved and thinking about the pain you are in. If you ask me, you both need to trust your guts, remember your training and fucking work together to sort this shit out. You can do it if you believe in yourselves and each other."

"Of course, I believe in him."

"And in yourself?"

"I can do this."

"That's fucking right!" Kate said slapping him on the back. "No one I would rather have looking for me and coming to save me. Prince Fucking Charming himself is riding in on his big white, ninety-five thousand horsepower jet plane! Everything a boy could dream of."

"You a such a romantic at heart."

"Yeah, but don't you fucking tell anyone!" Kate frowned playfully showing Max a clenched fist.

"Secret's safe with me mate," Max smiled.

"Now, can we talk about your batshit crazy plan?"

"Sure," Max said closing the door of the P-8A and sealing the rear compartment.

"Agent Shaw," one of the control room operators said from up near the front of the plane. "Agent Matthews, sorry for interrupting. We've found something."

"On our way," Max replied walking briskly towards the RAAF officer.

"This mean no discussion of your plan?" Kate asked quickly falling into step beside him.

"We can talk about it when we see what they found."

"We better," Kate said as they reached the control room.

"What have you got?" Max asked the officer who was taking her seat at a complex looking computer system.

"Sir, we think we've found the sub," the officer said pointing at various screens and explaining what they were looking at.

"How can you be sure?"

"Well about a minute ago the data lit up. The sonobuoys picked up what I can only describe as gunshots."

"You're joking?"

"No, sir. Several shots, followed by relative silence, but now we have locked on to the propeller's unique tracking signature."

"You can track it?"

"We know the sound of the propeller in the water. It's a classified secret, Top Secret in fact, but not from us, we know what we are listening for."

"Okay, well, what do you think happened?"

"We don't know what happened inside, but they would undoubtedly know we are here. That sub's got all the best radars and electronic warfare capabilities. It might be old, but it is just as capable as others in that department. They would have all of our planes on their radars. Best guess is they went dark, but the crew was smart enough to know we would hear the shots, so they fired her up and are moving to a new position."

"Go to war," Max ordered quickly moving for the door.

"But the fleet isn't in position."

"I'm not risking losing them again," Max said turning back to face the room. "Do it!"

"Yes, sir," the officer said barking orders at her crew as Max left the room.

"What are you doing, Max?" Kate questioned following closely behind him.

"You know what I'm doing," Max said striping off his borrowed RAAF bomber jacket.

"The plan was to wait for the fleet."

"There is no time, Kate. Blake is in trouble."

"I'm sorry, Max, but this is bigger than Blake."

"I know that, Kate. Flash is sitting on God knows how much of that Erebus shit, let alone the twelve Tomahawks. We've found him and we can't let him get away."

"This plan was crazy before, but it is simply suicidal now."

"My speciality," Max said gathering his gear.

"Then I'm coming too."

"No way," Max argued, stopping for a moment to look at Kate. "I might be willing to risk myself, but I can't ask you to do the same."

"Who said you were asking? And, who says I am either for that matter? I was there that day and pulled you away from Flash. I am just as much to blame as you and I have known Blake even longer than you have. So, I am coming, Max, and that is final."

"And if I ordered you to stay behind?"

"I would tell you to shove your orders up your arse. Boss."

"Okay," Max conceded. "I could use the help. Thank you."

"Too fucking right, you could. How many times has your dumb arse been knocked out in the last couple of days? You might be done, before we even start."

"I'll be fine."

"Yeah, well, I'm going to have your back just in case."

"Thanks, Kate."

"Don't thank me yet, the hard bit is still coming," Kate said changing and getting her gear ready.

Chapter Thirty-Six

"I don't want to hear fucking excuses!" Flash yelled. "It's a fucking sealed tube under the fucking ocean! There are only a handful of places he could be. Find him!"

"Yes, sir," one of the crew said running from the control room followed by two other men in combat gear.

"Sir," Pierre said, "they are moving in for another sweep."

"How many are there now?" Flash asked looking at the radar.

"Eight planes, six helicopters and we are getting periodic readings of very small blips on the radar, which I believe is a UAV. Could be more than one."

"Fuck."

"That's not all."

"What?"

"There is a carrier group sailing in from the south. It is still a long way out, but it's definitely on a straight line heading towards us. We are also reading the pings of a large number of sonobuoys."

"We knew Torres would come after us. We need to just find a new spot and go dark again. With some luck it will give us enough time to ready a couple of the Tomahawks which will give them something else to think about while we get away."

"I would rather not rely on luck, but I think we are going to need it," Pierre said nervously looking at the radar

"What do you mean, what is it?" Flash asked getting to his feet and walking over to the green radar panel.

"The other planes have stopped their grid sweeps and are moving into a rolling line."

"And?"

"They are moving in to attack."

"They know where we are?"

"Looks like it."

"Prepare us for war. Get the torpedoes into the tubes and ready a couple of the missiles."

"But the missiles are nuclear tipped or filled with Erebus."

"Use one of the empty ones! We need to send them a message – Plan C!"

"Yes, sir," Pierre said radioing the weapons room.

Flash watched the radar as the dots of the planes were moving into a line coming directly at them.

"Sir, one of the missiles will be ready in a few minutes," Pierre said anxiously, "but not soon enough."

"Hit the alarm!" Flash ordered as an alarm rang out throughout the sub and his microphone turned on booming his voice throughout. "Brace yourselves!"

Within seconds the first two planes passed over the sub's location and dropped torpedoes into the water. The radar lit up tracing the deadly weapons' progress through the dark ocean, speeding towards them. Every beep came quicker than the previous as the torpedoes got closer and closer, until they both exploded outside the sub.

The sound was deafening in the sub, like a giant hammer hitting the metal surface. The explosion rocked the submarine and the metal creaked and groaned from the pressure changes.

Several of the crew had been tossed around in their various compartments. They were getting to their feet as a second wave of torpedoes exploded nearby ripping small holes in the hull.

Blake had been hiding in a recess near the backup diesel engine when the torpedoes exploded wildly pitching the old submarine. One of Flash's men had entered the room just before the blast and he had fallen on impact. Blake sprung out from behind his cover and charged the confused crew member. He swung a massive steel wrench, which he had found in a toolbox in the engine room, and slammed it into the man's shoulder. He had been going for the head, but Flash's man had instinctively dodged the incoming blow, raising his shoulder to protect his head. It had saved his life, but not his arm.

Blake felt the bone snap and the guy cried out in pain dropping his pistol. Blake headbutted him then swung the wrench again, as he fell back, this time finding his mark. The big steel tool struck him in the side of the head making a sickening thud and crack as it broke his skull. He fell to the floor at Blake's feet. Blake didn't bother to check if he was dead, he knew he was.

Blake gathered up his former foe's pistol and put it in his belt, and went for the Steyr, but before he could unclip the weapon, two more men ran into the engine room and fired in his direction. Bullet slammed into the metal surfaces all around him. He abandoned the Steyr and ran using the backup engine for cover. He got to the hatch at the far end of the room and opened it making his way into a structural mess of steel in the void behind the hatch.

He used the steel beams to climb up towards the mess hall, praying another torpedo did not hit, because he knew it would have thrown him off the beam and down a couple of storeys to the bottom of the hull.

He used a beam to balance walk across to the wall of the mess and found a hidden panel in the steel. He unclipped it, letting it fall to the steel floor about two storeys beneath him. It bounced on several beams before slapping hard into the hull, making a hell of a lot of noise.

Blake quickly pulled himself into the crew's mess and went for the kitchen to find a spot to hide as another torpedo exploded throwing him off his feet onto the kitchen floor. He landed right beside one of the crew who had been bunkering in position, as the big boat let out a series of horrifying groans.

Blake wondered if this was the end, if he had been sacrificed to take out Flash and the Erebus. It made sense, it was the right play. But, he didn't have time to think about it. The crew member in the kitchen was moving fast for his own gun.

Blake scrambled forward on all fours tackling the man and the two wrestled between the benches on the floor, as another torpedo exploded and one of the cupboards overhead burst open scattering kitchen utensils and tools over the pair. They both covered their heads to protect themselves as the heavy items rained down.

Then for just a second, there was peace.

Blake looked over to the crewman on the kitchen floor and wondered, or more accurately hoped, to find him dead or unconscious. But he was not. He started raising his pistol and Blake flung a heavy steel saucepan into his wrist, freeing the gun from his grip, then he slammed the pan down on the guy's nose.

The impact forced him to the floor and Blake hit him over and over with the pan, spilling his blood on the floor, until he was dead.

Blake checked his pockets and found a few useful items, including a silencer, which he took as well as his pistol as spare and fled the room. He knew what he had to do.

In the control room, Flash was getting back to his feet. He had fallen and hit his head as the most recent torpedo exploded. He was dizzy and felt nauseous, but was coming good.

"Damage report?" Flash asked.

Pierre and another two of his crew were checking their panels and screens.

"They are detonating before they hit us," Pierre explained. "They are trying to force us to surface!"

"Don't you fucking dare!" Flash snapped.

"We will be a sitting duck if we surface, but we might not have any choice if they keep hitting us like this. This old boat can only handle so much, and we might need to get up there and start the pumps before they sink us."

"What about the missiles?"

"They are not ready yet!"

"Jesus Christ! We need to do better than this! Sort it out!"

"We are trying, sir."

"Well try harder!"

Blake had crossed the mess and made his way through the crew's quarters and passed the tiny bunks. As he was moving through the boat, he screwed the silencer he had found in the kitchen guy's cams on his pistol.

Quietly, he climbed the ladder up towards the top deck. He inched the hatch open and saw two men pressing themselves against the walls trying to brace for more attacks in the sonar room. He lined up the first one and shot him in the face. His head exploded over the nearby control panel and showered his comrade with blood. His companion jumped in shock trying to comprehend what had happened. He turned towards the hatch and no sooner had his eyes locked onto Blake, than a bullet tore through his eye socket and his brain, then pinged off the metal control panel. He sat perfectly still for a few seconds, before he slumped on top of his former crewmate.

Blake climbed into the room and locked the hatch. He secured the door and bolted it in place between his room forward control and missile rooms, then moved back to the two fallen men and stood over them getting control of his breathing.

Blake had served in the Navy for several years before being recruited to the AIS. He was trying to remember the layout of the boat's controls. He thought about the two men he had seen earlier at the helm. Put simply, the man on the right was controlling the steering, the Helm, and the man on the left was managing the big vessel's angle and buoyancy, the Outboard. He could hear Flash arguing with the Frenchman who was towards the back near the radar systems.

He moved closer to the door. Three, two, one.

Blake burst through the open doorway with both pistols drawn. He shot Pierre in the leg and he fell to the floor cursing in French. Flash was quicker than ever, he sprung from his chair and took cover behind it as Blake put two bullets into the chair where he had been sitting. The bullets didn't get him, but they would keep his head down at least for a few seconds and that's all he needed. He fired two shots in quick succession killing the Helm and the Outboard with his other pistol, while firing again at the captain's chair to keep Flash pinned down. He ran as he fired and arrived at the helm where he slapped his hand down on the emergency button or the chicken switch as it had become fondly known as over the years.

Instantly the sub responded as compressed air flooded into the ballast tanks at the front of the vessel and it began a rapid ascent towards the surface. Flash had been moving to fire at Blake, but the sudden change in the sub threw him off balance and he fell catching the big chair he had been in earlier. Flash held onto the bolted in chair, so he did not fall. Pierre was not so lucky, he slid across the floor and instinctively put out his legs to cushion the impact, sending pain shooting through his body, from the bullet wound in his leg, as he hit the wall.

Blake had run back to the front of the room, trying to get to the sonar room, but did not quite make it, given the speed of their ascent. Blake had spoken to a few of his former Navy colleagues who had experienced an emergency ballast blow and they had likened it to a rollercoaster ride. Now he understood why. The sub was moving fast and hard through the water – they must have been at four or five g-forces.

He laid against a nearby panel out of the line of fire, letting the machinery take his weight as the big girl rushed forward.

Seconds later, there was a brief moment where everything seemed to stand still and he felt almost weightless as the boat breached the surface, before it pulled itself hard back down towards the water where it bobbed and bounced, but held its course on the surface.

As soon as the g-forces had allowed, Blake ran for the door to the sonar room and disappeared behind the metal wall as bullets slammed into the metal. One of the bullets, hit him in the arm, the same arm that had been grazed earlier, but he kept moving. He needed to find a place to hide from Flash, not that it mattered though. He was sure that now the boat was in sight, the Air Force guys would sink it.

Chapter Thirty-Seven

Max and Kate were standing towards the back of the Poseidon. It had flown over the submarine's position and dropped a couple of torpedoes, before circling around to come back towards the sub from side on.

As Max's plane made its looping turn, the other planes came in and dropped torpedoes into the water around the sub.

Max had specifically ordered the crews to try to force the sub to the surface. He did not want to sink it and leave a dozen nukes and Erebus cannisters sitting on the bottom of the ocean. That and he didn't want to risk Blake's life.

He had struck a deal with Torres, he could lead an attack to reclaim the sub, but the first sign he had lost control or failed in his mission and she would give the order to destroy the vessel.

Max had agreed to the terms, and now he and Kate were waiting for their chance. They were both carrying hard backpacks for their gear and they were wearing black skin tight, but lightweight wetsuits designed for Navy Clearance Divers – Australia's Navy Seals.

"It's moving towards the surface," the RAAF officer shouted from the front of the plane. "Now's your chance."

"Thank you!" Max shouted over the air rushing into the cabin through the opened doors at the back of the plane.

"You sure you want to do this, Max?" Kate asked. "The fall could be enough to knock you out again from this height."

"I'll be fine, I promise. See you down there."

Max did not bother to try to talk Kate out of coming. He saw the determination in her eyes. So, he stepped to the door and leapt out in a pin drop position – legs and arms straight beside his body. Just before he hit the water, he opened his parachute to take some of the impact out of the fall.

As his legs broke the water, he cut away his chute, so he didn't get tangled in it. He sped deep into the water before finally coming to a stop. He kicked his legs hard, the big marine flippers he was wearing helping him back to the surface. As soon as he broke into the air, he kicked off the flippers and pulled on a pair of the Navy Seal's water boots, which had a grippy rubber sole, and he tossed his goggles into the water.

Off to his left he could see Kate. She jumped just after him and had resurfaced, a bit further away than they had planned, but it was still achievable.

Max pulled open his solid backpack and found his modified flare gun. He closed the bag again and put it back on his back, then lined Kate up with the flare gun. He sighted her waving, then pulled the gun up, so he was aiming several metres above her head, then he fired.

The modified flare shot out of the orange barrel trailing a rope, which was spooling off a metal reel attached to the top of the flare gun. A few seconds of spooling later and the line went taunt and Max gripped the handle tightly. The rope was fastened to the reel and held. For a moment, the rope almost hovered in the air as the energy flowed through it, keeping it in a straight line, then it fell flat on the surface of the water.

Max saw Kate in the distance swimming towards him and towards the end of the rope on her side. Before she got there, the six thousand tonne, billion dollar, 1980's built USS Pittsburgh broke the surface to his right. It smashed up from the deep ocean cascading, frothing and blasting the salty white water from is nose cone, like a jet breaking the sound barrier. The big sub launched a few metres in the air at the front, while dragged its big stern through the ocean. It slapped back down on the surface, shooting water out in every direction, then kept powering forward through the rough waters.

Max looked over to Kate who was still swimming hard for the rope while checking out the extraordinary sight to her left with each stroke. Before long, she disappeared as the sub sailed between them.

Max clenched the flare gun and the rope tightly, hoping Kate had made it, otherwise he was going to be treading water in the deep dark sea for a while having failed his mission.

The rope went tight and Max felt the big boat start to pull him through the water as it caught on the coning tower. Every passing metre not only pulled Max forward with the boat, but it also pulled him in closer to the vessel as the rope pinched around the coning tower in a narrowing V with Max on one end and Kate hanging onto the other.

Max arrived in the whitewash next to the sub and struggled to slide up onto the sleek surface. He looked over and saw Kate having similar issues.

"Use your boots!" Max yelled and Kate nodded.

In sync, both agents turned themselves around in the water, like a water skier bouncing their arses off the surface as their boots cut through the water.

"On three!" Max yelled. "One, Two!"

He took a breath and held onto the rope with all his might, then pressed his feet against the hull. The rubber gripped and he pulled hard on the rope and walked himself out of the water up onto the surface. Kate mirrored his moves and arrived beside him. The two agents smiled at each other, then when they were sure they were balanced, they walked forward still holding the rope, looking for the hatch.

Water was splashing up over the surface of the boat making their steps precarious, made worse by the rise and fall as the sub bounced through the rough seas. Max reeled in some of the rope as they moved forward.

When they found the rear hatch, Max took hold of both ends of the rope and supported Kate who was between his arms, using him as a pillar. She removed their guns from Max's pack and holstered them, along with their hunting knives, but before she holstered her knife, she cut away Max's now empty backpack and it fell into the water and rushed towards the back of the Navy vessel. It was sliced in half and dragged under the water by the huge propeller which was partially exposed. Kate knelt down opened the keypad panel and entered the open code. The hatch opened and Kate pulled her pistol and aimed down the ladder.

"All clear," Kate said and started down the ladder.

Max gingerly walked forward. He felt off balance and it was not just his un-acclimatised sea legs. The jump from the plane had shaken him up and his head was aching again. He slipped and fell into the water. Clutching at the rope. He caught the closest end, but the other shot off towards the conning tower. He looked back towards the propeller and his impending doom. Like the backpack, he was going to be sliced in half by the razor-sharp blades.

He kicked his legs wildly trying to get them to grip to the metal, but it seemed no use. He hopelessly grabbed the rope, but sprang into action when he felt it go taunt. Max looked down to see his legs only metres from the propeller, then looked up towards the hatch and saw Kate gripping the rope like a world tug-of-war champion.

Hand over hand she started pulling him in, straining against the water. When he could, he slid himself up onto the black metal surface. He laid for a moment to get his breath and shake off his headache, but he didn't get long. An alarm sounded and small red light started flashing inside the lid of the hatch.

"Run!" Kate yelled.

Max got to his feet and sprinted. The waves were crashing over the hull and the boat was rocking in all directions. Max pushed forward hard, running for the hatch. Kate disappeared inside and down the ladder as he ran, and the hatch began to close.

Two metres from the narrowing opening, Max slid like a baseball player for base. His legs forward. They went down into the opening, followed by his torso. His hands grabbed the second rung from the top of the ladder and caught his weight as the hatch closed above his head. Max felt the boat's angle change, it was diving again. He was hanging from the ladder as the boat sank beneath the waves and disappeared from the view of the planes above.

Max pulled himself in towards the ladder and climbed down. Kate helped him get in beside a metal wall leading to the manoeuvring room for support as the sub held its deep dive angle.

"Are you okay?" Kate asked.

"Yeah, thanks to you," Max said.

"What happened?"

"I slipped."

"You sure that's all it was?"

"Yep."

"Liar."

"I'm fine now, thanks again."

"Right. Well, what's the plan now?"

"I came up with that plan, what have you got?"

One of the crew came up through the hatch in the floor and started firing at Max and Kate. Max grabbed Kate and pulled her down to cover. He signalled for her to go to the manoeuvring room. She nodded and army crawled for the entrance.

Max got to his knee as the boat started to level out. He was using a small old electronics panel for cover, but he knew it would not be long before the gunman found him, so he moved first.

Max ducked around to the left and knelt with his face towards the grey metal housing of the panel. Quick as he could manage, he looked around the corner and saw the man heading around the opposite end searching for him. Max followed him around in a clockwise direction and, when he could, got to his feet properly and raised his silenced pistol. He fired two shots into the back of the guy's head just as he was about to investigate the manoeuvring room where Kate had just gone.

Max walked over towards the hatch and looked down, it was clear, so he headed for the engine room. He looked down the aisle between the rows of machinery. It was hot and there was some steam moving about in the small space as miniature valves released. It felt mostly deserted as he briskly moved between the machines.

A bullet hit the machine beside him. Max instinctively ducked and turned back. A couple of Flash's men must have come up the ladder and through the hatch. He turned and ran deeper into the engine room as bullets ricocheted and pinged off the little walls all around him. He ducked under some pipes and stepped left then right, running past a huge turbine.

As he got into a small clearing towards the stern of the boat, one of the crew launched out of the shadows and tackled him into the wall. He dropped his pistol as they wrestled against the wall. The guy had his wrists pinned to the metal and was kneeing him in the ribs and stomach. Max was straining against his assailant's grip, but he was bloody strong. He took a vicious knee to the stomach winding him and stopped straining for a moment against the guy's hands. Max felt him soften his grip slightly and ripped his right wrist free, tucked it against his chest for leverage and threw his elbow into the jaw of his attacker. The blow landed and the guy stumbled backwards. Max ran headlong into his immediate enemy driving his knee into the guy's chest knocking the wind out of him.

Max leapt forward off his left leg and drew back his right fist and thumped his attacker in the face, before landing and twisting drawing power up from his legs and throwing it out through his shoulder and slamming a left hook into the guy's jaw. He stumbled back and Max ran forward and jumped up kneeing him in the face. Max's attacker became Max's victim as he fell backwards into the space under the towering steel turbine's crankshaft. It rotated fast and hard, and before either of them could comprehend the situation, the massive steel rod pumped down obliterating him. Max grimaced at the sight, but was relieved.

While Max was under attack, Kate had crept into the manoeuvring room, unseen by the two man team inside running the boat's engines. She put a bullet into each of their heads, then got to her feet. She wiped the blood from the terminals and had a look for anything useful. She had never been in the Navy, she was Army through and through, and while she had been on a few boats and ships in her time, she had never been in the engine rooms.

There was only one obvious button. It was bright red and easily accessible from both positions. *Only one way to find out,* she thought to herself and slammed her fist down on the red mushroom button.

The effect was almost instantaneous. The boat started to slow. The red button had been the emergency stop switch and it had driven the control rods back into the reactor and flooded it with water, cooling and stopping the fission process, stalling the engine. She smiled to herself and headed for the door.

Max had watched as the big body crushing crankshaft and drive rod, slowed then stopped. Kate must have found a way to disable the sub. He smiled to himself then started sweeping the engine room.

Chapter Thirty-Eight

Blake had managed to get to a small medical centre, not far from the crew's quarters. He used a pair of forceps to retrieve the bullet from his arm, gritting his teeth and trying to muffle any groans as he dug around in the wound. He found the bullet and pulled it free in a wave of both pain and relief. He pulled out a pad and bandage, but did not get a chance to apply them as one of Flash's men dived over the operating table and tackled him into the wall.

Blake fell forward into the workbench smearing his blood over it and onto his mugger. He put his hands against the wall and the goon started throwing blow after blow into his back and kidneys. Blake threw a hard elbow into his nose breaking it and sending him back onto the operating table. Blake spun on his heal and threw a solid left jab followed by a haymaker right. It connected, but the blows hurt Blake just as much, if not more, from the bullet wound gash in his upper arm.

There was a stainless steel tray nearby which had neatly held some medical implements, before the emergency ballast blow, which had scattered them on the floor. Blake grabbed the tray and swung it hard into the guy's head and it rang out in the small space like a steel drum. He went for a second swing, but Flash's man caught his arms. He squeezed Blake's bullet wound and chuckled to himself as Blake screamed.

Blake threw a headbutt, landing it on his attacker's already broken nose. He fell back onto the bed and laid still. He was out.

Blake clenched his wounded arm; it was bleeding badly. He needed to seal it. He looked around and found a first-aid sign on a cupboard. He got a wound sealing powder sachet out of the kit, ripped it open with his teeth and poured it in the wound. It bubbled and frothed, until he put a medical pad and pressure on it. Blake scowled and clenched his jaw as the powder went to work.

He heard the man on the bed behind him move. Without too many sudden movements, Blake turned some dials on a machine in front of him then spun around and threw the remaining wound pounder into his target's eyes. He blinked and shouted as he tried to rub it out. Blake used the distraction to grab the paddles on the defibrillation unit he had just switched on and turned back to the bed. He had turned it up to the maximum. The attacker saw what Blake had in his hands and started wildly kicking trying to get them from Blake's hands, but in the process put both of his hands down on the metal bed. Blake pushed the paddles down on the metal bars and pressed the button. Electricity shot through the bed, up into his attacker's arms. He convulsed then fell back onto the bed as the shock stopped his heart.

Blake dropped the paddles and made his way back over to the first-aid kit. He bandaged his arm and taped it in position. He holstered one of his pistols, he was unable to use two, given the pain in his arm. He had practiced for years use using both hands and while two pistols would have been better, the pain was too great. So, he stuck to one and figured he could focus his shots better with one anyway.

He headed out of the little medical bay and made his way back through the crew's quarters.

In the bathrooms he found one of Flash's men and moved into position to take the shot, but the guy heard him approaching and spun around quickly, ducking the incoming bullet. It smashed into the plastic panel lining the wet room. The fanatic ran and dived for the shower cubicles as Blake unloaded three shots into the wall behind him.

Blake found himself staring at a row of cubicles, but before he got the chance to kick each one open to find his prey, they found him. Two of Flash's men jumped him from behind and he was forced to drop his pistol as they wrestled across the wet floors. Water splashed around them as they slid through the little room. The man he had been chasing burst out of a cubicle and joined the fight. He kicked and punched Blake as the other two men held him in position. Blood poured from Blake's mouth and nose, and his eyes started to blacken. He was on his knees and the men were holding his arms up above his head. The pain from his earlier bullet wound was still strong even over the pain of the beating.

The first guy wound up for another kick and Blake looked away, bracing himself for the pain, but it never came. A gunshot rang out from behind him and he quickly looked up to see the kicker standing perfectly still with a bullet hole between his now lifeless eyes. His knees collapsed and he fell backwards, crumpling in on himself. As he fell, two more shot rang out and the two men who had been holding Blake's arms fell to the floor dead.

Blake was not sure what had happened. He looked at the three men, then tentatively turned around to find Kate moving towards him. She knelt down on the floor in front of him and he collapsed into her arms.

"How you doing, kid?" Kate asked.

"I have been better, Kate, but I'm glad to see you," Blake said.

"Let's get you to the sick bay and fix you up. Can you stand?"

"I think so," Blake said taking Kate's hands to help him up.

She looped his arm up around her shoulders and supported his weight as they made their way back to the medical centre.

Inside they found the guy Blake had killed earlier still laying on the gurney.

"Some of your handy work?" Kate asked.

"Yeah, I hit him with the defibrillator," Blake replied. "Stopped his heart."

"Shocking," Kate laughed as she pushed the dead body onto the floor and Blake chuckled even though it hurt.

She found the first-aid kit and cleaned him up as best she could. She found some painkillers, but he refused to take them.

"I'll be fine," Blake said waving them away. "Lets me know I'm still alive."

"Let's keep it that way, shall we?" Kate said.

"That's the pain. Although the odds seem better now you are here to help. How did you get aboard?"

"Max and I were waiting in the water when you breached. We managed to get aboard before you dived again. Was that you, that breached it?"

"Yeah, I hit the chicken switch."

"The what?"

"The chicken switch. The emergency ballast blow switch. It pumped compressed air into the ballast tanks and caused the sub to rapidly ascend and burst up into the air."

"Well, it sure fucking did! Scared the shit out of me. Six thousand tonnes of black steel bursting out of fucking nowhere. Unnerving. Especially since I hate the ocean so much."

"Really?"

"Yeah, I don't know how you lot fucking do it. Couldn't think of anything worse than months on one of these fucking things. I mean look how low the roof is. I'd have a back injury from being hunched over all day and no doubt head injuries from whacking it constantly on all the hatches."

"I bet the sub breach would have been cool to see," Blake laughed holding his ribs.

"Yeah on TV or from a little bit further away," Kate huffed. "Not metres!"

Blake laughed and the pair sat in silence, while Kate placed the bandages. Blake gritted his teeth more than once as Kate's rough patch up pushed at his wounds.

"You said Max came on board too," Blake said as he started to pull his stained white shirt back on.

"Yeah, Prince Charming is here," Kate said. "I left him in the engine room. He's looking forward to seeing you."

"Me too," Blake acknowledged smiling broadly through the pain at the thought of holding Max again. "It was you guys who stopped the engines?"

"Yeah, I hit the emergency stop and shut it down."

"Well, unless they start the diesel, we will be floating here for a while."

"How come?"

"Flooding the reactor, stops the fission process. It will need a full shutdown, then a step-by-step system reboot. It will take a long while to get it up and running again."

"Hopefully, we won't need it anytime soon anyway. A carrier group is on the way and we have a dozen planes and helicopters overhead."

"Good."

"Well, it's mostly good."

"What do you mean by that?"

"Torres gave us a pretty short rope. Let's just say Max didn't make any friends at the White House."

"Well, I'm hardly shocked by that, Kate. He certainly has a way with politicians. I guess he doesn't trust them much."

"Who does?"

"True. Anyway, what sort of rope did Torres give you?"

"The any signs of failure and she's going to sink us kind."

"Short indeed. Well, we better get to work."

Blake jumped down off the table as four of the crew ran into the room. Blake ran forward for the first one through the door, pushing past Kate, but the intruder just pressed the barrel of his gun to Blake's forehead and pushed him back. Blake stopped in his tracks as they aimed their Steyrs at his and Kate's head. They were helpless and had no choice but to raise their arms in surrender.

"Hands behind your heads," the gruff crewman who had held his gun to Blake's head spat.

Blake and Kate complied.

Two of the men moved in behind them, keeping their rifles aimed squarely at their backs.

"Time to go see the boss," the crewman said leading them out of the room.

The team led the two agents towards the front of the big boat and eventually into the missile room. Occasionally along the way, Kate got lippy with her captors and she got prodded with the rifle to remind her it was there. There was also more than one threat to keep quiet or be shot out of the torpedo tube which she tried her best not to laugh at.

They opened the hatch and were paraded into the missile room. Flash stopped giving orders as former colleagues were marched in at gun point, surrendering, flanked by guards. He strode over and took Blake by the neck.

"You caused nothing but a delay and the loss of a couple of men with your little stunt," Flash said punching Blake in the face and knocking him to the ground.

Kate stepped forward to enter the fight, but several of the riflemen clicked their safeties off to discourage her. She stopped in place, but wore a furious look on her face. Blake held up a hand to get her to pull back when he saw the fury and rage in her eyes.

"Hello, Kate," Flash said jovially, "it's been a while."

"Not long enough, for a dead man, I guess," Kate grumbled, "but, not to worry, you will be proper fucking dead soon enough."

"Oh, I have missed your particular brand of cocky attitude. Always the Alpha. More macho than most of us in the team. I could have used someone like you in my current squad. Unwavering loyalty and drive. Tough as two bricks."

Kate spat in Flash's face.

"I would never join you, you fucking terrorist piece-of-shit!" Kate roared. "I would rather put a bullet in my head."

"Well, that can be arranged," Flash said wiping the spit from his face, dropping his grin as he wiped and placing his gun against her forehead.

Kate didn't flinch. She starred him down. Almost tempting him into taking the shot.

"Do it you soft prick," she taunted, locking in her deathly stare.

Flash pulled the trigger and the gun clicked, the safety holding the bullet in place.

"I want you to see this first," Flash said smiling.

"Pussy," Kate sneered after having not even blinked when the gun clicked.

Flash backhanded her and she bent to the side. She wiped blood from her mouth as she stood back up. Her eyes were full of hate.

"Why don't you tell your goon squad to put their guns down so you and I can go a couple of rounds," Kate taunted. "If that's all you've got, it won't take long to beat you and put an end to all this shit."

Flash rose to the jeer and dashed forward quickly throwing a punch at Kate.

Kate, the former Special Air Services Army officer and AIS trainer, dodged the incoming blow. She grabbed him by the neck and swung her foot around, taking him clean off his feet. She chocked him as he fell and slammed his back and head into the metal floor, but before she could finish the job Flash's thugs moved forward and pressed their rifles against her from all sides, warning her to stop.

Flash scrambled back away from her, crab walking backwards, embarrassed and annoyed.

"Lucky shot," he said getting to his feet and dusting himself off.

"Pig's arse!" Kate snapped, "I fucking trained you. I know all your weaknesses. Let me show you how weak you really are in front of all these cowards hiding behind their guns. Big pussies like their boss."

"Maybe later," Flash said shouldering past Kate.

"Soft as ever. I thought taking a bunch of bullets might have hardened you up, but no, still weak as piss."

Flash ignored the taunt this time and instead moved over to the nearby control unit and unceremoniously pressed the launch button.

There was a loud reverberating sound and short alarm, before the rumbling built and started moving up the room.

It was unmistakeable. He had just launched one of the Tomahawks.

Chapter Thirty-Nine

President Torres and her senior aides, as well as the United States' military leaders were locked in heated discussions with Prime Minister Ferguson and Hulk in the White House Situation Room.

"With all due respect to our Australian friends," the Chairman of the Joint Chiefs said, "this is an American decision. It is our boat and our soil, so it is our call."

"I don't deny that, Mr Chairman," Hulk said, "but the President was very clear. My team has the opportunity to try to get the situation under control and secure the weapons, which none of us want sinking to the bottom of the ocean. A search and rescue mission to get them back won't be easy."

"There is a madman on that sub with those weapons aimed right at us! A terrorist you trained for that matter. Why don't you want us to succeed here? Is there something I am not seeing?"

"I am going to let that accusation slide, because of our long history, Jerry, but let me assure you I will not sit here and be accused again. Not only is the thought preposterous and stupid, it is also insulting and unbecoming. I know you are under pressure. We all are. But, you only get one chance on a comment like that."

"Clearly, we can see where Mr Shaw gets his trademark style from," the Chairman said with a wave of his hand. "But you are right, I apologise I should not have accused you. I am just frustrated. Forgive me. But I stand by my recommendation to sink that submarine. Madam President, give me the go order before this escalates."

"Madam President, please give my team some more time. They are the best at what they do. We don't want to risk leaks from the damaged sub or worse someone else recovering the weapons before we can. We saw Max and Kate get onboard from the drone footage and the tracking sonobuoys have reported it has stopped moving. They are making progress.”

Torres sat thinking in silence at the points raised by both men. Ferguson sat in silence, almost blank. Hulk could not help but feel she was way out of her depth.

“I don’t believe our Australian friends have anything to do with this, Jerry,” Torres said finally. “I genuinely believe they are here to help us. Hulk has sent his two best agents in to rescue his number two and likely successor, if I am not mistaken.”

“Yes, ma’am,” Hulk nodded, “but that’s not the mission. It would be a bonus if we can get Blake back too, but the mission is to secure the devices.”

“Yes, I understand that and I believe you have the best intentions, but Jerry is right about one thing. The devices are an immediate, clear and present to the United States. If they fail, I will have no choice but to order an attack.”

“I understand ma’am, but give them time. They will get word to us somehow.”

An aide stormed into the room and pressed some buttons on the small black computer terminal in front of the President.

“Ma’am, you need to see this,” the aide said.

The screen changed to footage rolling in from one of the aircraft they had patrolling near the last known location of the submarine. A long smoke trail was arching across the sky. It had come from the ocean and was screaming across the blue sky.

“Is that what I think it is?” Torres asked not taking her eyes off the screen.

“Yes, ma’am,” the aide said. “It’s a Tomahawk missile. Fired from the Pittsburgh.”

“Target?”

“Still to be determined.”

“Jerry?”

"It is heading south west," the Chairman said holding a phone to his ear to get a live report. "Could be Atlanta or Miami."

"It's not coming for Washington?"

"No, ma'am, but they can change course," the Chairman said turning to the screen.

As if on cue, the missile arced in the sky, slightly changed course, racing away at an incredible speed.

"What is happening?" Torres asked.

"It has locked onto a target," the Chairman said. "Oh God."

"What is going to hit?"

The Chairman did not answer, the screen did the talking. The missile sliced into the cockpit of one of the P-8A Poseidons and detonated.

The shockwave rang out across the sky as a fireball raced up and away from the plane. The big jet fell from the air in chunks, engulfed in flames as a massive black plume of smoke extended up into the air as the aviation gas and the fuselage burned.

The camera footage rocked as the shockwave hit the plane, then the signal was lost.

"What happened?" Torres asked. "Was that a nuclear missile?"

"Yes, ma'am," the Chairman replied still with the phone to his ear listening to updates from the Pentagon. "It was a Tomahawk, but I don't think we are dealing with a nuclear denotation."

"How can you be sure?"

"The explosion was different. We did not see the normal mushroom type cloud we would expect to see."

"I want to be sure."

"The other planes are still in the sky. It was not a nuclear detonation. A nuke would have sent out an electro-magnetic pulse which would have shutdown their electronics. They would have all crashed, ma'am."

"I want a status report."

"Madam President, this is Commander Victor Cruise of the USS Harry S. Truman," Cruise said over the speakers.

"Go ahead, Commander. This is the President."

"Ma'am, a Tomahawk missile was fired from the Pittsburgh. It took out the RAAF Poseidon which was supporting our operation."

"Yes, Commander. I just witnessed it from one of our planes. What is happening there?"

"Ma'am, we are getting readings from the Tritons and the AWAC we have on site."

"Readings of what?"

"Nuclear material, ma'am."

"I thought it wasn't a nuclear detonation?"

"It was not a nuclear explosion, ma'am, but the readings may indicate a leak in the housing unit which holds the nuclear material. If that is the case, our planes and this carrier group are flying above and sailing into radioactive waters."

"Hold the line, Commander," Torres said muting the call. "Jerry?"

"An explosion that size, could have broken the core. Even if it wasn't an atomic explosion, some of the material could have leaked out."

"Advice?"

"Evacuate the area until we can be certain."

"And the sub?"

"There is significant risk to our troops. We need to hand surveillance over to the CIA using their new satellite and hope it can keep track of it."

"You don't think we should sink it?"

"Oh yes, ma'am. I do. But we should use the UAVs. They can get closer."

"But?"

"But they are not equipped with the right weapons. They need to be fitted with torpedoes."

"Alternatives?"

"Send a couple of the planes over to drop their weapons, but this time we let them hit the boat instead of exploding outside it like last time. But we run the serious risk of exposure. If the material is in the air our troops could be on a suicide mission."

"And the carrier group."

"Same advice, ma'am, move them out of the area until we know for sure. The planes are currently holding a safe distance away, but the carrier group needs to turn around now if that is your order. It takes awhile for them to change course."

Torres sat thinking about her options with the Chairman staring at her, willing her to make a decision.

"I don't have any choice," Torres said unmuting the line. "Commander, turn the fleet around. Get orders to our planes and helicopters to keep clear. The UAVs need to be fitted with torpedoes."

"Yes ma'am," Cruise said acknowledging his orders. *"We will fit the torpedoes on the UAVs as soon as they can land on deck."*

"As soon as they are fitted, you are to launch them again and they are to sink that submarine. Am I understood?"

"Yes, ma'am, it is a go on taking out the Pittsburgh."

"Thank you, Commander. Keep me posted."

"Yes, ma'am."

Chapter Forty

Max had killed several of the Pittsburgh's new crew and had made his way to the diesel engine room right at the bottom of the sub. One of Flash's men was swearing at the part of the engine he was working on. Max could not see which bit it was, not that he probably would have known what he was looking at anyway.

He took cover behind the solid metal engine as two more men came into the room.

"The boss wants to know why we are not moving yet," one of the men said. "He says I am to put a bullet in your head if it is not running in ten minutes."

"I am working on it, Bob," the original man replied. "This is a forty-year-old submarine and this is the back up engine. It has probably only run once year, if that, since it was built. And, it was being decommissioned. We will be lucky if it even kicks over."

"You will be a dead man if it does not work."

"I do not need the threats. I need someone in the manoeuvring room to start it. I cannot reach anyone. Maybe instead of being an arsehole, you can go and check who is up there and ask them to fire it up."

Bob nodded his head at his partner in crime, who jogged towards Max, heading for the ladder up to the room where Max and Kate had entered the old boat. Max knew no one was responding up there because Kate had killed them, but he did not want this guy to get up there and turn on the engine. Like Kate, he knew that they would be an easier target if they were immobilised. She had made the call and it had been the right one. If they failed, at least the military teams would have something to aim at.

Now he just hoped his team could finish the mission before Torres gave the order.

The crewmember ran past him. Max waited until the last possible moment, then threw his hunting knife as hard as he could. It spun end over end through the air, covering the short distance in no time at all. It speared into the fleeing guy's neck, right where it joined the base of his skull. The momentum threw him forward and he hit the floor hard, and slid forward coming to rest beside the ladder.

Max did not need to check, he knew the guy was dead.

"Mick?" Bob yelled out after him. "What the fuck was that? Did your dumb arse fall over? Mick!"

There was obviously no response. Max listened as Bob's footsteps got closer.

"Mick, you better be seriously hurt or dead, otherwise I am going to shove my boot right up your arse," Bob yelled in an agitated tone as he past Max.

"He is dead," Max stated calmly grabbing Bob by the neck from behind.

Bob jumped in fright, but Max had hold of him tightly.

"Where is Flash?" Max asked.

"Missile room," Bob replied nervously.

"And Blake?"

"He's there too, plus some huge angry bitch."

"Fuck," Max said under his breath knowing they had Kate too.

"You better hurry though, your friend Blake is bleeding pretty badly," Bob laughed.

Max did not bother to reply, instead he twisted Bob's neck with such force and speed it looked like it might come completely off his shoulders. There was a sickening crack as his neck broke. Max let his lifeless body fall to the floor before turning to face the man he had seen when he first came into the room.

"Please don't kill me," the mechanic said. "I don't want anything to do with these people."

"You stole a nuclear submarine and killed hundreds of people," Max said. "I don't believe you."

"I didn't sign off on this shit and I didn't sign up to killing all those people either. I joined to try to change the country. Go to a few rallies and marches to stop the government fucking interfering with our lives. But, I got in too deep and before I knew it I was swept up in all this and I'm sorry. I am so, so sorry. I couldn't get out. They would have killed me and my family."

"Let's say I believe you, for now. How do you know how to operate the engines?"

"I was in the Navy for fifteen years. We did some crazy shit, shit I didn't sign up for."

"Didn't sign up for this. Didn't sign up for that. Anything you do that you believe in?"

"I believed in the Navy until we were sent to rain bombs down on Baghdad and Afghanistan for oil. That's when I made the decision to get out."

"I understand your objections to some of the missions you may have needed to complete, but this is the opposite of that. Your crew rained down that Erebus shit on Seattle and wiped out a massive chunk of the city. Could be thousands dead."

"What?" he asked genuinely shocked.

"They used the chemical weapon they stole from the US Department of Defense on American citizens and your new commander set one of the cannisters off in the White House. He tried to kill the President. Doesn't sound very patriotic to me."

"He said we were only going to threaten them."

"You are an idiot if you believed that."

"That's fair," he said nodding with his head down and staring at the floor. "I was misled. How can I make it up to you?"

"I need to get to the missile room, stop the Erebus or nukes being released, and rescue my friends. You can start by showing me how to get there."

"Done," he said dropping his wrench and heading for the exit.

"Just a second," Max said running from the room to retrieve his knife.

He wiped the blood on Mike's shirt and holstered it, then ran back into the diesel engine room.

"Let's move," Max ordered as he followed the man from the room. "What's your name?"

"Sean," the supposedly reformed freedom fighter replied.

"I'm Max. I want you to know something Sean."

"What's that?"

"If I find out your lying to me, leading me into a trap or if you try to turn on me, I will kill you. Even if your whole crew unloads every bullet they have into my body, before I hit the floor and leave this world, I will kill you."

"Understood," Sean said fearfully ducking through one of the doors leading into the next room.

Each doorway was cut from the metal walls with a foot rise and fall from the floor and roof, respectively. It made it awkward for Max's large frame, let alone the low roof throughout the sub, which was ridiculous. Max was trying his best to forget about the claustrophobic feelings he was having and the horrifying thought of the impending missiles Torres was likely to send his way sooner rather than later. He had been in a lot of bad situations and had faced many difficult times where he thought he was done for, but the thought of drowning in the sinking submarine, really was not sitting well with him.

Imagining Blake drowning was devastating.

Max pushed aside those thoughts and followed Sean into the torpedo room.

Max grabbed Sean and ran forward holding his head down trying to keep him behind cover as bullet slammed into the metal surfaces all around them. As they got closer to the cover of the torpedo tubes the two men leapt forward and rolled, keeping low, as bullet pinged off the tubes.

Max snuck a quick look over the tubes. There were four guys all aiming their weapons at him. They had been loading torpedoes, but spotted Sean with Max in tow and had opened fire.

There was a ladder leading up to the next deck on the far side or the torpedo room.

"Where's that ladder go?" Max asked crouching behind the tubes next to Sean.

"Up to the missile room," Sean replied.

"Fuck," Max said firing blindly over the tube.

"What?"

"They would have heard the shots. They know we are here."

"Oh, fuck."

"Yep."

Max knelt and quickly ducked up to fire. He shot one of the men in the chest and he dropped his gun and clutched at his breast trying to stop the blood pouring from the wound. Max dropped back down as more bullets hit the tube.

"I need you to do something for me," Max said. "But I need to know I can trust you."

"You can. I swear on the lives of my children. I do not want this country attacked. I want to help you stop them."

"Good. Torres is going to sink this boat if I can't get a message to her that we are getting things under control."

"I cannot get to the control room from here."

"I know, that would be suicide. I'm not asking for you to do that."

"So, how can I get a message to the President?"

"I need you to get us back to the surface and I want you to permanently disable the ship's engines."

"I can do that."

"Good. I'm going to provide you cover, so you can get back to the door. When I say run, you will need to move."

"Alright."

"You will need to move fast."

"I will."

"Do you remember what I said about killing you earlier?"

"Yes."

"Good. Ready?"

"As ready as I can be."

"Three, two, one. Run!"

Max jumped up and started firing at the three remaining men in the room, drawing their fire. Two dived behind cover as the third spotted Sean. Max fired three bullets into him before he could get a shot off. He took cover again, as Sean ducked through the door, and waited for an opening.

In the room above, Flash had been congratulating himself with a long-winded speech about the genius of putting some of the radioactive water from the reactor into the Tomahawk. It was enough to set off the sensors in the planes nearby, but not enough to actually seriously spread any radiation. The fleet would be recalled and planes removed from the area, to protect the troops, giving them enough time to disappear.

Gunfire rang out on the deck beneath them. Flash grabbed Blake and used him as a human-shield.

"Lock it down," Flash ordered pointing at Kate. "You two, get her. Control room now."

"Yes, sir," the two men said pulling Kate up to her feet.

Flash dragged Blake for the door. Kate got to her feet and checked out both the men who had been ordered to escort her. She was easily half a foot taller than both of them. The guy on her left had his Steyr loosely in his right hand. It hung around his neck carelessly, without control. Kate dived for the rifle grabbing it, while at the same time kicking the guy on her right under the ribs. He fell into the wall hard as Kate spun the rifle towards Flash and opened fire. She pulled her shots to avoid hitting Blake, but she wanted Flash out of the room.

A couple of the other crew scattered when the shots rang out. The guy who's Steyr she was borrowing was trying to fight her off, but she was too strong. He had no choice but to be dragged around by the gun strap around his neck. She pulled the gun right and traced a line of bullets down her former guard who was struggling to get to his feet. She turned back to face her other guard. He was falling forward from her strength pulling down on the gun strap. His hands were trying to free himself from his makeshift leash, but Kate had a tight hold on it.

She pulled hard on the gun and the strap pulled him by the back of the head towards her. While he was falling forward, she violently reversed direction and crashed the rifle into his nose. She repeated the move three times, with volatile force, before his face exploded in blood.

He fell to his knees and she punched him as hard as she could right on the nose, then she drew her silenced pistol from his pants and shot him in the face with it. She yanked the strap loose as he fell.

Kate holstered her pistol and ran over to the hatch leading down into the torpedo room.

She laid on the ground and put her new rifle through the gap. She sighted one of Flash's men and not a second later his head exploded, spraying the nearby torpedo with his blood and brain. As he fell, Max ducked up from behind cover and dropped the final man in the room.

"Where the fuck you been?" Kate yelled down to him.

"Sorry, I had a few people that needed to be dead," Max said running for the ladder.

"Well, get your arse up here. We've got a couple of problems."

"Got it," Max said turning back to the door he had used earlier as two more men ran in.

They started firing at him, so Kate fired at them. They dived for cover as Max sprinted for the ladder. He climbed as fast as he could as the occasional, blindly fired, bullet pinged somewhere nearby.

As he got towards the top, Kate had to pull away to let him in. He dropped his pistol wielding hand to his waist and fired in his pursuers' direction, as he dragged himself up the last rungs, trying to force them to stay in cover.

Bullets clanged on the ladder as he pulled his feet through the hatch. Kate slammed the lid closed behind him.

"Where are we?" Max asked.

"They are losing numbers fast," Kate said. "Blake took down a few, I took down a few and you said you've shuffled a couple off the mortal coil."

"Good. Where is Blake?"

"With Flash."

"You spoke to him?"

"Yeah, found him downstairs and patched him up."

"Is he okay?"

"He is for now. Couple of broken bits and a bullet in the arm, but he's a tough prick. He will be fine."

"Next steps?"

"Got to be this," Kate said handing him her backpack.

"Really?"

"He launched one already. Full of radioactive water. It took down one of the Poseidons. Enough water to trick the sensors. The fleet would have pulled back and the planes too. Which may have bought us a little while longer."

"Probably not much though. Taking down one of the planes would be a signal we failed. Torres would have made the call."

"Probably."

"Okay, let's do this, in case he launches another one. Then we can go get Blake."

"Roger that."

Max took half of the contents from the bag and headed down the first row of Tomahawks as Kate headed down her row. There was a guy on the ladder at the far end of the row. He had been working to replace the nuclear material with Project Erebus and was coming down the ladder empty handed. Max fired two bullets into him and he fell the remaining distance to a hard slap on the steel floor.

Max used the ladder to climb up and fit one of the devices on the Tomahawk. He tagged the device and a set it as M1, then climbed down and dragged the ladder over to the next launch tube. He climbed up and he initially struggled with the latch on the tube. It was jammed tight, so he pulled out his pistol and used the butt of the handle as a hammer, and whacked it over and over until it gave a little. He holstered the weapon and used both hands to pry open the handle using a knee on the tube for more leverage.

He finally pulled the cover and fitted another device, tagging it M2.

After fitting the hatch back into position, he climbed down the ladder and the loudspeakers squeaked to life.

"You have been busy, Max," Flash said. *"A lot of my guys are unresponsive. I can only assume it's because you got to them and took them out, which is disappointing. I feel I'm going to be outnumbered soon, so maybe I will have to rebalance the ledger."*

Panic gripped Max as he realised what Flash was saying. He was going to kill Blake.

"I am going to give you four minutes to make your way to the control room," Flash explained. *"If you are not here by then, I am going to shoot Blake in the head and that will be two you have lost, Max. I have to say, you aren't a very good boyfriend."*

Max was mixed with emotions. Anger, fear, dread, hate, love. He checked his watch then dragged the ladder to the third tube. He fitted the third device, replaced the panel as Kate arrived having fitted hers.

"Go," she said to him. "I'll do the last two."

"Thank you," Max said marking the device M3. "M3 set."

"K1 to K6 fitted and synced. Ack M1 to M3."

Max climbed down the ladder.

"Go get that son-of-a-bitch," Kate said as Max passed her the remaining devices.

"Will do," Max said starting for the door. "When the opportunity presents itself get topside and get away."

"I won't leave you behind."

"This time it is an order, Kate, get yourself clear and watch for signals," Max ordered stopping and pointing to the launch tubes. "It's too important."

"Ack," Kate acknowledged with a frustrated nod.

"Thank you, Kate."

"Go get our boy back."

"That's the plan," Max said turning back for the door.

The loudspeaker crackled overhead.

"Max, I'm not sure you are taking me seriously," Flash mocked. *"Maybe I should cut something off him. Any suggestions?"*

"Don't do it, Max!" Blake yelled. *"It's a trap. Finish the mission."*

A gunshot rang out throughout the submarine over the tinny speakers. Max and Kate both froze in place, and time seemed to stand still. Horror and grief was all Max could feel.

"Oh well, you still had sometime left," Flash said a few seconds later as the speakers kicked back in, *"but whatever. You know where I am if you want to chat about dead boyfriends like days gone by."*

The speaker system cut out.

Max was nauseous. He gripped his pistol so tight he felt like he could almost crush it in his hand. Kate climbed down from the fourth launch tube and stood watching Max, feeling his pain. She was sad for the loss of her friend. She had known Blake for years and they were very close, but she also could not help but take on Max's pain.

Max turned to face her, his defeat and tears turning to burning anger. Kate did not know what to do. She wanted to kill Flash herself and wrap her arms around Max. He had lost so much and she wasn't sure what this was going to do to him.

She wanted to comfort him, but she had one device left to plant.

"Finish the mission," Max said through gritted teeth, "plant the devices and stay here. Hide until the sub surfaces."

"Surfaces?" Kate asked.

"I've got an inside man. I'm hoping he will do what he promised. When it surfaces get topside and get as far away as you can get. By now Torres would have made the call. Keep watching and do what you need to do."

"What are you going to do?"

"I'm going to finally bury an old friend."

"Good luck and Godspeed."

Max just nodded and turned back to the door. Kate could not see his face, but if she could, she would have only seen pain and anger.

Max crouch walked with his gun raised through into the officers' area on the sub. It was clear.

He led with his weapon through into the bathrooms and saw the dead bodies Kate and Blake had left there earlier, and continued passed into the crew's quarters. The tiny bunks looked like they were only maybe five-foot-long and maybe a foot and a half to two foot high. They had seat belts for rough seas, but Max doubted he would need one if he even managed to get in the bunk, because his six foot three frame would probably get stuck.

He kept moving, but then out of one of the high bunks one of Flash's crew launched down onto his shoulders and wrapped his arms around his neck. Max could feel the pressure instantly and started running backwards, slamming the guy into the wall.

He was pretty sure on the first go he had broken a rib. Max grabbed the goon's hand and tried to pry it away from his neck. The hand would not budge, so he thought he would try one finger at a time. He grabbed the first index finger and ripped it back hard, snapping it. His attacker screamed in pain as Max ran him back into another wall. He grabbed another finger and snapped it as the guy on his back was trying to get his breath back from the impact.

He finally let go in absolute agony and dropped to the floor. Max turned around to face him and without a word, put two bullets in his head.

In the wardroom, the officers' mess, was a long ornate polished table and leather chairs. It was no doubt nicer than the crew's mess, given it was for the higher ranked men and women on the ship. Max ventured in leading with his pistol, constantly scanning and sweeping the area.

As he turned to leave, the door swung open and three assailants ran in. He fired and took down the first guy, dropping him a foot from the door, but the second was quick and he dived and tackled Max against the table.

Max fell back and his new aggressor pushed him back hard against the table until he had no choice but to roll up onto it. His attacker was up and on top of him as soon as his shoulders hit the tabletop. He unleashed on Max with a flurry of punches, sitting on his stomach to pin him down. Max did what he could to block the blows, while the second attacker used a comms unit.

"We have him, sir," he said from the doorway. "Wardroom. Roger that."

Max struggled out from under his attacker and wrestled him onto his back, reversing their roles. Max unleashed his own series of violent blows, then he grabbed him by the sides of the face and repeatedly slammed his head into the table. Just when he looked set to pass out and the fight was leaving him, Max pulled out his hunting knife and with everything he had stabbed it down through his shoulder pinning him to the wooden table.

His pinned prey screamed in pain as his comrade took two massive steps into the room and levelled his gun at Max's forehead.

"That's quite enough," he said as Max turned his fiery gaze on his new quarry.

"Big man behind a pistol," Max taunted. "Put it down and let's see if you've got what it takes."

"I am not that stupid," he said raising an eyebrow unimpressed by his wounded colleague. "I was with MI6, I know who you are, Prince, and I know what you have done, but more importantly, I know what you are capable of. I think I will keep this pistol between us until he arrives."

"Flash?"

"Who else?"

"I've killed a couple of poms over the years, I now look forward to adding another one to my list."

"I am not an unarmed aristocrat. I am a trained spy. I will not go quite so easily."

"We'll see," Max said climbing down off the table using his knife to balance himself while twisting it slightly in the guy's shoulder and causing him to cry out in pain.

"Easy, stay where you are."

"So, what's the plan MI6? Where does this end?" Max asked flicking his knife to cause more pain as it wobbled from side to side in the wound.

"You can stop touching that knife to start with and move towards the back of the room with your hands over your head."

"Sure thing," Max smiled stepping back as the guy with the gun held his aim and walked forward.

When he got to his wounded colleague, he stopped and pulled the knife out giving his comrade a stern look which seemed to indicate displeasure, no doubt in his performance and getting himself stabbed. It was the precious moment Max had been hoping for.

An officers' mess was always adorned with relics and souvenirs, and a naval wardroom was no different. Max's alert mind always scanned and recorded a room, normally for exits and threats, but also for weapons. In this particular room, there was a proud glass display cabinet featuring a number of gold and silver relics. Cradled in the centre was a World War II

Japanese katana which had been taken from the captain of a surrendering Japanese ship.

Max elbowed the glass, shattering it, gripped the handle and swung it free of its brackets and brought it down on his captor's wrist removing his hand and his gun. The MI6 man stood for a moment in shock trying to comprehend what had happened, until pain and fear took hold of him as blood started pumping out of the wound. He looked up as Max took a step forward and drove the sword right through his chest. His new victim fell to the floor on his back with the sword still lodged in his chest.

The guy from the table scrambled off trying to get away from Max. He was clutching his shoulder, but let go to try one last chance haymaker. Max dodged the incoming blow and caught the guy by the back of the head and slammed his face into the big table, right next to the bloody hole his knife had left on its surface.

The wounded and semi-conscious attacker fell to the floor as Max gathered his knife and pistol. As he turned back, the wounded terrorist was trying to get to his feet. He had made it to his knees and was on all fours. Max stepped forward, put his thick rubber boot to his skin and drove his exposed neck onto the samurai styled sword which was still sitting upright. It instantly cut his neck and he started to squirm and moan in pain as the blade started to lower under his weight while slicing further around towards the front of his neck, then Max stomped hard on the back of his neck and blade cut deep, severing his windpipe and lodging in his spine. He kicked and fidgeted for a few seconds then laid still as his blood pumped out over his MI6 comrade and down onto the floor.

Max left the wardroom as Flash and a couple of his men entered the hallway near the bathrooms. The two former friends starred at each other for a moment, then Flash raised his pistol and started firing at Max.

Max turned and ran right through the storage room and into the crew's mess. He was right, it was no where near as nice as the ornate wardroom. It had long metal rows of tables and benches bolted to the floor, and an open window into the kitchen.

Two of Flash's men were in the mess waiting for him. They fired at him and he darted off to his right and dived over the bench into the kitchen. As bullets pelted the benches.

He shot blindly over the bench to hold the men off, but he knew he could only wait for a short period, before Flash and the other men joined in. He was pinned down and they would capture him soon enough.

He was hoping Kate had found a safe place to hide. It would be up to her to save the day and Max smiled knowing she was more than capable of doing so and wrecking Flash's plans.

Max could hear the men in the mess getting closer, so he fired again, then unexpectedly an alarm sounded and red lights flared throughout. Max did not let it distract him, instead he used it to his advantage. As the two crew in the mess looked around trying to figure out what was happening, Max leapt back over into the dining hall and shot them both, head and chest.

Max looked around for an escape point and found the hidden hatch in the wall which Blake had used earlier. He jumped through the gap as bullets slammed into the walls and flew over his head and pinged off the structural beams in the void.

Max landed hard on one of the beams just below the wall out of Flash's line of sight. His arms and legs were hanging either side of it, as the big sub rapidly shot up through the water. Sean had come through with the goods and it was surfacing fast. The g-forces held Max tightly on the beam, but he knew he could not stay there. He was a sitting duck.

He struggled off the side of the beam and dropped down to the next one. He hit even harder as the sub rushed for the surface – its ballast tanks filling rapidly with air.

Gunshots rang out above him as Flash arrived at the hatch. Max rolled off the beam as bullets slammed into it and he fell to the bottom of the sub as it breached the surface and floated in place. He hit with a thud and his body throbbed and his head ached, but he did not wait around. He struggled to his feet and ran for the diesel engine room and out of the line of fire.

"I will find you, Max!" Flash yelled, his voice booming and echoing off the walls. "You can't hide forever."

Max did not stop.

He ran through the engine room and found himself at the battery storage compartment. He stopped dead in his tracks as he saw the control panel. He started checking for labels. Some of them had worn with age, but he found the one he was looking for and pressed it.

Lights went off throughout the sub as he shut off the electricity.

Chapter Forty-One

"What do you mean you can't fucking fix it?" Flash screamed at Pierre in the control room having managed to find his way back in the dark.

"The electricity was cut at the source," Pierre said still limping in pain from the bullet lodged in his leg. "Someone must have turned it off in the battery compartment."

"Well, you need to get down there and fix it."

"I can hardly walk."

Flash huffed in anger. He pulled a small backup comms unit from his pocket and spoke into it.

"Can anyone read me?" Flash asked.

"Yes, sir," one of his men replied. *"What is happening up there?"*

"Nothing at the moment and that's the point. Someone turned off the electricity in the battery compartment room. I need you to get there and turn it back on."

"I can do that. I'm not far from the room. It will be hard to see without the lights though."

"Just get it done. We are sitting ducks here."

"Yes, sir."

Max had found one of the comms units on one of the dead terrorists as he made his way through the dark and eery submarine using the dull red emergency lighting as a guide. It was enough light to make out shapes, but not much more.

He found his way back to the torpedo room and headed up the ladder towards the missile maintenance room. He gently opened the hatch and climbed up into the missile room.

"Kate," Max whispered and listened for a response as he softly walked between the silos. "Alpha, you here?"

There was no reply, so he walked down the row into the pitch-black darkness.

"Kate, Alpha," he whispered again, but there was no reply.

Max turned back towards the main part of the missile room when he heard footsteps. He waited in the darkness, then saw a flashlight. One of the guards was sweeping the sub looking for him. He tucked in between two of the missiles as the light shone down the row and the footsteps started to get closer.

He watched the beam of light searching and bouncing with every step. When the source of the light made it to him, he took a quick breath. The torch's beam hit him and lit up his face.

"Hi," Max said frightening his would-be attacker.

The guy with the torch jumped and instinctively stepped back as he saw Max emerge from the shadows. Max did not waste the opportunity. He sprung out of the gap between the missiles and grabbed both of the terrorist's wrists. He pulled both arms to the side, digging his fingers into the pressure points on his gun wielding hand, twisting the wrist as he did. The guy dropped his gun, so Max focused his attention on the other hand which was brandishing a foot-long Maglite. Max clutched the big metal torch and threw it hard at the guy's face. He struggled against the blow, but Max was too strong. He staggered back slightly, but Max was relentless. He flung the flashlight forward twice in quick succession splitting the man's head open. Blood started pouring from the short cut down into his eyes. He was still struggling, but another blow from the hard metal light put him on the ground. Max then belted him four more times, until he was sure he was not getting up.

He got to his feet and headed back down the row and across the space for the sonar room. He used his new Maglite to light the way.

He softly opened the door and checked inside. It was clear, other than a couple of bodies laying on the floor. Max's breath caught in his throat when he saw one of the bodies had on black tuxedo pants and blood-stained white shirt.

It was Blake.

Max froze in fear, but then he saw Blake was strapped to the solid rods holding the chairs in place in front of the equipment. He would not need to be tied up if he was dead.

Max shuffled forward quickly and quietly, and knelt down in front of Blake. He turned off the Maglite, given he was so close to the control room where he guessed Flash would be. He didn't want to warn him.

Max put his hand gently over Blake's mouth and whispered his name in his ear, shaking him gently. Blake woke, frightened in the dark, until he saw Max's eyes in the soft red emergency lighting. His eyes welled with tears of joy and relief.

"Hey Mister," Max whispered putting his hand on Blake's cheek. "Ready to get out of here."

"Absolutely," Blake said softly. "Thank you."

"Don't thank me yet," Max said using his knife to cut the straps holding Blake's arms. "We aren't done yet."

"Let's finish this."

"You got it," Max smiled helping Blake to his feet.

"What's the plan?" Blake asked as the lights came on throughout the sub and the pair blinked getting their eyes to adjust.

"You are going to take this and shoot anyone who's not me or Kate," Max whispered passing Blake a Steyr he had taken from one of the guards. "Where is Kate?"

"Hopefully long gone."

"Good."

"Let's move," Max said sneaking into position near the door to the control centre.

Pierre was on his feet in front of a small radar screen which was flashing and beeping.

"What now?" Flash asked in frustration.

"There is a small plane, possibly one of the UAVs coming in and out of the radar," Pierre explained. "Couple of minutes out at the most."

"Fuck! We need to get back under the water."

"We cannot submerge. We do not have enough men left to crew the boat."

"Fucking Prince! I am going to kill him. Call in our back up."

"I have already made the call. That's it there."

Pierre pointed to another blip on the radar which was much closer and closing in on their position.

"Good," Flash said. "That's something at least. And, the missiles?"

"Ready to go," Pierre said. "Programmed for the cities we discussed."

"Excellent. Let's have some fun while we wait. Fire the first missile. Washington DC."

"Are you sure? They are already loaded and locked on."

"Yes. I would love to know it was in the air as we leave heading for that bitch Torres. Speaking off, you also need to take out that UAV."

"Understood," Pierre agreed moving to the weapons system.

He pressed a few buttons, but then Max and Blake burst in aiming their guns at the pair.

"Stop what you are doing," Max ordered staring down Pierre who looked to Flash then to his console. "Don't even think about it."

Pierre dropped his hand hard onto the terminal as Max fired four bullets into him. He fell to the floor, smiling as blood poured from his mouth. The terminal started counting down. Each missile tube was highlighted on the computer screen and was flashing with its own coordinates.

A small warning alarm sounded and the Washington bound missile launched from the sub.

"What have you done?" Max asked turning his aim to Flash.

"I just sent Torres a little present," Flash smiled. "Got to take out the leader of the free world if you want to free it and how good is it that it will be Erebus that wipes her out? It really is a perfect symbol. An ancient God from a fallen empire spreads its plague over the city and wipes out a modern empire which thinks they are Gods."

The radar picked up the retrofitted missile as it locked onto its target and sped across the sky.

"Erebus the personification of darkness," Flash said. "Can you imagine the horror this weapon was built to inflict on the enemies of America? It is insidious. Max, we didn't sign up to help people like them build weapons like this. It is repugnant and horrifying. They need to be stopped. They have lost their way. And, now their man-made plague of darkness is going to wipe them out, leaving those who remain to rebuild a society which can be thankful for their trials, but weary of returning to their greed and warmongering ways. No longer will they seek to rule the world, but instead be thankful for what they have."

The radar and weapons control systems where beeping tracking the missile, but then they stopped as it disappeared from the radar. Flash's smile vanished unsure of what happened. Max on the other hand smiled broadly for two reasons. The first was that he now knew Kate was alive and he was thankful for that. The second was that Kate had used one of the devices she and Max had planted on the missiles to blow it out of the sky.

"You've lost, Flash," Max said. "Get on your knees."

"I don't think so," Flash smiled looking over Max's shoulder.

Max spun around as three of Flash's men arrived at the door.

Max launched himself at Blake, dragging him down into cover behind one of the weapons panels. Flash checked the radar while Max and Blake were pinned down. Max saw him smile as he found whatever he was looking for on the radar, then he launched two torpedoes, before fleeing through the opposite door.

"He fired torpedoes!" Blake shouted over the gunfire. "We need to stop them. Cover me."

Max did not argue. He started firing wildly over the panel, forcing the three men back out of the room. Max stood and fired whenever one of them tried to enter as Blake ran to the weapons control system.

"One of the torpedoes is heading for a small object not far from here," Blake said typing franticly trying to abort the various weapons. "What could that be?"

"Kate!" Max shouted in panic. "I ordered her out to watch for missiles. She blew the last one up."

"Jesus!" Blake said typing on the small keyboard. "Please let this work."

He slammed his hand down on the mushroom button to his right.

The torpedo was still on course. Closer and closer it drove through the rough ocean towards Kate's life-raft.

Kate had managed to find her way through the dark sub to one of the rear hatches leading topside, while Max had been fighting his way through the mess and wardroom. She had found an emergency life-raft and, when the sub surfaced, she had paddled it as far away as she could, before she heard the missile burst out into the air from the bow of the sub. She had turned to see the Tomahawk trailing smoke, so she rifled through her hard cover backpack and found her tablet.

Kate unlocked the little computer with her fingerprint and opened one of the AIS apps. It filled the screen with eleven boxes, one of which was flashing *M1*, showing the missile which was in the air.

Kate tapped the box and a small pop up button appeared. *Proceed?* it asked. She pressed the button and the small device Max had placed on the missile exploded, blasting the navigation and targeting system from the missile.

Kate watched as the missile shutdown its engines, before it fell from the sky and splashed down in the ocean. She smiled. *Fuck you, Flash,* she thought to herself.

But, her joy was short lived as she saw a trail of bubbles rapidly shot out from under the sub.

Kate watched as the torpedoes trailed off through the water before they both started wide-arching loops. The first was only making very small arches, but the second was turning hard.

Within seconds, the second torpedo was racing towards her. She waited until the last possible moment then leapt into the water trying to hold the tablet out of the salty ocean.

The torpedo ran out of steam less than a metre from the raft and Kate saw it fall away into the dark abyss. It looked like it just stopped dead. Someone must have aborted it.

She breathed a sigh of relief, then climbed back into the raft and checked the tablet. It was blinking on and off. *Fucking piece of shit,* she thought to herself shaking it.

The screen went black.

"Fuck," she said to herself looking back to the sub as a helicopter came in low over the ocean.

Back inside the sub, Max had taken down one of the men in the doorway and was impatiently waiting to line up the others.

"You need to get out of here, Max," Blake said working on the weapons system. "I've got one of the missiles deactivated, but we've got a bunch more to do."

"What else aren't you telling me?" Max asked firing a round into the door to keep the men out.

"The second torpedo."

"Yeah."

"It's looping around and coming back for us."

"Can you disable it?"

"I'm trying, but it looks like its out of range. I'll have to wait until it gets back closer to us."

"Excellent," Max said sarcastically.

"You need to get out of here, in case I can't stop it in time."

"Fuck that. I'm not leaving you, Blake."

"I know, but Flash is going to get away."

"What?"

"There's a helicopter coming in from our south."

As Blake tapped at the controls, one of the other missiles launched.

"Oh shit," Blake said over the warning alarm.

"Where's it headed?" Max asked.

"It looks like it's locked onto the UAV," Blake started trying to disarm it.

"Kate will get it. You work on the others."

"Got it."

Blake went back to the torpedo with no luck, it was still out of range and rushing back fast.

"We've got a problem," Blake said as Max fired a round into the shoulder of one of the men at the door making him screech and scramble back to cover.

"What?" Max asked.

"The Tomahawk isn't stopping," Blake said tapping the screen as the big missile slammed into the UAV taking it down. "Kate must be compromised."

"The tablet could have been damaged."

"Yeah. I need to stop these from launching."

Max held his fire.

"Get down," he ordered as the two men burst through the door thinking he had run out of ammo.

Blake hit the ground and curled in behind the control panel for cover. The two terrorists ran in and unloaded their weapons into the various panels and control systems. Max ducked out at waist height from cover and fired three shot. The first two hit one of the guys head and chest. The third bullet hit the wall where the last guy had been standing. He had spun and taken cover against a table, with his back to Max.

Max drew his knife and leapt over the table with both arms out like superman. He clasped them tightly around the knife and, as he hit the terminal, drove it down into the top of the guy's head.

"Go, Max," Blake said getting to his feet. "I've got this. Go stop Flash. He's got more Erebus and he plans to use it. We can't let him get away."

Max jogged over to Blake and reloaded his pistol.

"I thought I lost you earlier," Max said. "I can't lose you, Blake."

"I'm not going anywhere, Max. I will be right here when you get back."

"Watch the doors. Watch your back."

"I will. Be careful."

"Always," Max lied with a smile. "See you soon."

"Go get him," Blake replied returning the smile and nodding for the door.

Max ran for the ladder and with one last look at Blake, climbed out of the sub. As he climbed out, he took in his surroundings. The wild ocean was lapping at the edges of the sleek black metal monster. It was pitching and swaying in the rolling swell. He was halfway down the big boat, just behind the sail. He looked down the long vessel's length to the propeller.

All clear.

As he spun to check the front, Flash swung his empty Steyr into the side of Max's head like baseball bat.

Max fell to the deck, clutching his head. He had been knocked out several times in the last couple of days and the blow to the head shook him up. His vision blurred and felt nauseous again.

Flash stood over him, then started laying the boot into him. With each kick, Max could feel his weary body giving in. He felt his stitches split above his ribs where he had been sliced open at the warehouse. He was glad he was wearing his Clearance Driver's wetsuit. It was thin making it easy to move, but it was strong. It would hold the wound together to some small extent.

"You just don't stop, do you?" Flash screamed over the sound of the approaching helicopter. "You know I thought about finding you these last few years. They said you had snapped and killed a Prime Minister and a Member of the Royal Family. I was impressed. I thought about trying to convince you to join me. To take down these arseholes who wronged us both."

"And why didn't you?" Max asked getting to his hands and knees holding his head.

"Because Jane died!" Flash said kicking Max in the ribs breaking one which made Max wince in pain and move his hand to the rib instead of his head. "And I remembered it was fault!"

"I didn't have anything to do with her death."

"You may not have killed her, but you weren't there to support her. She supported you when Lachlan died. We both did. But when she needed a friend you weren't there!"

"The Sixteen killed her, Jacob. Her brakes were cut."

"Liar!" Flash screamed running forward to kick Max again, but Max rolled into the blow, catching his leg and pulled Flash off his feet.

"I have never lied to you, Flash," Max said. "And, I never will. Regardless of what you have done. They killed her to control you. To make you do this."

"Why would they do that?" Flash asked getting to her feet. "I was complying. I was happy to help them take down the system. A system which created that Erebus shit. A system of killers and liars. They had no reason to kill her."

"For the same reason as they killed Lachlan, Jacob. To change us. They thought I would stop when they killed him, but instead it gave me purpose. It gave me focus and strength. They wanted the same reaction from you, to drive your hate, to make sure you didn't have a change of heart. To help you go through with all of this. To motivate and drive you. The Flash I knew would have been right here beside me trying to stop a madman from releasing a chemical weapon on innocent people, not trying to launch it."

Flash thought about it for a moment as Max managed to get to his feet, still holding his ribs.

"Even if that was true," Flash postured, "I still want to tear this all down!"

Flash ran forward and the pair started trading punches. They had been evenly matched throughout their months of training at the Wool Shed and in the years of missions they run side-by-side.

Flash the southpaw, left-handed, mirrored Max the right-hander perfectly like a mirror image of the each other. As one threw a punch, the other ducked or dodged throwing a counter punch to the sternum or ribs.

Elbows and knees were used as weapons when they locked up in a standing wrestle and they jostled trading blows, trying to get the upper hand.

"You don't have to do this, Jacob," Max reasoned. "I know we wronged you. I shouldn't have left you. I should have been there for you. I should have found you and saved you from whatever horror they put you through. And, I should have been there for Jane."

Flash threw short hard jab into Max's broken rib, winding him, then slammed his forehead down on Max's nose. Max staggered back, his head aching and spinning as the helicopter arrived at the bow of the sub. The wind was swirling and whipping the water and salt spray in the air.

"Move! Move!" Flash yelled waving at the helicopter as two of the missile bays opened only feet from the bottom of the chopper.

The big chopper pulled away just in time for two missiles to rush out of their tubes into the air. They flew off high into the sky as the helicopter rotated and took a wide arc around the submarine's sail down to the stern.

When it arrived, out of nowhere, it was assaulted with a barrage of bullets.

Max looked around and saw Kate on her little yellow raft firing wildly at the chopper. Most of the bullets missed, but in her defence, she was on an inflatable raft bobbing on the ocean aiming for a fast-moving, flying target. She did well to hit it at all.

Flash pointed at her and the pilot turned the big bird to face her.

Kate fired a few more rounds, before a line of bullets ripped into the water tracing a line towards her. She dived out of the raft and into the water, as the bullets tore into the raft, ripping it to shreds.

Max used the distraction to sweep Flash's legs out from under him.

Max was dazed and down, but not out. He dragged himself across the shiny metal surface and crawled on top of Flash, then unloaded blow after blow into his former best friend. Flash blocked some of the punches, but Max landed a fair share. His anger and grief flowing through his fists as if any one of his punches might bring his friend back.

Flash's nose broke and his eyes were starting to blacken.

When he felt the fight subsiding in Flash and his own crushing guilt pouring through every inch of his body Max stopped and rolled off onto the deck and got to his feet.

The big chopper swung towards Max and opened fire.

Max ran for the coning tower and slid in behind it, sliding in the water, as bullet slammed into the deck and sea beside him. Max saw something moving through the rough seas heading towards the boat. It was the torpedo trailing its way back towards him.

This was it. Blake was going to die and so was he. He closed his eyes and waited for it to hit.

But, it didn't.

Max opened his eyes and saw the trail falling away towards the ocean floor. Blake had saved them. He was relived, but it meant he still had a job to do. He ducked his head out from behind the coning tower as the incoming fire stopped.

Max saw Flash running for the rope ladder the chopper had dropped. Max pulled his pistol and fired hitting Flash in the leg and arm. He collapsed to the deck as Max fired at the cockpit forcing the big chopper to pull away out of range.

Max marched down the length of the sub, firing at the helicopter's windscreen, forcing it back further, until he got to Flash, who rolled onto his back laughing from the pain.

"Are you going to kill me, Max?" Flash asked, grinning wildly. "Do you even have it in you to kill your best friend?"

"My friend died on that cold London street years ago," Max said. "I held him in my arms as his world went dark. I don't know what they did to him, but I know you aren't him."

"I remember ever mission and every word we ever shared!" Flash bellowed launching himself forward and stabbing his knife down into Max's thigh.

Max roared and stumbled back as Flash got to his feet.

Both men were wounded and bleeding, but neither would give up. They traded blows again, matching each other as they tried to bounce on their injured limbs.

Flash hit Max in the face and Max felt like he was going to pass out at any minute. He fell flat on the deck and his face hit to ice cold water.

Flash grabbed the ladder as the chopper came back in over the deck.

Max rolled to his side, ripped Flash's knife out of his leg and threw it with all his might. It flew through the air end-over-end, then pierced through Flash's chest. Lodging itself deep.

Flash coughed blood and fell off the ladder. He landed on his back on the hard, cold surface of the submarine. Small waves crashed over the sides and splashed across him.

"I'm sorry, Jacob," Max said sadly, a tear rolling down his cheek as blood poured from Flash's mouth and wound. "I sorry I failed you."

Flash closed his eyes and his head fell to the deck, and he laid perfectly still. Max remembered the day he thought Flash had died in his arms in London. Sadness washed over him, but it was not the same as it had been that day. The man Max knew and the man laying on the boat in front of him were two different people. His friend was long dead. The man he saw now was nothing of his former self.

Max turned and started walking back towards the hatch. He stopped and watched as the two missiles which had launched earlier stopped in their tracks far off in the distance. Their smoke trails extinguished and they fell into the ocean.

The other missile hatches closed and Max smiled. Blake had done it.

Max took a step forward heading for the ladder, but felt a sharp stabbing pain in his back. He blinked as the pain set in and he fell to knees. He reached around and felt the knife buried deep in his back.

He pulled it out and dropped it onto the deck, his blood ran from the knife into the salty water washing the pink, salt water around his knees.

Max fell to on his hands, then to his side as the big chopper moved in hovering over Flash. Flash was smiling at Max's pain and suffering.

"Pity I didn't get the chance to kill Blake!" Flash yelled over the sound of the chopper, spitting blood as he pointed at Max. "Looks like I'm the one who finally gets to rid the world of the little Prince though, so I'll die happy!"

The pilot swung the big helicopter around readying its guns to take him down.

"No, you'll just die," Max counted drawing his pistol and firing until his clip ran dry.

The bullets tore into the windshield of the helicopter and the pilot slumped forward on the controls. The helicopter dived forward, its blades whipping through the air towards Flash as he screamed more out of regret since he would not get to kill Max, than from the fear of death.

The blades sliced into Flash and broke apart as they slapped into the deck of the submarine, tearing them off one by one. The chopper fell forward and collided with the deck, collapsing in on itself, before spewing gas, then exploded and burst into flames and fell on what was left of Flash's body.

The burning pile of twisted metal sent smoke billowing into the air as Max said a final goodbye to his old friend.

Blake ran across the deck and fell to his knees taking Max in his arms.

"Are you okay?" Blake asked, the fear and worry furrowing his brow.

"I am now," Max smiled, trying to reassure Blake.

Blake used his sleeve to wipe the blood from Max's face, then he sat his warm, loving hand on the side of his face. It was the same warm embrace Max had remembered from all those years ago in the Wool Shed during Max's training. He did not know what was in front of him then, but he knew now.

"I love you, Blake," Max said. "I'm sorry I didn't get to say it sooner."

"I love you too, Max," Blake replied with a mix of joy and pain on his face. "You are going to be okay."

Max reached up and pulled Blake in and they kissed.

"Well, fuck what a show, what'd I miss?" Kate asked climbing onboard drenched from her swim. "Oh shit, did I wreck the moment?"

"Well, kind of," Max laughed clutching his ribs, "but I am glad you're okay."

"I'm fine, other than being soaked to the tits from being in the water for so long. Fuck this bullshit, can we go back to land now?"

"That sounds like a good plan to me," Max said smiling at Blake. "How about you?"

"Sounds good to me too," Blake smiled holding Max tightly.

"But, one of you are going to have to carry me," Max laughed.

Epilogue

"It is with the pride and thanks of a grateful nation that I present you with the Distinguished Intelligence Cross," Torres said to the crowd gathered inside the White House. "This is the highest honour we have for intelligence agents in the United States and it is my great honour to award them today. Agent Kate Matthews, please step forward."

Kate in her Army dress uniform walked briskly and precisely over and bowed so Torres could hang the medal around her neck. She shook the President's hand and nodded before marching back to her chair.

"Real Admiral Blake Smyth," Torres said, "please come over."

Blake in his full Navy dress uniform walked over and Torres hung a matching medal around his neck. He too shock the leader of the free world's hand and said thank you before returning to his seat beside Max.

"And, Agent Max Shaw," Torres said. "Can someone help him over?"

Blake jumped up and reached down to grab Max's forearm to help him up.

"It's okay, Blake," Max nodded and smiled squeezing Blake's hand. "I've got this."

"Seems I do have time for your bullshit after all," Torres joked as Max hobbled over and Torres hung the medal around Max's neck. "Thank you for everything you have done, Max."

"Thank you, ma'am. Your bullshit's not too bad for a politician, I guess."

Torres laughed as Max shook her hand, then made his way back to his seat.

"Prime Minister Ferguson," Torres said. "I believe you have some announcements."

"Yes, thank you, President Torres," Ferguson said from her own lectern. "General Patrick 'Hulk' Scott, please step forward."

Hulk was surprised, but walked over to the Australian Prime Minister using his cane.

"General," Ferguson continued, "I am not long off the phone with His Majesty the King and Governor-General. His Majesty has appointed you as a Companion of the Order of Australia – our nation's highest honour. It is a fitting way to honour your lifelong service to our country and to wish you well as you move into semi-retirement."

The crowd applauded as Ferguson hung the large gold medal from his neck. Max and Blake exchanged looks, surprised by the announcement.

"Rear Admiral Smyth, will you join us again?" Ferguson asked.

Blake looked confused, but Max encouraged him to get to his feet and he walked over to stand beside Hulk.

"Admiral Smyth, His Excellency the Governor-General on behalf of His Majesty the King, has promoted you to Vice Admiral of the Royal Australian Navy," Ferguson said as Hulk removed Blake's epaulettes and replaced them with his new rank. "And, you have been commissioned as the new Head of the Australian Intelligence Service."

Blake looked genuinely shocked as the crowd applauded. Max smiled and clapped proudly.

"Agent Shaw will join you as Deputy Head of the AIS and Head of Field Operations," Ferguson said shaking Blake's hand. "And, Hulk here is going to run the recruitment and training for AIS, based out of the Wool Shed."

The crowd rose to their feet and started clapping.

"Congratulations," Hulk said smiling proudly.

"And you too," Blake said shaking his hand. "The Wool Shed?"

"Yeah, nice little place to retire in the countryside."

"Retire? I thought the PM said recruiting and training new agents?"

"I'll help the new recruits out when I can."

"What about me?"

"Nah, bugger that, you're on your own," Hulk joked patting Blake on the back.

The ceremony finished and they had a reception in the Rose Garden at the White House, but as soon as they could Max and Blake slipped away.

They had made their way back to the hotel and before long were naked in each other's arms. They made love for the first time, then held each other almost afraid to let go after years of longing and waiting.

"Congratulations," Max said while they laid in the massive king-sized bed at the Waldorf. "I guess I have to call you boss now."

"Only in the bedroom," Blake laughed playfully poking out his tongue.

They laughed and kissed passionately, then made love for the second time, before falling asleep in each other's arms.

The next morning Max woke at five, a habit he had never broken since his days training at the Wool Shed. He stood under the hot water in the shower letting the pain wash away. It had been a few days since the submarine and he had grieved the loss of his friend for the second time. Flash was dead and the intelligence teams in the US and Australia had set about finding the remaining cannisters of Erebus. They were getting close to a location on Franklin, and Kate and Jonnie were going to lead the operation to recover the Professor.

Blake joined him in the shower and the pair held each other for the longest time under the hot running water.

"That was nice yesterday," Blake said massaging Max's shoulders, "how the President gave a medal to that young guy who helped you on the train."

"Jim," Max said. "Yeah, he deserved it. He saved my life."

"Well, I'm very grateful to him."

"Me too," Max said nodding sadly. "I wish I could have saved him."

"I know you do," Blake said hugging Max and holding him tightly.

"I want to get in touch with his family today, to pass on my thanks and let them know he died a hero."

"That would be a very sweet gesture. I'll get the number for you."

"Thanks, Blake," Max said turning and passionately kissing Blake.

They eventually got out and dried, and Max offered to go out to grab them some coffees.

"We can just get room service," Blake said. "Just stay here. You need to get some rest."

"I think I need to go for a bit of a walk to loosen up," Max said, "I'm still in some pain from the last couple of days."

"Okay, well I'll come with you."

"Sounds great."

The pair dressed and headed out into the street. They walked hand in hand down the sidewalk until Max felt the hairs on the back of his neck raise. Instinctively he turned, pushing Blake away for safety.

A man dressed in black combat gear and balaclava had run from the shadows. He clubbed Max as a van pulled up. Two men similarly dressed jumped out and aimed their rifles at Blake. Blake stepped forward to reach for Max, but one of the men shot him in the leg. Blake fell to the ground clutching his leg in pain.

"Max!" Blake yelled trying to get to his feet as the men dragged Max into the van.

The door slide shut and the van sped off leaving Blake bleeding in the street.

"You did not think we would forget," one of the men said to Max inside the van. "You committed crimes on our nation. You killed our Prime Minister and a member of the Royal

Family. You will have to answer for those crimes and the various others you committed on our soil since."

"You shot my boyfriend," Max said his eyes ice-cold. "You will pay for that."

"You are hardly in a place to be making threats."

"Your Prime Minister and that other bitch were traitors. They got what was coming to them."

"Maybe so, but that does not give you the right to play judge, jury and executioner. You will be tried and prosecuted for your crimes."

"I hold the equivalent rank of a three-star General. I am an Australian citizen on US soil and I was pardoned by the President. She even hung a medal around my neck yesterday. You'll never get out of the country."

"Oh, Agent Shaw, don't be so naïve. Torres already cleared our plane for take-off. Our nations have a very special relationship."

Less than thirty minutes later, the private jet sped off across the blue sky bound for England.

The End.

Max Shaw will return in *Shaw Reclamation*.

www.jwpublishing.com.au